Winter Midnight

By Daphne C. Murrell

Mountain Paradise Publishers.

ISBN:0615950892
ISBN-9780615950891

Dedication

This book is dedicated to my soul mate, my kindred spirit,
my most definite other half, Rick. We have trudged through the
Winter Midnight and made it back into the sunshine of our own
mountain paradise. What a blessing to journey this life beside you.
It takes a special heart to appreciate an overly creative mind.
I believe God knew exactly what He was doing
when He linked us together.

Acknowledgments

Special thanks to Lisa Morrow Jackson who shared
her personal experience of cancer and recovery with me.

One

It was a typical winter morning—foreboding, gray, wet, the air thick and icy. Kyle stood just inside the window of the shop staring out at buyers rushing about three days before Christmas. It had been extremely busy that morning with parents purchasing instruments in high hopes of creating virtuosos. He remembered his first guitar; it had been a Christmas gift also.

As he lingered in the memory, the figure of a woman with long, dark hair and mirrored glasses grabbed his attention. His heart pounded as he stared in shock watching her dodge the rain to the door.

"Caryn?" he whispered, barely able to breathe.

When she entered, she looked over at him and smiled. Same hair, same height, but when she removed the glasses, his hopes vanished. Those were definitely not her eyes.

"May I help you?" he forced himself to greet her.

"I hope so. I need a special gift for my son. He really wants to learn guitar, and someone suggested Sarkos Music for the best deals."

Kyle felt his knees weaken. This was too much. He had to get away.

"Let me get someone to help you," he said as he turned toward the back of the store. Glancing through the massive room of musical paraphernalia, he searched desperately for a salesman who could take time with the woman. All were busy.

Please, God, let there be one person free to help her. Man, she reminds me of Caryn. I wonder if someday she'll be buying a guitar for her child also.

He rushed into the stock room and sighed with relief as he spotted Jamie lounging on a box drinking coffee.

"There's a lady out front that needs your help. She wants a guitar for her kid."

"And what's wrong with you?" Jamie griped hopping up from the box. "Aren't you the guitar guru around here?"

"Not today. In fact, I'm out of here. I'll be at the studio if anyone calls."

Jamie shook his head and cursed under his breath as he placed his coffee on the box and headed for the retail section. "Must be nice to be the boss's kid."

Kyle closed his eyes hoping to regain his composure. He went to the doorway and glanced through the store to watch Jamie greet her. She even moved like Caryn. Would there ever come a time he wouldn't think of her, wouldn't wonder where she was, wouldn't question why she did what she did? He turned away quickly, grabbed his coat and left through the back door. The rain had subsided to a drizzle, but its mixing with the cold made each drop feel like a pin pricking at his skin. Shivering in the mist, he hopped into the blue Jeep and dug the keys from his pocket. He had to get away.

He drove to the studio that bore his father's name also, Sarkos Recording. He jogged up to the front door and rushed inside hoping to conserve the warmth from the Jeep.

"Kyle! Whatzup?" Jed whipped his head around slinging the long dreadlocks across his dark face. His island accent was thick and cheerful, always accompanied with a bright smile.

"What are you doing here?" Kyle was surprised to find the studio's best sound technician sitting at the receptionist's desk.

"Doing Brandi a favor. She was wanting to shop; I got no one to record today—so here I sit."

"Nobody's recording?"

"It's three days before Christmas, mon! Where you been? Nobody's working unless it's at a store. Speaking of which, why are you here?"

"Had to get away." Kyle started for the hallway leading to the studios in the back. "I'm gonna chill just a bit. If anyone needs me, I'll be in Two."

"All right, mon. Take it easy."

He walked into Studio Two without bothering to turn on a light. The beam through the cracked door was enough to find his way to where several guitars sat. He dropped onto a stool, picked up the closest acoustic, and began to pick a tune that was purely melancholy. Caryn. She still plagued every thought.

How do you forget someone after ten years of marriage? How do you pick up and move on as though it's all water under the bridge?

The whole situation was driving him crazy—still. He struggled with simply living at this point. Until February, his life had been perfect, but after that unforeseen day, it had crashed and eventually burned. He was now lost: nowhere to go and nothing to do.

He stopped playing as his mind drifted to February 13. He had been in the kitchen preparing spaghetti. Caryn had been gone all day running various errands, most of which he was clueless about. He had called and confirmed their reservations the following night at the finest restaurant in Nashville, congratulating himself at how clever he had been to get them for Valentine's Day. This would be their best ever. He washed his hands and went into the living room to check the news. Their life wasn't perfect, but it was nice. It was comfortable, cozy, and nice.

The news was uneventful, so he had found himself staring at their wedding portrait hanging on the wall next to the television. Caryn had barely changed. She was still thin, with long, straight hair, and dark, exquisite eyes. He remembered the first time he had called them *exquisite*;

they had just met in college and had been studying at the same table in the library. He didn't even know her, but he'd already been taken by her beauty and poise.

He had changed considerably. His blond hair in the photo was long as he had just graduated college and wasn't concerned with appearance. By the time he had finished seminary, however, he had learned to look more presentable and respectable for church work.

When the front door flung open, Kyle looked back to see Caryn scampering in, purse falling from her shoulder, her expression frazzled and tense—very unusual for her.

"What's wrong, Babe?" he had asked as she hastily walked through the living room and headed down the hallway.

She said nothing. Kyle got up slowly and followed her to their bedroom. She was throwing clothes inside a suitcase.

"What's up?" he asked her this time, still not alarmed.

"I'm leaving, Kyle."

"Where? To visit your parents?"

She kept throwing clothes inside, drawer after drawer. "I'm just leaving. I'm going."

He assumed it was a joke. What was she talking about? "Leaving for where?"

She stopped shoveling clothes a moment as she closed her eyes in distress. "I'm leaving *you*," she said emphatically. "I'm going … somewhere … anywhere."

He stared at her and waited for eye contact. When she finally looked at him, he could see she was serious. He was floored. Where did this come from? They had a good life and a wonderful marriage. "What are you talking about?" He had tried to take her arm.

She jerked away and backed up against the chest of drawers. "Don't make me go into all sorts of gory details. Just let me leave. I'll send you the papers as soon as I get settled."

"Papers? What's going on here?"

"Divorce papers, Kyle." Her tone was exasperated as though he should know what was plaguing her. "I'll try to get them to you as soon as possible."

He then became angry. He was in utter confusion. When he had left for church that morning, everything was fine. She had kissed him goodbye and told him she would see him that afternoon. He knew she had a lunch date, so he hadn't bothered to call. When he'd seen the note that she'd be late, he didn't worry. Why worry? Things were great.

"Please offer me some kind of explanation!" he exclaimed as he moved closer to her. "I mean … can't you imagine why I might be confused about all of this?"

3

"I'm pregnant, Kyle," she said forcefully.

That statement slammed into his heart. After years of fertility sessions and major testing, the doctor had concluded that he could never father children. They had decided together this wasn't God's will for them, and they would let the kids and youth in the churches they served be their children.

"Wow." He was now more confused. "Was it some kind of miracle … or …"

"It's not yours, Kyle."

He had eased himself down to the edge of the bed. He couldn't process what he was hearing. Caryn was leaving him, she was pregnant, and the child wasn't his. She went back to throwing clothes into the luggage. With the first one filled, she went to the closet and brought out another.

"Whose child is it?" he had asked as he tried to get beyond the numbness invading his body.

"Do you really want to know, Kyle? Can't we just leave it at this and move on?"

"No." He was broken, pained. "How long have you been seeing someone else? *How* could you see someone else? I mean … I thought … things have been great between us. Why did you …?" He couldn't put into words the frustration rambling around his mind.

She had stopped for a moment to take a deep breath but still seemed unmoved. "Reese Weathers," she told him. "I've been seeing him for almost a year."

"Reese?" Kyle whispered in unbelief. "He's my …"

"Best friend. I know."

"Why?"

"Oh, Kyle …" She brought her fists up to her face and shook her head abruptly. "I can't explain my life to you."

"*Your* life?" Agitation pulsed through him. "I thought it was *our* life! For ten years I've lived by your side! We've had ups and downs, joys and disappointments, but nothing ever gave me a clue that you would … would … do this. What were you thinking?"

"Look, it just happened. Something between us died somewhere, and the next thing I knew, I was with Reese, and … well … it just happened, Kyle! I can't make any more sense of it than you can! Please stop questioning me! Just let me pack and leave."

"Something died? Wait … wait just a minute! At what point did something *die* in our relationship? You've been having an affair for a year, but there's been nothing different in any area of our life … *nothing*. If things were so bad, we could have gone to a counselor or something! But you never said anything! How was I supposed to know there was a problem when you … you … have acted like there wasn't?"

She had finished cramming the second suitcase and then went for her cosmetic bag.

"Don't I deserve an answer?" Kyle yelled after her as she went into the bathroom.

She returned with an armload of toiletry items and dumped them in the bag. "Yes, you deserve a lot more than I'm gonna give you. You're a wonderful man, a great music minister, and you've been a good husband, but it wasn't enough, Kyle. Try to understand."

He was bowled over. He couldn't believe this was happening. Caryn was packing and leaving him. There had been no hint or indication that anything out of the ordinary had ever happened. "How do you know it's Reese's baby?"

"Come on, Kyle!" she nearly screamed. "You heard the doctor! *You* can never have children! It's not going to happen! I've been with Reese for close to a year; it's his baby. Let's not go there."

"Is he gonna leave Alicia for you?"

"He doesn't know, and I don't want him to know. What's the point? I don't want him to leave Alicia. I don't want a life with him. I just want to be left alone."

"Why are you leaving *me*, then?"

"Kyle!" She turned to look at him in frustration. "I'm having another man's baby! You want me to stay with you?"

"No one would know. We'll raise it as mine."

She had turned to him with an open mouth. Her eyes began to brim as she stared in utter surprise. "You can't be serious. You would do that?"

He thought he might have broken through. "I'm not joking. I love you, Caryn. You're my wife; you're my life. I confess that all this floors me, but I don't want to lose you. We'll work it out."

He remembered her expression as she closed her eyes and shook her head. It was almost as if she had desperately tried to push him away and couldn't believe he would still want a life with her. She picked up the first of the luggage and headed down the hall.

"Caryn, I'm serious! Please don't go! We'll do whatever's necessary to work this out." He stopped her with his hands on her shoulders. "Please, don't go," he had whispered as he leaned his head into the side of her neck. "I love you. I forgive you. I don't want to lose you."

She paused but then broke free of his embrace. "It's over, Kyle." She walked resolutely to the door.

At that point he began to get desperate. He realized that she might actually leave. When she came back in for the rest of her luggage, he began to beg and plead for her to stay, for them to work it out, but she was adamant about going.

"Caryn, why are you doing this?" Nothing made sense to him, but she wouldn't answer. It was as if her mind had been set in stone.

As she walked out the door for the last time, she turned back to him and said, "I know all of this is sudden and confusing for you. I'm sorry. You're a good man, Kyle, and you deserve better than this, but ... well ... this is just how it's going to be. Really, I'm sorry."

And she was gone. She left Harvest Hollow, and as far as he could tell, never told Reese anything. In fact, Reese and Alicia went on as though life had not changed in the least. For Kyle, however, as a minister of music in a good-sized church, life changed drastically. He tried to pretend for a month that Caryn had gone to visit her parents in Martha's Vineyard, which she often did, but when the month passed, he felt it was time to talk to the leadership.

Dr. Carlton, pastor of Harvest Hollow Community Church, was gracious at first. He assured Kyle he understood the horrible incident wasn't his fault. As long as Kyle was willing, he could continue to serve the church and fulfill his heart's longing to lead others in worship. That lasted two months. Several church members began to get disgruntled at the idea of a *divorced* minister. Kyle understood; he'd felt the same way before his divorce. As the church began to push him toward resignation, he began to feel more and more helpless about his life.

Finally, in late April, he quit and moved back with his parents in Sheffield, Alabama, where he had spent his teenage years steeped in the music industry. They had been understanding and assured him he could stay as long as he liked. His father gave him a job at the music store, and he would occasionally sit in as guitarist or pianist for recording sessions. He was miserable, but at least the work could help take his mind off obsessing about Caryn ... until today, when that woman walked into the store.

***

At supper that evening, Kyle attempted no pleasantries. He was brooding, forlorn, and would barely eat. Bradley Sarkos was trying to be patient. His dark curly hair, salted with streaks of gray, was frizzy and unkempt from the day's humidity. The Greek descent was obvious. It was hard to believe Kyle could be this man's son based on appearance. But when his mother, Emma, entered the dining room with a freshly baked cheesecake, his resemblance to her was evident. She had always said *I'll be a beautiful blonde until the day you bury me. I was born blonde, and will die blonde.* She had even made them promise if she was ever put away in a home somewhere they would guarantee to keep her hair and make-up steady.

"Strawberry cheesecake anyone?" She placed the platter on the table.

Bradley nodded in delight. He loved dessert. "How did you find time to do this between shopping and ... well ... more shopping?"

"There's always time to make cake," she said warmly as she sat down. "Would you like a piece, Kyle?"

He shook his head. His steak lay barely touched on his plate.

"I know Christmas must be hard for you." His mother cut a slice of dessert and placed it on a saucer for Bradley. "Caryn always got into Christmas so much."

"Everything's hard," Kyle said mournfully.

"Even work, I suppose," his father said as he raised his dark, bushy eyebrows at him. "Jamie called and said you left today. They were really short-handed in the shop."

"I couldn't stay. This woman came in. She looked so much like Caryn that at first ... I thought ... then when I got a good look at her ... anyway, I had to get out."

Bradley sighed as he savored a large bite of cake. This was getting ridiculous. "At some point, son, you've got to move on with your life. It'll soon be a year since she left, and you're still struggling to keep your head on straight."

"Bradley, give him time."

"Time?" He couldn't hide his agitation. "People get divorced right and left, and they go on with their lives *and* their jobs as though nothing ever happened. All I'm saying, Kyle, is that you've got to get a grip on life and start pulling yourself together. I don't mind paying you a salary, and I don't mind you living in this house, but I can't stand the sulking and despondency. At some point you've got to move on emotionally."

Kyle nodded. "I know you're right, but I'm lost. My only goal in life was music ministry and church work, and no church will have me now. Then with Caryn having been a part of all that, going on without her leaves this gaping hole. I don't want to work at the store; I don't want to play at the studio. Most of the music is country anyway ... far from my favorite." He sighed. "I'm basically surviving, keeping my head above water so I won't drown in despair.

"You don't even go to church anymore," his mother added. "That's not like you, honey."

Kyle pushed his plate away and blew out a deep breath of frustration. "I know. I can't stand having people still coming up to me and telling me how sorry they are to hear about the divorce. At some point I imagined that I could walk into church and just worship and fellowship without having to face the degradation and frustration of my past, but it's worse there than anywhere else. Why are people still standing around gossiping about my life? Couldn't they just keep me on the prayer lists without having to hash over the details in their little prayer groups?"

"People are people," Bradley said matter-of-factly. "As long as you're here, Kyle, you'll be on somebody's *discussion* list."

"I know I need to move on, but what do I do? What's left for me? I'm thirty-one and my life's mission has been dissolved, not by my own fault, but because of the infidelity and unfaithfulness of my wife." He stood from the table. "I'm going out back for a little while. You're both right, but I don't know what to do." He rubbed the stubble on his neglected face. "I just don't know what to do."

Kyle walked out the French doors to the back yard which overlooked a massive cliff on the Tennessee River. He'd grown up here in luxury and had met numerous music stars over the years. His life had been charmed in many ways. He was the only child of a wonderful couple. He had developed musical talents early and been exposed to areas of music that most people could only dream about. He had been saved at fifteen and then gave his life to ministry shortly afterward. When he left for college, he had two goals: graduate with a music degree and get married. He had accomplished both, and then went to seminary to complete his education.

Everything had come easily for him. He was winsome, talented, and handsome. Caryn had been quiet, gentle and incredibly beautiful, a wonderful compliment to his ministry. She didn't want to work and was willing to do anything he needed to help along the way. She stayed home and created a beautiful house for them. She cooked and entertained, the perfect hostess. He had no idea that somewhere along the way she had grown discontent.

God, what do I do? I'm clueless. I don't even know where to go or what to think or how to start.

He leaned over the edge of the fence and stared down into the turbulent river. It was all he could do to keep himself from plunging over the side.

I know You haven't abandoned me, but I just can't see any reason for staying on this planet. What are You up to in my life, Lord? Help, please.

He knew he couldn't step foot again in his home church in Muscle Shoals. He'd had enough of that. He would have to try somewhere else and then attempt a new beginning. If worse came to worse, he could always teach music. It wasn't his first choice, but it was a viable option.

He had wanted to visit a church in the small town of Dockrey about an hour away. He understood that Stephen Williams' father-in-law was the pastor. Stephen had met the pastor's daughter and recognized her talent immediately. Being a world famous musician, he had offered her a place in his band and a spotlight on stage with his tour. She became an overnight sensation. Then, to top off the fairytale, the two fell in love and were married. Stephen had been one of Kyle's favorite musicians; he never missed a concert. When he found out that Stephen's wife was from Dockery, Alabama, he couldn't believe it.

Why don't we have people like Stephen Williams recording in Sarkos Studios?

As he stared out toward the horizon, he decided in that moment it was time to move on. His New Year's resolution would be to check out the church in Dockrey. If it looked like a good place to worship, he'd start with the church and then look into teaching possibilities somewhere in the area. Shivering in the darkness, the wind whipped his long hair, stinging his face. Perhaps this could be the wind of change.

Two

Cindy Marcum trembled from the cold as she unlocked the door to her mother's house after the first Sunday night service in January. It was cold, wet, and windy, and all she wanted was to thaw. She had said her goodbyes to Angie Wright Collins, her best friend in the whole world, who was returning to the Pacific island nation of Padawin as a medical missionary. Cindy would be left alone in Dockrey with her mother.

She placed her Bible and purse on the dining table and went to the kitchen for something warm to drink. Heating a mug of water in the microwave, she added a pack of caffeine-free hot chocolate mix. She would prefer coffee, but it had been hard to sleep lately. She grabbed her Bible and purse, mug in hand, and went upstairs to her childhood room. Nudging open the door she dropped her loose items on the bed, turning immediately to click on the television. If she didn't have something to occupy the silence she would burst into tears. How would she go through this without Angie?

At thirty, Cindy's life had finally begun to go her way—about a year ago. She had a great job, a great apartment, a great car, and a great man, all in Florence, Alabama, an hour away from the ho-hum life she had grown up with in small time Dockrey. But within a matter of months, everything had changed. Her father had died suddenly with a shocking heart attack beginning a series of events that slowly began to take the wind from her sails. The second blast came when her married boyfriend told her he couldn't leave his wife while she was struggling with a new baby. When she had mentioned this to Angie, she quickly translated to Cindy that what he really meant was he wasn't leaving his wife period. She accepted it, broke off the relationship and moved on. The final bomb dropped in early October: her mother was diagnosed with breast cancer. At first her mother refused any treatments whatsoever, but after some convincing words from Angie, Sue had agreed to both the surgery and the chemo. It was then that Angie explained how hard and impossible life would be for Sue on her own. The only hope for her survival would be for Cindy to leave her life and move back in with her mother to care for her through the hard months ahead.

As the credits to a movie ran in the background, she stepped into her bathroom. She removed her jewelry then took a brush to her growing blonde hair. She had hoped she wouldn't have to face this alone, but with Angie's leaving that left only Cindy and her twin brother, Billy. He was twice divorced, the epitome of selfishness, and unlikely to offer anything in the months ahead. She would be truly alone—again.

This isn't what she had wanted in life, but no matter how hard she tried, she simply couldn't find anyone, at least not anyone with whom she could fall in love. Perhaps that was what she enjoyed most about her relationship with Evan. Yes, he was married, but that took all pressure off her. She didn't have to worry about being forced into a commitment. No, she didn't care for the idea of sharing him with a wife, but there were no demands on her life or her time. Yes, she wanted desperately to share her life with someone, but no, it wasn't Evan ... or anyone else so far.

She carefully removed her eye makeup and began the nightly routine of cleansing her face. By the time she had finished, another movie had begun. She put a good bit of lotion on her hands and began to moisturize her arms and legs as she watched the opening scene. A predictable romance: *no thank you*. She needed no reminders of how other people lived happily ever after. At this moment, there was nothing happy about her life. The only comfort she could take was that she was sacrificing everything she had ever worked for so that she could tend to her mother and hopefully save her life—she hadn't been that fortunate with her father.

She picked up the remote and changed the channel to a comedy. She smiled at the actor, Martin Sartin. He had started on a late-night Saturday comedy show years ago and then moved on to star in feature films. He was hilarious. At the apex of his fame, however, he had been arrested for all kinds of drug involvement, from selling to murder, and locked up for a mind-boggling amount of time. The thought depressed her as she felt her situation was similar. She had been making vast amounts of money selling commercial real estate, living in an exclusive riverside apartment, and had everything she could have ever imagined, and all this without a college degree. Now she had another failed road she could travel if she lingered on the thought much longer.

Turning off the television, she decided to give sleep a try. She plugged her phone to the charger and set the alarm for the next morning—the first day of her new job as church secretary. She cringed as she realized the trust this church was putting in her, hiring her while she cared for her mother. Her father had been a deacon and her mother a faithful children's worker for over thirty years. When the secretary had retired in December, the church offered her the position temporarily hoping it would make staying with her mother more convenient. Cindy wasn't so sure about the arrangement now. After all, last year this time, she was having an affair, night-clubbing steadily, and as far from church as anyone could imagine. Had Angie not set her straight with several severe heart-to-heart talks, who knew where she might have been at this point?

She set her alarm for six thirty and then looked around the room for something, anything, to read. The only thing there was her Bible. She knew she should read it, but if she were honest, she was a bit angry with God at the moment. She glanced over at her computer displaying a picture of she and her father taken at Christmas last year. Tears began stinging her eyes. How she missed him. He had been gone for seven months, but the pain and loss hadn't eased any. In fact, since moving back into the house, the emptiness was stronger. As she stared at his smiling face, she could imagine him walking into her room to say goodnight.

Hey, Ladybug. I think you've made a smart choice in all of this. Working at the church, taking care of your mother—those are important things, Cindy. People are most important ... always remember that.

"I'll try, Daddy," she whispered as she sat down at the computer and traced his face on the screen. "I wish I would've remembered that while you were still alive. I always assumed there'd be more time."

She decided to check her Facebook. Perhaps she could lose herself in the triumphs or failures of her cyber friends. She would send Angie a message while she was at it so something from Dockrey would be waiting for her when she returned to Padawin. The internet was unmercifully slow. She would have to upgrade if she was going to survive here. She doubted her mother even turned on a computer anymore. Cindy moaned—Evan had sent another message. She wanted to delete it and move on, but she couldn't bring herself to. Instead, she clicked it first and began to read.

"Cindy, I wish you would just talk with me. I know that things were odd between us there at the last, but now that Christie is out of the picture, I would really like to get together with you and see if we can salvage us. We had a good thing, Cindy. Don't throw it all away because some missionary put a few righteous ideas in your head. Call me. Let's talk.

Love, Evan"

She couldn't believe how tempting it was to call him that very moment. She felt so disconnected from everyone in her life that even a night with Evan would seem comforting.

No! What am I thinking? Christie left him. She knew he was fooling around. He didn't leave her for me. He never did love me, and even if he did, what kind of man has a baby and a two-year-old and then an affair with another woman? This is crazy! Besides, she sighed, *I don't love him.*

She quickly deleted the message and went on.

There was also a message from Billy.

"Little Sister,"

She smiled. Although she was actually older than Billy by two minutes, he was nearly half a foot taller so he had always called her *Little Sister.*

"Little Sister, How's the church thing going? I'm still a bit shocked that you're doing all this, but I think it's a great thing. You're a better person than me. Much better, actually. The fact that you and Mom didn't even tell me about the whole cancer thing until Christmas sort of shows where my priorities are. I should have sensed something long before then. I tend to focus on me more than anyone else; at least that's what my ex-wives have told me. I have to confess to you that I'm still a bit bummed that Angie ended up with the missionary dude. Can you imagine that? Angie married to a missionary. But then, seeing that she's one herself, I guess it all makes sense. I think I'm the only person in the world whose life makes absolutely no sense at all. I know things are gonna be tough for mom after the surgery, thus things will be rough for you. I'll be at the hospital with you guys, but Cindy, I can't do the doctoring stuff and all ... I just can't handle that, but I'll be glad to buy dinner or whatever. Take care, and I'll see you in a couple of weeks. Love Ya, Billy"

Well, it was more positive than usual. At least he was showing some concern for someone other than himself. His ex-wives were right: he was an incredibly selfish man. How could two wonderful, godly, giving people have raised such a wayward set of twins? But Cindy was ready to put her waywardness behind and start a new path: the straight and narrow. However, it had been so long since she had been on that path she was scared to death she might lose her way.

Another message suddenly popped in her screen. Angie? She pulled up the note and began to read.

"Cindy, It was hard saying goodbye tonight, but I have to believe that God knows what He's doing. He could have easily worked it out for me to still be here during all that's about to happen with your mother ... but He didn't. Because of that, I want to tell you to get ready ... hold on to your hat ... because God must have something awesome in store for you. You've turned your life back over to Him, and He's about to work in it big time. Keep your eyes and your heart open these next months; God is up to something. Don't take anything for granted. When an opportunity presents itself, no matter how odd, remember that God is up to something. When it seems like everything is just about impossible to understand, get ready because God is up to something. Trust Him, Cindy, and trust Daddy. He knows you well, and he knows people well, and he's a man full of not only the wisdom of God, but also the grace of God. Daddy only expects perfection in his own children! Everyone else's is allowed their fair share of mistakes. He's a wonderful pastor, and he thinks a lot of you. Working for him these next few months may be just another way of proving that God is up to something. You can share your heart with Daddy, no matter how bizarre ... or even how wrong your thoughts might be. And of course, always remember that I am just a message away. Anytime you need a heart-felt friend, get on the Net and tell me what's going on. When it comes to mistake-making, I am the queen! You know that! If God can take me as far as He has—to mission work on a Pacific island—He can do anything. I'm always here for you. Take care, and please

keep in touch. With Much Love, Angie"

Cindy wiped the single tear that had managed to escape. She and Angie had been best friends in high school, and even though their lives had taken different paths, the bond had never changed. With Angie having been home the past three months, it was almost as if they'd never been apart. To have her leave again now was almost too much for an already struggling Cindy to handle.

God, I hope Angie's right. I hope You are indeed up to something. Right now, though, I confess that I see nothing. I'm thirty, I'm alone, I'm miserable, and I'm living with my Mom again—my sick Mom. Nothing looks right at the moment. All I know is to ask You for the patience and strength to get through these next months with my head on straight. I don't know how I'm gonna do this. I wish I had Angie's faith, but I don't. Yet I know I have her God, so Lord, I hope that somehow that'll be enough.

She turned off the computer and crawled into bed. Pulling back the comforter she gently slid beneath the warmed sheets. *Thank heaven for electric blankets.* She reached up to turn off the light and then snuggled under the warmth of the covers. Her heart still ached.

Just get through these next few months and everything will be okay. It'll all be okay someday. It has to be. It can't possibly get any worse than this.

Three

The drive to Dockrey on Sunday morning was liberating. Although it was still overcast, misty and cold, the heat was cranked up in the Jeep, as well as the stereo, and for just a moment, all seemed right in the world again. Kyle had decided against Sunday School on his initial visit to First Baptist; he wanted to check out the church first, see if it was a place he might seriously consider settling. If it seemed friendly enough, like he could fit in, then he would begin the process of starting over.

He smiled while driving past huge cliffs jutting out from the rolling hills. This place was almost worthy of a dotted trail on the map. As he observed the many varieties of country homes, he wondered how these people managed to build lives for themselves in the middle of nowhere. As far as he could remember, he'd never been on this road and he knew he'd never been to Dockrey. They'd often joked about the small town in high school; *Anyone from Dockrey is a red neck.* Why? Who knew? High-schoolers were skilled at insulting others to make themselves appear impressive. He was banking on the hope that not *everyone* there was a red neck, because if things turned out like he planned, he would begin teaching music in the dinky town, and that music would *not* include red neck anthems.

At the intersection, he turned right toward Dockrey. Once again, no hint of congestion. *Surely people build houses closer together in town.* As he crossed a long bottom where a sod farm grew during the warmer months, the whole area still looked rural. He could see the beginnings of the town up ahead and hoped that enough children resided here to actually consider music lessons.

Dockrey city limits. It actually was a pretty place, clean and manicured so far. Winter flowers laced the beds of various houses and the typical *Roll Tide* or *Auburn Tigers* signs were announcing allegiances. He passed two gas stations, a cemetery, and a flower shop before coming upon the Piggly Wiggly. Still no red light. When his GPS commanded he *turn left now*, he signaled quickly but did spot a red light farther on down Main Street. *Woo hoo*, he grinned. *That must be downtown.*

He wound around the curvy road which led him deeper into the country rather than on into town. He wondered how First Baptist ended up out in the middle of the woods. As he continued on, he passed the school and many more houses, then abruptly there was nothing again. He was now concerned that his GPS was mistaken or perhaps he had programmed the wrong address. After a couple more acres and eventually another house, he passed a massive twelve-foot fence with small crowds of people dotted beside it. *What on earth is that about? It's just a house ... in Dockrey.*

Not more than a quarter of a mile past the fence stood the church. It was a beautiful structure, quaint and rustic as it sat back in the woods. Cars were parked all over beneath large lines of cedars and pines, and people were congregating in various places between Sunday School and morning worship. It would be interesting to see how people in a community like this responded to a stranger. As he pulled to a spot *not* beneath the trees—he wanted no residue dripping onto his Jeep—people began to turn and stare. He grabbed his Bible and climbed out, taking care to make sure all saw him lock the door and double-check it. He wanted no *red necks* rummaging through his vehicle for whatever odds and ends they could find.

"Morning," smiled an older man smoking a cigarette before having to head back for the service.

"Good morning. This way to the sanctuary?"

"Yep," the man motioned toward the front of the church. "Just up those steps."

Kyle nodded a *thanks* and walked up to the large double doors. Two men greeted him, one shook his hand and the other handed him a bulletin while opening a door.

"Welcome to First Baptist."

Kyle smiled in acknowledgment and walked inside the church. It was much smaller than he was used to, yet it had a cozy feel. The interior was mainly exposed wood and beams, and the sanctuary was fanned. The choir loft was large, but the pulpit was nothing more than a small wooden structure in the midst of a large stage.

Plenty of room here for big musicals and productions, Kyle thought as he surveyed the area.

He also noticed three digital cameras. He was surprised. Were their services televised somewhere? Several more greeted him as he found a seat in the back. His hope was to sneak in unnoticed and observe without causing a big ado.

A black grand piano sat on the left, and a rather impressive organ on the right. The woman playing the pre-service piano prelude was doing an excellent job. She was blending hymns and choruses, easily changing keys as she flowed from one to the next. Whoever she was, she obviously knew music. There was something familiar about her. Did he know her? Had they been in college together? That long, dark wavy hair seemed so ...

Annie Wright! Stephen Williams' wife! No, it wasn't, but a very close resemblance. A *sister perhaps?*

Kyle glanced down at his bulletin and saw that Jonathan Wright was indeed still the pastor. He wondered what kind of man he might be. Was he dignified and unapproachable? Hiram Carlton had been. In fact, Dr.

Carlton had told Kyle that as ministers it was important for them to stay arm's length from the members. They needed to appear as *examples to the flock*, not as members of the same household of faith. Kyle couldn't buy it. He tried, but still found himself drawn into friendships and relationships with many church members, especially the Weathers ... Reese Weathers, his supposed best friend.

He looked through the announcements and weekly activities. For a country church, they stayed busy. There were many musical activities also: adult choir, youth choir, children's choir and senior adult choir. *Do they have that many people here?*

The prelude stopped and the choir began to assemble into the loft. It was massive! Kyle began to count: forty-five. *How could a church this size have that kind of choir? This music guy must be awesome.* Walking out with the choir members, the music director motioned for them to be seated then nervously dropped into one of the high-backed chairs. He sent an obvious wink toward the piano player. When she smiled back, Kyle knew the woman had to be related to Annie Wright Williams.

When the pastor finally stepped up to the platform to began announcements, Kyle was astounded. This man was the antithesis of Dr. Carlton. He had removed his coat and his tie was loosened slightly at the neck. Topping it off, the tie was not impressive or businesslike; it had vegetable characters dancing around on it. Kyle smiled. He had never seen a pastor quite as disheveled looking as Jonathan Wright. He shuffled a few papers, made a silly comment to the music director behind him, and had the choir cracking up over whatever had been said. He ran his hand through his thinning hair, obviously *not* to straighten it. Kyle couldn't help but notice his lips, the same lips as Annie Williams.

The pastor smiled endearingly as he began going over various announcements he felt warranted more than just a perusal from the bulletin or a glance at the Powerpoint. He made several humorous comments and took time to point out various people who could add to the information if needed. By the time announcements were over, Kyle felt like he had already made a friend without ever having spoken to the man.

Jonathan couldn't help being distracted. The young man on the back row with long blonde hair stayed foremost in his attention. It was nothing overt that he was doing that occupied Jonathan. Instead, it was the look of complete helplessness and hopelessness that encompassed him. Even while preaching, the man appeared to be questioning the tenets of his faith. What brought him here? Who was he? And why was he hanging on every word that came from his mouth? The longer the service prevailed, the more frustrated and confused the man seemed to become. At one point it even looked like he reached up to wipe a tear.

Who is this man, Lord, Jonathan prayed silently as he tried to continue his sermon, *and why is he here? Show me.*

When the service was over, Jonathan didn't stand at the front doors to greet members as they left. He immediately walked to the back row and reached out his hand to the stranger bearing red eyes and a defeated countenance.

"Jonathan Wright," he said as he offered his hand. "Glad to have you with us this morning."

The man nodded but wouldn't speak. He was obviously distraught.

"You want to step into a more private room with me for a moment?"

He nodded, blond hair sticking to his damp cheeks. Jonathan briefly touched the shoulder of the young man to lead him down a side aisle toward classrooms in the back. He directed him into a small room and closed the door.

"It seems like you really need to get some things together," Jonathan began. "Do you have some questions that you need to discuss?"

The man shrugged as he sat toward the front of the metal chair and put his face in his hands. He then began weeping. Jonathan had no idea what was happening or how to minister to him. Was he saved? Was he searching? Was he in trouble? Was he new in town?

"Take your time," Jonathan finally said sensing that whatever the struggle was, it was deep and bottled up and needed to be vented before any healing could take place. After a couple of minutes, he offered him a tissue from a box on the table in a corner of the room.

"Thanks," the man said taking deep breaths as he grabbed a few tissues. "Sorry about that. It's been a long year."

"That's okay," Jonathan said with a concerned smile. "Whatever the problem, I'll do my best to help."

"Whew," he sighed as he wiped his eyes and blew his nose. "That should've happened long ago. I don't know why the dam chose this day to finally break.""

"Emotions are a funny thing," Jonathan said warmly as he took a seat next to him. "Why don't we start over? I'm Jonathan Wright." He stuck out his hand again, and the young man chuckled slightly as he shook it.

"Kyle Sarkos. I'm from the Shoals area."

"Sarkos?" Jonathan questioned.

"Yes, sir. I always get that same look from preachers who know their Greek. My dad's Greek: my mom's not. I get my fair complexion from her."

"Were your ancestors butchers or something?" Jonathan wondered with a name meaning *flesh*.

"Spartans. Warriors. I don't even want to know how they ended up with the name. We've changed over the years, however. We're now either in the music business or the restaurant business."

"Sarkos Music," Jonathan said in recognition.

"And studios. You've been there?"

"This church and my children have probably bought you several cars and a couple of boats with all the purchases made there over the years."

"Not from me. Well … until recently, that is. Actually, it's all very complicated, Pastor Wright. This is one long story. I'm not sure if you really have the time right now for me to spill it all out."

Jonathan nodded as he stood. He ran his hand through his hair causing a few strands to stand on end. "Funny thing about today, Kyle. Normally my daughter and her family would come over for Sunday dinner, but it's her father-in-law's birthday. She's actually taking her four kids to a restaurant to celebrate. She's brave." He raised a concerned eyebrow. "The point being, by divine coincidence, Barbara and I are alone for lunch. Why don't you come home with me, have some dinner, and then we can talk through whatever it is you're dealing with?"

"Oh, I couldn't impose like that," Kyle said quickly as he stood to his feet. "I really didn't mean for all this to get as involved as it has."

"As I see it," Jonathan reiterated, "it's divine intervention. You're here, I'm free, and it would be a horrid waste for you to just drive off today. Let's go eat, son."

Kyle stood silently for a moment as he considered it. "Why not? For some reason all of this has happened at this time. I need help, Pastor, and I need direction."

Four

They walked down the hill to the house surrounded by the high fence. Jonathan punched in a code that unlocked a gate and motioned Kyle through.

"Lovely house," Kyle said sincerely. It was nothing grand or fancy like the homes in his parents' neighborhood, but it had a warming charm about it.

"Thanks. I built this over twenty years ago, raised my family here, and consider it my haven of all havens."

"That's what a home should be."

"Absolutely."

When they entered through the back porch, Kyle felt welcomed by the homey atmosphere of the great room. His first gaze took him to the fireplace and the large family portrait above it. He immediately recognized two of the three young ladies in the picture: one was Annie Williams, and the other was the pianist at church.

"The piano player was your daughter?" Kyle asked as Jonathan took his coat.

"Yes, that's Andie. She's on the top left up there. Next to her is Angie. She's a doctor now, working as a missionary with her husband in the Pacific islands of Padawin. The next one is Annie. She's quite the musician. Are you familiar with Stephen Williams?"

Kyle nodded. He was slightly embarrassed because the only reason he ended up here today was because he knew Jonathan was Stephen's father-in-law.

"She's Stephen's wife," Jonathan said as if it were no big deal. "Then the guy is Alex, my youngest and my only son. He plays bass for Stephen."

"Really?" Kyle was impressed. He hadn't known that.

"And I'm Barbara," said an attractive older woman as she walked out of the kitchen drying her hands on a dishtowel. "I'm the mother."

She was much shorter than her husband and her curly dark hair and dark eyes stood in contrast to his light features.

"I see where your girls get their beauty now," Kyle said smoothly.

"What are you talking about?" Jonathan shot back quickly. "Look at the lips on those girls. They're all mine!"

Kyle agreed. That seemed to be the predominant feature on each girl.

"This is Kyle Sarkos. He's from the Shoals and will be filling in for Andie and Doug's brood today during lunch."

"Wonderful!" she smiled. "Sunday dinner wouldn't be the same without someone here. The bathroom's just over there, Kyle. Why don't you wash up? It's ready to come out of the crock pot right now."

"Thank-you," he said politely as he headed that direction.

Inside, he stared at the mirror and asked himself what he was doing here. *This is crazy! I only came because I was curious about Stephen Williams' father-in-law. Then I cried like a baby when I met him, and now I'm about to eat dinner at his house. What am I doing? He seems like such a neat man … his wife too. They're so friendly and open.*

He laughed for a moment as he imagined Dr. Hiram Carlton sizing this man up. *He's not a minister; he's a joke,* Carlton would have said. He knew because he had heard him evaluate every minister they had ever met, and very few ever passed the test for impressive ministerial appearances. Kyle liked Jonathan Wright. His scruffy hair and Veggie Tale tie had won him over long before the firm handshake. *Why couldn't I have worked for a man like this? Why couldn't Caryn have had the privilege of being under a pastor's wife like Barbara?* Julia Carlton had been as stuffy and unapproachable as her husband, and had barely said a word to either Kyle or Caryn during their six years at Harvest Hollow. Maybe someone like Barbara could have been approachable enough to Caryn that she could have gone to her for advice … rather than winding up in the arms of her husband's best friend.

Sunday dinner with the Wrights was wonderful and animated. Before the meal was over, Kyle knew just about everything there was to know about the Wright family. Long after the eating was finished, the conversation lingered. He was impressed with how welcoming they remained without prying. Surely they were curious as to why he was here, but they only asked simple questions that revealed nothing more about him than the fact that he had grown up in the quad cities area and was of Greek descent on his father's side.

"Well, Kyle," Jonathan finally begin to change the course of the conversation, "I know you need to talk about some things. I don't have a clue as to what they are, but I'm anxious to find out why God brought you here today. Do you want to do this privately, or do you mind my wife sitting in?"

Kyle looked over at Barbara whose face was filled with the compassion of a woman who had raised three very spirited daughters and one sensitive son. He didn't mind at all if she stayed. In fact, he almost felt as if he had known these two for many years, not just minutes.

"I welcome her advice as much as yours, Rev. Wright."

Jonathan gave a warm smile. "What's your story, Kyle Sarkos?"

Kyle began with his call to music ministry while in high school. He took them through his college years and his three-year courtship with

Caryn. She had started as a freshman during his sophomore year, and they began dating immediately. Within a couple of months they had become inseparable, and Kyle had found in her a companionship that met many wants in his life. She was this wonderful, quiet person who seemed to compliment him in many ways. His parents, however, hadn't been impressed with her. She was indeed beautiful, exotically so, but they felt she lacked a certain *something* they could never name. They were wrong. She had been the perfect wife, at least for the ten years they were married.

He told them how Caryn supported him by typing papers and doing research for him while he went through seminary. He had suggested she get a job, but she said she was not meant to be the financial support for their marriage and insisted on staying home to be there for him each step of the way. She was willing to sacrifice financially, no matter what it took, in order to see them through those last two years of Kyle's schooling. When he finally finished his education, she became the perfect minister's wife—right up until the day she left him. Obviously, somewhere down the road, Kyle hadn't been what she needed. There was no talking, discussing or reasoning with her about her decision. And he hadn't spoken with her since the day she left. In fact, he had no idea where she was.

He then explained how the church at Harvest Hollow had supported him only briefly after his divorce. He was now struggling with what to do with his life. All he'd ever dreamed of being was a music minister in church. For now, he was living with his parents and working for his father until he could pull himself together and decide what to do next. The best he could come up with was to attempt teaching music somewhere away from anywhere he had ever been before.

When Kyle finished, both Barbara and Jonathan sat in thoughtful silence at what had been shared. Jonathan leaned back in his chair and once again ran his hand through his hair. "Wow," he shook his head, "that's quite a story."

"Quite a sad story," she added.

"There are several things that stick out to me immediately, however," Jonathan began. "The first is that your parents didn't really approve of her. That should've been a red flag to you."

"But they eventually did," Kyle defended. "They thought she was wonderful when they saw what a great wife she became."

"Perhaps, but second, why wouldn't she work? Even when you were in seminary and could've used the extra money, she wouldn't get a job. Why? It would've only been a few years, especially considering that you had no children. Had there been kids I could easily understand the sacrifice."

"That's just the kind of woman she was: devoted to me alone."

"It's just unusual. Most women today want a job *and* a husband *and* a family, sacrificing nothing for anyone." He shrugged. "Then one day she just walked out … no explanation about why?"

"Well," Kyle hesitated as he weighed the rest of the story, "there was an explanation—she was pregnant."

Barbara's eyes grew wide as she exclaimed, "She was pregnant with your first child and she left you!"

"She said it wasn't my baby. She claimed she'd had an affair with my best friend."

"Had you been … intimate with her?" Jonathan wondered.

"Yes. See, I had no clue anything else was going on. I thought all was well … life as usual."

"How did she know the baby wasn't yours?" Barbara asked.

Kyle stood up from his seat and began to pace. This had been the biggest disappointment in his life. Only Caryn and both sets of their parents, plus a few very close friends, knew the truth about his inability to father children. In fact, he had begun to wonder recently if maybe that had been the reason she was dissatisfied. Perhaps she had wanted children more than anything, and that was the one thing Kyle couldn't give her. He had suggested adoption, but she flatly refused. They had prayed about it and decided that the children they would invest themselves in would be those that came through the churches they served. She seemed content with that.

"The tests were all very conclusive," Kyle finished. "There's no way I can have children. I can't be harvested, pumped up, medicated or anything. I just don't have it."

Jonathan was silent again as he seemed to meditate on the facts. "Caryn's behavior and your description of her personality don't seem to match. I wonder if you put her too high on a pedestal all those years. Something's not right. But, let's move on. Why do you feel your ministry to the Church is over? Do you think your call has been rescinded?"

"I'm divorced," Kyle bemoaned as if that fact itself was enough.

"That's not the unpardonable sin, you know?"

"It is in the Baptist church."

Jonathan smiled and gave a humorous grunt. "I'll give you that one. As much as I don't agree with divorce, there are occasional circumstances that are above just being cut and dry. And as best as I can figure at the moment, you appear to be one of those. So you just gave up?"

"I didn't know what else to do. Harvest Hollow was like the ideal situation for me. If they *suggested* I resign, where else could I go? How do I handle the marital status part of a resume'? How do I answer the questions a committee would ask me about my failed marriage … the same questions my church asked? As I see it, I'm pretty much washed up."

"Hmmm," Jonathan continued to think. "But you're here on this second Sunday of January at First Baptist Church in Dockrey, Alabama. Why is that?"

Kyle blushed realizing his motive was about to be revealed. He was embarrassed to tell them what had brought him here because he didn't want them to get the wrong idea. But what did he have to lose? These people seemed sincerely interested in helping him, so why hide?

"Going back to my home church in Muscle Shoals has been miserable. People still talk about me, about the divorce, about my *special situation*. I can't escape anything there. Every Sunday I have to face the whole thing over again. I just gave up going. I knew you were Annie Williams' father. I thought, why not? It was the best lead I could come up with. I needed to go somewhere and start over again. I figured … give Dockrey a try."

At this explanation Jonathan actually laughed as Barbara clapped her hands in delight. Kyle was wholly confused.

"Amazing how God works, isn't it?" Jonathan's light green eyes twinkled.

"What do you mean?"

"I told you this was divine appointment. You came here out of blind curiosity to see Annie's father preach, but what you walked into was a situation full of divinely inspired opportunity or apparent coincidence—depends on how you look at it."

Kyle was bewildered. He had no idea what Jonathan was talking about.

"Our former music minister just spent his first Sunday morning at your old church in Harvest Hollow, Tennessee. Last Sunday was his final Sunday here," Jonathan cleared up.

"What? What about the guy who led your music this morning?"

Barbara giggled and Jonathan smiled big. "Doug? He's my son-in-law. He was coerced into this fill-in gig until we could find somebody else."

"He's not very musical at all," Barbara continued with the giggling.

"But he did so well this morning, and the choir was awesome."

"He did well because he's married to my Andie, a music major. She made sure he flapped his arms just right while he stood up there!"

"And that choir special was from the Christmas musical," Barbara explained. "They had just worked on it this past month."

Kyle nodded in understanding now.

"So you had no idea we were in need of a music man, did you?" Jonathan asked him.

Kyle shook his head. He was now more embarrassed over this than his actual motive. It would have been easy for the Wrights to think he had been trying to initiate some kind of invitation. "Wait a minute, I assure you I had no idea. I'm not here for a job, sir. I just need to get my feet on the ground."

Jonathan's warm laughter and smile assured Kyle they were convinced of his innocence.

"Look, son, you've been through quite an ordeal. I have to believe that all this was orchestrated by God, and the fact that I am Annie Williams' father was a wonderful catalyst. I'll have to tell her about this."

Jonathan now stood, running his hand through his hair again. He padded around the dining room as he considered how to handle the situation. "First, I'll need to speak with the deacons. A couple of them will buck me, but they always do. If the Lord Himself walked into a deacon's meeting with me and presented the date for the second coming, these men would argue with Him simply because it came from my side of the table."

"What do you mean?" Kyle asked, confused about meeting with deacons.

"You need to be here serving … at least for a little while," Jonathan explained.

"What? You want *me* to work in your church?"

"No," Jonathan said gently, "I want you to *serve* in this church. I want you to fulfill your calling until God calls you somewhere else."

"There's no way a church would hire me again. I'm divorced, remember?"

"Understand I'm not offering you a permanent position," Jonathan said soberly. "The best I can do is offer the interim job that Doug has unwillingly agreed to. You could live up there," Jonathan pointed to a door on the balcony, "and carry out the duties full-time. We'd pay you full-time, but the committee would still be formed and eventually pick out a replacement. But in the meantime, you can serve and build up a reputation as faithful regardless of your marital status. It'll also give you some good references for later on if you choose to continue in church work. And if you decide to teach music, you can begin building clientele while filling in here."

Kyle was stunned. This wasn't what he was looking for when he had considered *moving on*. It was almost too good to be true. "You think the deacons will go for it?"

Barbara laughed softly as she stood to clear the dishes. "Most."

"Would you believe I have a deacon's meeting this afternoon? If this is agreeable to you, I'll bring it up and see if we can get you started this Wednesday evening."

Kyle was dumbfounded. Could this be happening? No, it wasn't permanent, but it was *something*. If he could establish himself in Dockrey as a good musician, the transition to giving lessons should be a breeze.

"I don't know what to say," Kyle said as he stood to shake Jonathan's hand. "I didn't come here today expecting any of this. I just thought … well … I don't know exactly … that perhaps I would find a place where I could fit in and belong for a while. I never imagined … this."

Jonathan smiled as he shook his hand. "I had a sense about you when I first saw you. I knew God was up to something, but I didn't know what. Let me get your phone number, and tonight after church, I'll give you a ring. Hopefully it'll be good news."

Jonathan showed Kyle the upstairs apartment and then gave him a tour around the outside of the house. As they approached the front yard, several people at the gate began to yell. Jonathan rolled his eyes and sighed.

"Who are they?" Kyle asked him, dying of curiosity that a pastor's home in such a small town would have a huge fence with crowds gathering in front.

"Fans," he said bluntly. "Ever since Annie first went on tour with Stephen, they've collected there. I don't know what the deal is with their being here year round. When Stephen and Annie are here, *that* I get. When they're obviously in New York, I don't see the point. It's senseless and a huge waste of time."

Kyle nodded. That fact hadn't occurred to him: this was Annie's home. He felt sorry for Jonathan and Barbara who had to bear the brunt of this invasion into their privacy, and that it was senseless most of the time.

Jonathan took Kyle back to the gate which led to the church and pressed in the code to unlock it. He assured him that he would contact him this evening one way or the other, and that hopefully Kyle would be moving into the garage apartment within the week.

As he drove back to Muscle Shoals, Kyle found tears trailing down his face. He couldn't believe the possibilities that had been opened up to him. He had given up hope for any kind of tolerable future. But in one afternoon a man with a big heart for God had rekindled a sense of optimism that he didn't believe still existed. Perhaps God had not abandoned him after all.

Five

"What exactly are you purposing here, Jonathan?" asked David Deaton in a scathing tone.

"I thought it was pretty clear," Jonathan replied trying not to reflect the same sarcasm. "This guy has been beaten up emotionally. God has a call on his life. God brought him here. I believe God would have us pick this man up and save him from complete destitution."

"First, you get us to hire Cindy Marcum as a charity case to temporarily replace the secretary." David stood as he railed on about his concern. "Let's face it, as wonderful as her parents were, she and her brother were pretty close to delinquency."

Jonathan smiled to himself. David Deaton had no idea the stories he'd heard concerning the deacon's own children.

"Now you want us to hire a fellow who can't even deal with his own family, much less a ministry. Divorced?"

Jonathan thoughtfully considered his words before speaking. He felt it important to keep Kyle's situation in confidence, but at the same time needed the deacons to understand that it wasn't Kyle's fault.

"I think what you're missing in all this, David, is the purpose of the church." Jonathan stood to join him at the front of the room. "When we consider hiring people to work here, for some reason we want to look for perfection and for what benefits *us* the most. We go about it with the attitude of *what can these people bring to me*? I agree that Cindy Marcum hasn't been the picture of spiritual health for any length of time in her life. I'll also agree that Mr. Sarkos and his divorce seem to have a stigma attached to them that will now be attached to our church because people will be indelible gossips. However, Jesus said he came to heal the sick; they're the ones that need a doctor. As I see it, these two young people have received some pretty heavy blows in life, whether they deserved them or not, and God has placed within our church the opportunity for healing in a way they won't find anywhere else. I haven't asked that you hire either of them permanently. All I've suggested is that while these positions are open, and they have the abilities to fill them amply, that we become the vessel God uses to help put their lives back together again."

As he sat back down, he wasn't surprised at the expressions of the deacons. It was almost amusing to see how they were split in their responses. David Deaton and John Cramer both looked as though Jonathan Wright was about to hand deliver the entire church to Satan himself, whereas the other ten men appeared intensely compassionate. It didn't matter what the situation was, this was always how it turned out: two against ten. Without divine intervention, it would never change.

***

Kyle sat on the back patio that Sunday evening with his Bible opened. He had read and prayed, prayed and read for nearly two hours. Even if the Dockrey situation didn't work out, it was encouraging to know that there were men of God out there like Jonathan Wright. Kyle had come to believe that church work was just as much a business as any other organization. It was about appearances and impressiveness. He hadn't *wanted* to believe that, but that's just how it was. Six years under the leadership of Hiram Carlton had nailed down that fact over and over again. Why couldn't he have been in a church under a man like Jonathan Wright?

That's easy, Kyle scolded himself as he considered how he had chosen churches. *I didn't want a little church in the middle of nowhere like Dockrey where pastors such as Jonathan Wright thrive. I wanted a big church, an impressive church, a church where I could boast about having one hundred or more choir members and an orchestra. I never even considered small towns; that would be moving backward.*

As he remembered his first two churches, he thought of how he had loved those ministries. He'd served as youth and music minister in both, and even though they were much smaller, he had made friends, influenced young people to Christ, and done amazing things with the music ministries. The pastors and church members had been appreciative of his talents and work, and he was considered a *part* of the churches, not just the *staff*.

At Harvest Hollow, it had been a whole different story. He was paid well but was *expected* to perform a notable ministry in the church. There was little time for socializing, and Dr. Carlton had reprimanded him several times for *fraternizing with the flock*. He explained to Kyle that he was in the *big leagues* now and it was time to *grow up* in his ministerial demeanor. Translation: *you're too good to just be with anybody*. Kyle didn't want to agree, but his ego liked the church and the new notch it had raised him to in the Convention. He had to admit he took great pleasure going to meetings those six years, tossing out numbers and accomplishments to his friends from college and seminary who were still serving in *smaller* churches— churches like First Baptist of Dockrey. How was it possible that someone with such a love for the Lord and a heart for ministry could have transformed into such a pompous fool?

His phone sang, abruptly interrupting the memories. His stomach fluttered as he pulled his cell from the pocket and hesitated to click it on. He anxiously wondered what the verdict would be. He couldn't believe that he was hoping against all hope that God would allow him to serve in this small church after the accomplishments he had acquired at Harvest Hollow.

28

However, if the answer was *no*, he knew it would hurt. How time had changed things.

"Hello?" Kyle answered, nervous as a cat but trying desperately to appear confident.

"Kyle!" came Jonathan's robust voice. "Jonathan Wright here!"

"Yes, sir, I've been waiting for your call."

"I'm not gonna beat around the bush with you. I'd love to play with you for a while and let this thing become a teasing match, but somehow that just seems inappropriate for the moment."

"I appreciate that, but for the record, I normally do have a sense of humor and like a good joke as well as the next guy."

"I understand and will keep that in mind as I work with you over the next several months."

The statement registered immediately with Kyle. "Are you saying I got the position?"

"It's yours. But remember: it's only temporary. The committee is still going to be formed, and a music man will be chosen eventually. Your coming on board does allow the church to take its time in choosing a replacement. We'll be in no rush to get someone, and my son-in-law heaved a huge sigh of relief when I revealed the news to him tonight before church."

"I understand. And believe me, just this opportunity means so much. I'll do my best, sir."

"Somehow, I figured that," Jonathan laughed. "I told the church tonight after the service that an interim guy has been found, he'll be here Wednesday evening for choir rehearsal, and they're eagerly anticipating your arrival."

"Wednesday? You're ready for me to jump right in?"

"You *need* to jump right in. Start packing your things and try to be here for supper tomorrow evening, around five thirty, okay?"

"Sure. I didn't imagine this would happen so soon. Your church doesn't need to vote?"

"Not for an interim position; the deacons have full authority for that. It cuts through a lot of time wasting. On Tuesday, I'll show you the facilities, your office, and explain all the duties you'll be responsible for while you're here."

"Okay," Kyle said as he stood up and walked out toward the river. "I'll be there tomorrow afternoon … with bells on."

"Seeing that you're a music guy, I guess the bells will be fine. I'll leave your name with security at the front gate of the house. They'll let you in when you get here."

"Yes, sir," Kyle told him as he felt a smile growing from deep within. "And Rev. Wright?"

"Yes."

"There's no way I can thank you enough for this opportunity."

"You might be surprised." Jonathan was teasing him now. "As I see it, you owe me, son. I might come up with all kinds of ways for you to repay!"

"And I'll gladly oblige."

Six

As Cindy stared out the picture window to the breathtaking view behind the church office, she figured the former secretary must have personally designed it so she would see this from her desk every time she lifted her head. It was serene and comfortable here. Even though there was much work for her to do, it wasn't unbearable. Everything was manageable and even fun. She loved working with Pastor Jon. He was full of life and love and made every day wonderfully eventful. However, she'd only been here one week.

She looked back to the computer and began to sort through the contributions of the previous year in order to print out tax information. The former secretary had been highly organized and efficient. Cindy was thankful that her few years in real estate had been under a meticulous man who demanded well-kept records. Working at the church was a breeze compared to the pressure of commercial real estate.

The door flung open and in walked Jonathan, bursting with his usual energy and life. This Tuesday morning, however, he was followed by a stranger—a man Cindy knew would be the interim music minister for the next several months.

"Good morning, Miss Marcum!" Jonathan exclaimed as he spread cheer throughout the office. "Already up and at 'em, I see."

"Yes, sir," she said smiling in response to his joy. "Next week is mother's surgery, so I wanted to get as much completed as possible. All Mrs. Wright will need to do is answer the phone while I'm away."

"And she will appreciate you for that. You know she thinks computers are of the devil. She's concerned that her family uses them far too much for communication."

Cindy laughed. Barbara wasn't much for technology and was easily thrown into a fog. She could imagine how working on a computer would be overwhelming for her.

The young blonde fellow with Jonathan was carrying a leather briefcase and wore a tie with a dress shirt. She smiled to herself over his professional appearance. Pastor Jon was wearing his typical khakis and long-sleeved polo. The new guy looked more like a salesman coming to leave samples.

"This is Kyle Sarkos," Jonathan introduced. "He's the music man for a while."

"Hello," she greeted gently, wondering why the man had such a look

31

of defeat about him. "Welcome to First Baptist."

"Thank you."

"I've explained the wardrobe to him," Jonathan teased. "Tomorrow he should be a little more in sync."

"This was required wear at my former church," Kyle clarified.

"Well, not here," Jonathan grinned as he gently slapped him on the back. "Let me get you to your office, then we'll take a look at your responsibilities and check out the choir room."

"Sounds fine to me."

Kyle followed Jonathan to a large, beautifully furnished room. He knew immediately this belonged to the music man. There was an ample stereo along one wall, several pieces of framed cross-stitch with music motifs, and quite a collection of single volumes and pages of music that probably matched whatever was in the music library. The desk was massive, and he was somewhat shocked by the size and grandeur of the space. His office at Harvest Hollow had been half this size.

"Big room," Kyle mumbled as he sat his briefcase on the floor.

"It should be. A lot of work is carried on in this church where music is concerned. Without it, the whole ambience of our ministry would seem almost dry and suffocating. The music is what lets us exhale."

"Exhale?"

"Absolutely." Jonathan sat on the edge of the mahogany desk. "Church is about taking in everything. We take in the Word, the principles of the Lord, the facts about life and spiritual growth, and yes, a lot of food while we're at it. But music is what gives us the opportunity to let some of that out. It lets us breathe back to God creatively and expressively. The best thing I can come up with is exhaling."

Kyle liked that. In fact, it described very clearly what worship actually is. "I've never heard that before. It makes a lot of sense. Worship is the ministry of exhaling. That's a pretty good philosophy."

"No philosophy about it. That's pure fact."

"Yes, sir."

As Jonathan helped him settle into his office, he found himself more drawn to the man than before. He was warm and normal. He joked and laughed often, and seemed to find joy in almost everything he discussed. As he went on and on about his hobbies, his family, and various people in the church, he would occasionally throw in some responsibility Kyle would have. When he realized this was *the talk* about his duties at church, Kyle reversed his mind and began to jot down information on a pad of sticky notes lying on the desk.

"I have six grandchildren so far, with three more on the way," Jonathan said proudly. "You'll get acquainted with Andie and Doug's bunch real quick. They have four already, and one in the oven. You'll have the older boys, Adam and Arly, in children's choir. They meet on Tuesdays after school. Ashley's a preschooler, going on sixteen." Jonathan laughed at the thought of his granddaughter. "You don't have to do preschool choir. The teachers deal with them in Sunday School. Did you know Annie and Stephen are expecting another one too?"

"Didn't they just have a baby?"

Jonathan laughed again and slapped his knee. "So did Andie and Doug! Their youngest, Aimee, will be one-year-old next month. Little Stevie won't even be a year when Stephen and Annie's comes along in June. And believe it or not, Angie is pregnant too! What on earth are my girls thinking?"

Kyle wondered too. He was an only child, and with the fact that he couldn't father children himself, he found the idea of so many babies at one time a bit unsettling.

"You've got a pretty good group of teenagers here too," Jonathan went on. "Youth choir meets on Sunday afternoons at four o'clock. For now, we'll let Cindy be in charge of getting parents to provide them supper after practice. When you become more familiar with everyone, you can take that over yourself."

"Who's Cindy?" Kyle wondered as he wrote her name down on the sticky note next to *Youth Choir, four o'clock, Sundays.*

Jonathan looked over at him puzzled. "The girl out there: Cindy Marcum, the secretary."

"Oh, okay. I didn't get her name." Next to Cindy, he added, *church secretary.*

"Parents are good about the suppers. They're also good about making their kids show up at choir rehearsal."

Kyle nodded in understanding. Older teens had a tendency to slack off of church activities, especially choir, and parents often let them. It was nice to know he would have support from the households if he tried to do something big with the Youth.

Jonathan walked over to the computer and continued his talk about responsibilities. "Joe, that's your predecessor, left all the information you need about soloists and such on his computer."

Jonathan pulled open the top right drawer of the desk and retrieved a file. Handing it to Kyle he explained, "Everything you need to know is in this folder and on that computer. The folder will tell you all the programs and passwords. There're some ensembles in the church; he's got all that somewhere in here. We've got quite a few instrumentalists who like to do offertories and such; occasionally they'll play along with choir specials or something. All in there."

Kyle made a few more notes on the sticky pad.

"You ready for the choir room?"

"Sure."

"Follow me."

When they were back in the main office, Cindy stopped them.

"Mr. Sarkos," she said as she stood to hand him a form, "I need you to fill this out. It's for the payroll."

"He'll be staying in the garage apartment with us," Jonathan told her. "Just put that address down for now."

"Really?" Cindy raised her eyebrows. "Your wife too?"

Kyle hesitated as he bit his bottom lip. "I'm ...," he thought carefully, "... not married." He felt like the words were a lie. In truth, he was divorced, but to just come out and say it was still difficult.

"No dependents," Cindy checked a small box. "This should be really easy then. What about a phone number? Do you have a cell, or do you want me to put the Wright's number down?"

"Hang on," Kyle said as he walked to her desk and took the pen from her. He scribbled his number inside the tiny space provided.

"One more thing—Social Security."

"My Mark of the Beast," he mumbled with a smile as he scribbled again.

"I hope not," she teased back. "That may not put you in very good standing with our church."

"Then we'll just keep it between the three of us," Kyle winked.

He handed the pen back to Cindy and then looked toward Jonathan with raised eyebrows to ask what's next.

"Let's go see your laboratory," Jonathan said.

He led Kyle to the main part of the church building where the sanctuary was located. They climbed the stairs behind the worship center and entered yet another impressive room in Kyle's estimation. The tiered levels for seating, the incredible sound equipment, the bright and cheery decor made the room welcoming and functional.

"This is awesome," he said walking to the director's stool and looking over the sound equipment. "I've never seen a small church put so much money into its music program. How many do you run here?"

"About 150 in Sunday School, 300 or so in worship. It depends on whether it's hunting season or decoration time or summer vacation."

"You had forty-five in your choir Sunday. That's pretty incredible for a church this size."

"It all depends on what you emphasize as important," Jonathan explained. "Like I said, I see music as an exhaling, as something vital to the health and life of our church. Because of that, I give a lot of emphasis to its necessity for our spiritual expression, ministry and growth."

"You're a rare pastor, then," Kyle muttered as he walked over to the shelves of the music library.

"Well, perhaps, but I'm sure just as we may excel in our music ministry, there are many other areas where I've failed to lead adequately."

Kyle looked back and laughed slightly as he said, "And as the new music minister in your church, I would like to say, I don't care! I like your choice of emphasis."

Seven

As Kyle took another delicious bite of Beef Stroganoff that Tuesday evening, he felt guilty about eating his meals with the Wrights.

"I can cook really well," he told them as he reached for his glass of iced tea. "I know you have a little kitchen up there in the apartment. I'll be more than glad to keep to myself and cook and all. You don't have to do this for me."

"Whatever you prefer," Barbara said warmly. "You're no bother to us at all. But I'm sure after years of taking care of yourself, you'd probably like a little more privacy than this family is used to. We tend to intrude, blend and bond into each other's lives. You may have to tell us more than once to mind our own business, but don't think it's because we're nosey. It's simply because we care a lot."

"I welcome all the care I can get," he said while downing another forkful.

"Tell us that when you've been here for three months," Jonathan said skeptically.

Kyle laughed and shook his head in delight. Being around Rev. Wright was a breath of crisp, autumn air: you welcomed the cool after the hot, dry summer. Living with his parents again had been depressing. His father was a serious man, all business, and struggled to ever express anything emotionally. He believed life should be dealt with rationally and everything could be reasoned through. Even his Christianity tended to lack compassion and grace. Bradley Sarkos was a self-made man, and even though he acknowledged God's blessings in his efforts, he never failed to mention that it was he himself that had actually made the efforts. He had struggled with Kyle's inability to move beyond the divorce and the problem of serving in churches because of his self-imposed scarlet letter. He felt Kyle should pick himself up and start all over again in some other area of life. There was way more out there than just church work, and Kyle was too gifted a musician to sit around wasting his talents by pining and mourning his misfortune.

Kyle's mother seemed to float through life. She had no real responsibilities other than taking care of Bradley. It was hard for her when Kyle moved back home because her life was devoted to her husband, meeting his every whim, and to suddenly have to divide her time and attention became distracting. Bradley had noticed her struggle to perform top notch, so he began to give her busy tasks to keep her intact, or more

36

aptly, focused on him. During the months Kyle had stayed there, his father had insisted she remodel the entire downstairs of their mansion. Kyle couldn't tell if he was coming or going at times because of the unending mess and chaos in the living area. Because of that, he often retreated to his room, alone most of the time, where the emptiness and loneliness were even more magnified.

The Wrights' however, were a whole other level of existence. Their home lacked anything of the plush-ness and luxury Kyle had grown up with. In fact, had his parents seen this home, they would have immediately judged the Wrights as people with no taste or culture. The house was filled with books from top to bottom, not impressively bound volumes with decorative binders and classic titles like those of his parents. These were books that looked like a cur dog mix of Chihuahua and Great Dane: no sense, order or design. Each book was well worn, indicating it wasn't there for decoration, but for content.

The Wrights were openly warm and communicative. Their own exchanges indicated a deep love and respect for each other, the kind that comes when two people have shared many joys and trials in life. Barbara laughed at Jonathan's wit, and he appreciated every effort she made in service to others. Kyle learned quickly that Barbara hadn't officially worked since the birth of their first child, yet had remained incredibly busy serving others in countless ways through the church for years.

As the talk continued, he glanced up to the portrait over the fireplace and wondered how different his life might have been had he married someone like Andie, Angie or Annie after college. These girls had grown up in this family, with memories and a foundation of love and acceptance that pervaded all they did. Caryn had been an only child, but her relationship with her parents always seemed unnatural. In fact, for the ten years they had been married, he had seen her parents only five or six times, and that was with Kyle and Caryn traveling to Martha's Vineyard. The Carters never made a trip to Tennessee. Caryn traveled several times on her own each year to see them, and she used that as the reason why they never felt the need to travel south. She had been sent to boarding schools from the time she was in third grade. How she ended up at Furman University was beyond him.

She shared very few memories of her childhood. She loved talking about their years together in college and seminary, but anything before that she deemed boring and inconsequential. Her life had taken on new meaning in the relationship with Kyle—at least until last year—and obviously some time before. He was still baffled by the suddenness of her leaving and that he had never sensed anything wrong. Could anyone be that good at covering up bitterness and malcontent? Evidently so. Maybe his parents had been right about her all along.

Once again, the image of the three beautiful women over the fireplace haunted him. What would it have been like to have Jonathan and Barbara as in-laws, to be a part of this family? How would it have been to have a wife who spoke her mind … often … without holding things in to appear pleasant and content? According to Jonathan, his girls were beautiful, stubborn-headed, and opinionated, and they had no trouble letting anyone know what was on their minds. What would a relationship with that type of woman be like? Would his life be different now had he listened to those who had warned him about Caryn?

***

On Wednesday morning, Kyle appeared at the church office dressed considerably more casual. Cindy smiled as she complimented him on the change and then went back to her work at the computer. He nodded in acknowledgment and headed for his office. When he opened the door and turned on the light, he was again baffled at the size and the furnishings. Walking in and closing the door behind him, he took a moment to drink in the opportunity God had given him at this moment in time. He knew it was temporary, but at least he was here for now.

The ministry of music is the ministry of exhaling, Jonathan had told him. *I've never thought of it like that before. I have a lot to learn from this man, not only about ministry, but about life in general. Dear God, please don't let me miss a single lesson You've cut out for me by being here. Let me drink it all in … no … breathe it all in … and then learn to exhale as though it's just second nature.*

As the day drew on, he looked through books and listened to CD's located in his office. Joe had done an excellent job of chronicling when any piece of music had been done. He would start practice tonight with something familiar and then move on to new territory. As he thought about what the choir might sing on Sunday, he wondered if he could get copies of past bulletins to see how they generally scheduled their services. He checked his computer for some type of format but found nothing. Apparently Joe didn't save everything.

He peeked out of his office and asked Cindy, "Do you have copies of orders of worship for the past few months?"

"Why?" asked Jonathan who was getting a diet Mountain Dew from the small refrigerator in the outer lobby.

"So I can know how many songs I need to pick out and what order you do everything in."

Jonathan shook his head as he popped open the lid of the can. "No, just remember, we're exhaling. I never want our worship services to become predictable and routine. The best thing you could do for this church right now is put something together that we've never done before."

When Kyle hesitantly withdrew back into his office and closed the

38

door, Cindy looked up at Jonathan with wide eyes. "Are you serious? This church has been very routine and predictable for as long as I can remember."

"Pitiful, isn't it?" Jonathan said with a grimace as he went back to his own office.

Cindy found herself smiling at the thought of Kyle turning the services here upside down. His long hair and slightly hip demeanor just might have a positive effect on moving this church in a new direction. In fact, she had been so impressed with his unorthodox ministerial appearance that she was disappointed when he talked with her later that afternoon before leaving.

"Cindy?" he asked after he had passed her desk and then returned on a second thought. "Are there any hair places in Dockrey? I don't want a barbershop, just a regular salon. Where do you get your hair cut?"

"I get my hair done in Florence, but there are at least five different salons here."

"Really? Would you suggest one?"

"So, you're gonna cut your hair?" she asked him, let down that he would be turning himself into a conventional man.

"I should. I don't want to distract from what God might want to do through me. The long and shaggy look just sort of happened this past year. I'm afraid there are many that would immediately have to get over it before they could ever respect me in this church. It's the right thing to do."

Cindy nodded. She had never been in the habit of doing the right thing simply because it was *the right thing to do*. Her motto had always been to sort of buck the system whenever possible. Thanks to her influence, Angie Wright had been swayed from the straight and narrow quite often during their high school years. She wondered if Kyle had always been a man who did the right thing. And if so, what would someone like him think about someone like her? If she were smart, she would keep her distance from him and never let a real friendship develop. As the mental list of her discrepancies began to scroll through her mind, she shook the thoughts from her head. *You reap what you sow*, she thought to herself. *I never realized how much until now.*

Eight

Kyle dressed casually for Wednesday evening as Jonathan had suggested. He went with a pair of khakis and a blue button down dress shirt, no tie. He tried not to be nervous, but this situation was different than any prior. He had always been voted into a ministerial position at a church, and the position had always been permanent. He knew Jonathan had pushed him through the deacon board and then sprung him on the church. He wanted to believe that the church carried the same graceful openness as their pastor—at least he hoped it did.

As he walked into the sanctuary, it occurred to him that he had no idea what he was supposed to do during church. He had been so caught up in preparing for choir practice and Sunday's service that Wednesday's program just slipped his mind. *Great start, Sarkos.* He had almost decided to head back to the house to hunt Jonathan down when he walked through the door.

"Pastor Wright," Kyle said immediately with relief.

"I'm glad you've finally changed your address of me to something slightly less formal."

"Sir?" Kyle was confused.

"You've called me Rev. Wright from day one. You just called me Pastor Wright. You're improving."

Kyle smiled. Once again his thoughts went back to *Dr.* Carlton, who had insisted that he always be called by that title.

"What would you like me to call you?"

"Jonathan would be just fine. That's what the staff has always called me. We're co-workers, Kyle, laboring together for the kingdom. What I do, you won't do, and what you do, I can't even begin to do!" Jonathan laughed. "My kids are musical; I'm nowhere close."

"Cindy calls you Pastor Jon."

"Most people do. She was raised calling me that and feels more comfortable with it. By the way, that haircut looks great. I respect you doing that. That says a lot about who you are as a Christian. I've known a lot of Christian musicians who use their wacky appearance as an excuse to *quietly* rebel. They don't think of it that way, but that's what a lot of it boils down to."

"Would you have ever asked me to cut it?"

"Permanent staff member? Would have definitely suggested it. Interim and in your condition—not on your life. When you walked down the stairs

Tuesday morning in a dress shirt and tie, I already knew you weren't wearing the long hair out of rebellion and nonconformity. I could handle it if I had to."

Kyle nodded. He was glad now he'd gone ahead and cut it. Then he remembered his dilemma. "What do I do after church supper tonight?"

"That's up to you. Joe always went to the choir room and prepared for rehearsal."

"I don't need to lead any music for the service?"

"Actually, we don't have a service. We have a bunch of different groups that meet for various needs."

"Really?" Kyle was surprised again. He had never known a pastor to personally give up top billing. "What kinds of groups?"

"I teach a new Christian's class in here. There's a men's class, a women's class and a weight loss class—you don't appear to need that. Then there's a General Studies class. There's also a prayer group. And then usually a group of men stand around after supper and pretend they're doing something, when in actuality they're just jawing away about whatever. Just take your pick, son, or head on to the choir room and do any last minute preparations you might need to do."

"I'm finished with preparations."

"Let's eat, then" Jonathan slapped his back. "You can mull it over while you chew."

At the fellowship hall, Jonathan introduced Kyle to what seemed like half the church. He knew he could never remember all the names, but he took special note of those involved in the music program. He had never faced this situation alone before; Caryn had always been by his side. She was quiet, but beautiful, poised to perfection, with a gentle smile that seemed to disarm even the most resistant people. She had a calming presence, and at this moment Kyle's insides were churning. People were polite, he was polite, but nothing about it seemed peaceful. He wasn't here for the long run. He was nobody's golden boy this time. His purpose at this church was not to come in and dazzle them with his personality, charm and talent. He was just the fill-in man until the real one showed up several months later—or even sooner—to replace him.

"You look lost," came a vaguely familiar voice from behind his shoulder.

He turned to find Cindy and a compassionate smile. "I am lost," he confessed as he held his plate of chicken not knowing where to go.

"See that corner of the middle section of tables." She pointed toward the place. "That's where I'll be as soon as I get my food. If you want, you can sit with me tonight seeing as Pastor Jon seldom sits in one place."

"He doesn't even have a plate yet," Kyle noticed as he glanced to where Jonathan was laughing with several men.

"He's a social man. If I didn't know him really well, I'd think he was working the crowd. But he's not. He's a caring man who wants to know his people and wants them to know him."

Kyle nodded at the assessment and then sat at her suggested spot. He was relieved. Normally he would thrive in this kind of setting. He lived for these moments of meeting new people and getting to know others. But this wasn't normal. Normal was having Caryn by his side and being in a church that had called him. Normal was excitement about the upcoming first rehearsal knowing he would wow the people with all he had. He wasn't even sure how to handle this rehearsal. Should he be charming and cute and let them know they'd have a good time preparing for each presentation to come? Should he be laid back with a quiet confidence to let them know he could fill in until it was time to move on? He didn't want anyone to feel he was campaigning for the job. When Jonathan had first suggested this position to him, none of these dynamics crossed his mind. All he had seen was the possibility to work in a church again—if just for a little while.

Cindy sat across from him. "Hey, I see you found the place fine."

"Yeah," he said embarrassed, as his mouth was full with a huge bite of chicken.

"It won't take long for people here to know and accept you. This is a warm and gracious church."

"I'm not normally so … uncomfortable. This is sort of new to me."

"Really? You've never done church work before? I just assumed …"

"Oh, I've done plenty of church work. I've just never done it, well, like this … as an interim."

She nodded as she placed a small piece of chicken in her mouth. "Why did you stop doing it full time?"

He didn't answer. He felt his cheeks grow warm, and he put his fork down. When she looked at his expression after the awkward silence, she blushed.

"Did I say something wrong?" she asked gently. "I didn't mean to do say anything offensive or …"

He shook his head and motioned for her to stop as he swallowed his last bite. "It's complicated. There's a lot that's happened in my life this past year—things that have changed me. I'm just trying to find my way right now."

She nodded and went to another subject. "Your hair looks great, by the way, very stylish. I was sort of afraid you might buzz all those pretty blonde locks off all together."

"No buzzing for this head. I'm not a buzzing kind of person."

"Good," she grinned as she picked up another small bite of chicken. "I don't care for the buzz, but it seems to be all the rage right now. It'll be much more pleasant facing you each day at the office like this."

The rest of the meal was slightly awkward between them, but Kyle had to admit he appreciated how quickly she moved on past the changes he had spoken of but not defined. She had class, and was every bit as poised as Caryn, but they looked as opposite as night and day. Still, he was thankful Cindy had been here tonight to rescue him from his aloneness. He would owe her for that.

"Where are you going to class?" she asked as they threw away their plates. "Or *are* you going, I should probably ask. Joe never did."

"I'd like to be in a class, but I don't even know where to start. I thought the one with General Studies sounded safe."

"It's wonderful," she smiled at him. "Doug Mason teaches it. He's Pastor Jon's son-in-law."

"The one who led the music Sunday morning?"

She laughed and nodded her head. "If you only knew how much he hated doing that! You'll be like his eternal hero for getting him out of that job."

"I thought he did well."

"Then you're gonna love him as a teacher! He's actually pretty good at that."

Cindy was right on both accounts. When she introduced Kyle as the interim music minister, Doug actually fell to his knees and embraced Kyle's legs. It was a definite icebreaker for those already in the room. The lesson was just what he needed. He dealt with the reality of applying grace to our lives, realizing that this is how God deals with us, even though others around us may be calling for justice instead.

"It's easy to beat myself up," Doug told them honestly. "I'm a reactor, okay? You do something, I react. That's how I function. To make matters worse, I married a reactor!"

At this Doug looked over at Andie and winked. Kyle couldn't get over how beautiful Andie was having now seen her up close and how much she favored Annie.

"So imagine our home when the day has been stressful," he went on. "There isn't a lot of grace flying around there. Then add to that four kids and Andie's pregnancy hormones, and suddenly you have this recipe for complete chaos." Doug paused as he walked out to the middle of the room, in the center of twenty or so adults sitting around the perimeter.

"Sometimes, I'll wake up in the middle of the night ready to beat myself up over the fact that I did nothing to prevent the chaos. I could have, but I didn't. I felt justified to add my two cents in with everyone else when the complaining and griping started. But you know what? It's all over. The evening has passed, and no matter how much I may want to mourn over my mistakes, I can't take them back. And see? This is where grace comes in! God says, All right! You blew it! You know it! I know it! The kids know it! Andie knows it, and there's a good chance that any neighbor within a hundred yards of your house knows it too!"

The group chuckled at his expression. Doug was a very animated teacher.

"And that's when God tells me that He's erasing it because I'm confessing it. He's extending a huge amount of grace to me, not because I deserve it, but because He wants to. Now … I can keep beating myself up if I want, but that doesn't have God in it. That's just a Doug pity party, and Satan's name is scrawled all over that. See, grace means I can start over."

He went back to his little podium and glanced down at his notes. "It doesn't mean that Andie, the kids, or even the neighbors will forget what happened. Those scars will still be there when everybody gets up in the morning. What it does mean is that it doesn't have to happen again. I pick up right here, right now, and start over. It doesn't matter how bad I blew it. Grace is bigger than all my mistakes."

Doug leaned his arms on the podium and rested his upper body on them. "What have you blown?" he asked seriously now. "Do you think it's too big? Do you think that God can't extend enough grace to see you through it? If that were possible—the not enough grace issue—then Jesus wouldn't have said *it is finished* on the cross. He would have said, *Okay, I did my part. The rest is up to you guys.* He took it all, folks, every ounce of our failures so God could grant us grace instead."

He stood up again and walked in front of the podium this time. "To disregard God's grace for our failures is like slapping God in the face and saying, *No thanks, I'll take this one on my own.* We gotta let go of what we hold so that we can receive all that God's given."

Kyle enjoyed the class and loved Doug's teaching, but now he walked into the choir room slowly … almost forgetting why he was there. He was surprised to find most of the seats already filled with smiling faces looking at him with great anticipation.

"Wow," he said taken aback at the sight. "Are you the real choir or just some folks Pastor Jon hired to make me feel better about coming here?"

Laughter. His heart eased just a bit. He was shocked to see Cindy sitting right in the middle of the whole group. Did she sing? He didn't remember seeing her there on Sunday morning. Of course, he didn't actually remember seeing any of these people last Sunday morning. His mind had been somewhere else. He was pleased to see Doug find his seat on the front row, and his smile was bigger than the rest.

"Doug, if you have any pointers for me, I'd be more than glad to hear them," he said as he walked toward the director's stool and stand.

"Here's a pointer," Andie yelled out from the piano on Kyle's right. "Don't ask Doug for pointers when it comes to music."

"Oh, I've got a great pointer for you," Doug blurted out. "Always remember this: when the piano player ain't happy, ain't nobody happy!"

The room laughed and Kyle smiled at the give and take. "I assume you're speaking from personal experience?"

"That and large amounts of experimentation," Doug affirmed.

"Well, if the piano player doesn't mind," Kyle looked over at Andie with raised eyebrows in question, "I'd like to get started with rehearsal."

"Ready and willing," Andie said with a salute.

"Hey!" Doug called out. "You never say that to me!"

"You're kidding, right?" Kyle asked him. "Four kids and one on the way?"

At this the room roared with laughter, and Kyle found himself feeling as though his feet were beginning to be planted and his heart was beginning to be healed.

***

That night as Cindy lay in bed, she felt as though her heart would break. She wanted desperately to accept God's grace and believe He could look beyond her faults just as Doug had taught. But every time she prayed, all she could see were the sins she had willingly committed and wallowed in for many years. And she had not done them out of ignorance, but out of sheer rebellion. She knew the choices she had made, and she knew that wasn't how she had been raised to live. Her heart pounded heavily within her. She had felt hypocritical sitting next to Kyle, a minister, a Godly man, probably someone who had made right decisions all his life. He had even cut his hair because he didn't want to be offensive to the church. How would someone like him view someone like her? God's grace would have to be mighty strong to overlook the things she had done.

Nine

Cindy knew there was a Scripture about keeping your mind at peace, but for the life of her she couldn't think of it. Her brain was frazzled and her emotions shattered—the very idea of peace seemed impossible. Less than ten minutes ago they had wheeled her mother into surgery, and the doctor's words were still brooding around her head.

"I'm going to be honest with you two," she had told Cindy and Billy. "I'm not sure what we'll find when we get in there. Your mother put this off way too long. I've had cases before where the only thing I could do was sew them back up and send them home."

"Could it actually be that bad?" Cindy asked as panic rose in her throat.

"Absolutely. This isn't going to be an easy procedure any way we look at it, but your mother's choice to put off the surgery until after the holidays was ludicrous. She should've done this three months ago."

Billy now butted in. "Wait just a second here! Are you telling me that had this been done earlier she stood a better chance of survival?"

"A much better chance," the doctor replied sternly.

"Then you better hope everything turns out for the best, doc, 'cause there will be a lawsuit in this if it doesn't," he spat out.

"Shut up, Billy," Cindy snapped angrily. "You didn't even know three months ago that she had cancer. Had you spent enough time around her you would have figured out something was wrong. As it is, we're lucky she's even doing this. She refused any treatment all together at first. It if hadn't been for Angie, we wouldn't even be here. So save your macho baloney for somebody else. It's past time for showing you care."

Cindy felt cold and alone in the waiting area although she was surrounded by people who had been near and dear to her for most of her life. Jonathan and Barbara had been there waiting for the three Marcums when they arrived at the hospital. She had been relieved. She didn't know what to say to her mother, and with Billy added to the combination, the situation was even more uncomfortable. The Wrights had a calming effect; both humor and deep compassion flowed from them. Now the waiting room was full of deacons, friends and relatives, but she needed to be alone. She wanted to cry, she wanted to scream, and she wanted to drop from exhaustion.

"Hey, sweetie," Barbara said coming up behind her. "Could I get you something other than coffee? I know you've got to be drowning from it."

"No, thank you, but I appreciate it. If you don't mind, I might slip out of here for a bit and get something to eat."

"Absolutely," Barbara said warmly as she gently rubbed Cindy's back. "Head out for a while. If there's any news, I'll call you."

Cindy nodded, trying to hold back threatening tears. "Can I bring you something?"

Barbara shook her head and smiled as she walked her to the door.

***

"First Baptist Church," Kyle tried to sound cheerful as he answered the phone.

"I was wondering if there was any news on Sue Marcum's surgery," came an aged voice on the other end.

"All I've heard so far is that they took her in about two hours ago. My understanding, ma'am, is that the procedure is supposed to take ten to twelve hours."

"My goodness," the woman sighed. "We won't know anything then until tomorrow, I suppose."

"Actually, Pastor Jon said he would leave a message on the church answering machine when he returned tonight. You can call the church later this evening and probably get the full story."

"Thank you, so much. I'll do that."

"No problem. Have a great day."

He hung the phone up and sat back at his desk. He wished he had kept count of how many people had called to ask about Sue. He imagined it would be a blessing for Cindy and the family to know so many were thinking of them. He was antsy to call the hospital himself but knew Jonathan would keep him abreast as people would be worried and checking in at the office all day.

The phone rang again. Kyle breathed deeply as he reached for the receiver. He really wasn't enjoying manning the phones, but he felt honored he was able to contribute in some way.

"First Baptist Church."

"Kyle, it's Jonathan."

"Yes sir. How's it going in Tupelo?"

"Long and slow. So far everything's been routine. No problems to report."

"Glad to hear it. I'll pass the news on."

"Gettin' lots of calls?"

"Tons. People must really care about this family."

"Did you know Cindy's father died last May?"

Kyle was stunned. For some reason he had assumed Mrs. Marcum was divorced. He felt so emblazoned with his scarlet letter that he had refused to get to know Cindy. He didn't want to encourage any friendship or relationship with her to protect her reputation when the news of his status eventually leaked out. He had never considered the fact that she might have needed a friend.

"I didn't know that," Kyle finally answered. "How?"

"Sudden heart attack in the middle of the night. He was well loved at the church, a deacon, a Sunday School teacher, and a wonderful man."

"Wow, I ... uh ... I didn't know."

"Too bad you didn't get a chance to meet him. He was a good friend and a wonderful encourager to the ministers at the church."

"A rare man then." He shook his head sadly.

"I need you to do something for me, Kyle. I forgot the church credit card, and I was supposed to make a Sam's run today."

"Sam's run?"

"Sam's warehouse—that's where we get a lot of food and supplies for Wednesday night suppers. Because it's Tuesday, we have to get it today. I need you to get the card, come here by the hospital and get the list, and then go shopping for me."

"Okay," he said hesitantly. "Does that mean nobody will be here at the church?"

"That's what it means."

He paused for a moment and then asked, "Is that okay? Can we do that?"

"We can do whatever we want because Sue Marcum's in surgery. And as far as I'm concerned, you should've been here anyway. But since you offered to answer the phones, I figured why not. Sue and her husband, James, were pillars of this church. We should have a day named after them on the church calendar."

Kyle had to reset his mind to remember he was in Dockrey now and not Harvest Hollow. It seemed this church was not so much about appearances as it was relationships, and Jonathan Wright was the example the church followed.

"I'll do whatever is needed," Kyle told him.

Jonathan explained where the credit card was located and told him to head to Northeast Mississippi Medical Center in Tupelo. Kyle answered the phone twice more before he managed to get out the door.

Ten

Kyle found his way to the hospital and followed the directions to the waiting area. He slowly opened the door and peeked inside. There were many familiar faces, but he could only put names to a few. He edged his way in and began looking for Jonathan. He heard his laugh before he ever saw his face.

"I'm here," Kyle said softly as he walked up behind him.

"Great!" Jonathan said turning around. "You're a life saver, my boy."

"Kyle," said an older woman who was in the group that had been laughing. "I just wanted to tell you how much I enjoyed the services Sunday. Your order of worship and song selections were such blessings. You're a gifted young man."

"Thank you," he said humbly. "I really appreciate that."

"How did we manage to get you as interim?"

Jonathan cut in, "Right place at the right time," then quickly moved Kyle to another section of the room. "Have you had lunch yet?"

"No, sir. I was gonna grab a burger or something."

Jonathan raised his eyebrows in surprise. "You're in Tupelo and you're just gonna grab a burger? You obviously haven't lived in Dockrey long enough."

Kyle grinned. He understood. Getting out of Dockrey was a big deal to folks who had lived there for some time.

"I need you to do something," Jonathan said seriously this time. "Take Cindy to lunch. I think Olive Garden is one her favorites." He reached into his billfold and pulled out two twenties.

"Wait a minute, she doesn't want to be here?"

"She doesn't *need* to be here. This is really tough for her. She needs a change of scenery and company for a bit. She needs her mind off of all of this, even if only for a few minutes."

"Well," Kyle was still hesitant, "if you think so. But I can pay for it. No problem."

"I insist," Jonathan said as he pushed the bills into Kyle's hand. "I think you're just what the doctor ordered today. There's Cindy over there."

"What if she won't go?"

"She's ready to launch any moment—just waiting for the countdown. I don't imagine you'll have any problems getting her out of here."

He nodded and made his way to the other side of the room where Cindy was staring out a window at blank, sterile hospital buildings. He couldn't imagine what she might be feeling. Having lost her father in May, and now with her mother in surgery for cancer, it must be overwhelming.

"Cindy," Kyle said softly.

She turned quickly, not recognizing the voice, but then smiled when she saw it was him. "Hey," she replied wearily. "I thought you were answering the phone at church."

"I was. Jonathan forgot the credit card for Sam's. So, here I am."

She nodded and turned back to stare out the window.

"I was wondering," he began again. Why was this so awkward for him? "Have you had lunch?"

"That's questionable. I've snacked on a million things all morning."

"How about I take you out of here for a little bit … Olive Garden perhaps?"

This time she turned around with a little more energy and a genuine smile. "Are you serious?"

"I'm pretty hungry. Things are rather uneventful in here right now, and I've got my phone with me if anyone needs to contact you."

"You don't have to ask me twice," she grinned as she walked over to a couch to retrieve her purse; she didn't even bother to tell anyone she was leaving.

Kyle led her to his Jeep and unlocked her door. He went ahead and opened it for her and waited for her to get settled before he closed it. Was this okay? He should be a gentleman, shouldn't he? He climbed into his side and started the vehicle.

"I've never ridden in one of these," she said as he pulled out of the parking garage.

"What? A Jeep?"

"Yeah. It's actually a pretty nice car … vehicle. I never imagined it could be so well equipped. And I always thought they had canvas tops. I've never noticed one with an actual roof before."

"Actually, this one comes with both. During the summer I put on the canvas, and during the colder months I put on the hard shell." He stopped at the intersection and suddenly realized he had no idea where he was going. "So, how do I get to Olive Garden?"

***

Once they were seated and their orders taken, Cindy gave a huge sigh. She was glad to be out of the hospital for a short time. Her mother would be there for close to a week, which meant Cindy would be there by her side through all of it.

"Pastor Jon put you up to this, didn't he?" she asked Kyle as she put two packs of sweetener into her iced tea.

"He suggested it, but I'm glad."

She stirred her tea and took a sip. "I sometimes wonder if life can get any harder," she said as she bit her bottom lip trying to salvage her emotions long enough to get through a meal.

"I know what you mean."

"How could you? Your life is perfect. Good-looking guy, great talent, easy to get along with. What possible problems could you have in your perfect little world?"

Kyle stared at her for a moment.

"I'm sorry," she said meekly. "I didn't mean to be so rude. It's just hard for me to have gone from my life last year to my life this year. I sometimes feel like I'm swimming around in a murky pond and there's no relief in sight. I can't see; I can't breathe. And the worst of it is I don't know when it will end or how it will end."

He leaned forward into the table as he said, "Trust me when I say I can understand."

She looked up at him in confusion, "How?"

He closed his eyes. He was obviously struggling. "Did you ever wonder why I'm just the interim? Why I didn't put in for the full-time position?"

"Well, you came from Harvest Hollow; I just assumed you knew some bigger church was opening up somewhere and you wanted to be free when it happened. You resigned, took on this job, and you're waiting for the big kahuna."

"I'm divorced." He managed to squeeze the words out.

Cindy's eyes grew wide and her jaw dropped. For the first time in three months she actually managed to put the thoughts of her father's death and her mother's cancer out of her head. "No way," she said in disbelief. "I had no idea."

"My wife left me on February 13."

"Just this past year?"

He nodded.

"Why?" she wondered, now feeling guilty for beginning to pry.

"She said it was because she was having an affair with another man, my best friend, but then she didn't go to him, and she was pregnant." Kyle paused. "As the months go by, I'm beginning to wonder what the real reason was. None of it adds up."

"She was pregnant? Did you have any other children?"

"The baby wasn't mine, and no, we had no other children."

"How do you know it wasn't your baby?"

"I know," was all he would offer.

"I'm sorry. How long were you married?"

"Ten years."

"Well, you beat my brother," she half chuckled. "His first marriage lasted two years, and his second only nine months."

"I did everything I could to get her to stay. I didn't want the divorce. I was even willing to raise the child."

"Really? And she left anyway?"

"It was like her mind was made up and there was no moving her in any other direction," he explained as he relived the moments again. "I mean, the day before, life was great. On February 12, everything was like it had always been. We had breakfast together the next morning, and that afternoon she walked into the house, packed up her things, and left. And I haven't seen her since."

"Not at all?"

"I don't even know where she is. The divorce papers were delivered by messenger. She wanted absolutely nothing. She wanted no ties or anything, no pictures, no mementos. She just wanted the divorce."

"Well, what about your best friend? The guy she was supposed to be in love with?"

"Great guy," Kyle shook his head. "He and his wife seemed like these wonderful Godly people."

"Did you face him with it?"

"I didn't have the nerve. His wife was pregnant too. And Reese never acted weird in any way at all. I mean, even when it became common knowledge that Caryn had actually divorced me, he acted like all was well and tried to comfort me through it! It was nauseating."

"I can imagine! The very idea! Is he still in contact with her?"

"I don't know. The church pretty much forced me to resign after a few weeks. I anticipated it anyway. Not a very good image for a church to have a divorced guy on staff. When I left, Reese shook my hand and promised that he and his wife would be praying for me daily. It was like he had no idea. Surely he had to know she would have told me about the affair … and known that was the reason she left."

The word *affair* sunk into Cindy's mind like dead weight. The memory of her own life came flooding back. Here was Kyle, a wonderful, innocent man, whose life was literally wrecked over an affair. And hadn't she been guilty of doing this to someone else? If he knew her past, he would probably walk out of the restaurant in disgust.

"That explains the whole interim thing then," she sighed.

"Yeah. So you thought I was some hot shot looking for bigger and better things?"

"That was the best I could put together. I mean, you're very talented musically, that was obvious in choir rehearsal and then on Sunday. You're not obnoxious or anything, a well-rounded guy. You're handsome and polite, easy to talk to, good sense of humor—I never imagined there was a problem anywhere."

"Amazing, isn't it? I did have the perfect life, but the whole thing was ripped away, and I didn't even see it coming."

"No hint at all?" She still couldn't believe that his wife could have had an affair and him not have a clue.

"None."

"And the baby, I mean, could it possibly have been yours?"

"I can't have kids," he admitted softly. "I'm ... not able to ... have kids ... physically."

"Are you certain?"

"Trust me. I went through more tests than your mother probably did to determine her cancer."

Cindy nodded. What a bizarre situation. "Well," she finally smiled as she looked up at him, "you came to the right place for healing and encouragement."

"Dockrey?" he chuckled.

"Well, more like the vicinity of Jonathan Wright. Dockrey is far from perfect, but Pastor Jon has a way of seeing the best in everyone. Did you realize I'm only an interim myself?"

"Really?"

"Yeah, the secretary retired the last of December. Because I needed to move back in with Mother until she was through all of this, Pastor Jon came up with the plan of letting me fill in until she was better and I could move on again."

Kyle smiled. "Are we lucky or blessed?"

"Pastor Jon would say definitely blessed and all by divine appointment; he doesn't believe in luck."

"I don't think I've ever met anyone quite like him, especially a pastor."

As their meal came, the conversation became easier. It mainly consisted of small talk about various church members that Kyle could actually remember. By the time they were finished, both felt more relaxed, and the thoughts of Cindy's mother under the knife at that moment became less severe.

Eleven

After parking back in the garage and heading for the door of the hospital, Cindy stopped Kyle by gently grabbing his arm before going inside. She turned him toward her and said, "Thanks ... um ... well ... you know ... for everything."

He smiled shyly and nodded, still wishing he could have made it through lunch without having revealed his divorce. "Sure."

"I mean, it's nice to know, I guess, that I'm not the only one out here struggling like this."

"I understand. I would like to keep this info under wraps as long as possible, if you get my drift."

She nodded. "I won't say a word, but if the deacon body knows, it'll be out soon enough."

Kyle raised his eyebrows in question.

"All the men at First Baptist are not like Jonathan Wright ... or my father. If Pastor Jon's pulling for you, I can guarantee there are two pulling against you."

Kyle chuckled and shook his head. "At least it's deacons and not the pastor. And then again, I'm only the interim."

"Lucky for you," she grinned just as her phone rang. She quickly reached for her cell. "It's Cindy," she answered urgently. After a few short words she replied, "I'll be right there." She quickly turned toward the entrance. "I'm just outside the door. Make the doctor wait, please." She looked back at Kyle. "The doctor's on her way to the waiting area."

"I'm right behind you."

Just as the elevator doors opened to the third floor, Dr. Ashton was passing by.

"Doctor!" Cindy exclaimed as she grabbed the young surgeon's arm.

"Cindy!" the doctor said in surprise. "Just in time. Where have you been?"

"Olive Garden."

"Lucky you," the doctor smiled as she looked over at Kyle. "Another brother?"

"No," Kyle said quickly.

"Just wondering," the doctor said smiling at him while continuing down the hall. "The pretty blond hair and suave good looks just sort of made you fit right into the family."

He blushed for a moment as they headed toward the waiting area. Was the doctor flirting with him? He suddenly felt uncomfortable. His wide, golden wedding ring no longer hindered such advances.

The doctor motioned for Kyle and Cindy to stay outside of the room as she peeked in and asked for Billy and the Wrights to join them.

"She's smiling and cheerful," Cindy whispered to Kyle. "Everything must be okay. She was rather ominous this morning."

He nodded, but was still daunted by the attention the young doctor had given him. She was definitely attractive, and he was trying his best to not act as awkward as he felt.

"For starters," the doctor began, "it was considerably worse than October. But it wasn't beyond hope. We did well. I'd say her chances of pulling through this are high."

Sighs of relief and squeals of delight rushed from the group. Cindy closed her eyes and breathed a whisper of thanks.

"I'm not going to pretend, however, that any of this is going to be easy," Dr. Ashton continued. "You've still got the weeks of chemo; your mother isn't going to fare too well through that either. You guys are her support group. It's going to be up to you to keep pushing her. This next week of recovery is going to be a bear. She may even hate all of you a few days for making her go through this, but she'll pull through. The human body is an amazing thing."

"Great!" Billy nearly yelled. "We'll do our best. Thanks, Doc." He stuck out his hand and wildly shook the doctor's with excitement.

"So," the doctor eyed him slyly, "does this mean you're not going to sue me?"

Everyone glanced up at Billy who sort of shrugged his shoulders in response. As their attention was drawn toward him, no one noticed as Cindy began to sway slightly. Kyle looked back just in time to see her beginning to fall to the floor. He immediately jumped behind her and caught her in his arms. She was out in a flash.

"Just lay her down," Dr. Ashton said quickly as she knelt to the floor and grabbed Cindy's feet. "Let's get her legs elevated for a moment. I'm guessing she's had a short night and a long day."

"We all have," Billy said as he knelt down by the doctor.

"Here." She handed Cindy's legs to Billy and then moved up to her face. "Cindy? Come on, dear. Wake up."

Dr. Ashton looked up at Jonathan and said, "Get a cup of juice from in there, please?"

He immediately complied.

"She's lucky to have you here," the doctor said to Kyle as she glanced up at him briefly. "How long have you two been together?"

"We're not ... together," he said hesitantly.

"Oh," the doctor smiled now. "Then she's really lucky that you just happened by."

He was blushing again and wishing for his father's dark complexion to hide it. He tried to ignore the doctor, along with Billy's smirk, as he gave his attention to cradling Cindy's head in his arms. Her loose blond hair was baby fine as it draped over his hands and forearms, and he caught a stronger scent of her perfume that he had only faintly smelled in the office and in the Jeep earlier.

I'm going crazy with all this femininity, he thought to himself. *I was married for ten years, for crying out loud. You'd think I'd never been around women before!*

He noticed Cindy was beginning to respond to Dr. Ashton's words and touching. Her face was pale green and her lips nearly purple. The doctor didn't seem concerned by the whole incident, so Kyle didn't feel too alarmed. When Jonathan returned with the juice, Cindy finally opened her eyes.

"There you go," Dr. Ashton said with a warm smile. "Just stay down for a moment until you get your bearings. It must have been the Italian lunch … too heavy to combine with surgery." The doctor peeked up to Kyle and winked at the joke. He forced a smile, but still found himself concerned with Cindy's color.

As if reading his mind, the doctor offered, "She'll be fine. Let's get some of this juice down her. Cindy," she spoke directly to her now, "I need you to drink some of this wonderful OJ. The sugar should perk you right up."

Cindy furled her brows and shook her head slightly as she mumbled out, "Make me drink that after Eggplant Parmesan and you'll have to hold my head to throw up."

Kyle smiled at last; she was going to be fine.

"Oh, let's just give it a try," the doctor encouraged. "I've had much worse than vomit on me over the past several years."

She put the juice to Cindy's lips and helped her drink a couple of sips. To Kyle's relief, she held down her lunch. Slowly the doctor helped her to sit. As her hair slid from his arm, a strange sensation shot through his body so suddenly he nearly jumped in surprise. Both Cindy and the doctor glanced up at him.

"Off balance … a little," he said defensively as he got up.

A couple of minutes passed and Cindy's color began to return. Kyle stayed in the background as he watched the exchanges take place. Jonathan and Billy helped Cindy to her feet, wobbly at first, but quickly gaining her composure. She brushed back her hair and Kyle couldn't help but remember how soft the fine hair had felt on his arms. He twitched slightly at the memory.

"May I continue?" the doctor asked as Cindy seemed more stable. She nodded.

"Dr. Corts is performing the reconstruction now. This will be a longer process than mine. When the whole procedure is finished, they'll beep me back here and I'll monitor her vitals and see how she's doing then."

"How long will this part take?" Billy wondered.

"Who knows?" the doctor smiled. "You're mixing art and medicine now, and you know how artists are."

They all thanked her and then went back into the room, except for Kyle. He couldn't remember at this point why he was even at the hospital.

"I know you just ate at Olive Garden," Dr. Ashton said as she turned toward him, giving him a mischievous look, "but you could keep me company while I try to scarf down some of this great hospital chow."

He swallowed hard. He didn't know which would be more awkward: accepting or refusing.

"Don't think about it too hard," she teased him. "I don't have enough time to persuade you much. I've got another surgery in an hour and a half."

He shrugged and finally nodded in agreement. Why not? Lunch with two beautiful women in one day; he couldn't beat that.

The doctor told him to find a seat while she went through the cafeteria line. He sat nervously in the booth and wondered what on earth he was doing. When she finally joined him, she looked up at him and smiled before she started eating.

She offered her hand and officially introduced herself. "My name's Kate," she said tiredly. "I don't get out much, so pardon me for being a bit, well, *forward*, you might say."

"I can imagine," was all he could get out.

"It's been a long morning," she said as she stuck her fork into the meat loaf. "And meat loaf isn't the best option after hours of digging out cancer tissue."

He just nodded.

"So, how do you know the Marcums?" she asked.

"I ... uh ... work with Cindy."

"Real estate?"

"No." He was a little confused. "She's the church secretary."

"Oh yeah. She left the real estate thing to move in with her mom. Really admirable of her. I don't know many ladies her age would drop their careers to do what she's doing. So you work at the church too?"

He nodded again. Apparently Kate Ashton didn't need a whole lot of interesting conversation to keep her going; she did just fine on her own.

"So what are you? I know you're not the preacher."

"I'm the minister of music."

"Oh—so what is that? Do you like sing over the people or something?"

He chuckled at the thought and then shook his head. "I lead music, choirs, stuff like that."

"Does that pay well? I mean, do you actually make enough to earn a decent living?"

"It's no surgeon's salary, but it pays the bills," he said with a hint of defensiveness.

She laughed and took a swallow of her tea. "Sometimes, after all the gunk I've been through, I wonder if it's even worth it, the salary and all. Med school, internship, the whole shebang, the student loans, hah! I'll be working years before I finally pay them off. Did you go to school?"

"I have a Master's," Kyle said still feeling a bit defensive.

"Impressive," she nodded as she sat back for the first time. "I thought you looked like an educated guy. So, are you the creative type of musician or the perfectionist type?"

He thought carefully before he answered. "Are there any other options?"

"I don't know. You fill in the blanks."

"I like music. It's always been this huge part of my life. It comes naturally to me. I like the creative aspects, but I like perfecting it too. So what does that make me?"

"The worst kind! And to top it off, you're a minister. I was hoping we might connect somehow, you know, spend some time together on occasion. I'm guessing you're not that kind of guy."

"I don't know," he was a little confused. "What do you mean by spend time together?"

"Well, I'm not talking about dinner and a movie," she said as she raised an eyebrow at him.

He nodded slowly in understanding. "No, I'm not that kind of guy. Never have been."

"Too bad," she said almost sadly. "You would've been very interesting, a musician and a minister. That would've been fun."

"So you're not looking for a real relationship then? Nothing lasting or permanent?"

"Sure I am," she said seriously. "But you have to weed through all the preliminaries before you finally find that relationship. Until then, I'm sure having a great time in the process."

"Hmmm," Kyle mused as he rubbed his chin. "I'm not built that way."

"Too bad," she said as she shook her head and took another drink. "It would have been … interesting."

Kyle stayed with Kate a few more minutes and then remembered he still had to go shopping for the Wednesday church supper. He politely excused himself and went back to the waiting area. Cindy was standing outside in the hallway now, staring out a window blankly again.

"Hey, are you better?" he asked as he gently put a hand on her shoulder. She jumped. "Sorry," he said quickly as he pulled back his hand. "I didn't mean to startle you."

She closed her eyes and shook her head. "It's okay. Everything's got me jumpy right now. I've never passed out before. That was rather humiliating."

"You're an amazing lady, Cindy Marcum," he said with a sincere smile. "It takes a lot of character to do what you've done for your mother. You've been under a lot of stress from changing jobs, moving back home, and then having to deal with this cancer on top of it all after your dad's death. I think a little fainting attack was well deserved."

She smiled slightly and giggled, then reached up and put her arms around his neck to gently hug him. He was surprised but understood that this was completely different than Kate Ashton's advances. Cindy was genuinely thanking him for being understanding. He held her tenderly for just a moment, and then she pulled back.

"Thanks for everything today," she told him again. "They said I would have hit the floor hard had you not seen me and gotten behind me."

"Well," he glanced toward the ceiling, "I'm not normally in the habit of doing the whole knight in shining armor act, but I guess it was your lucky day."

"And I thank you greatly, Sir Kyle, for your chivalry. A concussion would have been the black cherry on the top of this day."

Twelve

The doctor had been right: Sue Marcum was ready to murder everyone who had talked her into surgery. The first three days after the procedure, her pain and recovery had been so intense she could say nothing positive. The throbbing was unbearable, and she swore that death would have been a more favorable option. After the third day, when some of the discomfort began to subside, she let up with her bitterness to a degree, but still refused to be glad she had gone through it all.

Cindy stayed with her the entire time, and the effects of little sleep, her mother's angry words, along with trying her best to make her mother comfortable, which was completely impossible, had taken their toll. When Barbara and Jonathan Wright walked in on Saturday morning to visit, Barbara immediately pulled Cindy from the room.

"You've got to go home and get some sleep," she insisted. "I'll stay here today and tonight."

"I can't do that. It would be like I'm abandoning her."

"Trust me, if you don't get away, we'll be finding you a bed in here next. This has been hard for you … the whole thing, from the beginning to the end. You've sacrificed everything to see your mother through this. Go home. Shower, sleep, and put on something ugly and comfortable."

Cindy smiled. It had been hard trying to keep up appearances with all the visitors the past few days.

"Eat some good food, and rest," Barbara continued. "Go to church in the morning, and then you can head back here tomorrow afternoon sometime. She's not even home yet, Cindy. When she gets there, your responsibilities will really kick in. Lean on others … okay?"

Cindy nodded as she let a small tear fall. Barbara was right. She told her mother goodbye and then made the hour-long trip back home. When she finally walked through the door, she went straight for the shower, then collapsed into her own bed without even drying her hair. Rest found her at last.

***

On Tuesday, Sue Marcum was released to go home. Her pain had subsided significantly, but four drainage tubes were connected to her body, and specific instructions for getting her through this recovery were weighing heavily on Cindy. She was thankful that people like Barbara would be in and out to see her through this.

The Wrights were waiting at the Marcum house when they arrived,

60

and Jonathan had even managed a wheelchair to help get Sue inside. Once she was settled, Barbara prepared a light lunch of tuna salad, and Cindy, Jonathan and Barbara sat at the breakfast nook eating while Sue slept in her own bed at last.

"I'll come over on Thursday so you can work on the bulletin for Sunday," Barbara told her. "Go ahead and plan to spend the whole day at church. I'll keep things up and running here."

Cindy was still exhausted from the whole ordeal. She thanked the Wrights for everything as they left, and sighed in despair as she remembered what still lay ahead of her. She peeked in on her mother who was sleeping soundly, and then went up to her room to shower again. She had forgotten to turn off her computer before leaving last time, so the first thing she saw was the desktop display of she and her father last Christmas. It was too much. Tears began to spill from her eyes as she fell onto the bed and cried herself to sleep.

***

On Thursday morning, she was thankful for the time to return to church and do something normal again. Barbara had assured her that her mother would be in good hands, and she knew it was true. As she caught up on a few things that had been missed during her absence at the office, Kyle came in.

"Welcome back," he said with a glowing smile as he came up to her desk. "Things haven't been the same with you gone."

"I'm sure," she smiled back at him. "But I'm only here for the day. Mrs. Wright will be answering the phone again tomorrow."

"How's your patient?"

"Miserable for the most part. I needed a reprieve."

"I can imagine. It was good to see you in church Sunday morning. I meant to speak to you, but you were gone before I got a chance."

"I needed to pack up a few things and get back to the hospital."

When the small chit chat was over, the silence became awkward. Kyle sighed and shuffled toward the door of his office.

"Um …" he turned back toward her, "I know we really don't know each other very well, and this church is full of people who've known you all your life, but if you need anything … anything at all, don't hesitate, you know, to call or ask or whatever."

She smiled warmly and nodded. "Maybe another trip to Olive Garden one of these days. That did me a world of good."

"I'll plan on it," he said as he opened his office door. "Just let me know when."

As the morning passed, she kept herself busy. It felt good to work, and there were even brief periods when she forgot that her father had died, that her mother was recovering at home, and that her life had been turned upside down. She knew time eventually would heal many of the wounds that were open and intense right now. Her biggest regret however was that she was going through all of this alone. Her twin brother had managed to avoid them since the day of the surgery. Had it not been for the church, she wondered how she could have survived. And had it especially not been for the Wrights, she knew she could never have stood it.

At lunch, Barbara had actually managed to get Sue to the glassed-in porch. The three ladies sat out there together and enjoyed a bowl of freshly made potato soup. Cindy loved this soup. She regretted never learning to cook, but it was one of those things that had always been low priority. To Cindy, if it could be bought or arranged for, there was no sense in doing it herself. She never cooked, cleaned, or did anything around her own apartment. Occasionally she would bring something home to eat from somewhere, but generally she just ate out with friends.

Back at the office, she worked hard to get everything finished knowing she would probably not be back again until next Thursday. As she typed out the bulletin, she noticed the choir would be singing one of her favorite songs this Sunday; she regretted not being able to be in choir during all of this. That would be something she could look forward to as her mother got back on her feet again. She put everything back in order on her desk, and then made another look around the office before she left. She hated to admit it, but she didn't want to go home; she didn't want to face her mother's negative attitude and misery again.

It won't be like this forever. God, just get me through it. Give me the strength to keep pushing along, and when it's over ... well ... just let it be over soon ... please.

As she prepared to leave, Kyle came in the door after being in the choir room and practically ran over her.

"So sorry," he apologized as he picked up her purse which he had knocked from her arm. "I forgot a CD over here ... I was in the choir room. I should have been more careful."

"It's okay. I was just heading out."

He glanced down at his watch and raised his eyebrows in surprise. "Wow! Four o'clock ... I had no idea. I guess it's time to leave."

"Time flies when you're having fun," she said trying to sound upbeat.

"Want to get a milk shake or an ice cream or something? You look a little, well, weary."

"Mrs. Wright's at home with Mother. I'd probably better go relieve her."

He nodded in understanding. They stood there awkwardly again.

"I appreciate your offer very much," she finally said.

"Well, it's not Olive Garden, but I'm learning how to make out with what Dockrey does have."

She chuckled tiredly.

"Do you want me to bring you something?" Kyle suggested this time.

"No thanks." She was glad to linger a bit. "People in the church are bringing things over all the time. They somehow even organized meals for us. It's been like having covered dish every evening."

"Baptists know how to deal with food."

"Tell me about it."

There was another awkward silence, and then Cindy finally waved a goodbye and headed out to her little red car.

Kyle watched from the office as she squeezed into her Thunderbird and then waved at her as she backed out. He had begun to feel some healing and relief in Dockrey, and it hurt him to know that she was so miserable. He wished he could help somehow, but he was really a stranger. He would just continue to pray.

Thirteen

The rest of the week and on into the weekend was more of the same. Sue Marcum was determined to hate her life. Cindy couldn't understand. Her mother had always been a wonderful, warm person. As a mother, she had provided for her children's every need over the years. As a wife, she had been the picture of perfection. As a preschool worker in the church, she had been faithful, innovative and loved. But as a widow recovering from a double mastectomy with chemotherapy on the horizon, she was a horrible person. Cindy had made a promise to herself: she wouldn't speak ill to her mother no matter how hard or impossible it got. Sue had put up with much disappointment in Cindy's life over the years—Cindy could hold her tongue for a few months if need be.

***

Late Monday afternoon, Kyle walked up the steps to his garage apartment. He had stayed later than planned at the church, but he was enjoying himself. To be back in ministry again—even for a little while—was invigorating. And this church had been so welcoming. They loved his innovative ideas for worship, and they appreciated how he blended many different types of music. Dr. Stanley at Harvest Hollow had insisted after a while that really Kyle should boil his music down to one style that suited the message and the ministry of the church. Kyle complied, but he always felt that many wonderful songs were being overlooked because of the *style* issue. It was almost as if being in Dockrey was the culmination of his many years everywhere else. Here he was able to have freedom to do what he had always dreamed of doing without the proverbial thumb holding him down.

Walking into his room, he removed his jacket and tossed it to the bed. He turned on the television to see if any news had developed worth hearing throughout the day.

"Kyle!" came Barbara's voice at his door along with a knock.

He walked quickly to the door and opened it. "Hey," he smiled at her.

"I need your help this evening. Are you busy?"

"Not at all. What can I do?"

"I've made a crock pot full of Beef Stew for the Marcums, but Jonathan and I are running late for the pastor's dinner in Russellville. Could you take the stew, a pot of rice, and the bowl of slaw over to Cindy's tonight? Maybe stay around and visit with them a little bit. She's going to go stir crazy if we don't get her out of there soon."

"No problem. When should I leave?"

"The sooner the better," she said heading back for the stairs. "I'm going to put the rice on now. When it's done you can head on over."

"Sure thing. Do I have time for a shower?"

"Twenty minutes!"

"Got it."

He showered and changed into a pair of comfortable jeans and a Furman sweatshirt. He helped Barbara get all the food together and then bid them a farewell as he headed out the door with a box of delicious smelling items. He took in a deep breath as he carried them to his Jeep. Carefully placing the box on the floorboard, he then began the ritual of leaving the house. He pulled up to the gate and waited for security to clear the drive out to the road. Once a way was made, a guard opened the gate and allowed him to pass.

These people are unbelievable, he thought to himself. *Stephen and Annie have been gone since Christmas.*

He made his way to the Marcum house following a scratched out map made by Jonathan, and was impressed with the majesty of the residence. It was a large, brick home with a beautifully manicured lawn of rye grass and winter flower gardens. He had no idea what James Marcum had done for a living, but he had obviously done well. Kyle parked his Jeep, retrieved the box of goodies, and then went to the front door. He managed carefully to ring the doorbell as he balanced the box on his knee. After a brief bit, the door opened.

"Kyle?" asked a worn and torn looking Cindy.

"In the flesh," he said with a bit of concern. "Are you all right?"

"That's debatable." She smiled wearily as she motioned him inside. "Did you cook tonight?"

"No, this is Barbara's stuff. I'm just the delivery boy. Where should I put it?"

"Follow me."

He had never seen her look anything other than perfect, so the disheveled appearance caught him off guard. She was wearing no make-up, an old, baggy sweat suit, and her hair was pulled back into a loose ponytail. He could still smell her perfume though as he followed her through the house.

When they walked into the kitchen, he had to force himself not to gasp. It was a disaster. Dishes and pots were literally piled on all the cabinets and inside the sink. Several bags of garbage had been tied up and leaned against the wall but never taken outside. There wasn't a free inch of space anywhere.

"Let me see," she mumbled as she tried to clear a spot on the breakfast nook for Kyle to place the box. "I think we can get it here."

He tried to keep his expression intact, but he was still shocked by the whole thing, beginning with Cindy and moving on to the kitchen. When she finally turned to look at him, he could tell she was exhausted and close to tears. He put the box down on the table and then looked at her with concern.

"Seriously, Cindy, are you all right?" he asked again.

"Honestly? I don't know how much more of this I can take," she said with obvious fatigue. "But if you would prefer pretense, I can tell you that everything's fine, Mom's getting better, and we should all be back to normal in a couple of days."

He stared at her a moment. It was hard to believe this was the same woman. Though her physical beauty was still very apparent, her eyes were dull and her demeanor was beaten down.

"How can I help?" he asked.

"Did you bring any valium with you?" she asked with a slight smile.

He chuckled and shook his head as he looked back around the trashed kitchen. "Nope, just food. If you'll point me to some clean dishes, I'll help you get your mom a plate and then you can sit and eat too."

She went to a cabinet next to the refrigerator and pulled out a stack of paper plates. "We're down to these."

He nodded and took them, really wanting to ask why she hadn't washed dishes for the past several days, but knew this wasn't the time. "Forks? Spoons?"

She pulled out a box of plastic utensils from the same cabinet. He took them over to the table next to the food. "Any glasses? Barbara sent a gallon of iced tea."

She turned back to the cabinet and brought out a pack of Styrofoam cups.

He helped her fix a plate for her mother and then followed her out onto the glassed-in porch where Sue was watching television.

"Suppertime, Mom," Cindy said cheerfully as she walked up to her mother. "It's Mrs. Wright's beef stew."

"Hello, Mrs. Marcum," Kyle said as he peeked around Cindy's shoulder.

"Kyle?" Sue asked in surprise. "What brings you here?"

"I'm the delivery boy tonight," he smiled as he handed her a cupful of tea. "How are you feeling these days?"

"I'm surviving," she said glumly. "The church loves what you're doing with the music there."

"And I'm loving the church. It's been a real blessing for me."

Sue slowly sipped her tea and then took a deep breath to savor the aroma of the stew. "This smells delicious. Barbara is quite the cook."

"Agreed," he said as he squatted down on the floor next to her. "Do you mind if I return thanks for the meal?"

"Not at all."

He said a sweet prayer. "If you need anything, Mrs. Marcum, just call, okay?"

He turned back to Cindy and gently took her arm to lead her back inside the main house. "Now, it's your turn," he said softly. "Who's been pampering you while you've been pampering her?"

"I don't think there's been a whole lot of pampering going on here period. Mother's been miserable. She was actually nice to you. She must think you came here out of the goodness of your heart rather than spiritual obligation."

"Then she's right," he said cheerfully. "Let me fix you a plate."

"I can get it."

"I *know* you can get it. You look completely capable. Just let me do this for you. Where are we eating?" he asked, knowing there was no free space in the kitchen.

"The living room, I guess."

"Go sit down, and I'll bring something out in just a second."

Cindy sat on one end of the white leather couch and laid her head back in fatigue. It wasn't the busyness that wore her out as much as it was the atmosphere and unending attitude of negativism from her mother. She hated to admit it, but she was beginning to believe this had been the wrong idea. She had these noble intentions of nursing her mother back to health and life, but as each day wore on, she wondered if it was reality.

She closed her eyes and tried to concentrate on something positive, something warm and wonderful. She imagined Angie in Padawin, basking in the South Pacific sunshine and healing people with her medical skills. By her side was her wonderful husband, Michael, who adored her as they anticipated the arrival of their first child. *That* was a nice image.

"Dinner is served," Kyle said cheerfully as he entered the room.

He had a tray carrying their plates and drinks. He placed it on the coffee table and then handed Cindy's to her. He sat in an overstuffed chair opposite her and got his own things as he settled in. He said another prayer, specifically mentioning Cindy this time, and they began to eat.

He talked most of the time about various things that were happening in the church. He was more animated than she had ever seen him and was thankful for his company and his endless chatter about this and that in Dockrey. She didn't know him well enough to know if he was doing this because he realized she needed it, or if he was a talker period. She had never known him to go on and on before.

When they had finished eating, they placed their plates back on the tray and sat quietly for a bit.

"Do you want to help me reclaim your kitchen?" he finally asked.

She looked up at him in astonishment. "What?"

"I thought the two of us together could get in there and bring it back to life."

She shook her head and said, "I don't do kitchens."

"Obviously," he snickered.

"Barbara Wright will be here tomorrow. She'll clean it."

He stared at her in near shock. "Are you kidding me? Your plan is to leave *that* for her?"

"She doesn't mind, believe me."

"It's not whether she minds or not. What about you?"

Cindy looked out the window toward the streetlight. "I told you, I don't do kitchens. And for the record, I don't do laundry or toilets either. So if you're bothered by the kitchen, I suggest you avoid the bathrooms altogether while you're here."

He said nothing, but she could tell by his expression he didn't approve.

"For the past six years, I've paid people to clean my kitchen, do my laundry and take care of my house. That's how I live, Kyle. This," and she motioned her arms around the house, "is a whole new ball game for me. I'm not the domestic type."

"So you would cook and someone else would clean it up?"

"I don't cook."

"Anything?"

"Nothing," she said flatly. "I do make coffee."

He nodded slowly and just stared again. "Let's go clean up your kitchen. I'll tackle your bathrooms when we've finished."

"You're kidding, right?"

He gave her a sober look and shook his head.

"I don't do kitchens," she reiterated.

"Then it's time you started," he said as he got up from his chair and offered his hand. "It'll be fun."

She sighed in amazement and finally took his hand, letting him pull her from the couch. She followed him to the kitchen where he immediately began to put a plan together. He had her tell him where the outside garbage was located, and he began by taking out all the filled bags while she unloaded the dishwasher. As the evening wore on, he washed; she dried and put away. She knew he was deliberately keeping the mood light, attempting to make her laugh, and she appreciated his effort. Cleaning the kitchen with Kyle actually was fun.

"This is really a beautiful kitchen," he said as they neared the end of the cleanup. "I love this color on the walls."

She nodded, but a lump began to grow in her throat. Seeing the kitchen clean again did bring a bit of relief and comfort. She should thank him, but she couldn't say anything.

"What's wrong?" he asked as he put down the dishcloth and walked over to her.

She shook her head; she still couldn't speak.

"Cindy?" he asked again.

She took a deep breath and tried to explain. "This is all so hard for me, Kyle. It's like my life is in a winter midnight. It is the coldest and darkest point possible. The only way it could be worse is if I were living at the South Pole."

He nodded in understanding. "Winter midnight, huh," he said as he gently pushed a strand of hair from her face to behind her ear. "I can relate to that."

"I sometimes wonder where I'll find the strength to go on. I fall into bed at night and just pray I have what it takes to get up the next morning and do this all over again. And it's so hard because ... well ..."

"Because you're alone?"

She nodded.

"I know," he said tenderly. "I know this is different than what I went through, but believe me I understand the aloneness. Only with me, I had never been alone. I'd always had Caryn. She shared everything with me. Now she was the one who hurt me, and I had no one to turn to. Everyone kept telling me to just get over it, but you don't turn off ten years of your life and pull out the next rabbit from the hat. And Cindy, you don't just leave your great life that you had and waltz back here to Dockrey and *get over it* either. I know how hard it is for you."

"I feel so exhausted ... in every way possible," she said as tears started trickling down the sides of her cheeks. "I'm emotionally depleted. I'm physically worn. I'm out of my element, Kyle—like a fish out of water— and I don't know what to do to get myself back together."

"Well, let's think of it more like you're a fish that's been put into a different tank."

She looked up at him and grinned slightly.

"Try and look at it this way," he continued. "You're still in the water. You can breathe, you can swim, and you can still do all your little *fishy* things. You just have to do them in a different place and in a different way. For starters, we cleaned your fishy kitchen. When you bring in a plate or a glass or a pot in this particular fish tank, you rinse it off and put it in the dishwasher. When it gets full, fill it with fishy soap and turn it on."

She now giggled a bit and felt her cheeks flush in embarrassment at how horrible the kitchen had gotten.

"Don't let things get big and out of hand," he went on. "Keep it all under control little by little. When Caryn left, I couldn't find a reason to make my bed. I kept telling myself I just got back in it every night, all alone, to mess the sheets up again. What's the point? Then there came this issue of self-respect. I did it because I was alive, and because it felt good at night to pull back the covers and climb in exhausted."

"I do make my bed," Cindy said in weak defense.

"Good," he smiled at her. "Then you're not a total loss. And see, when you cook …"

"I told you, I don't cook."

"What do you mean exactly—don't cook what?"

"I … don't … cook …" she looked seriously at him and finished with, "… anything."

"Nothing?"

"Nada."

"Well," he sighed and raised his eyebrows, "then it's time you learned. Did you ever plan to get married at some point in time?"

"I considered it, but the opportunity never presented itself. Besides, it's just as easy to order out for two as it is for one."

"But not near as much fun." His blue eyes twinkled. "Haven't you ever cooked with anyone? Planned and prepared a meal together?"

"With Angie Wright, I have, but that was a bigger disaster than this kitchen was!"

"I hope I get to meet these other Wright girls before my stint is up here," he laughed. "The more I hear about them, the more curious I become."

"They're a hoot all right," Cindy smiled as a few memories raced through her mind of various shenanigans she and Angie had pulled over the years.

"Okay, look," Kyle headed back to the sink, "let's finish the dishes and then we'll tackle the bathrooms … and I suppose, the laundry?"

"You don't want to see the laundry."

"I didn't want to see your kitchen either, but look at the miracles we've performed in here already."

When the kitchen was finally spotless, they headed to the downstairs bathroom. Kyle had Cindy carry the dirty clothes to the laundry room while he looked for cleaning supplies. When she returned, he told her to go ahead and gather all the laundry from around the house and let him know when it was collected. He had time to clean the toilet before showing Cindy how to divide the laundry into piles.

"But all our towels are white," she protested as he insisted they start a linen pile. "Why can't I just wash them with these other whites."

"'Cause it'll get lint all over your clothes. Trust me on this: towels need their own pile, especially ones as thick as these."

"Okay," she sighed as she started tossing towels into another heap on the floor.

"What I'll do is help you get started here, then you can catch up tonight and tomorrow. What do you need washed more than anything else?"

"*Personal* items," she said with a slight laugh.

"Very well. Get all the *personal* items you want to wash together first. I'm adding a cap of this detergent to the machine and then turning it on. See?"

Cindy watched and nodded. She then picked up various pieces of underwear, slips, bras, socks and hose and began tossing them into the machine.

"When it gets to about here," he said as he pointed inside the machine, "stop loading stuff and put down the lid."

They continued until the sorting was done, and then Kyle made her help him in the bathroom by cleaning the mirror and counter while he washed the tub. Next they made their way up to her room. When they walked inside she was very relieved that she had indeed made her bed that morning.

"Pretty room," he said as he looked around. "Did you fix it up yourself?"

"No, Mother did all of this after I moved out. It looked considerably different when I was a teenager."

"Is that your father?" he asked as he pointed to the picture on the computer screen.

"Yes," she said softly. "That was last year at Christmas."

"What an expression on his face. He looks awfully proud to be next to his daughter there."

"Daddy was wonderful. If he were here now, Mother wouldn't be in the shape she is. He would've pulled her out of this."

"No," Kyle said quickly as he turned back to Cindy. "I'm willing to bet that's all backward. Your mother is in the shape she's in *because* he's not here."

"Yeah, you're right."

"Where's your brother been in all of this?"

"Doing what he does best, avoiding conflict, confrontation or responsibility. He stays in Florence ... calls now and then with some lame apology."

He pointed toward her bathroom. "Is that the dungeon of terror?"

"It's not *that* bad!" she exclaimed.

"Let's see about that," he grinned as he carefully opened the door.

Thankfully, it wasn't that bad. It was neat and in order, unlike the kitchen. He handed her the cleanser and the sponge and then took the toilet cleaner for himself. "Start on the counter," he told her as he grabbed the toilet brush.

"Okay, this is wrong," she finally blurted out. "I can't let you clean my toilet. You're not the hired help; you're a friend. Besides, you already took me to Olive Garden; I owe you. If I let you do this too, I'll owe you big. I don't like being in that position."

"Doesn't bother me," he grinned as he knelt down and began to spray the cleanser inside the rim.

After finishing the bathrooms, they sat in the living room and turned on the television. Kyle agreed to help her through a couple of loads of laundry before turning her loose on her own. They watched some sitcoms and then folded clothes before he noticed that she was extremely tired.

"Let me help you get your mother back to her room, and then I'll be on my way," he told her.

"That's okay. I can get her."

"There you go again," he said shaking his head. "When help is offered, just take it. Let's go get your mom."

To their surprise, she had actually left the porch on her own. Cindy tiptoed to Sue's bedroom and saw that she had already tucked herself in and gone to bed. She left the door cracked and went back to say goodbye to Kyle.

"Thank you for tonight," she said sincerely. "I actually feel like I might make it through this thing now. I wasn't so sure before you came."

"Mission accomplished then," he said cheerfully. "But I want you to know something, I am going to teach you how to cook ... whether you like it or not."

"Good luck. No one else has succeeded."

"I am like no one else."

"So I've noticed. And for the record, I don't really know anything about Caryn, but she's obviously not very bright and part blind."

"Why would you say that?"

"Because if she really knew the treasure she had in you, she would have never left."

He smiled at her and shook his head as he said, "Obviously I wasn't everything I seemed to be to her when we first married."

"Or maybe she wasn't everything that she seemed."

Fourteen

Cindy heard noises downstairs the following morning as she struggled to rouse herself from bed. Her first thoughts were that everything was still normal, her mother was making breakfast, and she should get up and shower for school—then she remembered reality—it was fifteen years later. She glanced at the clock: six forty-five. Someone was in their house! She jumped from her bed, pulled on her robe, and then dug through her closet for an old tennis racket. She quietly opened her door and crept down the stairs.

I'm an idiot. So what do I do when I catch him? Whack him with this racket. Stop sir! Or I'll serve!

She decided her best bet was to sneak around to the laundry room and peek in from that direction. When she finally edged past the piles of clothes she and Kyle had sorted the night before, she tiptoed to the hallway that led to the kitchen and tried to keep her breathing to a minimum. When she finally saw the culprit, she was in complete shock.

"Mother?" she exclaimed.

"Oh," Sue said with a start. "Good morning, dear."

"You're up?" Cindy said slowly as she walked on into the kitchen, racket still in hand.

"I figured this morning, I'm not dead yet, why act like it?"

"Mother! Of course, you're not dead."

"I kept hoping, waiting, and assuming, but apparently I'm actually going to recover from this. I felt like dying, you know? That surgery was horrible."

Cindy just nodded, still amazed that her mother was up and about and making coffee.

"I still ache, and it's hard to lift my arms, but other than that, I feel like I need to move around. I couldn't believe the kitchen this morning! I actually expected to find it in total disarray."

Cindy smiled. No need to tell her mother it took Kyle's prodding and help to remove the disaster rating it would have received last night.

"I guess you finally did grow up some," her mother continued talking. "Now Billy, that's another story. He still hasn't shown up, has he?"

Cindy shook her head. She was actually embarrassed for her brother. At least he did make it to the hospital.

"Kyle stayed over for quite a while last night, didn't he?" her mother asked.

"Um … yeah, he did. We ate and watched a little TV."

"He's a fine man. Makes you wonder about his wife, doesn't it?"

"You know about his wife?"

"Barbara had shared it with me the week the church called him. She said we should be praying for him that God would do whatever needs to be done in his life while he's here."

"It's hard to imagine that someone could be married to him and then just take off and leave like she did. I know none of us know him very well, but he doesn't seem like an unreasonable guy. Surely they could've gone to counseling or something and worked it out."

"That's pretty much what everybody thinks. Could you reach the bread for me? Feel like sausage and eggs this morning?"

"Are you cooking?"

"You're sure not!" Sue laughed. Then looking at the racket she asked, "Playing some tennis today?"

***

"Everything looks great," Dr. Ashton told Sue and Cindy at the six-week checkup in mid February. "I think we're ready to start the next step."

"I'm not looking forward to the next step," Sue said soberly.

"It's not as bad as it used to be, Mrs. Marcum. There are a myriad of medicines available now to help ease the nausea."

"I wasn't talking about the nausea. I was sick the entire nine months of my pregnancy. I was more concerned with the hair loss."

"Well, that is a side effect, but on the positive side, all that hair should grow back. We'll give you four treatments at three weeks apart— beginning Thursday."

Sue sighed. Cindy understood. It would be hard to go through the hair loss. In fact, Cindy wondered if she herself could take such a drastic extreme.

"Ladies!" Dr. Ashton exclaimed. "Pull yourselves out of this! Consider this a hard year, okay? This time next year, Sue, you'll be well! You'll have hair, a great set of new boobs, and you'll be cancer free! Cindy, you'll have your life back. It's just for a period of time right now. The alternative to what you've chosen was death. You'll get through this—trust me."

Cindy smiled at the doctor's enthusiasm. Yes, the alternative was death, and that was why she had sacrificed everything. She had no hand in helping her father. No one even knew he was sick. But she had the privilege of seeing her mother through this, and she was thankful God had given her this opportunity.

"Before you go, Cindy," Kate said as she took her aside, "could I please have your work number? You're still at the church, right?"

"Yes," Cindy replied a bit puzzled. "But I always have my cell with me."

"Oh," the doctor laughed, "not to contact you. I'd like to call Kyle up some time. He peaked my interest significantly during our little lunch after your fainting session."

"You had lunch with Kyle?"

"Well, *I* had lunch; he just watched. I've been meaning to get back with him but haven't had the time."

Cindy wrote down the number as a twinge of jealousy chewed inside.

Why am I feeling this way? I told myself from the moment I saw him there could never be anything between us. He's a Godly man with a good heart; I'm an adulterer. He's someone who's made right decisions his whole life; I've constantly chosen the path of a rebel. He deserves someone smart and professional like Dr. Ashton, not a first semester college dropout like me.

"Here you go," Cindy tried to sound perky. "Kyle's in from around nine to three. He takes his lunch break at noon."

"Great," Kate nodded as she placed the number in her pocket. "Give him my regards, would you?"

"Sure will." Her face went warm.

Fifteen

Cindy sat at her desk on Wednesday morning wondering if this would be her last day of peace until her mother's chemotherapy was finished. Sue's first treatment was scheduled for tomorrow morning, and even though Dr. Ashton had assured them all should be fine, she still found herself drowning in uneasiness. She had heard horror stories of people on chemo, and after the bout with surgery, she wanted to assume the best, but found it impossible.

"Hey, beautiful," Kyle called out as he entered the office that morning.

"Hello, handsome," she replied as had become their habit.

"Any messages?"

"Jennifer's mother called. She's got strep throat and can't sing Sunday morning."

"Rats," he mumbled as he took the note. "Why don't you sing?"

She laughed and shook her head as she reminded him for the fiftieth time, "I don't sing."

"You sing in the choir."

"There's a reason for that. I sound wonderful in a choir ... with many other voices around me ... to drown me out."

"Okay, okay, I give up. How'd your mom's appointment go yesterday?"

"She starts chemo tomorrow. I hope it goes better than the surgery."

"Me too," he joined her mood. "Should we cancel Friday night?"

He had come over to the Marcums each Friday after the kitchen cleaning fiasco to teach her how to cook. They had forged a wonderful friendship through that, and she actually was learning to cook in the process. He also had the chance to get to know Sue better. Between the three of them, all hurting for different reasons, they had found some peace and hope in each other.

"Let's not cancel just yet," she suggested. "Dr. Ashton seems to think she'll be fine. Go ahead and plan ..."

She stopped mid-sentence as his expression grew grim.

"What is it?" she asked.

"Dr. Ashton? Is that the one who did her surgery?"

She nodded. Apparently Kate Ashton had made an impression on Kyle also. There went that surge of jealousy again.

Kyle is my friend and only my friend. I should encourage him in other relationships so he can move on beyond Caryn.

"She said to give you her regards." She tried to sound positive. "She's very attractive, isn't she?"

"Right." He started for his office. "Okay then, I'll plan for something Italian on Friday." He was obviously distracted now. "Does your mom have a favorite Italian dish?"

"As you've noticed, my mom enjoys anything she doesn't have to cook herself."

He chuckled as he went into his office and closed the door. Cindy's smile, however, faded. She didn't want to have feelings for him. Maybe she was just being protective. He was out of her league; he was a *good* man, a Godly man. Had she met someone like him in college, perhaps she would have stuck with her education and done better. But at thirty, her mold had been cast. Shoot! The last man she had dated was married!

Even if Kyle were ever attracted to me, I could never let things develop; I'd be a worse blot on his life than Caryn. I need to keep my head on straight where he's concerned. In fact, the best thing I could do for him would be to encourage a relationship with Dr. Ashton.

Her opportunity came. Later that morning, Kate called the office to speak with him. Cindy transferred the call and then congratulated herself for being able to let it go so easily.

"Kyle here," he answered.

"Kyle, it's Kate Ashton. How are you?"

He was silent for a moment. Why hadn't Cindy mentioned who it was?

"Remember me?" she asked.

"Yeah ... uh ... sure. You're Sue Marcum's doctor."

"I've got some time off this weekend, and thought we might try and get together for a little while."

"Well, what did you have in mind?" He felt uneasy. He hadn't dated in over fourteen years. He also knew that his ideas of dating and Kate's were drastically different.

"How about dinner and a movie?" she proposed.

"Really?" he was caught off guard. "I thought you didn't go in for something that simple."

"Well, you're a different sort of guy. I'm willing to try an old routine if it means I get to spend some time with you."

He was now on the spot. He didn't want to see her. She wasn't the kind of woman he would ever be interested in, but he felt uncomfortable telling her that.

"What do you say, Kyle?" she pushed him. "You could drop by my place, we could pick out a movie, and then we could decide on somewhere to eat. No pressure or anything like that."

"Well, the truth is," he was stammering now, "I already have plans for this weekend."

"Oh, come on, Kyle. I'm sure that spending some time with me would be way more fun than whatever you've got planned. You can cancel. I don't get off very often like this."

He blew out a breath as he tried to think of what to do. The truth was, he had plans with the Marcums. Another truth was, he would much rather spend the evening relaxing and laughing with Cindy and Sue than being uptight and on his guard around Kate. Nothing obligated him to be with Kate, and from everything he could tell, she wasn't the kind of woman he needed to spend time with.

"Don't deliberate too much," she cautioned him teasingly. "The offer won't stand forever."

"The truth is," he said, wondering how much of the truth he would actually give her, "I really do already have plans for Friday. I don't *want* to break them because they're plans for pleasure and not for work."

"Okay then, how about Saturday? We could meet in the afternoon, still do the movie and dinner thing, and get you home in time for beddie-bye so you can be fresh and snappy for Sunday morning church."

That did sound like a safer offer: afternoon rather than night.

"Okay," he agreed.

"Great! Let me tell you how to get to my place."

"How about another meeting place?" he said, still feeling the need to guard himself. "Meet me somewhere for lunch."

She was silent. That was obviously not what she had wanted. "Okay," she moaned. "You win. Where do you want to meet?"

"I only know where Olive Garden, Sam's and the hospital are. How about Olive Garden around one o'clock?"

Kyle thought on the conversation long after he hung up. He didn't need to be with this woman. Even as a high school student he didn't date non-Christians, and here he was a minister, a year off of his divorce, and the first woman he was going out with was an obviously forward doctor with different ideas about relationships. What was he thinking?

***

Cindy sat nervously in the room as the nurses began hooking IV's to her mother.

"These two medicines are anti-nausea," the nurse explained. "We're going to begin them now. In a little while we'll start the actual ones designed to kill the cancer."

Sue seemed to take it all in stride. She smiled politely at them and acted as though being jabbed with needles was a normal part of life. Of course, for her, it was beginning to become that. When Dr. Ashton came in, she monitored all that was happening, and then made some notes on Sue's chart.

"If there are any problems, you need to call my office," Dr. Ashton told them. "You also need to be prepared for chunks of hair to begin falling out, oh, anywhere from three to five days."

Cindy felt a knot hit her stomach. Sue closed her eyes and nodded.

"Make the best of this, ladies," the doctor told them again. "See the humor in it. Keep your morale up."

"We've bought a wig," Cindy said, mainly to remind her mother. "When things are totally … uh … gone, we'll stick the wig up there."

"Good for you," Dr. Ashton told them. "Because it'll all be gone in about ten days."

"Ten days?" Cindy exclaimed in surprise. She thought it would be gradual.

"But remember, it all comes back," Kate said with a silly smile. "Usually."

***

Cindy was thankful when Kyle came to the door Friday evening. Her mother had practically vomited non-stop from the moment they had entered the house. Thankfully, the doctor had prescribed some new medicine that knocked her out, and Cindy kept it down her as often as possible.

"How's the patient?" he asked quietly as he walked inside with grocery bags in hand.

"Really bad. She can't stop throwing up; the nausea is horrible. It's everything I ever imagined it might be … and more."

"Well, at least you kept the kitchen clean this time," Kyle grinned as he placed the bags on the counter.

"You bet. I wouldn't dare let you walk in here again and see my kitchen in that kind of shape."

"*My* kitchen? *My* kitchen? Are we beginning to feel more at home in the kitchen now? Taking a little ownership of the area, are we?"

"Don't give me a hard time," she pouted. "I'm starving. What are we cooking tonight?"

With an Italian accent he replied, "Spaghetti with meatballs, garlic bread, and a tossed green salad."

"Wonderful!" she clapped. "How do we start?"

"We make the meatballs first. Get out that large saucepan and a medium sized bowl."

***

When Sue woke up, she was violently sick again. Kyle helped Cindy through the episode and then helped get another dose of medicine down her. When Sue was settled, they collapsed on the couch and Cindy turned on the television. An old movie caught their attention, and soon they were enmeshed in the plot of mystery, romance and intrigue. It wasn't until Kyle

79

saw her asleep that he realized how draining the past two days had been for her. He turned off the TV, covered her up with an afghan, and then locked the door on his way out. He whispered a prayer for both of his good friends as left the house for his garage apartment.

Sixteen

"Come on, now, it wasn't near as bad as you thought it'd be," Kate joked with Kyle as she took his arm while leaving the theater.

"The movie?" he asked.

"No, the whole day," she clarified. "Lunch was interesting, and then spending the afternoon at the park and the mall was fun. Admit it."

He laughed nervously and nodded. Kate snuggled deeper into his arm and laid her head on his shoulder. As tempting as it felt to have Kate on his arm like this, he was uncomfortable. He knew she would suggest more if he didn't cut the ties quickly.

"Yes," he finally verbalized it. "I had fun. You're quite a woman, Kate Ashton. However ..."

"Oh, no howevers, please," she groaned as she lifted her head, stopped walking, and pulled him back to her by the arm. "Just say we had fun and that I'm quite a woman and leave it at that."

"However ...," he said again very deliberately, "... I need to get home."

"It's only seven," she complained as she pulled him closer. "The night's still young."

"It's an hour's drive to Dockrey. I need to get back so I can get ready for tomorrow."

He tried to inch away from her, but she just moved in closer, taking both of his hands and intertwining his fingers with hers. She stepped up to him until her face was just inches from his. Her eyes were suggestive, and the scent of her perfume along with strands of her long hair blowing about were beginning to intoxicate him. The night was cold, but as she moved in closer he began to warm immediately. Kate was merciless in her pursuit. He tried to pull away politely, but she merely pulled him back.

"I think you know I'm uncomfortable with this," he finally said to her.

"I think you should just relax and enjoy the moment. You're so uptight about things, Kyle. We've had a great day, have we not?"

"It's been nice, but I'm not ready to do this with you right now."

"I'm not pulling you into bed with me. All I want is to kiss you for just a bit ... to let you know how much I appreciated the day."

"Kate," he pulled her hands together and took a step back, "a simple *I appreciated the day* would suffice. I don't do relationships like this. I take my time, build something, and then begin ..."

"I'm not being overbearing, Kyle. I just want to express to you how I felt about our time together. Do you think a kiss is too much?"

"For me, it is," he said as he took another step back. "I'm not ready for this. It's too much too soon, and I'm not even sure this is something I want to share with you."

"A kiss? I think I'm being very lenient here."

"I'm divorced, Kate," he finally blurted out. "And you're the first woman I've been with since her. She left me last year, and it's just not natural being with anyone else yet."

She pulled back this time. "I'm sorry. I didn't realize … I mean … I just assumed. You haven't dated for a year?"

"No. I wasn't sure about spending this day with you, but it seemed safe—in the daytime, nothing too much too soon."

"And then I came on like Papa Bear," she said as she threw her hands up in disgust. "Why didn't you tell me, Kyle? We spent the whole afternoon talking about our lives, and you conveniently failed to mention you were just divorced! What was all this to you? A game? So we were supposed to pick out selective parts of our lives to share? I didn't get that memo!"

"I wasn't trying to deceive you. I didn't think I was ready for this anyway, but you kept pushing. I didn't have the umph to tell you I wasn't ready to go out with anyone again."

She put her hands on her hips and closed her eyes. She was obviously upset with the way things had turned out.

"You scare me somewhat," he confessed. "You're not like any woman I've ever known."

She laughed sarcastically. "Heavens, Kyle, I don't know if that's good or bad. You've been talking in mysteries all day long. I just assumed you were playing with me for a while, but I realize now you're totally hung up on too many things. I should have stuck with my original plan and made you bend."

"What was your original plan?"

"To get you to my place," she grinned.

"I would never sleep with anyone outside of marriage."

"Seriously? You really hold to that? Do you mean to tell me that you were a virgin when you got married?"

"Yes, I was. And I've never slept with anyone other than my wife."

"You're kidding? And you don't intend to sleep with anyone again until you get married again?"

"If … I get married. Right now I can't imagine being with anyone else."

She nodded as the truth of the situation began to sink in. "You and I want totally different things from a relationship."

"That's what I tried to tell you at the hospital."

"Yeah, you did, but I somehow thought I could pull you out of your little shell. I thought it was a *shy* thing. I didn't realize your were … well … *damaged* emotionally."

"Damaged?" he nearly exclaimed.

"Oooo, hit an open nerve there, did I? Yes, Kyle, you're damaged … like abused goods. See, that's what I'm trying to avoid. You can condemn me for my sexual freedom, but I'm not walking around with my heart on my sleeve either. Maybe I've given myself to a few too many men in your opinion, but I never gave myself so much that it hurt. You, on the other hand, played by all the rules, and look where it got you."

The words stung him deeply. He had thought about that very fact often. Yes, he had played by all the rules. He had saved himself for marriage, and then he had given himself completely to his marriage. He had done everything the way he was supposed to do it, but God had still pulled the carpet from beneath him It wasn't fair, but he was helpless to do anything about it.

"I'd better go," he said in defeat as he began to walk back to the Jeep.

She followed him. "I really didn't want the day to end like this."

"I bet you didn't."

"I didn't mean it like that. I just meant I'd hoped we could see each other again."

"Why?" he asked in unbelief. "So you could try and seduce me out of my *damaged* mind?"

"Look, Kyle, say whatever you want about me, I don't care. But you really need to look at yourself first. I may not be a *safe* person to you, but it doesn't seem to me that anybody is *safe* for you right now. Some day you're going to have to open up your heart again if you want to do more than just exist in this life. I'll be glad to help, but don't blame me for being too forward or too bold. We did a whole lot more today than just something physical, and you didn't even have what it took to be honest then."

"You want me to take you to your car?" he asked with no emotion.

"I'll walk myself," she responded in like manner.

He unlocked his Jeep and jumped inside, immediately cranking the engine and then pulling out. He wouldn't even look into the rearview mirror to watch her disappear. This had been a big mistake.

Seventeen

By Sunday evening, Sue's nausea had subsided. She was tired and weak from the ordeal, but at least she was in the land of the living again. She was impressed when Cindy brought her a cup of broth to drink, both hoping that she could finally keep something on her stomach.

"It doesn't take a rocket scientist to drop a bouillon cube into a cup of hot water," Cindy told her mother concerning her ability to brew broth.

"No," her mother smiled, "but in your case it does take a bit of a miracle. I need to remember to thank Kyle once again for getting you into the kitchen."

"Why don't you tell him tonight? We've missed discipleship training, but we can still make it to worship."

"I probably should go," Sue laughed. "It'll be the last time I see any of these people for a while with my real hair still in place."

"Mother! That's not funny!"

"Right now, dear, I feel so much better that I could find walking over hot coals funny."

***

After the evening service, Kyle found Cindy immediately. "Hey beautiful. I can't believe you two made it tonight. Your mom must be doing better."

"This afternoon it was like a miracle struck or something."

"Great! Let's celebrate!"

"I'll pass," she said quickly. "I think going home and putting my feet up sounds much more pleasant."

"Oh, come on. You don't have to go far. The youth are having a fellowship tonight. They're playing volleyball. You'll love it!"

"I don't do youth, and I *definitely* don't do volleyball."

"Yeah, but you used to not do kitchens, toilets and laundry, and look at you now."

Kyle could be very persuasive when it came to Cindy, and she almost hated the fact that he had that kind of power over her. "Are you trying to reform me, Reverend Sarkos?"

"Trying really hard." His eyes sparked with mischief. "Is it working?"

"Apparently. Let me see if mother can get a ride home."

"Just give her the keys; I'll take you home when it's over."

Cindy hadn't eaten pizza in over two years—partly because it was fattening, and partly because she didn't care much for it. But as she took a second piece, she was beginning to wonder if perhaps she had denied herself the eighth wonder of the world. When it came time for volleyball, she protested vehemently, but Kyle had a way of talking her into things for all the right reasons.

"Kyle, I didn't even play the games when I was *in* youth group, much less now at thirty."

"Oh, I see," he said knowingly as he shook his finger at her. "So you were one of those *too cool* girls that sat on the side while everyone else had a blast."

"Basically, yes. Give me one good reason, and I stress *good*, why I should start playing with teenagers now."

"See all those girls sitting over there?" he said as he nodded to one of the tables. "You know those girls?"

"Most of them, yes."

"They think you're the grandest thing since sliced cheese," he whispered to her.

"Get out'ta' here! Those girls are wrapped up inside their own little worlds."

"That's what they want you to think. Half of them are hoping like crazy they can look like you when they're thirty, and the other half are arguing that there's no way you could be thirty."

"You won't sweet talk me into this game, Kyle."

"I'm not kidding, Cindy," he said as his expression became more serious. "The best thing these girls can have right now is a good influence in their lives. They need to see adults who are committed to the Lord but know how to enjoy life at the same time. You may never teach them a single Bible lesson in their lives, but if you show them some positive attention and then back that up with faithfulness to the Lord, you've accomplished something huge."

She sighed deeply and looked over at the table of girls. One of them looked up and smiled at her. She felt like the last person in the world who should try and influence teenage girls for Christ, but Kyle was probably right. He usually was.

"Besides," he said with a big grin now, "the ball is massive. No one can miss it."

"You haven't seen me play."

She removed her high heels and stepped onto the cold gym floor as Stephanie Freeman and her husband Danny rolled out a beach ball that had to be a whole yard in diameter. Stephanie and Danny were one of two couples who volunteered to work with the youth at First Baptist. As they explained the rules, which were minimal, Kyle smiled at Cindy from across the net. She shook her head in doubt at him.

"It's not all that hard," said a girl's voice from beside her. "If you just hit it up and run out of the way, someone's bound to get it over."

"Can you tell I'm nervous?" Cindy asked her.

"Naw, I just remember how stupid I felt the first time I played," the girl, Kaleigh, told her. "I knew I would look ridiculous trying to bop that thing around, so when it came to me, I just whacked it like crazy and it went flying up into the air. Some big guy spiked it over when it came back down and everyone thought it was so cool."

"What if I'm not as *blessed* as you and I whack it and lose a point?"

"Then they'll hate you forever." Kaleigh said grimly.

Kaleigh and Kyle had both been right: it was too big to miss, and if you hit it straight up, someone else could finish the job. As Cindy began to break out in a sweat, she found herself actually enjoying the game. She took a tumble once, and the entire team rallied around her to get her back up. The bump had hurt, but she found herself laughing so hard that it was easy to talk it off as nothing serious. By the end of the evening, she was a pro at Beach Ball Volleyball.

"You've got to admit that was fun," Kyle said as he pulled out of the church parking lot to take her home.

"Okay, I admit it. It was fun. I didn't know I could still have fun."

"It felt good to release some tension, didn't it?"

"Speaking of tension, you seemed rather tense today? What was up?"

"Wow," he said more under his breath than openly. "A lot."

"Really?" She edged nearer to him in the Jeep to hear his story.

"I spent the afternoon yesterday with Kate Ashton."

"Ashton? Dr. Ashton? Mom's doctor?" Her heart sank an inch.

"The one and only. It was an uncomfortable day to say the least."

"She's very pretty ... and very smart." She was trying to sound encouraging and positive. "I imagine the conversation was interesting."

"Well, not in her opinion."

"Come on, it couldn't have been that bad."

"By the end of the date, she told me I was damaged goods. Is that what I am now, Cindy? *Damaged goods?*"

"No ... Kyle." She was stunned. "You're ... you're..." *wonderful, incredible, amazing,* "... you're this great guy ... really good guy. I mean, you're a Godly man who chooses to do right. You have character and honesty, and you care for people in ways that they don't have to guess what you're up to. Just because you may be hurting, which by the way, all humans have permission to do, doesn't mean there's anything wrong with you. It means you feel deeply—you give deeply. I don't see anything about you that's damaged. I think you're ... well ... as close to perfect as a man could be."

Kyle pulled over and stopped the Jeep. He looked to his right with a smile. "Thank you. Even if you don't mean it all, I still thank you. It's good to hear an encouraging word now and then."

"Why wouldn't I mean it?"

"Well, how can one woman one day tell me I'm *damaged goods*, and then another the very next day tell me I'm great?"

"Because one woman doesn't know you at all, while the other one has been privileged to see inside your heart."

He still wouldn't drive on. He just sat, staring out the front window, apparently contemplating her statement. He finally nodded.

"Cindy," he said softly, "I did something wrong with Caryn— something drastically wrong. She was sweet, quiet, and gentle. She lived to please me. We seldom spoke a cross word to each other. But when she left that day, she was hard, cold and bitter. It was almost as if she wasn't the same person. *I* did that to her." He turned to look back at Cindy. "I changed this dove into a raven, and I don't even know how."

"Kyle, you can't blame yourself for something you knew nothing about. She lived with you for ten years and acted as though everything was fine. If she wasn't happy, it was her job as your wife to communicate that to you."

"But what if she tried and I didn't listen? I had to have missed something! I drove her away somehow!"

He put the Jeep back into gear and finally drove on. Cindy wished she could talk to him, wished she knew the right words to say to comfort and reassure him, but when it came to relationships, she was batting a big, fat zero. Every single relationship in her life she had selfishly destroyed in some manner. She could start with her parents, move on to her friendships, and then end with any guy she had ever dated. She was a taker, never a giver, and she had a life of emptiness to show for it.

The rest of the drive to Cindy's was silent. Kyle huffed in exasperation, and she bit her lip wishing for the right words to say. When he pulled into the drive, he parked and turned off the engine. She took that as a clue he wasn't ready to leave yet.

"Do you want to come in for a glass of tea or something?" she asked.

He shook his head and stared out his window. "I want to know what happened to my marriage. I want to know what I did wrong. If I never know what happened, then how can I move on? How can I know that if I were to find someone else and marry again, it wouldn't happen all over like before?"

"Kyle," Cindy turned to him in her seat and took his hand so he would look at her. "There's an element in here that you keep missing: *Caryn* left. She gave you no real reason, and she gave you no clue"

"I haven't missed that! It's the one obvious thing that keeps creeping up in my mind!"

"No, that's not what I mean. She didn't *want* you to know anything. When women get mad or hurt, they want revenge. They want the culprits to suffer just like they did. All she wanted was out of your life. Didn't you say you haven't seen or talked to her since she left?"

"Nothing. I don't even know where she is."

"And she didn't leave you for the guy she had an affair with?"

"He's still with his wife as far as I know."

"When she left, it wasn't about *you*. If it were, trust me, she would have laid it all out. She would have made demands. There was something in her Kyle that either snapped or was repressed ... or ... whatever—I don't know. But she didn't leave you because you were a jerk. She left you because *she* wanted out."

"But *why*? Why did she leave?"

"You can't answer that. She's the only one who can, and if she doesn't want you to know, chances are you never will."

He sighed, squeezed her hand and then released it. "So you really don't think all this makes me damaged goods?"

She smiled and giggled a little as she said, "Not at all. It just makes you a more *sensitive* man, and you know how the chicks love that."

"Chicks, huh. I'm not *even* ready to get back into the dating thing again. Besides, I don't know where I stand biblically with all this. Am I considered an adulterer if I marry someone else while Caryn is still single? Or since she committed adultery, am I released from the marriage? I've heard so many different takes on what's right and what's wrong; I don't know where I fit in! I know this: no one wants me as their minister anymore."

"Jonathan Wright does," Cindy piped in quickly.

"Yeah, but he only has enough power to get me in as an interim. What do I do after this?"

"Well, if Angie was here, I know what she'd tell you."

"The missionary?"

"Oh, don't let that title fool you. Angie is one tough and spirited character. But when it comes to the Lord, her head is screwed on straight."

"What would the *spirited* Angie tell me then?"

"She would say *God is up to something*. She would say you're here for a season and a reason and to be careful not to miss it."

He thought on that statement for a moment and nodded in agreement. "She ever said that to you?"

"Last thing she said to me," Cindy smiled. "I treasure her words too. She's a woman of faith, someone who overcame many obstacles to follow God's call on her life. I would've thrown in the towel years back, but Angie was firm on what God wanted of her. I would give anything to have that kind of spiritual foundation and backbone."

"If it helps, you've been a wonderful backbone for me these past couple of months." His expression was gentle again now. The anger and frustration had subsided, and compassion shone in his eyes once more.

"Oh, Kyle, I don't know how you could say that. You've been so good to me and Mother through all of this. We were for all practical reasons strangers to you, but you came into our lives and picked us up. You filled a spot that my father had always filled, and that my brother refused to step into. If for no other reason than that, I thank God that you're here. I've been no backbone, Kyle. You've been the one to hold me up all this time."

"I had no idea I meant something to you. I just thought you were letting me commiserate with you."

She laughed and shook her head in amazement. "We're downright pathetic! We're hurting so much we can't see beyond our own emotional instability."

He laughed with her. "No wonder you don't think I'm damaged goods. You're as bad off as I am."

"Or worse. I've never been married, proposed to or even come close to discussing wedded bliss with anyone. At least you've been in some kind of life commitment. I'm just floating around out here."

"You're picky, I guess."

"About men? Heavens no! I pick the biggest losers in the world. I pick guys that I would never want to marry, guys that are … unavailable, so to speak."

"I doubt that. Give me an example."

"The tennis pro," she immediately thought. "Real hot shot, actually played on the pro circuit for awhile. He was hired at our country club—this was like three years ago. He was so stuck on himself, but I was determined to be his girl. He was a complete moron intellectually and emotionally. I might as well have talked to a tree as to try and carry on a conversation with him, but he was so dog-gone good looking! All I wanted was the image thing. So I went after him."

"Did you get him?"

"Yes," she sighed deeply. "For nine long, miserable months. The whole time I dated him I kept thinking how nice my life would be again when we finally broke up."

"You're kidding!"

"No! That's how shallow I am! And that's how I've managed to avoid marriage. Every single guy I've ever been with, I start the relationship by thinking of all the reasons why it won't work. Then I endure the thing until it's over."

He just stared at her and then said, "Wo. That's not right. It just doesn't seem like you, though. You're full of life … and so giving. I can't imagine you being, well, emotionally unavailable like that."

"I've changed a lot … especially recently. There's so much about me,

Kyle, that you don't know. You see me as the church secretary with a very sick mother I'm caring for. I probably seem vulnerable and needy right now. But that hasn't characterized my life all these years. In reality, I suppose I'm a self-sufficient pig who has wanted everything my own way. I didn't live to please God. I just lived ... I guess ... to please myself."

"You may not believe this," Kyle interjected, "but as I look back at my six years at Harvest Hollow, I really think that's where I was headed. The church was no longer a ministry, but a profession. Appearances and professionalism began to usurp the real reason I was in ministry to begin with. Only I didn't see it until I came here."

"I can't imagine you being selfish."

"Neither can I imagine you. I guess maybe God is in the process of weeding that selfishness out of us, because right now, you're the person who knows me best in the whole world. And if you don't see it, then maybe God *is* up to something."

"Ditto," she said with a knowing nod.

Eighteen

Dr. Ashton finished the follow up exam on Thursday and asked, "How are you ladies fairing with the hair loss?"

"On Tuesday several huge clumps came out at one time," Sue told her. "Scared me to death!"

"I heard her scream and went running into the bathroom." Cindy actually laughed about it now. "She was standing there with this mass of hair in her hands."

"We sort of looked at each other and cried for a bit. I told her it was time to start pulling out the hats and scarves."

"We started giggling then," Cindy added. "I don't really know why."

"Cancer has a way of putting you through the gamut with emotions," Dr. Ashton told them. "It looks like you're pretty much bald right now. Some patients find the itching unbearable and will actually shave their heads at this point."

"Never!" Sue exclaimed at once. "I will scratch my scalp off before I shave my head!"

When Mrs. Marcum left to make her next appointment, Kate asked Cindy to stay behind for a moment.

"Is there a problem?" Cindy asked with concern.

"No, it's nothing like that," Dr. Ashton assured her. "I just wanted to let you know I spent the day with your co-worker on Saturday—Kyle."

"Yeah, he told me about it."

Kate's eyebrows raised immediately in surprise. "Really? He actually talked to you about our date?"

"Yeah, he didn't elaborate ... well ... he wasn't exactly *comfortable* with it ... your date, that is."

"Tell me about it! I was there. I guess I'm shocked that he talked about it to someone. He seems so bottled up. I assumed he was like that with everyone. Do you guys talk often?"

Cindy thought before she answered and then said, "Yeah, we really do. We talk a lot now. The longer we work with each other, the more we seem to get along ... I guess."

"Hmmm," Kate murmured to herself.

"But that's it," Cindy added quickly. "I mean ... we're not ... well ... he's not interested in me or anything."

"Are you interested in him?"

She didn't want to answer that, but she had the pat reply down in her mind well. "I'm not the kind of person Kyle needs. He's a wonderful man, but he needs something more than I can offer him."

"Don't be so sure," Kate said cautiously. "Look, he was like a sick clam in a glued up shell on Saturday. If he really opens up to you, then you're meeting a need in his life that nobody else is at the moment."

"I agree, but that's all it is … and it's only for the moment."

***

As they headed home, Sue talked non-stop about practically everything. Cindy was thankful she was feeling better, and she tried to concentrate on her mother's conversation, but her talk with Dr. Ashton concerning Kyle kept running through her mind. Even if Kyle had an interest in her, she was *not* the right person for him. First, she would be responsible for trying to make him forget the love of his life, Caryn. She couldn't compete with what had been the perfect wife for him. Second, she had never been a woman of character or Godliness. She was trying with all her might to change that, but her past was her past. To be linked with Kyle would be like smearing mud on a white steed, and she could never let herself do that to him. And then third, he was deeply hurt. As wonderful as he was, and as incredibly handsome and compassionate as he was, there would be parts of him that she could never reach because of his previous marriage and unanswered divorce. Cindy would never be able to handle those dark recesses. She needed to put him out of her mind once and for all, and then force herself to remember her resolve during those moments when his blue eyes pierced her soul and his gentle words brought peace and healing to her life.

Nineteen

Easter would be early this year. It was to be the last Sunday of March which meant it would still be cool. Cindy had much to be thankful for this Easter, and she almost felt shallow as she searched for a dress. The meaning of the season had really taken root in her heart, and somehow the idea of picking out something bright and cheery seemed superficial compared to what the death and resurrection of Christ had come to symbolize for her.

I wish you were here, Daddy, she thought to herself. *Mother took her second treatment last week and she's doing wonderfully. I'm working in the church now and I'm actually walking with the Lord. All those years when you would ask me how my relationship with the Lord was, I would always smile and say that God and I had things in hand. I lied, Daddy. I knew nothing about the Lord. But now, He has become my life. I'm learning and growing so much, and I'm struggling hard to understand His forgiveness. I strayed so far from what you taught me. How God could actually forgive me and wipe my slate clean is beyond my comprehension.*

"You're deep in thought," Sue said as she came up behind her with an armload of dresses. "You're not even looking at clothes. Where are you?"

"My mind's just wandering. Are you buying an Easter dress or an entire new wardrobe?"

"It depends," Sue said as she turned to the fitting rooms. "If I like them all, then I suppose a new wardrobe!"

Cindy was thankful for the new relationship with her mother. For the first time in her life they had become a dear friends. Sue could trust her now, not having to worry where she was, who she was with, or what she was doing. She had told her last week during the chemo treatment that just Cindy's presence and encouragement in her life had been a huge source of healing and motivation.

Then there was Kyle. He had filled up a lot of the emptiness left by her father's death and Billy's obvious absence. He had become a regular on Friday nights, Sunday dinners, and often visited during the evenings. Playing Liverpool Rummy had become a ritual and they even bought a special notebook just to keep up with the scores. He was also a great handyman, fixing many of the things that had fallen in need of repair over the past year, and he always had a cheerful attitude whenever he worked. Sometimes Cindy would hand him various tools or items he needed, while at other times she would just sit and watch. He was comical, fun and easy to be with. He had even admitted that some of his intense feelings about Caryn were beginning to fade.

Preparations for the Easter musical found Kyle and Cindy spending much time together at the church building sets, gathering props, and organizing the program. She hadn't been a part of an Easter presentation since junior high, and she was excited about this one. The music was beautiful and lively. It captured the essence of Easter in a bright and inspiring way. The drama combined ancient scenes mixed with present situations to help bring the soul of Easter into a modern context. Kyle had pleaded with Cindy to take a larger part in the drama, but she had never been one for being on stage. Instead, she agreed to play the part of the woman caught in adultery. Every time the rocks began to drop and Jesus reached down to take her hand and lift her up, she felt as though Christ Himself was actually touching her life once again and bringing another depth of healing.

***

"Where are we going?" Cindy asked Kyle on the Friday evening after Easter as they headed toward Sheffield.

"Somewhere different." He only smiled, refusing to give away his surprise.

"I can't believe we're actually headed this way instead of Tupelo. Why the change in direction? You've avoided the Shoals area since I've known you."

"Well, I need to pick up some papers from my parents' house, and I've wanted to do something special for you because of all your hard work in the Easter program. I'm killing two birds with one stone."

"Ooo," she squirmed at the expression. "I don't want to be a part of anybody *killing* anything."

"Okay, bad example. Ever heard of *Oh! Bryan's?*"

"Oh, my gosh, yes! I love it!"

"You've been there?"

"Twice. I went there once with my girlfriends for my birthday, and another time with ... well, a date. The girlfriend thing went great; the date thing ... disaster."

"Are the memories too unpleasant to try it again?"

"Not on your life! Maybe you can be charming enough tonight to make up for his blustering through my evening."

"Heavy responsibility, but I'll give it a try. Then down on the corner from the restaurant is this book store ..."

"Coldwater Books? The two story place with the wooden floors and little coffee shop!"

"You've been there too?"

"I love it! I've only been there once but have been dying to go back!"

"I guess my surprise isn't working too well." He was obviously disappointed.

"Trust me," she smiled at him as she reached over and rubbed his arm, "it's a wonderful surprise."

"But you've been to both of them."

"Not with you."

Kyle first went to his parents house. Cindy was dazzled by the home.

"I've seen this house many times from the bridge. I always thought it was gorgeous. I never imagined I would actually know anyone who lived here," she said in awe.

"I grew up here."

"You're kidding?"

He parked the Jeep in the front and hopped out. Cindy hesitated, however. Kyle opened her door and she stepped out slowly. He was taken by her beauty again. Her hair had grown longer and now the breeze from the Tennessee River was blowing it gently behind her. Her blue eyes sparkled from the setting sun, and her mauve, cashmere sweater and white slacks made her look like Miss America stepping out for the night.

"You really look beautiful tonight," he told her sweetly. "My parents will be impressed."

She looked at him funny. He couldn't read her reaction very well. "Or not?" he hesitated. "You look ... uh ... rough?"

"Oh, I'll take beautiful over rough," she said as they walked toward the huge portico at the front of the house. "You just sounded so ... serious."

"It was a serious compliment."

She looked over at him again, same strange expression.

"Okay!" he exclaimed. "I'll stop!"

"I'm not complaining," she said as she bit her lip. "I'm just ... I don't know ... uncomfortable with you saying things like that ... about *me*."

"Why?" he asked as they stopped at the front door. "I call you beautiful each morning. It's never bothered you before."

"I guess I'm just ... I don't know," she tried to sound light about it. "Let's go meet the parents."

Kyle shrugged his shoulders as he opened the door and motioned her in.

"Mom! Dad!" he called out. "Where are you guys hiding?"

The couple emerged from their den and greeted Kyle with warm hugs. Cindy was as impressed with his parents as she had been with the house. Bradley Sarkos was an incredibly handsome man with obvious Greek features. His dark hair, wavy and unusually long for someone of his age, was sprinkled with strands of gray. Emma was tall, yet thin, with blond hair, blue eyes and pale features just like Kyle. She was poised and gracious and Cindy found herself smiling at the motherly embrace she gave her son.

"Mom and Dad, this is Cindy Marcum," Kyle introduced. "She's the secretary at the church."

"Wonderful to meet you at last, Cindy," Bradley said as he shook her hand gently. "Kyle has told us much about you over the phone. I'm actually a bit shocked to see *him* here in person."

"Gotta get those papers," Kyle explained. "I also thought I'd treat Cindy to *Oh! Bryan's*. She helped me an awful lot with the Easter production."

"Hello, Cindy," Emma said as she gently hugged her. "So nice to meet you."

"It looks like the renovation is finished," Kyle said as he glanced around the downstairs. "Can you guys actually live in here again."

"At last," Emma sighed. "I don't want to go through that again."

"Your house is beautiful," Cindy said breathlessly. "I've noticed it on the cliff from the bridge many times. I can't believe I'm actually standing inside it."

"Would you like a tour?" Emma asked.

"Oh, my, would it be presumptuous of me if I said *absolutely*?"

Emma laughed and took Cindy's arm as she said, "Not at all! Come with me."

"I'll get those papers and catch you later," Kyle said as he headed for his father's study. Bradley followed.

"Ooo la la!" Bradley exclaimed after closing the door to the study. "You work with that girl? That's the face you get to see when you walk into the office every morning?"

"Nice, isn't she?" Kyle said preoccupied as he glanced through the stack of mail he knew to be his.

"Nice?" Bradley asked in astonishment as he turned Kyle toward him. "Nice doesn't even begin to describe her. I bet it's been a lot easier to put Caryn out of your mind working with her."

"It's not like that, Dad. I'll admit, being around Cindy and her mom has helped me forget a lot about Caryn, but there's nothing going on between us. We're really good friends ... and I'll be honest with you ... I think that's pretty much how she wants to keep it."

"Come on, Kyle," his father was starting to sound exasperated. "I would swear to you that she's the most beautiful woman I've ever laid eyes on. And her spirit! I could see it in her eyes the moment I met her! *That's* the kind of woman you *should* have married!"

"What?" Kyle turned around stunned. "Why would you say that? You were so dead set against my marrying Caryn. You never really did warm up to her. Why all of a sudden do you think Cindy's the *right kind of woman* for me?"

"Not the *right kind of woman*, Kyle. She's *the* right woman," Bradley clarified.

"You don't even know her!"

"No, but I know you. Caryn was dark. She had this brooding melancholy about her that just wore you down. But you worshipped the ground she walked on and did everything she wanted."

"Obviously, it wasn't enough," Kyle mumbled.

"Or perhaps it was too much. I think she lost her respect for you. You two never *lived* together. You were always like these two separate entities who shared a name. Your marriage was never a normal marriage."

"What? You don't know what you're talking about! Caryn and I had a great life! In fact, it was as close to perfect as it could be!"

"Then why did she leave, son? If things were so great, why did she walk out on you and never look back?"

He dropped his head and sighed. He had no idea. When his father had first met Caryn he warned Kyle that she wasn't the woman for him. He suggested Kyle break off the relationship immediately and move on. Kyle said he wasn't serious about her but just had a good time being with her. Before he knew what was happening, however, weeks turned into months, and then months into three years, and the next thing he knew, he was graduating from college and proposing. Sensing his parents' disapproval, they eloped to Martha's Vineyard and were married at her parent's house.

"You never liked Caryn," Kyle said with pent-up bitterness.

"No, I didn't. And apparently I was right."

"You never gave her a chance."

"I gave her thirteen years, Kyle, and I never saw her treat you in a way that a woman treats the man she adores. I've been married to your mother for over thirty-five years, and she still has this way of making me feel like the king of the world when she walks into a room."

Kyle leaned back against the wall as he pretended to go through his mail again. He flipped one envelope after another although he wasn't reading any of them.

"Now, Cindy," Bradley moved on in the subject, "there's a woman who could make a man feel like a king. She's beautiful, Kyle."

"So was Caryn." And she was. Caryn's long dark hair and dark eyes gave her a beauty that was almost exotic. She looked like a woman from some island that had been transported to the states. Her exquisiteness had been the first thing that captivated Kyle.

"But Cindy has an inner beauty that literally lights up *your* eyes. When you introduced her, Kyle, you were oozing with pride."

"She's a friend, Dad. Even if I wanted to make more of this relationship than it is, I really don't think she'd be interested. And I'll be honest, I don't know if I could do the whole love and marriage thing again."

"Oh, I think you could. In fact, I sometimes doubt you ever did it for real to begin with. When you find someone who really completes your life, it's worth fighting for. You didn't fight for Caryn, Kyle. All you did was brood."

When Kyle emerged from the study, he saw his mother and Cindy still arm in arm. Emma was explaining some of the large framed photographs in the great room, pictures they had taken over the years at various vacation spots around the world. Cindy was awed, and as Kyle watched her, he had to agree with his father: she was beautiful. Every now and then, he wanted to reach up and touch her hair again, the baby fine hair that had swirled around his arm that afternoon she had passed out in the hospital. Cindy and Emma were clicking too. His mother was animated as she described each photo, and Cindy's expressions of delight just encouraged her all the more.

"I hate to end this budding relationship," Kyle said as he walked up to them, "but dinner is at six."

"So you're going to steal her away from me?" Emma protested.

"Did you take any of these, Kyle?" Cindy wanted to know as she pointed toward the photographs.

"Oh, yes!" Emma exclaimed. "The Parthenon. Isn't it beautiful?"

"Wow," Cindy said in awe

"And I took this one too. It was at Arches National Monument."

"You're very good," she said as she turned to him. The genuine admiration in her eyes nearly sent his knees buckling.

"Thank you," he replied humbly. "I consider you a woman of great taste, so a compliment on my art means a lot."

"Goodness, Kyle," she whispered to him, "your creativity impresses me constantly. I just assumed it was only with music. Apparently you have a lot of unseen talent hiding back there."

"Naw. I was just like messing around with a camera now and then."

"How old were you when you took these?"

"The Parthenon was sixteen," he said as he tried to remember. "I think Arches was when I was thirteen."

She shook her head in amazement and looped her arm through his as she said, "You are a truly gifted man."

Bradley and Emma stared in delight. They had endured thirteen long years of watching their son's demise because of a woman who never knew how to be a wife, and before their eyes they were seeing him transform. Who was this angel on his arm, and where had she been all these years?

Twenty

After being seated at a booth in the corner of *Oh! Bryan's*, Kyle immediately began humming along with the tune playing through the speakers. He ordered an appetizer and their drinks, un-sweet tea, without even asking Cindy. After spending so much time with her, he knew her favorites well.

"How many instruments do you play?" she asked as he continued to hum.

"Hmmm, hard question."

"How can that be hard? Count them up on your fingers. Or even better, you list and I'll count."

"It *is* a hard question. I play some instruments well, you know, have a good command of them; others I just piddle with. I can play around with just about anything. So making a count of them is close to impossible."

"Let's try," she pushed. "I'm just curious."

"Okay, I'll play along. Piano and guitar are at the top. Then you have to think about those instruments that sort of go along with them: chimes, bass guitar, xylophone, hammer dulcimer."

"What the heck is that?"

"I'll show you some time. Then I do pretty good with the saxophone, and the flute is really close to that with fingering and all, although I struggle somewhat with intonation and technique with the flute. I wouldn't want to actually play that publicly unless I had to. I'm okay with the trumpet as long as it doesn't get too high and fancy. And I can do the baritone and the tuba too. Then the French horn some—it's fingering is very similar to the trumpet. Uh, all the percussion instruments. I'm not that good with drums, mainly because I can't sing and play at the same time. But I can generally get by with just about anything else in that family."

"Okay, I give up!" Cindy stopped him. "I don't have that many fingers! How did you end up doing church stuff? You could have done anything you wanted?"

He looked at her funny and cocked his head to the side. "What do you mean *end up doing church stuff?* That's what I've always wanted to do. From the time I was in high school all I ever wanted was to lead worship and train choirs in churches. It's like, I don't know, a life calling or something."

"I believe it. You and Angie and your calls. I obviously don't have one because I've never felt that convicted or sure about anything in my life. You guys would move heaven and earth to do what you feel called to do."

"It's strong," he admitted. "And I'm in such a quandary right now because the call is still strong, but my credibility is lost. No one wants a divorced minister in their church—they just don't."

She nodded. She'd heard church members talk about him, and sometimes the conversations bordered on gossip. No one really knew his situation, but they enjoyed speculating. She knew more than most, but even she was in the dark about his marriage and his life with Caryn. He swore to her that everything had been fine and perfect, but she couldn't imagine how Caryn could just walk out on him if that were really the case.

They ate their meal and then moved down the street to the Coldwater bookstore. They ordered coffee and began to browse among the books, enjoying the archaic, dark atmosphere. The wood-lined floors and set back shelves made them feel transported to another time and place. They wound up on a brown leather couch upstairs looking through a book of black and white photography. As they glanced through it, Kyle would occasionally comment on a picture.

"Why do you like black and white so much?" she asked as they were about half way through the book.

"Hmmm ... never thought about it. I guess because it's more of a pure image. See the lines here? You're not distracted by color or anything. It's like all you see are the various icons in the photo. And then look at how everything moves toward this one spot. It's almost like it's pointing you there. Your eyes are drawn to particular things without all this busyness going on that color can cause."

Cindy followed his finger as he pointed out the lines and nodded in understanding. "I can see that. But doesn't the black and white seem so ... well ... gloomy? Even a sunny day in black and white can feel dark and dim. Look at this picture." She flipped back a couple of pages. "Here's the sun, and these children are obviously laughing as they play. But it looks so foreboding."

"It looks foreboding," he said as he touched a child in the corner, "because this kid is miserable. He can't play with them for some reason, so his misery is what pervades the picture. It's not the color."

"Or lack of it. For the record, I like color, and lots of it."

"I see," he nodded as he turned a few more pages in the book. "So if a guy were to give you flowers, you would rather forego a dozen red roses in favor of a more colorful bouquet with a variety of less expensive blooms?"

She looked up to the ceiling and thought about for a moment. She had never before considered that. "I think you're right. I think you're definitely right. I'm envisioning now a dozen red roses on the dining table in your parents' home. It would make it look so ... staunch, you know? But imagine a vase of glorious wild flowers. The room is now warm and inviting. Yes! I go with the assortment of cheaper flowers."

Kyle reared his head back and laughed loudly.

"Shh," she hushed him quickly as she put her finger up to his mouth.

"This isn't a library," he told her.

"No, it's worse," she said seriously. "People actually pay to get books from here. The management might throw us out."

She self-consciously whipped her head around to see if Kyle's outburst had caused any concern. A few strands of hair strayed across her face. He put his arm behind her on the couch and carefully moved a piece back behind her ear.

"What are you doing?" she asked him as she moved away slightly.

"Why didn't you ever get married?"

"I told you; no one ever asked."

He moved back to his side of the large loveseat. "But why? I can't figure out how anyone could date you and never fall madly in love with you."

"Why would you say that?"

"Because, well, look at you. You're beautiful, you're wonderful to be with, easy to talk to, and you have such a tender heart. How could someone spend time with you and not be swept off his feet?"

She chuckled as she pulled a foot up beneath her. This was an uncomfortable conversation. "My relationships were always with men who were … uh … sort of unavailable. I told you about the tennis pro. They were all pretty much like that. I entered a relationship knowing I didn't want anything more out of it than a few weeks of a good time. No one ever got close."

"Why? Didn't you want to fall in love and build a life with someone?"

"I guess not. That whole concept scares the daylights of me. I suppose it doesn't help that my brother has been married and divorced twice already. It's such a huge commitment—saying you're ready to be with someone for the rest of your life."

"You never fell in love, then," Kyle said knowingly. "When you fall in love, all you can think about is that person. You want to be with them constantly. You try to create ways just to spend time with them."

"You're right. I've never been in love then. I've always enjoyed my space and my freedom. I don't want to pin myself down to one man. It's claustrophobic."

He now gave her a confused look.

"What?" she asked him.

"But that's how God designed it. He placed within us the desire and need to be with someone else—to have a helpmate."

"He placed it within *some* of us … obviously not all of us."

"Something happened to you. That's not normal. Why don't you *want*

101

to fall in love?"

She closed her eyes and sighed deeply. She didn't want to get into this discussion with him. All she wanted him to know about her life was the here and now. He was good. He was Godly. He made right decisions and chose to follow the Lord. She didn't want him to know about her past, her life, and especially the men she had known.

"It's complicated," she tried to put him off.

"I'm fairly intelligent," he pushed. "Try me. Open up to me, Cindy."

She looked up at him. There he was again, tender, compassionate, his blue eyes beckoning to pierce her deepest secrets. She needed to keep up the boundaries. This was a man who was about to tear down her defenses, and she found herself trembling at the thought. But he didn't know her. If he did, he would change his mind. Maybe her best defense was to be brutally honest with him. If he knew what she was really like, he would stop looking at her like he did, he would stop thinking she was beautiful, and he would go back to only wanting to be her friend … or maybe not even that much.

"In high school, Billy, Angie Wright and myself pretty much ran the social code," she began. "We were the *good-looking* people. Why that gave us such power, I don't know. But I was full of myself. I played no sports, no instruments, did nothing but twist myself around school. The teachers liked me, the students adored me, and I dated anybody I crooked my finger to. Life was just too easy.

"Then I left for college, UNA, and my life fell apart. I was a nobody there. I shared an apartment with two friends who took their studying seriously, but I was out for a good time. The only problem was, I didn't know anybody, and nobody gave a flit about me there. By the end of my first semester, I was miserable and bored. I ended up with a B, three C's, and a D—and the D was out of the goodness of the professor's heart. I told my parents I was quitting college and was gonna get a job instead. Talk about a major disappointment. They were devastated."

"Did Billy finish college?"

"No, but he did make it through two years. I got a job in a department store at the mall. I did really well. I had a knack for selling stuff. Because my roommates were still in college, they had college guys over occasionally. The guys acted like I didn't exist. I couldn't figure it out. What had happened between high school and college? I was telling these girls about it one day and they explained that college guys required a lot more from girls than high school. If I wanted to date older men, I was going to have to move a little faster in the relationships."

"Cindy," Kyle began to interrupt, as his face grew alarmed.

"It was true, Kyle," she stopped him. "All I had to do was sleep with one guy and my whole life changed."

"Cindy ..." he said sadly now.

"Now I was back to my old charm. I could date anyone I wanted, and by the end of that semester, I was dating the quarterback, a junior. Life was very different for me now. By Christmas of the next year, he was beginning to think about the future, and a red flag went up immediately. I was nineteen and nowhere near ready to settle down. Besides, I didn't like him all that much. I liked the *image* of dating the football star, but I liked my freedom too.

"As a joke, there was this really good looking smart guy in my roommates' science class, and they dared me to ... well ... you know."

Kyle shook his head in unbelief.

"They talked him into helping them study one night at our apartment, and by the end of the night, I had him in bed too."

Kyle closed his eyes in hurt and disgust, shaking his head at the thought.

"We dated the rest of the year. I liked him, but I was restless and ready to move on. That became my pattern. Then after a couple of years, Louis Tsaveres' wife came into the store to buy some special outfit for a big awards thing in Las Vegas."

"Tsaveres Real Estate?" he asked. She nodded and a light appeared to turn on in his head. "Is that who you worked for, Louis Tsaveres, when you went into real estate? He's like a mogul in the Shoals area."

"She was incredibly impressed with my sales abilities. So much so, that she went home and told Louis he needed to get me on the team. He came in the next day. I had no idea who he was, but he was insistent on buying this ugly suit. I wasn't even supposed to be in his department, but somehow there I was, convincing him to get something much nicer. By the end of the little rendezvous, I had sold him a $1500 suit, and he was impressed. The next day he came in with his wife, introduced himself, and offered me a job."

"You worked for Louis Tsaveres," Kyle said mainly to himself.

"I sold houses for a while and did great. Then he decided to just try me with commercial buildings. On my first attempt I sold a $4.5 million office suite to a new business moving into the area."

Kyle's eyes grew wide in unbelief.

"Needless to say, my career in real estate took off. Now I had everything: an apartment on the river, a nice car, lots of money, great clothes. I went night clubbing a lot, and I met a lot of guys there. I dated a few guys, superficially, and had a good time. That's all I wanted."

Kyle was now folding his arms. His expression was stern, and his face was nearly pale.

"Then I met Evan Clark," she said softly.

Kyle looked up at her and raised his eyebrows. "You're actually mentioning a name?" he said somewhat sarcastically.

"He was a kind of turning point in all of this."

Kyle just nodded for her to go on.

"He worked at another of Louis' offices. We met at a monthly briefing of everyone on Louis' staff. He was a little older, very charming, settled and very sure of himself professionally."

"Very different from the other guys in your life so far?"

"Very," she nodded. "We went out for a drink that afternoon, and before I knew it, we were back at my place. He just wanted to see it. He knew the cost to live in one of those apartments."

"And you slept with him," Kyle said under his breath.

"Yes," she admitted shamefully. This was harder than she had thought, but it was working. Kyle was appalled. "It wasn't until the next week that I found out he was married."

At this, Kyle nearly came off of the couch. "Cindy!" he exclaimed. "How could you not be more careful? You didn't even know him! He could have been some lunatic and could have ..."

"I surmised it was the perfect relationship for me," she said firmly.

His gaze grew even more dumbfounded.

"He was the ideal guy: charming, mature, intelligent, and completely unavailable. I only had to see him occasionally, and when we were together, I felt on top of the world."

"And when you were apart, how did you feel?"

"Great," she said plainly. "It was everything I wanted. Great guy, no chance for commitment, and everyone lived happily ever after."

"So what happened?"

"Angie Wright," she said with a smile.

"The missionary Angie?"

Oh yeah," she nodded. "When Daddy died, Angie had just finished seminary. She was home for a while and we spent some time together. I confessed my relationship to her and she went ballistic."

"Good for her."

"She raked me over the coals. It was easy for me to feel guilty then because my father had just died, and I knew he would be major disappointed if he knew what my lifestyle had become. She told me to break off the relationship, get back in church, and start turning my life around. I tried. I ended it with Evan, much to his dismay."

"I can imagine," he murmured.

"I started going to this huge church, but it felt so impersonal. Then when mom found the lump and we learned it was cancer, my world fell apart once again. I decided I really needed to get things together with God, and First Baptist of Dockrey was my best option. I started going back home on the weekends and attending church. Then the secretary position became open, and well, as they say, the rest is history."

Kyle was quiet. His arms were still folded, and his eyebrows were furled in frustration. She couldn't read what he was thinking.

"You had an affair with a married man," he finally stated.

"I didn't realize it at first."

"But you knew eventually. Cindy, you slept with him! Over and over again! How many times?"

"I don't know, Kyle. It was how I did relationships. It was just how I did them," she paused. "I'm not proud of it. I wish I'd been like you and saved myself for one man and one marriage, but I didn't, and I can't change that now."

"Even when you found out he was married you kept on seeing him?"

"I was messed up," she stood up and walked toward one of the windows. He followed her. She stared out and said, "I thought it was right for me."

"But you were sleeping with some other woman's husband! Someone believed he was her life, and you were out there … putting it out for free … while she's at home trying to be faithful and true! How could anyone resist you, Cindy? Don't you know how incredibly beautiful you are?"

She turned around to face him. "Yes," she confessed. "And I hoped my outward beauty could cover up all the inner ugliness that was there."

"Oh, Cindy," he breathed as tears welled in his eyes. He reached up and took a strand of her hair in his hand. He turned it between his fingers as he came closer to her. "You are so beautiful, inside and out," he whispered as he drew even closer.

"No, I'm not, Kyle," she said nervously. "I just told you …"

"It's not what you did that makes you ugly inside," Kyle said softly. "Satan deceived you big time. He convinced you of things that weren't true. No wonder you hated yourself. You gave yourself too soon and too often."

His face was closer to her than ever before. His hand still kneaded her hair, and Cindy felt she couldn't breathe. All she wanted at that moment was to hold him and to love him. It had happened. She had fallen in love, and this wasn't the man with whom she wanted that to occur. She wanted someone with a past to match her own, someone she wouldn't feel unworthy being with, but this was Kyle. She looked up into his eyes and her heart began to melt.

"What is going on?" she asked him as she tried to pull back. "I don't want this to happen, Kyle. I don't want to feel this way about you?"

"Neither do I. I didn't want to feel this way about anyone ever again."

"Then stop," she said, barely able to speak. "Move away and let's pretend it's not happening."

"I can't," he confessed as he moved closer.

His lips were now touching her forehead, and he gently let them brush a kiss over her.

"Kyle," she tried to protest, but when his eyes met hers, she stopped talking.

This time he leaned down and tenderly found her lips. She tried to feel nothing, but tears began to flow as she leaned into him and lingered in the kiss. As his arms came around her neck, and his hand caressed her hair fully, she grabbed the shirt on his chest and clung to him now. She pulled him closer and began to kiss him in a way she had never kissed any one in her entire life. So this was love.

She finally managed to pull back, tears streaming down her face and confusion eating at her heart. He looked down at her and his eyes once again melted any defenses her mind was trying to hold onto.

"Kyle," she pleaded in a whisper.

"Shh," he said as he put his finger up to her lips, "just a minute."

He left her and went over to the loveseat to grab their jackets. He helped her with her coat, put on his own, and then took her hand to lead her down the stairs.

"What are we doing?" she asked as he went for the door.

"Getting away from here," was all he said.

Once outside, he continued to hold her hand as they walked to the Jeep. The air was crisp and chilly, unusually cool for the beginning of April. The warmth of his hand felt good, but she was now thinking more clearly, and the defenses and barriers were going up again. She stopped quickly and jerked her hand from his.

"We can't do this, Kyle," she said as she closed her eyes so she couldn't face him.

"I agree," he said as he motioned her toward the Jeep. "Let's just drive for a while and then talk through all of this."

Twenty-One

The drive back to Dockrey was uncomfortable. The silence was hard, and the conversation and laughter that always came easily to them was now stifled by tension. Cindy couldn't stand it.

"I shouldn't have let that happen," she finally said.

"It wasn't your fault. Cindy, I never meant to fall in love with anyone, least of all you. I don't want to mess with what we have."

She turned her head quickly to look at him. He glanced back.

"Come on," he said impatiently. "Don't try to pretend you don't love me too. I was married for ten years and never had anyone kiss me like you did back there."

She felt her face go warm. No matter what words came out of her mouth, she knew that kiss would paint them all as lies. Even as she thought about it, her mouth went dry.

"I don't *want* to be in love with you," she finally admitted. "I don't want to be in love with anyone, but especially not you. I want your friendship, Kyle. I don't want what has happened to ruin what we have."

"Then that makes two of us."

There was silence again as they both tried to process what the next step would be.

"Cindy, you're my lifeline right now. Your friendship is all that's kept me going sometimes. I'm nowhere near ready to be with anyone again. I have no future. I have nothing to look forward to. I have no idea what kind of job I'll end up with after the church finds a permanent music minister, and I don't know where I'll be. I can't do a relationship with all that doubt hanging over me. And then there's the whole Caryn issue. Can I even have a legitimate relationship while she's in the picture? What if she walks back in my life? Is there an obligation to her? I don't know what to do, Cindy, but one thing I do know, I can't be *in love* with you."

"Thank goodness," she sighed with relief. "I don't want things to change, Kyle. How do we handle this? Do we try to pretend it never happened? Do we talk through it? What do we do?"

He reached up and scratched his bushy hair. It had grown out some since his one haircut in Dockrey. Cindy had commented on how much she liked the longer locks, and he hadn't cut it again.

"I guess pretending it never happened is a viable option," he finally said. "I don't know if I can do that … honestly. That was some kiss."

"Okay," she was agitated. "Let's just stop talking about the kiss."

"Agreed!"

More silence.

"I just want to know," he broke the quiet, "and I'll never bring it up again."

"What?"

"Was that just an average kiss to you?"

"Kyle!" she exclaimed. "I don't want to talk about it anymore."

"Agreed," he said quickly, "but just answer that one question. Was it just me?"

"No!" she said in exasperation. "It was … awesome, okay? It was like nothing I've ever experienced before. I could have died at that moment—and died happy."

He laughed at her description, but she was being serious. As she thought about what she had said, however, she began to laugh too.

"Can you turn your back on that kiss?" he asked without laughing. "I'm willing to try. I'm not ready for love, Cindy, and especially not with you. I need you desperately to remain my friend."

"Then we're agreed," she said as she offered her hand to shake.

He took it and shook it, but just touching him like that brought a whole rush of feelings again. She would make a mental note: don't touch him … ever.

When they pulled into her driveway, he walked her to the door as usual. They stood awkwardly on the porch as they tried to act as though nothing had happened.

"We could give it another try?" he asked with a silly grin.

"The kiss?" she asked astonished. "Are you kidding? That would be like nailing the coffin of our friendship."

"Maybe not," he suggested. "Maybe the store was just a fluke. What you told me was very emotional for both of us. Maybe we were just reacting to that moment. Maybe we're not in love? Kiss me goodnight. Maybe there's no magic. Try not to feel anything this time."

"Are you crazy?" she asked him as she bit her lip. "That's the most ridiculous thing I've ever heard."

"Come on, it's worth a try. It would put all our fears to rest."

"Or compound them," she said as though she were the only voice of reason.

He nodded and turned to go, but turned around to see her face again. She was still staring at him in unbelief. Her head was telling her to go inside and run for her life, but her heart was racing at the thought of feeling his lips on hers again.

"Oh, what the heck," she mumbled as she walked over to the steps of the porch. "It can't hurt, can it? I mean, the damage has already been done."

Kyle stepped up to the top step and she remained on the deck. Their eyes were even. He reached up and took her hair in his hand again and leaned in slowly, watching her eyes as he drew closer. Before he ever touched her lips, she knew she had made a mistake. She'd only imagined a simple kiss, but it quickly became more. She felt the passion surge through her and wished she could simply erase Caryn from his memory.

She knew it shouldn't have happened. She wanted to pull away and laugh as though she felt nothing and that the whole thing was just a silly misunderstanding, but with his hands in her hair, and his kiss continuing, she found herself putting her arms around him instead. She was lost in the emotion, but what was more, she had no doubts about her feelings for Kyle: she was in love.

"I felt nothing," she giggled as she finally pulled away from him. "What about you?"

"Not a thing," he said as his blue eyes pierced her again. "Except I don't think I can breathe right now."

"Me either," she confessed as she placed her forehead against his. "I don't like the way this feels, Kyle. The way you're holding me, the way you touch my hair ... this isn't friendship."

"I know. I guess I was wrong about our little experiment," he whispered. He kissed her again, and she pulled him even closer.

"Where do we go from here?" she asked this time. "Before, I could pretend. Now ... I don't know."

"I'm not ready for this," he said honestly. "But I don't want to lose you. How do I keep you in my life?"

She looked deeply into his eyes. She knew the feeling. She backed away this time, but he kept one hand on her silky hair. She gently took his hand from her hair and kissed it tenderly before putting it back by his side.

"No pretending," she told him carefully, "but we don't do this anymore. We stay with others; we don't go it alone, just the two of us."

"Good idea," he said as he stepped down a step. "I can still come over, as long as your mother's here."

"And leave when she goes to bed," Cindy added.

"And we don't talk about this ... or ... that," he grinned referring to the two kisses now.

"No," she smiled back at him. "We talk about the things we've always talked about before."

"And we move on," he agreed.

Twenty-Two

Kyle and Cindy didn't call each other on Saturday. Sue wondered about Cindy's unusual mood and asked about it several times, but she always made up an excuse. She was torn. She did *not* want to feel like this toward Kyle on one hand, but on the other she was practically walking on air. She couldn't think straight, and she actually found herself cleaning the kitchen floor to occupy her mind.

When there was nothing else to do, she went upstairs to her computer. Smiling again at the picture of her and her father, she got online and went to Facebook. Nothing newsworthy with anyone else, but boy did she have news, only she couldn't share it. Her life was full and she had no need of anyone other than those who were there right now, namely Kyle and her mother. She clicked on Angie's name to send a message. She was safe; she was on the other side of the world. How she wished Angie was sitting beside her to give some advice. A letter would be the next best thing.

Dear Angie, You're probably going to die when I try to tell you all of this, but I really need to talk right now. You promised me you would always be a click of the mouse away. Without a bunch of mumbo-jumbo, here's the bottom line: I've fallen for Kyle Sarkos. I didn't mean for it to happen, in fact, I tried to avoid it. From the first day I met him I told myself he was out of my league and out of my reach, but something happened. Yes, I know what you're thinking, and he does feel the same way. This isn't all in my head, but here's the deal—we don't WANT this! It's hard to explain, but we just don't. We only want to remain good friends. I haven't seen him since all of this happened, but tomorrow is church. I'm wondering how I'll make it through choir and worship with him standing in front of me the whole time. Angie, when he kissed me, I thought I would melt into oblivion. It was like nothing I've ever known before. And then there's this whole thing about his wife! How do I deal with that? I don't want to be in love with a divorced man whose wife could walk back into his life at any moment. And Kyle's the kind of guy who would go back with her in a flash, regardless of his feelings, simply because it would be the right thing to do.

Give me some wisdom, Dr. Ang. I need one of those good old no-nonsense talks you're so capable of. I know it's the middle of the night where you are, but I will be waiting on pins and needles for your reply, so unless you have some major surgery in the planning, you'd better write back immediately!! Lost in Love, Cindy

***

Angie rolled over sleepily as the sound of the river beckoned her back to slumber. Michael was already up, and she knew she would find him reading his Bible and praying on the back deck. She reached down and gently rubbed the small bulge that was finally showing in her tummy. Her smile grew as she pulled herself over to the edge of the bed.

"Hey, sweetie," she said as she waved while passing the door to the back. Michael looked up and smiled adoringly. "Don't stop praying on my account."

She went to the kitchen area of their squared house and poured herself a glass of juice trying hopelessly to wean herself off her morning coffee addiction—she was avoiding caffeine while pregnant. She sat down at the computer and logged onto Facebook.

"Cindy Marcum," she smiled as she read the message alert. "Something big must be up in your life to actually write me." As she read, her eyes began to grow wider. "No way."

"No way, what?" Michael asked as he walked inside.

"News from home … big news."

"What is it?" he asked as he came over and kissed the top of her head.

"Cindy Marcum is in love."

Dear Cindy, You're as full of paradoxes as ever! What am I going to do with you? I finally get you straightened out, and then you go and fall for a divorcee! Just kidding. First, let me say that what you and Kyle feel for each other is probably NOT love. If it were love, you wouldn't try to be reasoning each other out of it, at least that's my experience. When I realized I was in love with Michael, you could have chained my feet to a cannonball and threatened to drop me in the ocean and I wouldn't have recanted. I think that perhaps what you two have discovered is a wonderful friendship with some deep emotional attachments due to your unique situations. The very fact that you DO NOT want to be in love is a good indication that you probably aren't. My best advice? Avoid being alone together. Pray a lot. Enrich your lives with each other, but avoid places where emotions might take control. Think with your heads and not your hearts for a while.

As Michael read over her shoulder, he frowned. "I thought you said she was in love?"

"She is," Angie said as she continued to type.

"Then why are you telling her she's not?"

"Because that's what she wants me to tell her."

"No, she wants you to give her advice. That doesn't sound like advice."

"Trust me, Michael, you don't know Cindy like I do. She doesn't want to be in love with him right now, but the evidence is obvious."

"So, why aren't you telling her that?"

She turned around and glared at him for a moment. He put his hands up in surrender. "I don't understand women, right?"

"Remember that, will you?" she said as she turned around to finish the

111

When you love someone, they consume your every thought. You don't want to do anything or go anywhere without them. Things that used to seem mundane now take on this great sense of excitement when you do them with the one you love. So, don't worry! You're not in love! When your every waking moment is wrapped up in him, when you can hardly wait to see him again, when the very thought of him makes your heart race, then you'll know you're in love. For now, keep your infatuation at bay by sticking to groups. That's my advice.

***

Sunday morning was a trial for Kyle. As soon as Cindy came into the choir room he knew it. He could smell her perfume above all others, and he forced himself not to turn and look at her. The scent reminded him of Friday night, and as he thought of holding her in the bookstore and on her porch, he found himself rubbing his fingers together as if her silky fine hair was still there.

She did an excellent job avoiding his eyes as he directed the choir through a quick run of their morning special, but when it came time for the actual performance during the service, they found each other. He smiled weakly and directed his attention to the basses who were struggling to get out a particularly high line. He was thankful for the first time in his ministry that the basses needed his help.

***

As was the norm, he went to the Marcums for Sunday dinner. For the first time, Cindy had prepared the entire meal herself.

"I had a lot of time on my hands yesterday," she said as a response to his question concerning her meal while they cleaned up the kitchen after dinner. "I looked through some of Mother's cookbooks and found this recipe."

"I'm proud of you," he said warmly, keeping his distance. "I guess I did well. I suppose you don't need any more Friday night lessons."

She started to protest and then realized this was probably his way of easing out of their spending so much time together. "Probably not. I'm not ready to cater any church dinners, but I think I can hold my own now."

"I don't know. You did awfully well on this one. I would put you up for a catering job."

She laughed as she rinsed out a plate and put it in the dishwasher. "Your faith in me is rather amazing, wouldn't you say?"

"Hmmm ... it might be faith in myself. After all, I was your teacher. Does that make me arrogant?"

"There's not an arrogant bone in your body, Kyle Sarkos," she said with a warm, heartfelt smile.

His eyes nearly melted her defenses ... again.

112

***

Sunday night after church was another youth fellowship. Cindy didn't have to be asked twice this time. In fact, she came prepared. She wore jeans and tennis shoes and was determined *not* to take a tumble during this game. After two slices of pizza and much laughter, she was ready to go, but Stephanie Freeman needed to talk first.

"Is there a problem?" Cindy asked as Stephanie took her aside in the gym.

"Not really," Stephanie said in secret. "I just needed to talk to you about a situation."

Cindy could feel her face blushing. Did Stephanie know about her and Kyle? Had someone seen them on her porch, or at the bookstore? Was she about to get a lecture about something?

"I'm pregnant," Stephanie said instead.

Cindy's eyes grew wide both from surprise and relief. "Stephanie! That's wonderful!"

"Shh!" Stephanie hushed her quickly. "We're keeping it quiet for now. I'm a little over four months, but the last two times I was pregnant, I lost the babies."

"Oh, I'm sorry. I didn't know."

"We don't want to tell anyone this time in case … well … you know … if I lose the baby again."

"I understand, but why are you telling me?"

"You know I teach senior high girls in Sunday School right?"

Cindy nodded.

"I mentioned to them this morning about getting someone to take my class while we go on this cruise. In truth, I was feeling them out for when the baby comes. For one week they could go into the junior high class, or even mix with the boys for that matter. But I really wanted to hear their responses. If the baby makes it, I'll need a couple of months off."

"I understand."

"The girls all agreed they'd like you to teach them."

Cindy's mouth dropped. What? Did she hear her right? Teenage girls wanted Cindy to teach them the Bible? Surely this was a joke. "I've never taught anything in my entire life."

"These are teenage girls," Stephanie said in a way that sounded as though that should clear up any uncertainty.

"Heavens, Steph, that's even scarier."

"The only lesson they need is for you to share your life with them. Tell them how to be committed to Christ in today's world. Answer their questions. You don't have to do a whole lot of preparation to teach them, just a whole lot of prayer. Sometimes one simple statement will start a discussion that takes the entire class time. What they need is honesty and commitment … and love."

Cindy swallowed as she considered the thought. She peeked around Stephanie's head to the older girls who were still congregating at a table. They looked awfully intimidating.

"Let me think on it," Cindy told her.

"That's why I'm telling you now. They want you, but you need time to decide if you want them."

"You could have phrased it differently than that." Cindy rolled her eyes.

"I could have," Stephanie was grinning. "But it sounded much more persuasive the way I said it. Wouldn't you agree?"

"Definitely."

Cindy couldn't believe the girls had actually asked for her. She felt honored in her heart, but sick in her stomach. She wasn't the one to lead impressionable girls in their walks with Christ. Or was she?

Are You up to something, God? Angie would say You are.

Cindy's thoughts faded quickly as Kyle came up next to her on the court.

"Are we on the same team tonight?" she asked as she lightly punched his arm.

"Careful. That's my spiking arm. And yes, I'm on your team, so you don't want to damage the star player."

"I'm feeling very fit and lucky tonight," she told him with a wink. "Just try and steal my thunder if you want."

"On top of the world, are we?"

Yes, and I have been since Friday night.

Twenty-Three

On Monday morning Cindy was stunned to find a sheriff's car from Tennessee parked at the church office. She stepped out of her little red Thunderbird cautiously wondering why someone would be here from out of state. Gathering her purse, she walked up to the door where the sheriff was waiting.

"Can I help you?" she asked as she reached for the office key. "Is there some kind of trouble?"

"I need to speak with Kyle Sarkos," the man replied. "Does he still work here?"

"Yes. He probably won't be here for another hour. He usually comes in around nine."

"Do you mind if I wait?"

"He lives just down the hill," Cindy pointed toward the Wright house. "You could see him now if it's urgent."

"Too much security." The sheriff was shifting his feet uncomfortably. "I don't want to stir any rumors or cause a raucous."

"A sheriff's car from Tennessee parked at the church office in Dockrey?" Cindy laughed. "If you didn't want to cause a raucous, you've already failed—I can guarantee that. I'd better start answering the phone now. Do you have a suggestion for a reply when they start asking?"

"Just tell them it's official business."

Cindy opened the door, put down her things and went immediately to start the coffee. The sheriff followed.

"Beautiful view out there," he commented as he walked to the window that overlooked the valley.

"Yes, it is."

"Nice place to work, I imagine. How's Kyle doing here?"

Cindy looked up at him. Did he know Kyle? Was this a personal visit? "Is Kyle in some kind of trouble?" she asked.

"I'm not at liberty to discuss that, ma'am," he said going back into law enforcement mode.

She nodded. "Okay, it just seemed that you knew him by your question."

"I did know him. I was a member at Harvest Hollow."

Cindy's eyebrows flew up. "So, is this personal business or police business?" She was too curious now.

He just shook his head.

"Right," she nodded slowly. "You're *not at liberty to discuss* it."

She got the coffee going and then went to her desk to turn on the computer.

"Kyle's doing wonderful," she said.

"Excuse me?" he asked as he moved closer.

"You asked me how Kyle was doing here. He's doing wonderfully. He's a very talented man with a heart for God and worship. Your church lost a treasure in him."

"Believe me, many of us know that."

"How's Joe working out?" she asked him. "Did you know he was here before going to Harvest Hollow?"

"When a few of us heard that this was where Kyle had ended up, we thought it was rather ironic."

"So how's Joe doing?"

The man smiled and shook his head briefly before he answered. "He's not Kyle. There'll never be another Kyle."

"You're right about that."

Time passed slowly as the sheriff drank two cups of coffee with her. She learned during that hour that he had just recently become sheriff and was now working with county cases. She wondered what he wanted with Kyle. It would put a damper on their greeting this morning. She was curious as to how it would go. Would he still call her *beautiful*, or would it be different. He'd been the same old Kyle last night at the fellowship, but her heart had jumped into her throat during both services any time their eyes met. She did take consolation in Angie's words: they were probably *not* in love. It was possible to be attracted to someone and not be in love. She of all people should know that. But what she felt for Kyle was different from what she'd felt for anyone else. At least he didn't consume her every thought. Or did he?

When the door finally opened and Kyle walked through, the recognition was immediate.

"Davidson!" Kyle yelled as he walked over to the man and embraced him. "What brings you to Alabama?"

"Kyle, good to see you again. You look amazing, in fact, better than ever I believe."

"It's the company I've been keeping," he winked at Cindy. "What do you need? I'm assuming this isn't a pleasure call."

"Can we go somewhere private?" the sheriff said lowly. "This is ... odd."

"Anything you want to tell me you can say in front of Cindy." He walked over to her desk.

"I think you would prefer me to do this in private," the sheriff insisted.

"And I assure you that it's fine for Cindy to hear whatever it is you have to tell me." He now put his hand on her shoulder. She could feel her face grow warm at his touch. How could he do that to her so easily?

"Okay," Sheriff Davidson said as he cleared his throat. "You might want to sit down then."

"What on earth is going on?"

The sheriff bit his lip, crossed his arms, and looked up at the ceiling as he chose his words carefully. "There's no easy way to tell you this."

"Then for heaven's sake just spit it out! What's happened?"

He hesitated as he said, "Caryn was … murdered last night."

Cindy watched as Kyle grabbed his heart. His face went pale, and his eyes began to tear.

"What? Why? How?"

"We have very few answers," the sheriff explained. "It was all rather odd how we found her."

"You were there?"

"I recognized her address, and her situation. She was living in a nice apartment complex just outside of Franklin. I'd seen her there on a previous call to another apartment in the building. I had talked with her and asked her how she was doing. She was very guarded, not happy at all that I knew where she was. She was also … very pregnant at that time."

"I knew she was pregnant when she left. She still wouldn't stay."

"The call came in last night about eight forty-five. A neighbor heard the baby crying, and she said that baby never cried. The lady listened for noises through the front door that would indicate that Caryn was taking care of the baby, but the crying just got worse and the baby more hysterical, and no other noises were heard. She knocked and knocked on her door, but no answer. That's when she called us."

Kyle took a deep breath, his face still ashen and his heart pounding in his throat. Cindy couldn't help it; she stood up next to him and took his hand. He squeezed it back.

"We had to break in the door, and what a sight it was," Bob said as his voice began to choke. "There'd been no struggle. Whoever shot her wasn't a stranger. She'd been shot three times, obviously in a torturous manner."

"What? Why?" Kyle asked as he put his head down in his hands.

Cindy reached up and smoothed back his hair and then began to rub his back. She had never seen this kind of hurt in anyone's eyes.

"I was hoping you could give me something … anything," Bob said as he held out his hands. "Whoever did this did a deliberate job."

"What happened?"

"She was shot first in the upper leg, right near the thigh," Bob said slowly, not wanting to give out these details. "The second shot went to the abdomen, and then finally, her heart."

"Good heavens!" Kyle nearly screamed out. "Why? Who did this, Bob?"

"Like I said, there was no evidence of struggle. This was professional. A silencer had to have been used, and Caryn had to know the person. From the blood patterns, and the position of her body, it doesn't appear she even fought the execution. She just stood there, let whoever did it finish the job, and then she sat down on the couch and died."

Kyle erupted from the desk in a scream, obviously trying to control the anger that was now surging through his body. "What happened, Bob? Somebody had to see something? Who had been visiting her? Who was in her apartment yesterday?"

"Everyone around gave the exact same answer: she kept to herself and no one came in or out."

"Then somebody's lying!" Kyle insisted.

"I agree. None of it makes sense. But I have to continue with the reason I came." He walked over to Kyle. "I have to ask where you were last night."

"What?" Cindy yelled this time. "Don't tell me *he's* a suspect."

Kyle shot a glance of unbelief at Bob.

"It's routine, Kyle. It's what I do. This is just procedure. You're the closest legitimate relation to her, and you have the possibility of a motive."

"You think I killed Caryn?" Kyle asked astonished.

"No," Bob said quickly. "But this is modus operandi. I have to ask you this, and I need people to back up your alibi."

"I can tell you exactly where he was until nine thirty last night," Cindy jumped in. "From six o'clock on, he was at the church. He led worship in front of a hundred people, and then he was at the gym with three other adults beside me and about twenty-five teenagers."

"Could I have the names and contact information for those other adults?" Bob asked her.

"You know it," she said and then immediately went to her computer to look up the names of Stephanie and Danny Freeman and Jared Smith.

"There's more, Kyle," Bob said as he crossed his arms again.

Kyle's eyes grew wide from emotional shock. "More?"

"It's the baby, Kyle. You have to take her."

Kyle shook his head and sat down on the desk.

"Kyle," Bob said more seriously, "the baby is yours."

"You don't understand," Kyle tried to explain. "It's not my baby. I can't have children."

"Oh, I remember the testing. I was in your prayer group when you found out. I prayed many nights for you and Caryn. But this is *your* baby."

Cindy printed out the information and went to the printer to retrieve the paper. She took it to Bob Davidson and then went back to Kyle who was staring in shock.

"It can't be my baby," Kyle insisted.

"I've seen her, Kyle, and there's no way under heaven that this little girl isn't yours."

"It's Reese's baby," Kyle choked out. "She was pregnant with Reese's baby when she left me."

"You're crazy, Kyle!" Bob said this time. "Reese and Alicia are as happy as ever. They have a new baby of their own."

"I know what I'm talking about. Caryn had an affair with Reese. That's why she left me. She was pregnant with his child, and she wanted out of our marriage. I guess she had enough diplomacy in her not to force the issue on Reese since Alicia was pregnant too."

"Kyle, I've seen the baby," Bob said again. "She looks just like you."

Kyle's expression was one of total confusion. He ran his hand through his hair and just shook his head.

"But you understand Kyle *can't* have children," Cindy reminded him. "There's no way this baby can be his."

"I know what the facts are supposed to be," Bob told her, "but I also know what I saw. Those were Kyle's blue eyes, and those were *his* blond locks."

"Blue eyes and blond hair?" Kyle asked him. "How? Caryn and Reese were both ..."

"I know," Bob nodded. "Dark hair, dark brown eyes, it doesn't make sense. But look, I didn't know about the Reese connection here. This makes everything even harder for you then."

"Why?" Cindy asked.

"I took the baby to Reese and Alicia's," Bob said in embarrassment. "I needed to put her into someone's custody until I could contact you."

"I'm not taking this baby," Kyle said firmly. "I don't care what you say, she's not mine. It's impossible."

"Did you sleep with Caryn anytime before your divorce that could have possibly fathered that child?" Bob asked bluntly.

"I slept with her the night before she left me! That's why I was so flustered when she walked out! Our life was fine! I had no clue!"

"This is your child, Kyle," Bob insisted again.

"It's not my baby. It's impossible."

"Your name is on the birth certificate."

"What? Are you kidding me? Why would she put my name on the birth certificate?"

"Maybe she knew it was yours, Kyle," Cindy suggested.

"How?"

"If she looks like you, she must have known."

"The baby looks just like you, Kyle," Bob said again. "But maybe there's more to it than just that."

"Like what?"

"Like what if she and Reese were never together. I don't have to tell you; you know what kind of man Reese Weathers is. He's a good man, an honest man, a man of integrity. He loves his family and adores his wife. He's a doting father and husband. Maybe she just threw that name out for some reason. Maybe she just wanted you to let her go with no questions asked."

"She wouldn't do that," Kyle said insistently. "She wasn't that kind of woman."

"She walked out on you after ten years of marriage and gave you no chance to work through it," Bob reminded him. "She was *that* kind of woman."

Kyle began to pace. Cindy's emotions were so jumbled she didn't know what to do. So much for an easy friendship with Kyle—for things going back to like they were. Whatever happened from here on out would be nothing like what things were before. And right now all she wanted was to hold him and tell him all this would work out for the good.

"You're the official guardian of the baby, Kyle," Bob went on. "You have to take her. Your name is on the birth certificate as her father. And besides, she even named the baby after you."

Kyle looked up at him again and shook his head.

"Her name's Kylla. I'm telling you, she's yours."

Kyle walked over to the window and looked down at the valley that had become a huge part of his peace and healing the past two and a half months. Even its serenity couldn't calm the storm brewing in his heart. He closed his eyes and wondered if possibly this were only a dream. He had tried to convince himself that his Friday evening with Cindy had only been a dream, a wonderful dream. But this was a nightmare. Caryn had been murdered, she had put his name on the baby's birth certificate, and now he had legal custody of a child that wasn't his—a child he didn't even want to see, much less hold or raise.

He glanced over at Cindy. Her eyes were red with compassion and his heart gelled within him. Yes, he loved her. It hadn't been a dream. He had tried to be casual with her last night, but all he wanted at this moment was to grab her and put his arms around her and make her promise to never let go of him again. How did life go from being almost right again to complete disarray in a matter of three days?

"What do I need to do?" Kyle finally asked in surrender. "I don't want the baby, Bob. I don't care whose name is on the birth certificate."

"Take her for the moment. If you absolutely don't want to keep her, then you can begin some kind of adoption proceedings or something. But take her briefly or she goes into custody of the state."

Kyle nodded in defeat. He looked over at Cindy in utter helplessness and shrugged his shoulders. She walked over to him, put her arms around his waist and pulled him close. He began to sob into her hair on her shoulder. She cradled his head and gently spoke words of encouragement in his ear.

"We'll get through this, Kyle," she whispered. "God is up to something. We'll get the baby and then take it from there."

Suddenly Jonathan Wright sprang through the door. "Morning, everybody!" he said brightly. "What's with the Tennessee sheriff parked out …"

He stopped as he took in the scene and recalculated his bubbly intrusion. "Cindy? Kyle? What's happening here?"

"Sheriff Bob Davidson," Bob said as he offered his hand. "Kyle, you want me to tell him?"

Jonathan was floored. It took him a few moments to imagine something like this could be reality. He looked over at Kyle and Cindy and his heart was struck at the sight. These were two hurting people who had found healing in each other, and this latest incident was going to draw them even closer together.

When Kyle excused himself to the restroom to wash his face, Jonathan motioned Cindy to him.

"You need to go with him, Cindy."

"To get the baby?" she asked in a near panic. "What about the phone here?"

Jonathan gave her a sharp look. "I can answer the phone; Barbara can answer the phone. Any monkey on the moon can answer the phone," he said sarcastically. "But neither of us can be the support he needs during this unbelievable exchange. To top it off, Cindy, he has to pick up the baby from the man who supposedly had an affair with his wife. Everything in this spells trouble and heartache. He needs you."

"But," she looked around helplessly as she searched for her explanation, "I don't need to be the one with Kyle."

"As I see it, you're the only one who needs to be with Kyle."

"You don't understand," she said as she sat down and gave up. "Nobody does. I don't even think I do."

"Let me tell you what I *do* understand," Jonathan said as he sat on the edge of her desk. "You and Kyle have forged a relationship that's done you both a world of good. A relationship is easy when there are no barbs or obstacles to test it. Well, here's your chance. Kyle needs you right now, Cindy, just like you needed him after your mother's surgery and chemo treatments."

"But I don't know any more about babies than he does," she protested. "Pastor Jon, I've never even changed a diaper!"

"I'm not sending you with him for the baby," he said gently. "I'm sending you because you will be the pillar of support that gets him to Harvest Hollow, drives him to that house, stands by him as he faces that man, and props him up when he sees that baby for the first time. You'll be the one to hear his heart going and coming."

Kyle came out of the bathroom obviously trying to put on a positive face, but he was still pale from the shock. "It's a six hour drive. I'd better get going."

122

"We'll have the crib up in your apartment when you and Cindy get back," Jonathan assured. "Take your time."

"Cindy?" he asked confused.

"I'm going with you," she said as she stood and got her purse.

His look of relief and delight was more than enough to convince her she was doing the right thing.

"You'll call mother?" she asked Jonathan as they started to leave.

"She'll be praying with us," he assured them both.

As they climbed into the Jeep, Kyle just stared quietly for a moment.

"Are you okay?" she asked him.

"This is not how I imagined this day going. I thought we'd banter a little bit, try to pretend Friday was just a good joke. I'd convinced myself that I didn't need you, and even more, that I didn't love you. I was determined to make it this week without going to your house or leaning on you in any way."

She smiled and nodded in understanding.

"But now, I'm thinking, Cindy, if you weren't going with me right now, I don't know if I could do this."

She reached over and took his hand, gently kissed it and then placed it next to her cheek. "Kyle, you have me for as long as you need me and for whatever you need me," she promised him. "Forget Friday. This is Monday—and things are very different for you on Monday."

"Are they different for you?" he asked her with pleading eyes.

She kissed his hand again and just nodded. "Crank up the Jeep, handsome," she tried to lighten the mood. "We've got a baby to procure."

"Yes, ma'am, beautiful," he said as he reached up to touch her hair again.

They let their eyes meet briefly, and then they were off.

The beginning of the trip was light and things almost felt normal between them again, or at least comfortable, but the looming of what was to come dampened the mood. She could tell when he would sink back into a melancholy doom, and she would try to bring him out for a little while. As awkward as it was right now, it would be even more so during their return—they would have the baby with them.

"I'm not very good with babies," Cindy began at one point after lunch. "I've never even changed a diaper."

He laughed. "I'm not surprised."

"Really? Why?"

"You've never cooked, never cleaned a toilet, I would guess babies and diapers would have been close behind that list of," his voice went high pitched as he mocked her, "*things I don't do.*"

"I'm serious about this, Kyle. I can't help you one iota when you pick her up."

"Can you hold her?"

"Of course I can *hold her.*" She bit her lip.

"I can change a diaper. Caryn and I baby-sat a lot ... even Reese's oldest boy."

He grew silent again. She saw how just mentioning Reese's name made a vein pop up in his neck.

"How do you feel about all this?" She finally asked what they had been avoiding all day.

"All what?"

"Caryn's death. You being listed as the baby's father. The fact that we're going to be at Reese's in about two hours to get her. Any of it—all of it."

He sighed before he spoke. "Caryn's death, or more aptly, her murder, leaves me, for lack of a better way to describe it, disappointed. Somehow, I always imagined meeting up with her again and getting some answers. I figured things would cool off, we'd move on, then we'd happen on each other, and I would learn the truth. That'll never happen now. And then this whole bizarre thing with her being murdered. What's that all about? Who would murder her? Why? Did she know this person before she left me? Did she think I was in some kind of danger? And if so, why didn't she worry about the baby? If there was really someone after her, why didn't she get rid of the baby, give it up or something? None of this makes sense! Or did she get involved with this person last year? Maybe he's the baby's father! Too many unanswered questions to begin with, and now the list just gets bigger.

"Then the whole father thing," he shook his head. "Did she do that to maybe get back at me? Was it like a joke or something ... putting my name down as the father on the birth certificate? The best I can figure is that when she told Reese about the baby, he must have flipped. He told her no way would he claim it, and she was on her own. When the baby came, she just put my name down, knowing that if anything happened ... man ... like a murder or something ... I'd do the right thing because..."

"... because that's the kind of man you are," Cindy finished the sentence.

"Yeah," he nodded as he turned off the interstate onto an exit ramp. "Good old Kyle, a sucker down to the very end."

"You're no sucker. You're a wonderful man. Don't ever sell yourself short. I never want to hear you say anything like that again."

"The only good thing that came out of any of this is that I met you," he told her as he pulled into the gas station. "And it seems the deeper I get into this, the more I need you beside me."

He pulled up next to a gas pump and shut off the engine. Turning to her, he reached out for her hand. She gave it willingly. He held it for just a moment and then asked, "Want some M&M's?"

"I'll get the M&M's, a big bag of 'em, and you pump the gas," she suggested.

"Thanks," he said tenderly.

"It's no big deal, Kyle. I can afford snacks, you know?"

He just smiled at her. They both knew that he wasn't talking about the snacks.

Twenty-Five

Cindy noticed the vein in Kyle's neck beginning to throb again as they entered the city limits of Harvest Hollow. This wasn't a normal town, at least nothing like the towns in northern Alabama. It was manicured, cultivated, and looked almost surreal—like a setting in a movie. The people moved along the exclusive storefronts in perfect clothes with expensive baby strollers and kids in designer outfits. Had Cindy seen this place a year ago, she would have longed to move here. Each building followed the same motif of design, sporting an adobe type style with some slight difference to set it apart. It was charming, but sterile somehow. It lacked the character that old towns like Dockrey had aged into, something that took time, birth, life and death to create.

When Kyle pulled onto Dogwood Street, he slowed down in front of one of the smaller houses. It was a beautiful classic brick home with a perfect lawn and single-colored mums poking out from the various flowerbeds.

"That was my house," he said weakly.

"It's beautiful."

He rounded the next corner and pulled into the driveway. After turning off the engine he just sat there.

"They lived really close to you guys," she commented.

"Closer than I imagined."

"Are you gonna be all right?" she asked as she reached out for his hand again. He took it and shrugged his shoulders.

"I'm here, Kyle. I'm just a hand away at any moment, okay?"

"Let's do this." He took a deep breath. "Let's make this as quick as possible."

"I'm with you."

They climbed down from the Jeep just as a man walked out the front door.

"Kyle?" he asked as he shaded his eyes from the sun.

He was very handsome, considerably shorter than Kyle, and opposite in features. He had a gentle look about him, and Cindy couldn't imagine that this was the man who had stolen Caryn's heart from Kyle.

"It is you," Reese said as he approached Kyle with open arms. "I'm so sorry about all of this."

Kyle pulled back when Reese tried to embrace him, and Reese stood there stunned.

"I'm Cindy," she said trying to stop the potential volatility she knew was rising.

"Nice to meet you," Reese shook her hand. "Reese Weathers." He took a second look at Cindy and then turned back to Kyle. "Are you okay?"

"If I were half a man, I'd punch the crud out of you right now," Kyle said through gritted teeth. "This whole thing is absolutely ridiculous!"

"What in heaven's name are you talking about?" Reese asked as he took a step back, obviously concerned by Kyle's attitude.

Cindy came up behind Kyle and took his hand, reminding him that she was on his side.

"I know everything," Kyle told him. "I didn't say anything before because I was living in a state of shock and trying my hardest to keep my job. But you might as well know that I know."

"Know what?" Reese was utterly confused.

"That this is *your* child," Kyle hissed out. "That you and Caryn had an affair."

"What?" Reese said with a tinge of anger. "What are you talking about?"

"Caryn told me the day she left that you and she had been together for several months. She explained that it was your baby and that ..."

"Are ... are you kidding me?" Reese stammered out. "You've got to be out of your mind! I never had any kind of ... of ... thing going on with Caryn. I would never do that! What kind of man do you think I am?"

"Well, I certainly didn't think you were the kind who would steal a man's wife and then abandon her when she was carrying your child!"

Kyle was in Reese's face, towering over him with a foreboding expression.

"Hang on just a second, man," Reese said as he put his hand to Kyle's chest to move him back. "This is news to me. I never did anything with your wife. I love Alicia with all my heart and I'm totally committed to her. Did you think all that time after Caryn left that I was playing some kind of game with you? Pretending to be your buddy after sleeping with your wife?"

Kyle only nodded. The anger appeared to be leaving and that look of hurt and devastation reappeared.

"Kyle, man, I never, I swear to you, never laid a hand on Caryn or even considered it," Reese said as he put his arm on Kyle's shoulder. "Please tell me you believe me. I don't know what possessed Caryn to make that up, but you've got to believe that I would never do that ... first of all, to my wife and family, but then to the Lord, and especially not to you ... my friend ... my brother in Christ."

"Be up front with me, please," Kyle said as he leaned into Reese. "If you did, it's over. I'll somehow put it behind me. But I need to know the truth—I need to know at least one thing in all of this that is the truth."

"Kyle, never," he assured him. "Never."

Kyle now reached out to Reese and pulled him close in an embrace. He turned back to Cindy with tears in his eyes and suggested she go on in. He needed to talk to Reese in private. She understood, reached up and touched his cheek, and then moved to the front door. This was awkward for her. She had never seen Alicia in her life, and this whole situation was uncomfortable. She was glad for Kyle's sake that the affair with Reese appeared to be something Caryn concocted to abet her leaving. But she also realized this meant there would be more questions now than before.

"Hi, I'm Alicia," said a petite lady probably in her late twenties. "You're with Kyle, aren't you?"

"Yes," Cindy walked inside the house. "I'm Cindy."

"I bet this is all so hard on him," Alicia said as she offered her a seat on the couch.

"Very," she nodded.

She could hear the voices of small children, and she saw their evidence: toys and things were strewn throughout the living room, but she didn't know where they were. She wondered if Kylla was one of the happy voices, and would Kylla be as happy when she and Kyle took her away from here.

"I'm sorry it's a mess," Alicia began to apologize.

"Oh, don't be sorry. I'm sure your life has been turned as upside down as Kyle's this morning."

"Started last night with us. The sheriff called us around ten thirty to explain what had happened. We got a neighbor to watch our kids—she knew Kyle and Caryn real well, and we went to pick up Kylla. She's beautiful ... so beautiful. She never cried once. She came home and we put her in the crib with our baby, they're so close in age, and she slept through the night. Not even my baby does that yet!"

"How old is she?" Cindy wanted to know. They knew nothing about the child except its name.

"I'd guess around nine months. But she's so good ... and so beautiful."

Cindy sat quietly for a moment. She wasn't sure what to do next. She glanced out the door and saw Kyle and Reese deeply involved in their discussion. It didn't appear it would end any time soon. She looked over at Alicia helplessly.

"How do you know Kyle?" Alicia asked her.

"I'm the church secretary. He's working as an interim there. He's very good."

"He's exceptional. I could've died when Harvest Hollow made him leave. Reese and I left the church after that. So did a lot of other people."

"Really? Kyle doesn't know that."

"He stopped returning calls or communicating with anyone when he moved back with his parents. We understood: he wanted to put all the hurt behind him, and unfortunately, a lot of that hurt included what the church did to him."

"He's come a long way. He's been wonderful at Dockrey ... and he's been wonderful to ... well ... to me and to my mother. She has cancer. My father died last May, and it's been a miserable year for us."

"My heavens," Alicia gasped in compassion. "How did you survive?"

"With Kyle's help."

Alicia nodded. They awkwardly attempted small talk, but having no real connection except the obvious strange situation they were all facing, there was more silence than speech.

"Could I see the baby?" Cindy found the nerve to ask.

"Oh, off course. I didn't know how this should work, if you were waiting for Kyle or what."

"Me either, but I have to confess, I'm dying to see her. I don't know why, maybe it's a morbid curiosity."

"Not at all. There's nothing morbid about it; you want to see Kyle's child."

"It's not Kyle's."

Alicia looked at her in complete surprise.

"He can't father children," Cindy reminded her.

"So they said. I promise you, this is Kyle's child. Come on."

Alicia got up and Cindy followed her down the hallway to a room with an open door. It wasn't hard to separate the children when Cindy looked in. The two brunette Weathers' children were facing her on the floor as they sorted blocks into little colored boxes. Kylla, however, had her back to Cindy, but her gentle blond curls stood out in stark contrast to the other two.

"Kylla?" Alicia called out sweetly.

She knelt down by the baby and held out her arms. The little girl turned to her and lifted out her hands to be held. Alicia picked her up and nuzzled her naturally to her breast. Cindy walked over and stood beside Alicia so she could get a good look. When the baby turned to see who was there, Cindy gasped in surprise. There was no doubt; this was Kyle's child.

"Oh, my gosh," she whispered in shock. "Those eyes. Those precious eyes. So blue, just like Kyle's. And her little lips. Those are his lips. I've never seen a baby look so much like a parent in my entire life." Cindy looked down at Alicia in complete bewilderment.

"Obviously she's a miracle baby," Alicia said.

"But ... how?"

Alicia just shook her head. "Why don't you take her?"

The thought petrified Cindy at first, but as the baby looked up at her with the same expression and piercing gaze as Kyle, then held out her arms, she gently reached for her and pulled her close. She was so light and dainty and continued to look into Cindy's eyes with an intense stare.

"I bet she's amazed by your blue eyes," Alicia told her. "Caryn's were almost black, and all of us, well, no one will ever mistake us for Germans."

Cindy shifted Kylla to one side and then gently took her tiny hand in her own. Kylla smiled. She was Kyle made over—the smile cinched it. She tenderly kissed her little hand and then touched Kylla's hair. "Your daddy is going to love your hair," she said softly. "You're an angel, aren't you? You're a little gift from heaven."

"When you think about it," Alicia interrupted her, "that's the truth. She's this miracle. Kyle couldn't have children, yet here she is. But now Caryn is ... gone ... and she's Kyle's. I can't explain this whole mess of events, but I know that this little girl has been through who knows what. She was in the room when Caryn was murdered."

"No," Cindy gasped again. "In the room? She saw it?"

"Unless she was asleep. All we can do is pray."

They heard the front door open and Cindy's heart began to pound. How would Kyle react?

"Maybe you should take her in there," Cindy suggested, but Alicia shook her head.

"I don't think so. She belongs with you now. Take her to her father."

Cindy took a deep breath and looked back down into those sweet blue eyes and prayed in all earnest that this innocent child hadn't seen her mother killed. Kylla smiled at her again, and nestled her head on her shoulder. Cindy almost felt as if she could cry. She forced herself to move out of the room and down the hall toward the men's voices. When she reached the living room, Reese stopped talking and motioned for Kyle to turn around. When he saw Cindy carrying this bundle of blond hair, tears began to form in his eyes.

"Meet Kylla," Cindy said as emotion stalked her voice.

Kylla then turned around and saw Kyle for the first time. When his eyes met hers, he stopped cold. It had to be like looking in a mirror. He walked over slowly and reached up to touch her hair first.

"Told you," Cindy whispered to her. "He has a thing about hair."

Kyle looked at Cindy and rolled his eyes, but then gazed back down at the baby. He smiled gently and began to examine her face more closely. "You are so beautiful, Kylla," he said as he ran his finger down her cheek.

She smiled when he spoke her name. He laughed softly but continued with his inspection. He touched her hair again and then glanced back up to see Cindy biting her lip.

"You hold her," Cindy said tenderly.

Kyle reached out his hands and Kylla easily went into his arms. When

Cindy saw them together for the first time, her heart nearly burst. She brought her hands to her mouth hoping to control her emotions, but tears began to flow and small sobs made their way out. Kyle looked at her, his own eyes brimming, and he smiled. He knew this was his baby. He held Kylla close and whispered soothing thoughts to her as though he had known her all her life.

"Everything's fine now," he told her. "Daddy's here. We're gonna be all right."

Cindy was fighting not to cry. In the thirty years she had lived on this planet, nothing had ever touched her as much as this moment. She would never forget it. She saw all the resolution and resentment Kyle had toward this child melt in a matter of seconds, and the man that she knew he was—compassionate, tender, and loving—was now being showered on this innocent life. She tried to regain control, but she couldn't. It was too overwhelming.

"Come here," Kyle said to her as he held out his arm.

She moved toward him and let him embrace her along with the baby. This feeling was indescribable, and it scared her to death, because now she found herself falling in love all over again. Not only with Kyle, but with this little child that bore his resemblance impeccably. She reached up and gently ran her hand along Kylla's hair, only to realize that Kyle was doing the same with hers. She looked up at him and melted again as his swollen blue eyes gazed at her. Her life would never be the same. Never.

Twenty-Six

Reese and Alicia insisted Kyle take one of their car seats. They buckled Kylla into the back with Cindy sitting next to her and settled in for the long drive to Dockrey. It wasn't long before Kylla was asleep, so Cindy crawled back up into the front next to Kyle.

"This is crazy, Cindy," he said softly so as not to wake the baby. "How can that baby not be mine?"

"She's yours. There's no doubt about that."

"But what all the tests—and the doctor I went to? He made it very clear, not only could I not father a kid normally, we couldn't even do a test tube thing or harvest anything; he said I had nothing to get."

"Obviously he missed something."

"You don't know how emphatic he was. When we left after our final session, there was no room for hope. It was plain and clear, he was sorry, but facts were facts."

She looked back at Kylla and felt her heart flip again. "She's so beautiful, Kyle. She looks like an absolute angel right now. I could almost swear if we took her little dress off we'd find wings sprouting on her back."

He laughed gently. "I don't know what I'm gonna do, Cindy. I only thought things were complicated where you were concerned. Now I have a baby, no wife, no real job, and no certainty about my future. It's as though I've stepped from the frying pan into the fire."

She turned back around and patted his arm. "You don't just have any baby, Kyle—you have the sweetest one in the whole world. I don't know about you, but I think I've fallen in love with her already."

"How could I not love her?"

"Man," she whispered in awe. "God, what on earth are you up to?"

For supper, they stopped at a small Italian restaurant just off the interstate. Kylla had at last woken up, and still only smiled at the attention. They had no idea what to feed her. She did have a few teeth, so they cut up some spaghetti and Kyle did his best to give her small mouthfuls. Every bite she took, every gesture she made, and every expression she gave sent their hearts into orbit again. At one point during supper she sneezed, and they both oohed at its cuteness.

"New parents are always so funny," their waitress said as she handed them the tab. "You two are acting like this baby is the best thing since the wheel. I'll say this: she's adorable—looks just like you two."

132

"And she's the sweetest thing I've ever seen," Cindy cooed as she reached up to wipe off a smattering of sauce on Kylla's chin.

It was almost one thirty in the morning when they pulled through the gate at the Wright house. Kylla had fallen asleep long ago giving Kyle and Cindy the opportunity to talk. There were many things to do and many plans to be made. They had to get clothes, baby supplies, someone to watch the baby, so many things that it had become dizzying. As they pulled up to the house, they were practically giddy from tiredness and overwhelmed at all that lay ahead.

"My mother's car is here!" Cindy exclaimed in surprise. "Pastor Jon said they would be praying, but I didn't realize he was organizing an all night session."

Kyle reached into the back seat and unbuckled Kylla then gently took her from the Jeep. Her eyes opened as he pulled her to his chest, and she mumbled some undecipherable sounds as she looked around in the dark.

"We're home, little one," he said softly as he closed the door.

Cindy watched from behind the vehicle and waited for him to join her. She still felt a lump in her throat when she saw the two together. He was so tender with her, the perfect father. He had told her before how desperately he and Caryn had wanted children, and how heartbreaking the doctor's news had been. He had gone off alone and cried one night so Caryn wouldn't see how devastated he really was over the fact that he could never have children of his own. As he cradled Kylla and continued to whisper warm words to her, Cindy knew that part of this was a dream come true for him, even though the circumstances were horrendous.

When they opened the door and walked inside, they found Sue Marcum sitting at the dining table having coffee with Jonathan and Barbara. Immediately the three jumped up to greet them.

"Hello, everyone," Kyle said proudly as he turned the baby around to face them. "Meet little Kylla."

"Oh, Kyle," Sue said breathlessly. "She's so beautiful. She looks just like you."

"She has to be yours," Barbara said as she reached over to stroke the baby's hand. "What is going on here? I thought …," Barbara stopped and everyone exchanged strange glances.

Sue was nearly crying as she reached out to take the baby. "Please let me hold her if she'll let me."

"She's the sweetest thing, Mother," Cindy yawned. "She hasn't cried the whole time, and she goes to anybody."

Kylla went easily into Sue's arms, and she hugged her gently. Kylla reached up and touched her glasses as though they were a toy just for her. Sue said nothing and let her put her hands all over them.

"I guess I need to begin making some arrangements," Kyle said tiredly. "There's so much I need to do."

"All you need to do right now is sleep," Jonathan said as he put a strong arm on Kyle's shoulder. "Tomorrow we'll begin sorting through all that. The baby's bed is ready upstairs, and everything you need to get through the night is there."

Kyle nodded and yawned. He was exhausted.

"I need to get my car," Cindy said as she stretched her arms above her head.

"I'll drop you off," her mother offered as she continued to make on over the baby.

"No," Kyle said quickly. "I'll walk her up there. I need to get something from the office."

"Surely, it can wait, Kyle," Barbara said trying to help.

"I'll only be a minute," Kyle assured them. "Can you watch the baby until I get back?"

"You know it," Barbara smiled as she reached out to take the baby from Sue. "I've been dying to get my hands on this little angel since you brought her in."

Kyle and Cindy walked Sue to her car, and then headed up the hill to the church. He unlocked the gate and locked it back, a habit that was irritating, but necessary. They walked quietly to her car, and she dug through her purse to find the keys.

"Do you need my office key?" she asked as she pulled out her key chain.

"No," he shook his head with a silly grin. "I don't need to go to the office."

"But you told Barbara …"

"I think I lied," he said as he took her hand. "I just needed to thank you … alone … for all you've done today."

"You don't have to do that," she squeezed his hand. "We're friends, remember?"

He pulled her close and reached up to feel her hair. She was too tired to pull away. She laid her head on his chest and just sighed for the moment.

"Things will be so different for us from now on," he said softly. "Time alone together probably won't happen often. But I want you to know that I'll be thinking about you and I'll be wishing I were with you … even when I'm not."

She found the energy to pull back and look up into his face. His eyes were tired, and his blond locks were flowing in the gentle breeze. She reached up and ran her fingers through his hair and then down his cheek. As he smiled, she traced his lips with her fingers and was amazed again at how Kylla's were identical. He moved his hands to her waist and she found

134

her head beginning to spin with emotion. He slowly pulled her to him and she was lost again. He kissed her forehead, and then rested his chin on the top of her head.

"I don't know where to go with you, Cindy Marcum. And the thing about my whole life at this very moment is that nothing will ever be the same again. Anything I ever thought my life would be this time yesterday has suddenly changed, and I'm powerless to go back and start over."

She looked up at him and locked her arms around his neck. "I'll be here, Kyle. I'm in no hurry to do anything. I'm as overwhelmed as you, and I don't think I could reason straight if my life depended on it."

"We'll just take everything one day at a time. Just promise me we'll take it together."

"Promise," she smiled.

"You'd better go or we may find ourselves in a repeat of Friday night."

She nodded and released her arms as he released her waist, but in her mind she was longing for a repeat. She stared briefly at his lips again and then turned her head to go. She unlocked her car and sat down behind the wheel as he held her door. He closed it and gave a small wave as she backed away. Where did her life go from here, and where would Kyle fit in? At some point in the near future, this entire arrangement would change. He would have to leave as they called a new music minister. She would have to leave as they hired a permanent secretary. Then what? Right now her life was very convenient, but the future was so unsure that she was beginning to feel uneasy in the present.

Don't borrow trouble from tomorrow. Do what's placed before you right now. Do your job, love your mom, and support Kyle as much as possible.

Kyle. Kylla. From now on they would go together. Even as she drove away, she ached for both of them. Angie was wrong: she *had* fallen in love, because the thought of being away from either of them was breaking her heart, and she'd only known Kylla for an afternoon. For the first time in her life, the idea of being alone forever was frightening, and even more frightening was the idea of living her life without Kyle Sarkos. She needed to separate herself from him as much as possible, because when the day came that he left or she left, it would be unbearable.

Twenty-Seven

"What are you doing up, Mother?" Cindy asked in surprise as she found Sue already making coffee the next morning before Cindy had even made it down the stairs.

"I thought I would go over and help Barbara with the baby."

"You what?" Cindy laughed. "What makes you think Barbara will have the baby?"

"Oh, please—did you see her with that child last night? She was gushing all over it. She'll shoo poor Kyle out of the house before he knows what's hit him, and she'll have the darling all to herself."

"And so you're going to what? Rescue Kylla?"

Sue turned to her daughter and raised a finger as she said, "Barbara Wright has more than her share of grandchildren—with a whole other passel of them on the way! At the rate you and Billy are going, I'll never be a grandmother. Kyle is like a son to me, and this little girl may be the closest thing I ever get to a grandbaby."

"Thanks for the vote of confidence. I'd like to get married before I start producing your grandkids."

"Me too, but you don't seem to be making any progress on either account."

***

"What are you doing here?" Jonathan asked Cindy as she came into the office right at eight o'clock.

"I work here ... don't I?" She was confused because he was never there that early.

"Not this morning. After your day yesterday I assumed you would come in dragging. Surely you're exhausted?"

"Coffee does wonders. Have you seen Kyle this morning?"

"Bright and early. He and Kylla were downstairs cooking eggs when I left."

"He's got her cooking already?"

"Sitting right up there next to the stove telling her every single move he made as though she was studying for culinary school."

She imagined the scene easily and smiled as she sat and turned on her computer. Kyle loved to cook and had loved teaching Cindy the basics. She could see him explaining every little detail to those sleepy blue eyes as he scrambled a couple of eggs.

When Kyle finally came in, close to ten o'clock, he was bubbly and

136

excited. "Hello, beautiful," he said cheerfully as he walked in and sauntered over to her desk.

"I take it you had a good night?"

"She was incredible. I didn't even want to put her in the crib; I just wanted to lay her down next to me. Her eyes were so heavy, and when she saw the crib up in our room, she held out her arms to it. Barbara and Jonathan had the cutest little sheets with bunnies and such, and then a little stuffed pink bunny was in the corner. She took the bunny, curled up to sleep, and just drifted off."

"How about this morning?"

"I woke up and looked over at her and she was standing up in the crib staring at me. I said, *Good morning, Kylla,* and she squealed out this silly little sound. Changed her diaper, got us both dressed—Barbara had a couple of little outfits laid on the dresser—and we went downstairs to cook up some eggs."

Cindy sighed at the thought. She was a beautiful baby. "You certainly look like a proud papa."

"I didn't want to believe this baby could be mine," Kyle said seriously, "and now I'm scared to death she might not be."

"How could you think she's not yours?"

"Regardless of how much she looks like me, Cindy, the fact still remains that I can't have children. Maybe Caryn did have an affair with someone ... only he was blond headed and blue eyed like me."

"Kyle, there's no possible way that she isn't your child. It's not just the *nature* of her features; she actually looks like you. Her eyes, her little gentle curls, her lips, they're identical to yours. I bet if we compared your baby pictures to her, they'd look exactly alike."

"Baby pictures," Kyle sighed as he scratched his head and winced. "I have to eventually let my parents know about this. Wow, this thing just gets a little deeper each moment, doesn't it?"

***

Cindy wanted to make herself stay away from Kylla that day, but when her mother called to say Barbara had made egg salad for lunch for everyone, what choice did she have? She walked with Kyle and Jonathan to the house and enjoyed a meal that mainly consisted of everyone mooning over everything Kylla did. And when work was over, Kyle talked her into going shopping with him and the baby to get clothes and whatever else was necessary to raise a little girl. They drove to Russellville and had to watch themselves to not spend too much on a baby that would be growing quicker than they could imagine. Several stopped them in the store just to adore Kylla's beauty, and they proudly showed her off.

On Wednesday evening, Cindy ended up staying at the Wrights all afternoon instead of going home to change before the evening activities.

She walked with them up to the church and beamed as everyone made-on over little Kylla. She volunteered to stay with her in the nursery, but the nursery staff shooed her away, so she reluctantly went on to class and choir.

***

After two weeks of seeing Kyle and Kylla every day, Cindy was beginning to feel as though she were having withdrawals whenever she left. She had become so attached to Kylla, that she had even considered asking Kyle to let her spend the night occasionally. She found herself thinking of all the little things she did that absolutely melted her heart, and even while simply shopping in the grocery store, she would pick up something for her: a toy, a cookie, a jar of juice, it didn't matter.

Kyle's parents had been on spring vacation in the Caribbean, so he hadn't told them about Caryn's death or the baby. When they called to let him know they were back, he asked if he and Cindy could come over for dinner to see them. They were thrilled at the prospect of seeing Cindy again, so they agreed immediately.

When Bradley Sarkos answered the door, his smile changed to confusion when his eyes passed from Cindy to Kylla.

"Hi, Dad," Kyle smiled. "Guess what happened while you guys were basking in the sun?"

"Kyle! How did this come about?" his mother exclaimed after he explained the story.

"Which part, Mom? The murder, the baby, or my becoming a parent?"

"Good heavens," she dropped down into her seat. "You can't have children!"

"That's what I thought too," he said as he shrugged his shoulders.

"She has to be your baby."

"Does she look like Kyle when he was a baby?" Cindy wondered.

"Oh, my gosh! Exactly!"

"Either way," Bradley said as he curled one of Kylla's silky locks around his finger, "she's our granddaughter, and that's just incredible."

"You *are* going to keep her, Kyle?" Emma asked him. "Even if you find out she's not actually yours?"

"How could she not be?" Cindy wondered again.

"All I know is that Kyle went through major testing, and the results were really unpromising," Emma reminded them. "Isn't there some way to find out for sure?"

"Yes," Bradley said. "A simple blood test should prove it. If that's not conclusive, there's always DNA."

Everyone looked over at him.

"I work with musicians. Paternity suits are a common item ...

unfortunately."

The rest of the evening was spent around Kylla, as usual. Emma and Bradley fell in love with her, but they were just as impressed with Cindy. She was the antithesis of Caryn. It was almost a miracle itself watching Kyle and Cindy interact. They noticed the intimate glances that were exchanged from time to time, and the way both of them oozed with delight any time Kylla did anything. On occasion, Cindy would gently rub hs back or touch his arm, and more than once he would reach up and smooth her hair or lean into her as he laughed.

"Did he say anything to you about their relationship?" Emma asked her husband as they climbed into bed that night.

"Nothing. I think for the moment, they're more wrapped up in Kylla than they are each other."

"Do you think that's good?"

"I think anything that brings them together is good," he said as he reached over to kiss his wife goodnight. "She's right for him, Emma. He glows around her. He doesn't have to try and *sell* her to us like he was constantly doing with Caryn."

"And she's so wonderful. I would like to think I'd feel the same about her if she wasn't so beautiful …"

"You would. You're not being shallow."

She laughed and wrinkled her nose at her husband. "She's so beautiful, Brad, and so is that baby."

"Maybe all that praying we've been doing is finally having an effect."

Twenty-Eight

The following Monday morning at the church office, an FBI agent made a visit. Agent Ben Hall was the definition of FBI: tall, dark hair, dark glasses, all of which matched his dark suit. He seemed young for an agent, but he was very confident and austere. He insisted on speaking with Kyle alone, and followed him into his office. Kyle sat nervously at his desk as the agent pulled out a file and began thumbing through pages of notes and documents.

"We're in a mess," the agent finally told him after several moments of silently reading his information. "We've tried to keep you out of this, knowing you're just the ex, but the whole baby thing, and then your wife's identity ... the bottom line, Mr. Sarkos, is that we're just jumbled up all over the place and we have nowhere else to turn."

"I don't understand. What's the problem?"

"Do you know you're wife's social security number?"

"No idea. It would be on our marriage license, wouldn't it?"

The agent raised his head in hope as he asked, "You have that?"

"Not here, but I'm sure it's gotta be in my files back at my parents' house."

"That's ... uh ... Sheffield, right?" the agent said as he looked at a paper.

"You know where my parents live?"

"I know everything about *you*, Mr. Sarkos. It's your wife I can find no information on. Do you realize her body is still sitting in the morgue? We can't find anybody to claim her."

"You're kidding me! Her parents live in Martha's Vineyard! Bill and Linda Carter. I've been there many times. They haven't claimed the body?"

"Got a number for them?" the agent asked as he flipped over several pages and readied his pen.

"Uh ... no, but I know where they live."

"Got an address?"

Kyle sighed and shook his head. "I could draw you a map from the airport to their house, and even describe the house to a tee, but I couldn't tell you the street to save my life."

"More dead ends. Here, take this paper and draw that map. Write a description of the house."

Kyle complied, and the man sat silently the entire time it took him to create it. When he finished, he handed the paper back to the agent who studied it carefully and then nodded.

"You pay special attention to details. This should get us there fine. Now, I have some questions for you."

"Shoot," Kyle said off the cuff.

The agent raised an eyebrow and glanced up at him.

"The questions … shoot the questions."

The man thumbed through his pages again, stopped at one, and looked up at Kyle as he asked, "Was her name Caryn Carter before you married?"

"Yes."

"When did you meet her?"

"Fourteen years ago at Furman University."

"When did you marry?"

"June 21, eleven years ago."

The man wrote down the information and then turned a few more pages. "When did you divorce?"

"She left me February 13 last year, and I never saw or spoke with her again. Her lawyer brought me the papers to sign sometime in March."

"Did you have a lawyer look over them?"

"No sir. She didn't want anything from me. She asked for no money, no possessions—just the divorce. I signed the papers."

He nodded as he wrote down a few more notes.

"Can I ask what the problem is?" Kyle wondered as he began to feel antsy. "I mean if you can't get in touch with her parents, it's highly possible they could be out sailing or something."

"The problem, Mr. Sarkos, according to the system, is that your wife, Caryn Carter, did not exist. We have no record of her life, no birth certificate, no marriage license, no divorce papers. The only thing we do have is her baby's birth certificate, and on that she put no social security number."

"So what does that mean? No license or papers or stuff?"

"It means that your wife was in all probability *not* Caryn Carter."

Kyle leaned back in his chair as his face contorted over the prospect of yet another mystery surrounding his ex-wife. If she wasn't Caryn, who was she?

"Your wife barely left her apartment after she left you," the agent said as he now put down his pen and closed the file. "She never saw a doctor during her pregnancy. She just showed up one night in labor, gave birth, and left with the baby the next day. She had her groceries brought to her, and she did all her shopping on the Internet. No one ever went in, and she never went out. The only exceptions were noted by the neighbor lady that had called the police. She said Caryn had taken the baby out a couple of days when the weather was really nice in March. No stroller or anything, she just held the baby close to her. When the neighbor tried to talk with her and make on over the baby, Caryn got really nervous and politely went back to her apartment."

"Do you think maybe she was whacko or something?" Kyle wondered.

"Do *you* think she was? You were married to her all that time. Did she seem off balance, insane, paranoid, anything like that?"

Kyle thought carefully and then shook his head.

"Then there's only one other option if she wasn't *psycho*," the agent sighed. "She was hiding. Her name was an alias, and the baby was apparently a big mistake."

"This is preposterous!" Kyle exclaimed as he threw up his arms. "How could she not have been who she said she was? I was married to her for ten years! She was Caryn Carter, her parents live in Martha's Vineyard, and she left me and then divorced me because she had an affair and was carrying another man's child!"

Kyle stopped ranting quickly as he remembered his conversation with Reese. "Wait a minute," he said more to himself than the agent.

"You remembered something?" the man asked as he immediately pulled out his pen and opened the folder again.

"I talked with the guy she claimed to have had an affair with. He swore his innocence."

"You believe him?"

Kyle looked through squinted eyes, thought for a moment and then answered, "Yeah—yeah, I do."

"And the baby? You think it's yours?"

"Man, I don't know. She sure looks like me."

"Can we order a paternity test? Would you mind?"

Kyle hesitated on that one. If the test proved that he wasn't Kylla's father, it would crush him. Yet at the same time, this little girl had been dropped into his lap, and after losing her mother, how could he let her go? He would have gladly raised her as his own during his marriage if Caryn would have agreed to it, and that's all this would amount to if Kylla wasn't his. Then there was the fact of all his fertility testing; if the doctor had been right, there was no way she could be.

"What would proving paternity do for your case?" Kyle wanted to know.

"For starters, it would tell us whether your wife likely had an affair or not. If it's not yours, we work on finding out whose it possibly is."

"Do I retain custody?"

"Your name's on the birth certificate. Unless you give her up, she's yours. But there's another twist to this too: if it *is* yours, the chances are high that she lied about the affair and felt the need to get away from the marriage because of the pregnancy."

"But why?"

"That's what we've got to figure out. She wasn't Caryn Carter; I'm fairly sure of that. She must have been trying to cover her identity for some reason. The more facts we uncover, the better chance we have of finding out who she was and who it was that pulled the trigger that night and chose to leave your baby alive for the time being."

The blood left Kyle's face at that thought. The killer knew Caryn, killed Caryn, but didn't kill Kylla What if he had? Why was Kylla left alone?

"Do you think someone might be … I don't know … tracking Kylla or something?" Kyle asked cautiously.

"It's possible, although we've noticed no one at the moment."

"You've been following me?"

"We've been keeping eyes on the baby. Lucky for her you happen to live with Stephen Williams' father-in-law. Right now the fact that she spends most of her time behind that twelve-foot fence is a big deterrent for anyone who might have nasty ideas."

"What kind of *nasty* ideas might this killer have?"

"That's what we're trying to figure out, Mr. Sarkos. I'll call you when we set up the paternity test. After that, we'll have an idea of what direction we need to take. For now, we'll work on locating her parents in Massachusetts. As soon as we find out anything, we'll let you know. Whether you like this or not, you're wrapped up right in the middle of the whole conglomeration, and that little girl may end up holding one of the major keys to unlocking it."

"I have to be honest with you; I don't like this at all."

The agent stood. "That's because you're a good man, Mr. Sarkos. You've been checked out to the nth degree, and basically, you're squeaky clean. You're the typical Mr. Nice Guy who appears to have been drawn into one huge ring of deception. You've never even made a late payment. If you ever leave the ministry, you might consider the agency."

Kyle raised his eyebrows in question.

"Just kidding, Mr. Sarkos. You don't have the constitution. I was joking," the agent said with no laughter in his voice or hint of a smile on his face.

"Ha ha," Kyle mocked weakly.

***

"Do you think Kylla's in danger?" Cindy asked in horror as Kyle laid out the conversation with the FBI agent. "Should we do something to protect her?"

"I have no idea, and neither does he. He doesn't even know who Caryn is … was … or anything."

She stood and began to wring her hands as she paced. The thought of anyone harming Kylla sent chills down her spine.

"Do you know how to look up people on the Internet?" Kyle asked as an idea crossed his mind. "Let's just see if we can find Caryn's parents. I know their names, and I know they live at Martha's Vineyard."

"If the FBI can't find them, surely you're not gonna pull them up."

"It's worth a try."

She nodded and sat down at the computer. She went to a people search and started by trying to find a phone number.

"What are their names?"

"Bill and Linda Carter."

She typed in the names and the location and pressed the search button. Nothing.

"Let me try William," she suggested.

Nothing again.

"Can you remember a street name or anything?"

"No," he said with a sigh. "It never occurred to me I would have to know."

Twenty-Nine

After telling the Wrights along with Sue Marcum at lunch about the meeting with the agent, it was decided that the best course of action would be to keep Kylla behind the fence as much as possible. It would be easy for someone to blend in with the crowds that always gathered, but it would be impossible for someone to penetrate the perimeter. Jonathan decided to call Stephen and see if he could suggest more safety measures.

"Unreal," Annie said as she and Stephen shared a conference call with her father. "That's even scarier than what Stephen and I put up with."

"What do you think, Stephen? Should we beef up security?"

"If it were my child, I definitely would. What we need to do is go ahead and station guards at both of the other gates also. We'll put two armed guards at the gate that leads up the hill to the church, and then stick two more at the back gate. Because people are hardly ever there, that would be the best place for someone to try and sabotage the system. I'll call the security company and have things in place before the day is up."

"I wish you two could see this little girl," Jonathan told them. "There's something special about her. She's the most beautiful baby I've ever seen, and that includes my own children and grandchildren. She has the sweetest temperament and is so loving. She's been here for two weeks and I haven't heard her cry once."

"She sounds special, Daddy," Annie told him. "I bet Moms is having a ball with a baby in the house again."

"She has to fight Sue Marcum for her. She's here every single day. Sue has sort of claimed a *grandmothership* type of possession over her. She thinks the world of Kyle. He's been good to her and Cindy during all of this cancer business."

"How is Mrs. Marcum doing?" Annie asked.

"Remarkably well. And this baby has just raised her recovery several notches."

***

The extra security made everyone feel better about Kylla's safety, but they still took her to church with them for every service. It was almost as if little Kylla had five bodyguards with her at all times. Jonathan spoke privately with the nursery workers about the delicacy of the situation so they would always be on guard against anyone unusual trying to get close to her. They promised to protect her with their lives. It was as if anyone who had contact with the baby immediately fell in love with her.

Sue and Barbara claimed they were too nervous for Kylla to be in the nursery during the worship services, and then added that being in the sanctuary with so many people would be much safer for her. The result: Kylla sat with Sue and Barbara during church now. Cindy could no longer concentrate on the sermon Sunday mornings. Instead, she smiled and stared at Kylla. On Sunday nights, she now sat with her mother and Barbara so she could get her hands on the baby also.

***

As the month of April came to a close, a permanent routine had developed among the Wrights, the Marcums and Kyle. Sue or Barbara kept the baby during the day, lunches were always at the Wrights, and Cindy and Kyle gave her all their attention when they left the church.

"When is her birthday?" Cindy asked Kyle one afternoon as they sat on a blanket in the back yard of the Wright's house.

"I have no idea," he said as he laid back and dangled Kylla above him. The tiny girl squealed in delight and wiggled all over as he swayed her back and forth.

"She's probably 10 months old now," Cindy surmised from remembering her conversation with Alicia. "We need to know when her birthday is. We have to celebrate."

Kyle laughed as he brought Kylla back down to his side. She immediately crawled up into Cindy's lap and put her arms around her neck for a hard embrace.

"I love you so much." Cindy closed her eyes as she gently returned Kylla's hug. "When is your birthday, little bit? What would you like? Hmmm?"

A loud scream of youthful energy burst from the screened-in back porch of the house. They looked up to see Andie's two oldest, Arly and Adam, running from the porch toward the blanket. Andie followed wobbling at a more settled pace.

"Can I hold her?" Arly asked as he plopped down on the blanket. "I'll show her the flowers and even let her pick one."

"And I won't let her eat any no matter how much she wants to," Adam added.

"Why would she eat flowers?" Cindy wondered.

"All kids do," Adam said as though this were common knowledge. "Ain't you ever eat a flower?"

"Not that I recall," Cindy laughed slightly.

"Here you go," Kyle said as he lifted Kylla up into Arly's arms. "And I'm holding you guys to the not letting her eat flowers thing."

"You can count on us, Mr. Kyle," Adam said very grown-up as he gave a quick nod.

"Enjoying this gorgeous day?" Andie asked as she carefully made her way down on the blanket with them. Her baby was due in two months, and both Kyle and Cindy were amazed that she even opted to join them on the ground.

"I can't believe you got down here," Cindy laughed.

"Me either," Andie grinned. "You both may have to pull me up when I leave."

"No problem," Kyle said as he looked at her with admiration. This would be her fifth child.

Something stung his heart as he thought about the fact that he hadn't been with Caryn while she had carried Kylla. He would have doted on her hand and foot. He would have been by her side during the delivery, and all of that would have happened even though he would have believed the child wasn't his. What if she had known it was his and told him? He couldn't imagine the joy he would have felt. But that wasn't reality.

He glanced at Cindy who was now feeling Andie's stomach and screaming in delight as the baby kicked her hand. He tried to imagine Cindy pregnant; it was easy to do. She'd practically become a mother to Kylla. He imagined how beautiful she would look carrying a child. In his opinion, no woman ever looked more attractive. There was something to him about carrying new life inside a body, and he loved watching pregnant women negotiate and navigate as they carried that life.

"What *are* you thinking about?" Cindy asked as she settled back next to him.

Her perfume carried to his nose and he smiled at the thoughts he'd been having about her. "Choir practice," he winked.

"Not with that expression, you weren't."

"I'm a man dedicated to my work."

"I suppose," she said as she reached up and tweaked his nose. "But if that's the kind of look you get thinking about your work, I think it's time for you to get a life."

He grabbed her hand from his nose and then remembered Andie was with them. He looked over to see her grinning at their exchange, and then quickly let go of Cindy's hand.

"What brings you here to our humble spring outing?" he asked, hoping to take his mind off Cindy.

"I have a proposition for you," Andie replied. "I want you to give my boys music lessons."

"Like I have time to give lessons."

"I'm serious. I can teach them school right now, but I don't want to teach them music too. You're very talented, Kyle, and you're a wonderful teacher, not to mention the fact that you're a man. It would be a good thing for them altogether. They both have good musical aptitude, and they've expressed an interest in learning. Arly wants to play piano, and Adam the guitar. You could give them a great start."

"When would I do it?"

"After school and work one day a week."

"Do you have a day in mind?"

"Thursday," she smiled.

"You've put a lot of thought into this already."

"I'm a thorough sort of person. I was thinking twenty to thirty minutes apiece. Does that sound about right?"

"Hey, I haven't even agreed to this yet! I have to make arrangements for Kylla."

"Arranged!" Cindy jumped in. "I could actually have her all to myself for one hour a week. That would be like heaven."

"Gee, that's one obstacle conquered," Andie smiled. "Any other problems you need Cindy and me to work out in order for my sons to become virtuosos?"

"Apparently not," he said shaking his head and feeling as though he had just been railroaded.

Thirty

Cindy was thrilled to have her hour alone with Kylla each week. As the end of May approached—nearing the first anniversary of her father's death—she took comfort in the new life she had found in her relationship with Christ and with Kylla. She never imagined wanting to be a mother, but the little girl had changed that. As she thought back on the prior year, she was amazed at how much her father's death and her mother's cancer had altered her life. This time last year, she had been in a relationship with Evan, and she had convinced herself all was perfect. They would get together on occasion, leave town for the evening, sometimes the whole night, and then she may not see him again for days or weeks. She didn't have to worry about marriage, children, or changing her perfect selfish life for anyone. However, that life seemed far from perfect now.

***

When Kyle finished lessons with the boys, he walked down to the gate now patrolled by two armed guards.

"Good afternoon, Mr. Sarkos," one of them said as he punched in the code for the entrance to slide open. "Have a good evening."

"You too." He headed for the house, and for Kylla, although the fact that Cindy would be there too made him smile even more. He walked inside and looked around for the girls.

"They're up in the apartment," Barbara said as she handed him his phone. "You left this on the table from lunch. It's been singing that goofy song all afternoon. It appears someone is either trying desperately to contact you or drive me insane."

"Sorry about that." He looked at the display: voice message. "Whoever it is left me a message."

"Whatever happened to a simple ring-a-ding-ding?" She shook her head.

He chuckled and started up the stairs to find Cindy and Kylla first. The door was cracked, so he sneaked inside the room to get a peek at the two. The vision nearly caused him to swoon. They were on the couch, Kylla in Cindy's lap, reading a book containing bold pictures. As Cindy would say a word, she would help Kylla point to the picture.

"Hey, beautiful," he said as he walked over.

"Dadda!" Kylla squealed.

"Did you hear that?" he yelled in delight. "She spoke my name!"

"Of course, she did," Cindy grinned as he walked around the couch and sat beside them. "We've been working on that. Watch this."

Cindy pulled a photograph from the end table of Kyle and Cindy that had been taken by one of the teenage girls at the last church fellowship.

"Who's this?" Cindy asked Kylla.

"Dadda." Kylla said sweetly. He melted.

"And who's this?" Cindy asked as she pointed to her own picture.

"Indee!" Kylla called out as she bounced on her lap.

"That's amazing. I had no idea she could learn stuff already."

"That's nothing. Watch this."

Cindy sat Kylla down so that the baby straddled her.

"Where's your nose, Kylla?" she asked her. "Where's your nose?"

Kylla reached up and touched Cindy's nose.

"No, silly. That's Cindy's nose! Where's Kylla's nose?"

Kylla grinned big and reached for her own this time.

"Good girl!" Cindy clapped and Kylla clapped with her.

"Where's Kylla's eyes? Show me your eyes."

She squealed again and then reached up to touch her eye.

"Eye," Kylla said.

"When did she start talking?" Kyle asked in amazement. "I had no idea she could do all this!"

"I bought this book. It told about all the things she should be able to do developmentally, so I thought I would give it a try. Kyle, I think she might be exceptionally bright. I didn't start doing this stuff with her until today, and she's an old pro already."

"Dadda!" Kylla said again as she climbed over onto his lap.

"That's right," he grinned proudly as he leaned in to kiss the baby. "You're a smart girl, aren't you?"

He then looked over at Cindy and said, "And you are a smart lady."

She smiled proudly.

"Indee!" Kylla squealed again as she crawled back into Cindy's lap.

"You're my smart little angel, aren't you?" she cooed as she held Kylla up to her chest.

Kyle put his arm up on the back of the couch and moved next to the girls under the pretense of being closer to Kylla, but when he reached down to take a strand of Cindy's hair, she looked up at him and grinned.

"What is your Dadda doing?" Cindy asked Kylla as she leaned into her for another kiss. "Is he playing with Indee's hair again?"

"He can't help himself," he whispered as he leaned down next to her and breathed in the perfume. "Sometimes all this femininity just gets the best of me."

"Dadda!" Kylla called out again and then jumped back onto his lap.

"Dadda has to make a phone call," Kyle said as he pulled out his cell.

"To whom?" Cindy asked as she leaned over to see the number.

"I have no idea," he mumbled, more interested in her leaning into him than the phone call. "Why don't we find out?"

"Why don't we?" she said as she looked up at him with a twinkle in her blue eyes.

"If I didn't know better," he pretended to be serious, "I'd say Indee was flirting with Dadda."

"It's a good thing you know better then. Let me take this girl off your hands so you can dial easier."

He pulled out his phone and closed his eyes for a moment as he tried to put the scent and nearness of Cindy out of his mind.

"Forget how to punch a number?"

"Hmph," he mumbled as he stood up and waited for his voicemail.

The message was from FBI agent Ben Hall. He needed him to call as soon as possible. Kyle frowned wondering if there was more news concerning Caryn's death. He pressed the number and waited.

"Hello?"

"Yes, this is Kyle Sarkos. I'm returning your call."

"Mr. Sarkos, glad you got back so quickly. This is agent Ben Hall, FBI. We've arranged for that paternity test. We had to make sure it was a safe place."

"Okay," Kyle was nodding, even though he didn't understand what a *safe place* was about. "What do I do?"

"There's a clinic in Huntsville."

"Huntsville? That's so far. We've got a doctor here in Dockrey."

"Didn't I mention the words *safe* and *place* to you?"

"Oh yeah, sorry."

The agent gave him the address.

"Take the blond with you," Ben Hall told him. "Sign in as Mr. and Mrs. Sarkos."

"Cindy?" Kyle asked in surprise.

Cindy stood up with Kylla and walked over to him as she raised her eyebrows in question.

"Yes, bring Miss Marcum," the agent replied. "And bring the baby, I assume you know that. We'll draw blood and compare that at first. It should take care of it."

"You're gonna have to stick Kylla with a needle?" Kyle was almost panicked.

"Several. She has no record of any immunizations. This doctor will take care of that too."

"You're kidding me? This is gonna be like a torture session for her!"

"One thirty on Friday," the agent said with no nonsense.

"This Friday?"

"Yes. Is that a problem?"

"No, we'll be there."

After the agent gave directions, Kyle hung up, walked over toward the bed and tossed his phone on top.

"What's wrong?" Cindy asked following him.

"We do a paternity test on Friday ... in Huntsville."

"Okay. Why Huntsville?"

"Because it's a *safe place*. You have to go with us."

"Why?"

"I don't know," he sighed as he sat on the bed. "We have to sign in as Mr. and Mrs. Sarkos."

"He knows we're not ... married ... or anything, doesn't he?"

"He knows. He called you *the blond* at first, and then referred to you as Miss Marcum."

"The blond?" She was a little offended.

"They're also going to give her some immunizations," he said reaching for Kylla. She climbed onto his lap and said *Dadda* again as she put her arms around his neck.

"Eye," she said clearly as she poked at his eye.

"That's right," he smiled even though his heart broke at the thought of unending needles on Friday.

"At least we'll find out once and for all if Kylla is yours," Cindy said gently as she sat down next to him and began to rub his back,

"Yeah," he nodded. "I'll die, Cindy, if she's not."

"No you won't, Kyle. I *know* she's not mine, but I feel like she might as well be. I couldn't love her any more had I carried her and given birth to her myself."

He softly kissed the top of Kylla's head. Cindy was right. It would be a huge let down if Kylla wasn't his, but it wouldn't change his feelings for her. She would always be his daughter, blood relation or not.

Thirty-One

Kyle tried to enjoy the drive to Huntsville. Here he was with his two favorite people in the world, but the looming of needles ahead kept his mood down. Cindy spent most of her time turned around in her seat talking with Kylla. He enjoyed listening to the exchanges between the two and had to admit a secret delight at the thought of signing in as married. He wished with all his heart that he had some kind of settled future. If anything firm were on the horizon, he wouldn't hesitate to develop this relationship with Cindy. In fact, with Caryn now being totally out of the picture, all he could think about was being with Cindy. But he had nothing to offer her. She was a woman that knew what she wanted in life, had worked hard, done well, been very successful, and now was caring for her mother, although Sue was surviving just fine on her own it seemed. He couldn't imagine leaving Dockrey and taking Kylla away from Cindy … or Sue.

They had lunch at Shogun, and Kylla once again delighted them as she responded to the chef and his shenanigans as he cooked on their table. She sat in her high chair between them and ate bites of rice as she watched the cooking show. The waitress gave her a tiny umbrella from the bar and Kylla squealed out a barely discernible *pretty* as she carefully opened and closed it.

"Eye," she said at one point as she pointed to Kyle's eye. "Dadda eye."

"Yes," Kyle smiled at her and kissed her hand.

She then turned to Cindy and said, "Indee eye?"

"That's right," Cindy said as she clapped. "Where is Cindy's nose? Can you touch Cindy's nose?"

"Indee no'ee," Kylla repeated as she touched her nose.

Kyle found the clinic easily, but his stomach churned as he pulled into the parking lot. Kylla had fallen asleep in her seat from the restaurant to the clinic, and he dreaded waking her up to be stuck with needles over and over again. He wouldn't move after turning off the engine; he didn't want to go in. Cindy reached over and took his hand squeezing it firmly.

"Let's do this, honey," she winked as he glanced over at her.

"Honey?"

"We're supposed to be married, aren't we?" There was that twinkle again; he loved it when she teased him.

"Yes, *sugar-pie.*"

"Sugar pie?" she grimaced. "Did you ever call Caryn that? No wonder she left you."

He laughed as he squeezed her hand and then opened his door, but the truth was that he and Caryn had never had pet names for each other. For some reason, it would have seemed very odd. He reached back and unbuckled Kylla, and then eased her out of her seat. She was a limp noodle and never once opened her eyes. He was glad she was resting.

Once inside the clinic, Kyle gave the baby to Cindy as he went to the receptionist's window to sign in. He wrote down *Mr. and Mrs. Kyle Sarkos* as he was told, and then started to leave, but the receptionist stopped him quickly.

"Mr. Sarkos," she said urgently. "Would you step back here please?"

Kyle nodded in confusion then pointed toward Cindy and Kylla.

"Just you," the lady whispered. She motioned him toward a door.

He went through and found Ben Hall along with two other persons, a man and a woman.

"Mr. Sarkos," Ben stuck out his hand. "This is agent Morrow and agent Sparks." They shook his hand also. "Enjoy your lunch?"

Kyle only nodded. He supposed they knew where he had eaten. In fact, they probably knew more about him than he did at this point.

"The Wright house is being cased," Ben said sternly.

"Excuse me? What do you mean?" Kyle was puzzled.

"There are people there who are watching you and following every move you, Cindy and the baby make."

"Your people?" Kyle asked.

"Our people and ... them," the agent clarified.

"Can I sit?" Kyle asked beginning to feel faint.

"Actually, you need to get back out there with *Mrs. Sarkos* and Kylla," Ben said as he walked him to the door.

"They have to know we're not married," Kyle whispered.

"They think you're separated," Ben explained. "They think Caryn was some kind of caretaker for Kylla that you two had hired while you worked out your differences ... or something along that line. Figured it was a way for her to make a little cash. Right now, they think you're trying to work things out for the sake of the baby."

"That's bizarre! Why would anyone do that? It doesn't make sense—hiring someone to take your kid while you try to fix a marriage?" Kyle swallowed hard then looked back at the agent to ask, "How do you know that?"

"It's my job to know," the agent said as he stopped Kyle at the door. "For now, that's a good thing. They can't get their hands on any legal documents at the moment because the FBI has all of them tied up—yours, what little there are of Kylla's, and even Miss Marcum's. Caryn did no talking, so they have no idea about the baby. However, it would be really helpful for us if we could see any copies you have of legal pieces. You mentioned your marriage license and divorce papers. Have you found them?"

"I'll drop by my parents on the way home and see if I can dig them out."

"Great. Get back to your wife and baby."

"Should we ... act married ... or separated?"

Agent Hall cracked open the door and peeked out at Cindy and Kylla. "Take your pick. But if I had a woman that looked like that willing to play the part of my wife for the day, I would prefer acting *married*."

The agent actually winked at him, and Kyle chuckled. Did this man have a sense of humor under all that black and white?

He walked back into the waiting area and sat down beside the girls. Immediately Kylla reached out to him and began to touch his eyes again.

"Dadda eye," she said sleepily.

"What's going on?" Cindy asked him.

"There are three agents back there," Kyle whispered with a smile as he leaned into her ear. "We're probably being followed right now. The ... whatever they are ... the enemy, I suppose ... thinks we're married, but separated, and are trying to work things out because of the baby."

"You're tickling my neck when you breathe on me like that," she giggled.

"Pretend you like it," he said as he kissed her hair. "We're working on our marriage, okay?

"Pretend?" she raised an eyebrow. "If you do it again, I might possibly pin you down on the couch. You found a very sensitive part of my anatomy there."

"Is that right? I'll remember that."

"Indee!" Kylla squealed.

"Mama?" Kyle said softly to the baby. "Dadda," he pointed to himself. "Mama," he pointed to Cindy.

Cindy gazed at him puzzled. She had never been referred to as *Mama*. But suddenly Kylla's expression changed significantly. For the first time since they had known her, she had a look of fear in her eyes.

"Don't do that again," Cindy whispered. "She must remember Caryn. Something struck her with that name."

"I agree. I was just trying to play the part."

"We'd better stick with Indee for the moment."

After close to twenty minutes, they were called back. Kylla had nestled herself into Cindy after the *Mama* fiasco and quietly gone back to sleep. Kyle helped her up and put his arm around her waist as he led her to the door. When they entered the back of the clinic, the three agents were waiting there again. They escorted them to a room and then closed the door. Shortly after, a doctor entered along with Agent Hall.

"Hello, Miss Marcum," Ben Hall said as he shook her hand. "We really appreciate you playing along with us right now."

"No problem."

"As long as they think you two are married and that this baby is not Caryn's, we stand a chance of staying one step ahead of them."

"Why are they interested in Kylla?" Cindy wanted to know.

"It obviously has to do with the fact that she was with Caryn. Or maybe they're curious about Kyle? We don't have all the facts yet, but this little test today should get us moving in the right direction."

"I'm Randy Jeffries," the doctor told them. "I'll be performing the tests—beginning to end; the fewer people we involve with this the better. I am curious, Mr. Sarkos, why do you have doubts about being her father?"

Kyle sighed and went through the quest for a baby while married to Caryn.

"From what you've told me, it appears impossible that she could be yours. What makes you think she is?"

"You haven't got a good look at her yet," Cindy said instantly. "She's his."

"We'll see, but I'll be honest with you, if what you're telling me about the fertility testing is true, you need to be prepared to accept that biologically she isn't your child."

"I understand," Kyle said as his hopes began to fall again.

Cindy reached over and took his hand. He squeezed it hard as the doctor began to prepare the needles and vials to be used for the testing.

"How are you doing?" Cindy asked him as they sat quietly in the little room, finally having calmed Kylla from all the needles. Kyle paced.

"I'm ... I don't know," he confessed. "I'm trying not to get my hopes up. So much lies on the outcome of this test."

"Not really, it doesn't. She's still yours, Kyle."

"I know that, but I keep thinking in the back of my mind, that if I fathered one child, maybe I could have more. Maybe there was a mistake with all of this. Maybe I can have a real family one day."

Cindy patted the chair next to her, reached out her hand, and pulled him back down beside her. "Kyle, there are other options even if you can't. You're not married to Caryn anymore. Other women have no problem with adoption, or fertilization. If it were ... me ... *hypothetically* ... as your wife, I would do anything you wanted to build a family. I know how much you love Kylla, and I also know how much you've always wanted a family."

Kyle leaned over and gently kissed her cheek as he reached up to caress her hair. "Thank you. I'll try to keep that hope in mind for the moment."

"I'm not offering myself up for the position, though," she added as he continued to rub her hair between his fingers

"I'll keep that in mind too," he smiled as he kissed her forehead. "But I must confess it's been lots of fun playing your husband for the day."

She giggled and then looked down to see that Kylla had finally fallen asleep again. She brushed her lips over Kylla's soft hair. After another long wait, the doctor finally opened the door and walked in ... alone.

"The tests are conclusive," the doctor said as he sat down with several sheets of paper. "This baby is most definitely yours."

"Yes!" Kyle jumped up and pumped the air with his fist. He then leaned down and kissed Cindy right on the lips. "She's mine!" he said to her as he closed his eyes and kissed her again.

Cindy leaned back in the seat and found herself dizzy at Kyle's explosive response in the kiss.

"I'm curious, though," the doctor said as he pulled off his glasses, "who was your doctor—the fertility guy who ran all these tests?"

"Dr. Abraham Camp," Kyle said quickly. "He's in Nashville."

"Listen," Dr. Jeffries said, "I'm really curious about all of this. Have you ever had any problem performing sexually?"

Kyle and Cindy both blushed. They avoided eye contact as Kyle shook his head.

"Look, do me a favor. We could settle another question very easily here," the doctor grinned.

"What?" Kyle asked.

The doctor pulled an empty vial from his pocket and handed it to Kyle. "Let me do a brief fertility test of my own. I know your case. I'm not even a doctor here; I work in DC. I think your wife lied to you."

"But the doctor ..."

"I'd be willing to bet money that there is no Dr. Camp in Nashville."

"But I went there ... for months."

"Yeah, yeah, yeah," the doctor shook his head. "Your wife was one smart cookie. We can't find anything on her, yet she managed a marriage and a divorce all beneath the system."

Kyle took the vial and stared at it for a moment. He knew what the doctor was suggesting.

"Where should I go?" Kyle asked him. "She's not really my wife, you know?"

Cindy blushed so red that even Kyle felt sorry for her.

"Follow me," the doctor said.

When Kyle walked back into the room after what seemed like an eternity, he was beaming like Cindy had never seen him before.

"Was it that much fun?" she asked him in near disgust.

"I saw the slide," he said as he knelt in front of her. "Little guys were swimming all over the place. They were strong, healthy, and looking for someplace to go."

Cindy felt her cheeks blushing again.

"And ..." he continued, "there's no Dr. Abraham Camp in Nashville ... never was."

"Kyle? How did this happen?"

"I have no idea. All I know is that I feel like I once was blind, but now I see. Not only is Kylla mine, but I can have all the babies I want."

Cindy reached out and pulled him down to the seat as close to her as she could without bothering Kylla who was sleeping in her arms.

"I'm so happy for you, Kyle. I can't imagine how you feel right now."

"No one can, Cindy. It's like I've been released from prison."

Thirty-Two

Kylla slept through the rest of the office visit as well as the transfer to her car seat, then all the way back to Sheffield. Kyle was dropping by his parents' house in hopes of finding legal documents concerning his marriage. As was with most people, they were thrilled to see Kylla, although her temperament was fussy for the first time any of them had seen. She clung to Cindy the whole time and wouldn't speak or point to parts of the face. It crushed Emma that she couldn't hold her, but for today it was enough to just see her. She had burst into sobs when Kyle told her she was officially a grandmother.

"Here we go," Kyle said as he found the particular file he had been looking for packed up in a box in the attic. "Everything should be in here."

He opened the folder and found the divorce papers right up front. After a few more seconds, he pulled out a copy of the marriage license.

"I need to call Mr. Ben Hall and let him know I've got these," Kyle said as he pulled out his phone and punched in the number.

Bradley glanced into the box and noticed tons of photos, a couple of picture albums, and a candle he recognized as one Caryn and Kyle had bought on their honeymoon. He wondered why Caryn hadn't taken anything with her when she left. But even more, he wondered why she had used a fake name, why she had lied to Kyle about being unable to have children, and why she had left Kyle when she knew she was carrying his child.

When Kyle hung up his phone, Bradley asked him, "Who was she, Kyle? You were married to her for ten years, but she wasn't even Caryn—who was she?"

"I have no earthly idea. At this point, Dad, I almost don't care anymore. It's amazing, this time last year I was devastated. My wife had left me, and I had no reason to go on. But after all this, I don't even know how to process it! Caryn wasn't Caryn, she lied to me about having kids, Kylla *is* my baby, and now Caryn has been murdered."

"Have you thought about the ramifications all this brings?"

"Like what?"

"Your ministry, for instance," Bradley said as he dropped into an old chair causing a cloud of dust to rise. "You're not divorced anymore; you're widowed."

"Well, officially, I'm both. However, my situation may seem a little more sympathetic now."

"Especially with Kylla. And if you were to add Cindy to that combination, I think it would be a win/win situation."

Kyle stared at his father with a strange expression. "What are you suggesting?"

"You love her, don't you?"

"Well, I haven't *tried* to," Kyle answered.

"Tried to? What does that mean?"

"It's just been too complicated for us. Our existences are in complete disarray, and neither one of us has any permanent future plans. It's like our lives are on hold for the time being, and we've trying to make sense of where we are."

"You don't make sense out of love, Kyle, but I guess you wouldn't know that. You were chained to Miss Whoever for thirteen years."

"It really seems like that now. As I look back, there were all these gaps in our life, in our relationship, but they were things I never questioned. I just thought I had married this beautiful, shy woman who needed someone to believe in her. She was a good wife, you know, in the sense of staying home and … well … being at home. She sort of made me feel like I could do anything, and I guess I thought that's all she wanted. When it came down to it, Dad, I actually believed I was her entire life—that if I weren't in her life, she would have nothing."

"And what do you think now?"

"I'm still working on that."

***

Kyle drove Cindy up to her house and started to step out to get her door.

"You don't have to do that," Cindy said as she held his shoulder back.

"I don't do it because I have to. I do it because I'm honored to do it."

"It's been a long day. I'll keep the thought of honor in mind as I open and close the door myself. And I'll probably even carry it with me as I walk into the house and up the stairs to my room where I'll collapse on my bed and close my weary little eyes."

"Thanks for all you did today," he told her as he reached over and ran his hand down her hair. "You went way above and beyond the call of duty."

"Yeah, I'll have to agree with you there. I've never been a *wife* before. I've been a lot of things, but never a wife."

"How'd you like it?"

She smiled and sighed, "It was fun, but I don't know if it was being your wife, or being Kylla's mama … or both."

He nodded.

160

"Mama," came Kylla's little voice from the back seat.

Kyle and Cindy jerked around quickly. Her blue eyes were smiling sleepily and she was reaching her hands out to Cindy. Cindy looked at Kyle with her mouth open in shock.

"Mama," said Kylla again, reaching toward Cindy even more.

Cindy reached back, took her from the car seat, and placed her on her lap. Kylla looked up at her and gave a big, toothy smile. She then reached up and touched Cindy's eye.

"Mama eye?" she asked Cindy.

Cindy couldn't speak. She kissed the top of Kylla's head and pulled her close as tears began to sting her eyes.

God, I can't lose this little girl. Please don't tell me that you brought her into my life just to take her away.

Thirty-Three

On Saturday morning, Agent Ben Hall sat with Kyle and Jonathan at the dining table as they looked over the documents Kyle had dug up. Barbara walked around the house with Kylla, thrilled to have her all to herself for a change. No Sue Marcum, no Cindy, and the men were occupied with *important stuff* so she was able to hug and squeeze the little bundle to her heart's content.

"Can I take these with me, Kyle?" Ben asked. "I'll make copies if you need them now for some reason."

"I don't need them. And as far as I know, I probably never will. Now that Caryn's ... dead ... I don't imagine I'm going to have to produce any of these papers for anyone ever again."

That statement sparked something inside Jonathan's head. Kyle was right. Caryn was dead; his divorce was moot for all practical purposes. And with a child in his possession, *his* child from his marriage to a woman who had passed away, Kyle was now a family man. His reputation as a free and single divorcee' had significantly changed.

"That lead you gave us about her parents? Big dead end," Ben said shaking his head. "The place you described housed a couple, but no Bill and Linda Carter."

The agent turned back in his folder to some scribbled notes and gave him the names, "Jackson and Miranda Malone live there."

"You've gotta be kidding!" Kyle shook his head. "You must've gotten the wrong house. I've been there several times."

"It was the right house, believe me. They'd never heard of a Caryn Carter, and they'd never heard of you. They had no children."

"That's crazy!"

"Perhaps, but we did a little more snooping. I showed photos of you and Caryn around the neighborhood—interesting results there. No one ever remembered Caryn ... period. And the responses were always pretty much the same. *I'd remember a girl who looked like that.* But two men remembered you. One was a neighbor you had spoken with down at the dock one day. You probably didn't even realize he lived near the *supposed* Carters. The other was a man you had talked with while walking down the street one evening. Said you were a really nice guy and a minister."

"Well, I'll be darned," Kyle scratched his head in disbelief. "Come to think of it, Caryn never would get out unless we were going on the boat. I loved the climate up there. I'd beg her to take an evening stroll with me, but she'd never budge. I went out alone several times."

Jonathan crossed his arms and leaned back in his chair as he looked at Kyle and asked, "Did you ever wonder what kind of a loony woman you were married to?"

"It never crossed my mind that anything was abnormal. I didn't know. I didn't have any sisters, just a mom … and she can be moody when she wants. I just figured maybe Caryn was a little moodier than most. Women are moody; you can't understand them. I've heard that my whole life."

"There is a positive aspect in this dead end, however," Ben told them. "We can know with one hundred percent certainty that Caryn Carter was *not* who she said she was, and the lack of parents was the final proof."

"But they knew Caryn," Kyle insisted. "We were there. She went there four or five times a year to spend a week with them."

"Maybe …?"

"What? You think she went somewhere else?"

"She had a real name and a real family somewhere. If the Carters were just a couple of people working with her on this, then she was probably going who knows where during those supposed visits and living a whole other life."

Kyle leaned his elbows on the table and placed his face in his hands.

Ben Hall reached into his briefcase and produced a photograph. Handing it to Kyle he said, "Jackson and Miranda Malone."

Kyle's jaw dropped as he stared in bewilderment. "That's the Carters."

"I'm gonna begin a check of these documents you gave me through the system," Agent Hall said as he stood from the table to leave. "As you can tell from setting up the paternity test, these things take time to work through. If I find out anything, I'll let you know. Until then, keep Kylla here as much as possible, and be seen with Miss Marcum as much as possible."

"Why?" Kyle asked.

"Because there are eyes just beyond that fence who are trying like crazy to figure out who your little girl is. I don't know why, but they are. And for the moment, they believe she's yours and Cindy's. That seems like a safe assumption."

"What do you think would happen if they found out she was Caryn's?" Kyle wanted to know.

"Who knows? But look what they did to her mother, and try to explain why they're following her now."

"Who are *they*?"

Ben frowned as he replied, "Some mega drug cartel. That's all we know right now. As for their interest in your little girl—we're clueless."

***

Cindy sat at her computer on Saturday and read through the news. She was trying with everything within her to forget Kylla had called her *Mama*.

When Kyle had tried to get her to say it at the clinic, the baby became reserved and uneasy. Did she remember Caryn was her mother? Had Caryn called herself *Mama* to Kylla, and even though she had been dead for almost two months, did she remember that word? Was *Mama* a name to Kylla, or was it a title? Had she come to think Cindy was now her mother since she was the significant female person in her life?

She tried to push the thoughts from her mind because they all pointed back to one big question that was haunting her like mad: had Kylla seen her mother murdered? Bile rose in her throat every time that thought crossed her mind, and the deeper this investigation went, the only things that turned up were more unanswered questions. The single thing that had been settled was that Kylla was Kyle's, and that he could indeed have children. But then again, more questions were raised. Why had Caryn lied, and why had she gone to such great attempts to deceive him?

She fought the temptation to call Kyle. Their role-playing yesterday had been uncomfortably comfortable. Pretending to be his wife, having him touch her and kiss her so freely, and then acting as though she were really Kylla's mother had all made Cindy feel like she was walking in the clouds. But the reality of it, the down to earth facts, came out to the simple truth of what Cindy knew in her heart: Kyle would leave Dockrey, and most probably it would be soon. He would take Kylla with him. Who knew where he would go or what he would do? Then she would be replaced with someone permanent at the church office, and she would have to start all over again. She couldn't stay in Dockrey without them; it would hurt too much.

You love him, she bemoaned to herself. *Why did you have to wait all these years to give your heart away, and then finally give it to someone you can never have?*

Why did Kyle have to be so wonderful? Why didn't she go to Furman and meet him instead of Caryn? Why hadn't she listened to her parents, and to Angie, and chosen to live a life of purity and holiness so that when she did meet him, she had something more to offer him than used goods? Funny, but all those years that she lived so loosely, her life had never bothered her. But now, she saw each past relationship as another huge blot on her life that pulled her farther away from the Godly woman Kyle needed, and the Godly influence he would want for his daughter. She had been brutally honest with Kyle, and he had overlooked it. No matter how much she asked for God's forgiveness and cleansing, her conscience would not give her peace.

She had indeed fallen in love, but she couldn't let it go any further. It had to stop now.

***

"Where were you yesterday?" Kyle asked Cindy as he walked into the office Monday morning. "I looked for you all day. I called your cell but got

164

no answer. Kylla misses you."

His trump card, Kylla. All he had to do was mention her name and Cindy's insides began to fall apart.

"I think Friday took more out of me than I realized." Not true.

He nodded and leaned against the counter of the kitchenette. "It's my fault—I know it is."

"Why would you say that?"

"I took too many liberties with you. I wish I could say I couldn't help it, but that's not true. When Ben Hall told me to act like we were married, it was like I lost my head. You do that to me, Cindy, and I don't know how to handle it. You have to realize how different my relationship to you is than my relationship to Caryn. When I found out Kylla was my child, it was almost like finding out she was *our* child. That's what it felt like to me. It was as if she had been handed to *us*, not just me alone. You've been with me from the very beginning with her, even before that. It seemed only right … when I found out … to … to …"

"To kiss me?"

"Yeah," he closed his eyes in embarrassment. "That was just my first reaction."

She nodded but didn't respond. She was tired of trying to keep Kyle at bay, her heart intact, and her attachment to Kylla minimal

"I know what you're doing, Cindy," he said as came over and sat on the edge of her desk. "I've tried to do it too to a certain extent."

"And what is that, Kyle?" she sighed as she looked up at him tiredly. Sleep had not been easy the past two nights.

"You're trying to disconnect from us."

Her face remained blank. She took a deep breath, looked out the window at the peaceful valley and then nodded her head.

"Let me ask you something." he said gently. "What difference does it make to you if you walk out of our lives today, or three weeks from today, or three years from today? Is it gonna be easier when we move on simply because you chose right now to say goodbye?"

Cindy's heart was breaking. She never wanted to say goodbye. "I doubt it," she confessed as the ever-familiar lump started creeping up her throat again.

Kyle got off the desk and knelt down in front of her. He turned her chair around so that she would have to face him.

"Don't do this, Kyle," she pleaded.

"No, Cindy, don't *you* do *this*. Kylla needs you. You've come to mean something in her life that is desperately important. Don't abandon her."

Cindy choked back her emotions. *Mama.*

"And I need you," he said as though he were coming clean. "I don't know where we'll stand tomorrow, but right now I need you. If I have to leave in a month, then I'll deal with losing you then. But for now, here I am. And I couldn't go on here … without you."

A tear slid down her cheek as she reached down and gently stroked his hair. He took her hand, tenderly kissed it, and then placed it back in her lap.

"And I'll keep my hands and my lips to myself from now on," he promised.

She nodded, but her hand was still tingling from his touch.

Thirty-Four

May 29. James Marcum had died one year ago today. Cindy remembered being called at five fifteen that morning. She had been with Evan that night, and because his wife was visiting her parents for the week, they had actually spent the night at her place and not an out-of-town hotel. They had stayed up late, enjoying a rare sense of freedom because Evan had nowhere to go. They had ordered supper and watched television all evening, lounging around on her couch and being more romantic than Cindy had ever remembered being with anyone before.

The phone had rung many times before she answered because she was so exhausted she could hardly find her bearings.

"Cindy, this is Jonathan Wright. It seems your father had a severe heart attack."

"What?" She was groggy and unsure of what was happening.

"You need to get to Dockrey. Your father has died."

She began to wake up. "I thought you said he had a heart attack."

"That's what they think. It appears he died immediately. There was nothing anyone could do."

Cindy now sat at her desk and felt humiliated as she remembered Evan trying to pull her back into bed, clueless that her father had just died. She had jerked away from him and ran to the bathroom to collect her thoughts, and that was where the reality had hit her. It reminded her of a youth conference where the speaker had told the teenagers to watch their behavior; how would they feel if Jesus came back and they were in the middle of something questionable? How did it feel to be in bed with a married man at the moment her Godly father left this earth? Horrible.

The phone rang, pulling Cindy back to the present. She was thankful. She may have to live with the memories of her past, but she took solace in the fact that her present had been right for some time now.

"Good morning, First Baptist Church," she answered cheerfully.

"Hey, Cindy! Is that you?" came a lady's voice.

"Yes, it is."

"Stephanie Freeman here."

"What can I do for you, Steph?"

"Glad you asked." Stephanie gave a small laugh. "How about a trial run?"

Cindy turned to the window as she wondered what on earth Stephanie was talking about. "Where am I running?" Cindy watched a hawk swoop down into the valley.

"Our cruise is coming up. I need a fill-in teacher for my Sunday School class."

"Oh," she said slowly. She had forgotten all about *that* discussion with Stephanie.

"You could teach them that one Sunday, and it would sort of let you get a feel for what it'll be like when the baby comes."

"Uh … yeah. I hadn't really thought that much about it."

"Well, it's time to start the thinking. Look, Cindy, it's not that hard. I've tried to tell you how easy these girls are to teach."

"Teenage girls? Are you kidding me?"

"For Pete's sake! You're not teaching them algebra! It's just sharing with them how to stay on course with Christ."

Cindy frowned at the mention of algebra. Stephanie had been in Algebra Two with her in high school, and she never got it. She almost failed the course that year.

"The difference here is that no one in their right mind would ask me to teach algebra," Cindy tried to reason. "You of all people should know that. But you *are* asking me to teach a group of girls about being faithful to Christ. I hardly think I qualify for that either."

"It's not ten years ago, Cindy. And besides, these girls think you're great. I could get others to fill the spot, but even if they taught with the wisdom of Paul, yet didn't connect with them, it would be worthless time spent. However, they admire you, and anything you'd say to them would fall on eager ears."

Cindy bit her lip as she struggled with the decision. She didn't feel at all ready to lead others spiritually especially after reminiscing her relationship with Evan that morning.

"Are you saved, Cindy?"

"Barely, but yes, I'm saved."

"Do you believe that a life of obedience to God and his Word is the best path to take?"

"Yes." She closed her eyes and leaned her head back. Stephanie was going to win.

"Then you're qualified."

"Okay, okay. Please tell me you have some kind of literature to use."

"Yee haw!" Stephanie laughed into the phone. "The girls will be absolutely thrilled. And yes, I have literature. But like I told you before, you can't plan a whole lot with this group. Most of the lessons end up in discussion, and you'll find yourself stressed out if you try to cram it all in. Just let the lesson flow."

"Right," she said mournfully. There was no possible way it could be that easy.

It was close to lunchtime and Cindy wanted to visit her father's grave. Her mother had gone this morning and she had offered to go with her, but Sue preferred to be alone. She understood. She needed to run by the post office, so she decided to leave a little early and drop by the cemetery before going to the Wrights for lunch.

She grabbed her purse and started for the door when Kyle came in. It was eleven twenty-five.

"What have you been up to this morning?" she asked him. "Been working in the choir room?"

"Kylla's sick," he said wearily. "I've been up all night with her."

"Oh no! What's wrong?"

"Bad stuffy nose and a rough cough. I ended up putting her in bed with me. We both got a little more rest after that."

She smiled at the vision and then commented, "Lucky you. You got to snuggle with her all night."

"Trust me: it was *not* fun," he yawned. He noticed her purse. "Are you leaving already?"

"Post office," she explained as she held up the mail. "Have you been to the doctor?"

"That's where I was this morning. She's on all sorts of medication."

"Can I get you something and bring it back with me? Do you need anything personally?"

Kyle smiled and shook his head as he went for his office.

"What's so funny?" she asked.

"I was mentally going through my list of things you could do for me *personally*."

She glanced back at him and caught him grinning.

"Goodbye, Kyle. See you at lunch."

***

Cindy stood at her father's grave and stared at the marker a long time. It was strange seeing a tombstone for someone she knew so well. She had never experienced death as closely as this. In fact, the only people she had ever known that had died had been either very old or very sick, and none of them had ever been involved in her life in any significant way. When she lost her father, there were many other things she lost as a result. Some of those things she needed to lose, but she hated the fact that it took the death of someone so dear to make her see the light about what is most important in life.

Daddy, I miss you so much that I sometimes find myself talking to you in my dreams. I'll be having this conversation with you about something I'm struggling with, but before I hear your advice, I wake up. It's like I have to grieve all over again. I hope there's some way for you to know that I've turned my life around—that things are drastically different for me. I also hope that you never lost faith that I would change. It would kill me to know that your last thoughts of me were despair and anguish.

You were a wonderful father, and when you left, I wondered if I could actually keep going. For two weeks I could hardly sleep. I walked around in a daze trying to decipher what was real and what wasn't; you couldn't be dead, I kept telling myself. But I soon realized that all of it was real, and I had to force myself to move on.

It's easier now. I don't know how. They say time heals all wounds, but I couldn't believe it was possible. But here I am, not thinking about you as much, not missing you as much, and realizing that my life really will go on without you.

As she continued her thoughts, she noticed a man moving near her in the cemetery. She glanced up to see if she knew him, and he stopped suddenly to begin viewing a grave. She knew the grave; it was Dr. Dampier's. The man standing there now was no one she knew to be related to the late town doctor, but he did seem familiar.

She leaned down to her father's grave and removed three dried leaves that had blown upon it since she'd been there. As she knelt, it was then that she realized who the man was. She stayed down and acted as though she was doing something else, but as she pushed her sunglasses up higher on her nose, she kept her head pointed toward the ground and her eyes looking through the dark glasses focused on the man. Sure enough, that was he. She could tell by the swatch of gray at the very front of his head in an otherwise extremely dark mass of hair. He was the pharmaceutical salesman at the clinic when Kyle had gone for the paternity test. She remembered him because of the unusual gray in his hair.

Maybe he's another agent? No, Kyle said there were a total of three in the back already. Surely he would have known about a fourth.

She stood up and continued to keep her head looking down toward the grave, but with her eyes hiding behind the glasses she watched him closely. He was definitely interested in whatever she was doing. He would look at Dr. Dampier's grave briefly, then he would gaze back at her. She looked up once to see what he would do, and he immediately jerked his head down and did the sign of the cross. She had to force herself not to laugh; there were few, if any Catholics around Dockrey. The nearest Catholic church she knew of was 50 miles away.

She decided to do a little investigating on her own. She would pretend she had no idea who Dr. Dampier was, and casually offer her condolences to the man. Maybe she could discover something in the process that could help Kyle.

Kyle. So he had a list of things he would like her to do *personally* for him. She smiled at the thought as she bid her father farewell and headed for the strange man in black.

"Hi," she said as she walked right up to him. She looked at the tombstone and shrugged her shoulders as she shook her head. "Dr. Charles

… uh, how do you say that last name?"

The man was startled and obviously nervous, but Cindy pretended not to notice.

"Dampier," the man replied with an unusual accent. Northern? Definitely—with something ethnic added, Italian maybe? "You din't know 'im?" the man asked her about Dr. Dampier.

"No. I've never even noticed the grave before. My father died last year." She pointed toward the marker. "I never came out here until then. I know some people like waltzing through graveyards just to read the tombstones. Not me. Sort of freaks me out."

"Yeah, I know watcha mean. Dis guy, he was an uncle, but he was more like a fathah to me. Know whad-I mean?"

Cindy nodded, but on the inside she was amused. Dr. Dampier was a man bred, born and raised in the South; he had no relatives on this planet that sounded like this guy.

"I'm Cindy Marcum," she smiled as she stuck out her hand.

He shook it and hesitated as he answered, "Uh … I'm … uh … Joe Jones. Yeah."

"Nice to meet you, Joe. You're not from around here, are you?"

"No," he laughed a little. "Guess dat's obvious, huh?"

"Well, we do tend to have accents a little different than yours."

"Yeah, I noticed. Sometimes it's a little hard to figure out what yous guys is saying."

"I can imagine."

She let the silence linger for a bit before she acted as though she had come up with an idea.

"Joe, you want to get a coffee or something? I'm on my lunch hour."

"Wo, really? I mean, wouldn't there be like a jealous husband or boyfriend ready to tie me up or somethin'?"

Think, Cindy. They think you're married to Kyle.

"Oh, there's a man all right." *Good girl, use man, not husband or boyfriend.* "But I doubt he'd be jealous."

"I can't imagine that, you bein' so beautiful and all."

"Well, thank you. It's nice to hear that now and then. I try, you know, to look good, but he gets so preoccupied with other things … oh, never mind. You don't need to hear this."

"Well, he's gotta be blind to not see what's right in front of 'im."

"That's sweet of you," she said with her saddest smile. "How about that coffee?"

"Well, I got uh … well, I gotta place I need to be in just a few minutes. I's just coming to see Uncah Cha'lie before I took off again."

She nodded in understanding and tried to look disappointed as she stuck out her hand again and said, "Nice to meet you, Joe. Thanks for your kindness."

"Don't mention it."

She walked away slowly, but inside she was ready to run like crazy. This man was obviously following her, or following those in contact with Kylla somehow. She felt as though her skin would crawl away if she didn't move fast. But she kept up her slow pace, remembering not to glance at any tombstones because she had told him that felt *freaky* to her. When she reached her little red car, she took her time getting in, and glanced around to see where Joe was. He was still standing by Dr. Dampier's grave, but he was turned toward her. She started the engine, put the car in gear, and slowly pulled away.

Thirty-Five

"Are you crazy!" Kyle yelled at her. "Did you not remember that these people murdered my ex-wife?"

"I didn't do anything overt!" Cindy insisted.

"I need to sit down," Sue said as she put her hand up to her forehead. "Cindy, I don't think that was a smart move at all."

The lunch gathering at the Wrights had become frantic when Cindy came in and told them her story. Kyle was pacing, Sue was laid out on the couch now, Barbara was praying, and Jonathan was running his hand through his hair every minute or so.

"I'd better call Agent Hall," Kyle finally decided. "He needs to know what you did."

"I might can help him with some information also," Cindy said a bit stubbornly. Why was everyone flying off the handle? She didn't do anything drastic.

Kyle now had the number for the FBI programmed into his phone.

"We're familiar with him," Agent Hall explained. "You probably won't see him again; I can almost guarantee that. When they find out he had contact with Cindy, they'll do away with him right away."

"Who are *they*?" Kyle wanted to know. "And for that matter—who on earth was Caryn!"

"We don't know a name yet. She covered her tracks well. I guess with twelve years behind her, the trail grew more faint with each passing year. Don't worry though, Kyle. We'll figure this out. It'll take time, but we'll get to the bottom of it. Now can I talk with Miss Marcum, please?"

Kyle turned to Cindy and handed her the phone. "He wants to talk to you."

She took the phone, inhaled deeply, and then said, "Mr. Hall."

"Yes, Miss Marcum. Thanks for this info. It tells us that they're not just following Kylla alone. There are probably tails assigned to both you and Kyle. Now, what you did was wrong—not because you talked to him, but because you had contact with him. His people will probably have to pull him, which means that someone new will be assigned to you if that's the case. What I want you to do is keep your eyes open for the new tail, and for any tail that might be following Kyle when you're together. But this time, ignore them at all costs. Just report to us any strange fellows that keep popping up like this one."

"I understand; I'll do what I can."

"And thanks for trying to help," he said thoughtfully. "But from now on, let us do the planning. We try to weave a web, Miss Marcum; that's how we work. We'll be arranging several more things for you to do for us, but things like you did today can throw weeks of planning into the toilet. Do you understand?"

"Yes, sir. I just wanted to do something to protect Kylla."

"We know. But until further instruction, act ignorant when you see some guy for the tenth time while you're grocery shopping."

"Got it."

***

That afternoon in the office, Cindy was ready to strangle Kyle. He walked around in a huff, in and out of his office, slamming cabinet doors, sighing heavily every chance he had. She got it: he was upset at her for what she'd done, but it was over, and she'd learned her lesson. As he walked by her desk one more time, deliberately not saying anything to her, she'd had enough.

"Would you get off it!" she finally declared. "I made a mistake, I realize that, and there's nothing I can do to change it!"

"I still can't believe you did it," he bemoaned as he pulled a can of Diet Mountain Dew from the small refrigerator. "You could have been ... well ... I don't exactly know what—that's what makes it so difficult! We know what these people are capable of, but we don't know why they're so interested in us."

"They're interested in us because of Kylla. They're not out for you or me; they're just trying to figure out how we relate to her."

"We don't *know* that, however. We're just *assuming* that."

"Okay, Kyle," she blew a wisp of hair from across her face, "it's over. I've learned my lesson. It won't happen again."

"It's over? That's like saying that a hurricane or a tornado is over! Yeah, it's passed on by, but who knows the devastation and damage that was caused as a result! You don't just ..."

"Enough Kyle," Jonathan said sternly as he appeared from his office. "It *is* over. You can stop chastising her now."

"Thank you," Cindy expressed.

"I'm not chastising her. I'm ... well ... worried. I mean, Kylla's safe behind the fence; Cindy isn't. There are agents watching our house; no one is watching Cindy, except ... *them* ... the bad guys ... the people who murdered Caryn. How am I supposed to think clearly when Cindy's out trying to play detective? I can't protect her like that!"

"It's not your job to protect me!"

"Well, it needs to be somebody's!"

"Calm down, you two," Jonathan spoke above their yelling. "Look, we move on from here. The FBI is aware of everything, and who knows, maybe Cindy's little conversation today will be helpful in the long run."

Kyle and Cindy were silent for the moment, but Kyle was obviously still agitated.

"The best you two can do is be seen together ... a lot," Jonathan reminded them of Agent Hill's instructions. "For now, these people think you're probably married, or at least a couple trying to put their lives back together. Concentrate on that."

"Fat chance," Cindy murmured.

Kyle glared at her.

"Besides," she reasoned, "they can't be total morons. Surely they've dug into our private records and know we're not married."

"Wrong *again*," Kyle shot back. "They know nothing. The FBI has anything about you and me tied up in some kind of non-accessible lockdown."

"Look," Jonathan continued, "there's a Gideon supper this Thursday evening for the city's ministers; Kyle's going. I'll give them a call today and tell them he's bringing a date."

"That's my favorite night of television," Cindy pouted. "I don't want to go."

Both men looked at her with irritation.

"Hey! I'm a woman," she defended. "I have a right to be difficult now and then."

Jonathan smiled and chuckled. "Even *I* know how to use the DVR. I'm calling the Gideons, okay?"

She bit her lip as she pretended to think on her decision. She finally nodded, and Jonathan went back to his office. Kyle stared at her for a moment and then shook his head as he blustered back to his own office.

"What time will you be picking me up?" she called out to him, making sure the agitation in her voice was clear.

"Quarter after six," he yelled back, finally closing his door—rather hard.

***

On Thursday evening, Kyle showed up at the Marcums with his black suit and tie; the Gideons' supper was semi-formal. He was still perturbed with Cindy; she refused to see the seriousness of what she had done. He wished she could understand that the reason he was furious was because she had scared him to death. It was hard for him to concentrate, or even sleep, as he imagined what other impulsive acts she might try to pull. As he walked up to the door, Sue was on her way out.

"Going to watch my baby," she smiled at him as she came onto the deck. "My! Don't you look handsome! You are one good looking guy, Kyle

Sarkos."

"Why, thank you, Sue, although I wonder if you're being serious or just buttering me up because you get to baby sit Kylla tonight."

"A lot of both," she laughed.

"Is Cindy ready?"

"Fair to partly cloudy. You'd better ease up on her or she's liable to knock you for a loop."

Kyle nodded as he waved goodbye and then ambled on into the house. It was quiet. Should he let Cindy know he was there, or just wait until she appeared? He walked into the kitchen and smiled as he saw it was spotless. He wasn't sure if it was because Cindy was in on the work now, or because Sue was feeling great. He shuffled slowly back into the dining area and then glanced into the living room. He started to pick up the remote to watch some TV when he heard a door slam upstairs.

"The prima donna has emerged," he whispered to himself.

He turned to look upstairs, and the sight he found nearly made him lose his balance. Cindy looked more beautiful than he had ever seen her. Her hair was put up, but several long strands of spiral curls hung down around her face. She was wearing a dark navy dress made of shimmering material that clung to her body and looked liked liquid jewels flowing down around her. He tried to remember he was mad at her, but all he could see was her beauty.

"Ready?" he asked smoothly.

"Let me get my purse."

He waited for her at the door as she went out to the glassed-in porch. When she came back, it took his breath yet again. She refused to make eye contact with him, but he continued to be polite. He opened the door for her and gently put his hand on the small of her back as he followed her out.

"Got your keys to lock the door?" She reached into her purse, removed her key chain, and dropped the keys into his hand. As he locked the door, she went on down the deck and walked toward his Jeep.

"Why don't we take your car," he suggested as he searched for the key on her chain. "Somehow getting all decked out like this and showing up in a Jeep seems like a travesty."

"Whatever," she shrugged as she strolled over to the Thunderbird.

He opened her door and waited for her to get to the car. When she arrived, she just stood there, not getting in.

"Problem?" he asked her.

"Yeah, there is. You're holding the door open for me. You told me you did that as an honor, but you haven't been very honorable toward me of late. So I'm wondering now: are you doing it out of obligation? Because, if that's the case, I would much rather walk back into my house and turn on the television."

He closed his eyes and sighed. "I don't want to dishonor you, Cindy. In fact, right now my heart is in my throat and I can barely catch my breath because of your beauty. If I could take back every word I've said to you this week, I would in a minute."

"It's not just your words, Kyle. It's everything. I've been ready to crawl under a rock because of how you've treated me. A person can only take so much disdain."

"I didn't mean for it to be like that. I just … well … Cindy, I care for you so much that I'm scared. Fear can drive a man to do strange things."

"I don't care if you do *strange* things. Just stop doing *mean* things."

He reached out for her hand and moved close to her. He could smell her perfume and see the intense blue of her eyes again. Being close to her erased his reasoning. "I'm sorry."

"Can you put the whole incident behind you? Please?"

"I can do anything you want me to do."

She finally smiled at him, and then as if to taunt him, she stepped right up to him so that she was barely an inch from his face. "Then maybe tonight won't be so bad after all."

The Gideon supper turned out to be just what everyone needed. The speaker was a potter from Mississippi who used his wheel, clay and talents to talk about how the Lord relates to His children. As he took a lifeless clump of brown clay and began to work it on the wheel, Cindy could almost feel the hands of God transforming her life. Within a few minutes, the potter had formed a beautiful, large urn that could be used for anything from decorating to watering a garden. He explained the processes of painting and firing that would eventually follow, and how all of these elements worked to make the urn not only beautiful, but also useful for the master.

She desired with everything inside her to be beautiful and useful for God. She had made so many horrible mistakes in her past that sometimes it was hard to believe God could do anything with her again, but as she thought about her present, she realized that God was truly a God of forgiveness. She was a church secretary, not permanently, but still the fact that God would place her there was encouraging. She would be teaching a high school girls' Sunday School class in a little over a week; who would have thought that? And she was learning to find strength and wisdom in the Lord rather than looking for fulfillment in the world. Yes, the hands of God were on her life, and He was molding her into something He could use.

She waited for Kyle to open the car door when they arrived back at her house. He held his hand out and pulled her up from the seat. She thanked him politely and started for the house.

"Hang on," he said as he caught up with her, "your keys."

"Oh yeah."

"We ought to get that potter guy at our church some Sunday evening. I thought he was great."

"He was marvelous. It's comforting to know that God is the Potter who is forming our lives, isn't it?"

"Very."

"I mean, sometimes he has to crush us and start over, but at least we know He's not given up and is always in the process of molding us into something."

"I know what it feels like to be crushed," Kyle confessed as they walked up onto the deck. "But as I look back, I realize how much I needed that. Cindy, I had gotten so cocky in my ministry. God had to remind me what true worship is, and He had to bring me back to the point of being able to worship Him privately again before I could lead publicly."

"I know the feeling. Not leading in worship and all, but being crushed so God could bring me back to what really matters in life."

Kyle took her keys back and unlocked the dead bolt and doorknob.

"Want something to drink?" she asked him.

"Yeah. I think it would be good if I stayed here until your mother gets home. Got any iced tea?"

"Be right back," she nodded heading for the kitchen.

As he watched her walk away, he was again taken by her beauty and poise. When she had appeared on the stairs tonight, she could have been a high-end model for all he knew. To have her with him at the banquet had made him feel like a king. He smiled. His father had told him that was the key to true love—finding someone who made you feel like a king. But did he make her feel like a queen? He knew he had been harsh with her this week, but she had scared him. He had lost Caryn to these people, not only by her murder, but years before. She'd been running from them, and he had no idea who the woman was that he had married. For all practical purposes, his marriage had been a sham.

When Cindy came into the living room with the glasses of tea, he walked over to her, took them from her, and set them on the coffee table. He then took her hands in his and looked as deeply into her eyes as he could.

"You're not going to kiss me again, are you?" she asked hesitantly.

"Not that I wouldn't love to, but no," he said as he leaned his head down to her forehead. He lingered there a moment and then pulled back. "I'm really sorry for how I reacted this week. I get so confused where you're concerned. There are so many things I feel for you, but there are so many barriers in our lives. I wonder sometimes why *we* couldn't have met in college. Life back then was so free and easy."

"Maybe you could have coaxed me into staying in school."

"And maybe I would've kept you from a lot of decisions that messed up your life."

She nodded regretfully and laid her head on his shoulder. He put his arms up around her back and gently ran his hand over the fluid material. Holding her was like nothing he had ever known before. She seemed to melt into his embrace. Caryn had always been stiff and unsure. No wonder … she had probably never really loved him.

"I wonder what it would have been like to have married you instead," he imagined as he began to think aloud. "I could've known your father."

"He would've loved you," she smiled as she eased her hands inside his coat and around his waist. "Mom already does."

"We'd probably have a house full of kids right now."

"But I wouldn't have this same figure after carrying them all," she snickered.

He pulled back and looked into her eyes again as he said, "But your beauty would be even deeper. Just watching you with Kylla brings out a whole new spectrum."

"I love her, you know?"

"I know." He pulled her back to him again. They just stood there silently enjoying the embrace. Imagining their possibilities of years before was more disheartening than it was positive. The truth was, they hadn't met, their lives had been ruined to some degree, and they each held wounds they would carry with them from here on out.

"What are we doing, Kyle?" Cindy asked him softly. "Why does this feel so right on one hand and so wrong on the other?"

"I don't really know. I wish I could make sense of anything in my life right now. If I could, then somehow I could figure out where *we* fit into it."

The door opened, and they knew that Sue was home. They backed away from each other quickly, but held their gaze until she walked in.

"Jonathan and Barbara said the evening was wonderful," Sue remarked. "Did you two enjoy it as well?"

"It was splendid," Kyle told her. "Jonathan wants to bring him to our church some night."

"Kylla would love that," Sue said energetically. "She is so smart, Kyle. And she's going to be walking soon. She cruised around that house all night long. I could barely keep up with her! Barbara's going to bring out the little gates they used for Andie's kids to block the stairway tomorrow. I'll sleep better knowing she can't get up there."

Sue sighed and then yawned. "I'm a bit tired. I'll think I turn in. Good night, all."

"Night, mom."

"Good night, Sue," Kyle added.

When she had closed her door, Kyle and Cindy looked at each other again.

"I should go," he reasoned. "It's late."

"You didn't touch your tea."

"No, but I touched you, and it was much nicer."

Her cheeks grew pink for a moment, but she held his gaze. "I'll see you to the door," she said as she motioned him out of the living room.

They walked slowly, neither really wanting the evening to end. It was almost dreamlike. They were dressed in their best, and the mood prior to Sue's entrance lingered.

"I feel like I'm in a soap opera," Cindy said as they reached the door. "We look so elegant and all. It seems like we should say something dramatic and then ..." She stopped.

"And then what?"

"You know soap operas. Just fill in the blank."

"I'll do that." He turned to open the door, but twisted back around. "Did I tell you how beautiful you look tonight?"

"I don't recall. But sometimes being repetitive isn't all that bad."

He smiled at her honesty, took her hand, and pulled her close to him once again. "You looked more beautiful tonight than anyone I've ever seen in my entire life," he whispered to her. "You take my breath away."

She grinned up at him and said, "I know you never said *that*. Thank you."

"I could say it again if you want?"

She traced his lips with her fingers and then reached up to caress his hair. His head was swimming with emotion again, and he desperately wanted to kiss her. Instead he remained the gentleman, took her hand and kissed it, and then bid her goodnight.

Be still, my heart. Sarkos, what are you doing, man?

Thirty-Six

On Saturday morning, Kyle helped Jonathan in his vegetable garden. This was a first for him having never so much as planted a flower or picked a tomato. He found getting dirt under his fingernails invigorating. Maybe he would take up gardening some day, when he was settled, when he had his own home, his own family, a life.

"Have things smoothed out between you and Cindy yet?" Jonathan asked as he brought out a bag of fertilizer.

"Yeah ... finally. She really scared me when she pulled that stunt at the cemetery."

"We saw that."

Kyle reached into the bag and grabbed a can full of fertilizer. "Can I ask you something about Cindy?"

"Sure. What do you want to know?"

"She shared with me a lot about her past. I know she was ... well ... far from perfect, let's say. But her mom is so good, a woman of faith. And everyone says her dad was this great and godly man."

Jonathan nodded in agreement.

"How did Cindy and her brother turn out like they did? How did they go so far from what they were raised to be?"

"Well, the Marcums had a rough time having children to begin with. When Sue actually carried the twins close to full term, and then had two healthy babies, it was almost a miracle ... well, it was a miracle. They knew these would be the only children they ever had, and felt unbelievably blessed to have had a boy and a girl. In a lot of ways, the Marcums were a bit too tolerant and a bit too giving, but I don't know if you can really blame the twins' rebellion on that. They were just sneaky kids."

"Sneaky?"

"Okay, take my kids, for example. Angie was my rebellious one. Alex had a little bit of it in him, but nothing compared to Angie."

"The missionary?" Kyle asked surprised. "She was a rebel?"

"Always," Jonathan cackled at the memories. "But she was overt with her rebellion. She didn't agree with our rules or our standards, and she made no bones about it. She was out to find her own way ... and she was helped along by Billy and Cindy. Now, don't get me wrong; I'm not blaming them for her rebellion. She probably pedaled them down the path as much as they did her. It was definitely a *symbiotic relationship*. But Cindy and Billy were different. Their parents had no idea how wild they were. For example, when we would have family worship on occasion, Angie made no attempts to cover up how miserable she was with it. We'd ask, *Angie, you want to add something?* No. *Angie, would you like for us to pray about anything?* No. *Angie, what did you get out of Sunday's message?* Nothing. We knew exactly what was going on with her. But she told me that Billy and Cindy actually tried to outdo each other in impressing their parents. Long prayers, deep descriptions of Sunday School lessons, actually telling their parents they had witnessed to kids at school."

"You're kidding! That's horrible." Kyle was astonished and a bit repulsed.

"So when they moved away to college, these kids had no real foundation for anything. They had so buffaloed their parents, that when they got out from under their protection, they went wild. Cindy lasted one semester, and Billy two years."

"Did the Marcums get it then?"

"Slowly, but it took Billy's two failed marriages and a huge," he paused and sighed, "revelation at Cindy's apartment one day to make them see the real extent of their ungodliness."

"Wow, what happened at Cindy's apartment?"

Jonathan paused. "I don't really know if this is something I should share with you."

"She's told me a lot already. I can't imagine there could be any worse."

He sighed. "James had gone on a business trip for a week, so Sue went up to Florence to stay the week with Cindy. Cindy had given her this rewritable disc to record a certain show that was coming on that day about real estate selling tips. Cindy wanted to be able to transfer it to her laptop and edit it to show some of the salesman at work … extra credit type of thing … trying to look good to the boss. Sue popped in the disc when the show was about to start, and you know how some machines start playing the DVD automatically?"

Kyle nodded.

"Well, that's what happened. Sue was about to turn it off until she realized what it was."

"Which was …?"

"Cindy and a … boyfriend."

Kyle thought for a moment, and then the truth registered. "Oh, man!" he exclaimed slowly. "Poor Sue."

"Oh yeah. And the thing about it, rather than turn it off, she just watched the whole thing. It was obvious this was not Cindy's first experience."

Kyle leaned back on his knees. He couldn't imagine Sue's devastation … or Cindy's, for that matter. "It's hard to believe she ever lived like that. She seems so pure, almost pristine. She has this beauty that's wholesome and unspoiled. It's almost as if she was somebody else during that time and now the real Cindy is back."

"That, my boy, is the power of the blood of Christ," Jonathan contended firmly. "Her forgiveness *is* complete. The cross provides a cleansing that is above and beyond anything human minds can imagine. God literally makes all things new, and in Cindy's life, that has most certainly been the case. The sad thing, however, is that no matter how thorough God might be, people will fall way short of that. There will always be those who are skeptical of her because of her past. Cindy herself has a hard time believing she's worthy of God's attention."

"How? The transformation is so complete."

"That's called *reaping what you sow*, Kyle. Forgiveness and cleansing are complete, but the effects of sin will always be hanging over her head like a neon sign flashing *not worthy*."

Kyle nodded. He understood that allegorical sign very well, only his was announcing *divorce*. The thing Kyle struggled with concerning his own life was that he was actually innocent when it came to the divorce. He had not expected it, not wanted it, not planned it or even encouraged it. He had wanted to salvage the marriage, right up until … until he had met Cindy.

"Do you think?" Kyle began a thought. No. "What if?" No. "Let me pose you a hypothetical situation."

"Baloney," Jonathan grumbled.

"Excuse me?"

"Don't give me hypothetical. Hypothetical means you're going to ask me something that involves you intimately but you want both of us to pretend it's not about you. Am I right?"

Kyle chuckled and shook his head. "That's exactly what it means."

"Then how 'bout you just give it to me straight."

"Imagine," Kyle began, hesitating slightly, "that when Dockrey finally gets a music guy, and I have to move on … well, Cindy's this—I don't know how to say it—professional type woman, you know? She's classy, sells million dollar buildings to corporate executives and all. She's used to having lots of money in her hands and doing pretty much whatever she wants with it. I mean, she's single … no husband or kids—no responsibilities."

"That's pretty much her," Jonathan agreed.

"Well, do you think she could ever go for someone like me? I'll never be in a huge church again, if even a church, so my salary won't exactly be *comfortable*. I've got a kid now. It would mean a big change in everything she's pursued to be with a guy like me."

Jonathan leaned on the handle of his hoe and stared out beyond the garden to the lush woods. "I think you're asking the wrong thing. It isn't if she could go for a guy *like* you; you're being hypothetical again. The bottom line is could she change her life for *you* specifically. See, it isn't the circumstances that dictate love; it's the people. If she loves you, Kyle, she'll follow you anywhere. If she doesn't, she'd better not even try."

"But everything is so hard right now. Neither of us has a future, we don't know when our jobs here will end, and absolutely everything about who we were and who we're becoming is totally unsure. I mean, we can't even begin to think about anything between us right now; it's too complicated."

"Who ever told you love was uncomplicated?" Jonathan crowed. "Like I said before, you don't look at your circumstances, you look at the people. Do you know what life is all about, Kyle?"

Wow. What a loaded question. What is life all about? "I won't even try to answer that."

"Relationships. That's it—that's the bottom line. You relate to God, you relate to family, and you relate to others. Everything else we do, from career to recreation has very little meaning if our relationships are minimal. See, you're looking at the meaningless stuff right now. A job, money, convenience—all those things are nominal when you compare them to the meaningful relationships in your life."

"But you have to look at things realistically."

"Absolutely! But what is real? Money? Is that the meaning of life? Career? Comfort? Is that what it's all about for you Kyle ... for Cindy?"

He thought for a moment. Apparently it was. He and Cindy both seemed to be dancing around each other because they feared that being together might eventually be worse than being apart. Being together might mean having to change their lives. And as he thought about it now, it still scared him.

"But isn't it irresponsible to just throw caution to the wind and pursue a relationship without thinking about all the ramifications?" he appealed.

Jonathan laughed again as he stuck the hoe into the earth to make another furrow. "Love really doesn't give a flip about responsibility. In fact, when love is the controlling factor, every inch of sensibility seems to just fly out the window. And as for your circumstances, the ministry, the baby—those are *not* reasons to love or not love someone. They're a part of who you are, and if someone really loves you, Kyle, she accepts those things too ... because those things are now the essence of *you*.

Thirty-Seven

Cindy locked her car nervously and then shuffled through her papers as she headed for the church. She was teaching Sunday School today; this was a milestone. Had someone told her this time last year that God would have worked so much in her life that she would be trusted to teach teenage girls, she would have laughed in their face. But here she was, trembling both with the weight of the responsibility and the sheer fear of facing these girls.

"Morning, beautiful," Kyle said as he came up behind her. "Ready?"

"Are you kidding? I've think I've actually lost my mind. Why did I ever agree to do this?"

"Because it's the right thing to do, and because it's *time* to do it." He reached up and cupped his hand on her shoulder. "You're ready for this."

She took a deep breath and tried to nod bravely, but her mind was racing with every reason in the world why she should *not* be doing it. "Where's Kylla?" she asked, thinking of the one person who could take her mind off the bigger people she was about to face,

"Barbara's bringing her up to the church. I needed to set up the mics for the ensemble, so I came on up a little earlier. Want me to pray with you for a moment? God set this up, you know? He'll see you through it."

"That would be wonderful." She felt relief as he led her to a room off the sanctuary where they prayed briefly for God to give her wisdom and an extra set of nerves.

"Okay, Stephanie said we're supposed to talk about making right choices today. Does that sound on track?" Cindy asked the class of eight girls ranging from tenth through twelfth grades.

"We have no idea," Kaleigh stated from the corner. "We don't have books."

"Stephanie threw those out sometime last year," Lori explained. "She said it was a waste of money."

"We never read them anyway," Kaleigh added.

"And the lessons were kind of ... well ..."

"Boring," Keisha put in. "I mean, the Bible isn't supposed to be boring, is it? And Stephanie said we could do whatever we wanted."

"I want to go to MacDonald's," Lauren said out of nowhere.

Cindy looked at her confused, then giggled nervously as she said, "Me too. I'm so nervous about teaching you guys I could probably eat an Egg Mac Muffin or two just to calm my nerves."

"*You're* nervous?" Keisha asked. "About teaching *us*?"

"Extremely," Cindy confessed.

"Why?" Lauren wanted to know. "We should be the ones who're nervous."

"Why should you be nervous? I'm the one who's got to talk in front of all of you and try to pretend I've got my life together."

"Trust me on this one, Cindy," Kaleigh said knowingly, "this will be way easier than your first beach ball volleyball game. And look how you did with that? You're a pro now."

"Cindy's played with the big ball before? When?" Lauren was impressed.

"At all those after church fellowships you never come to," Cindy smiled at Lauren.

Lauren grinned and blushed a little bit. "I don't do youth fellowships much anymore."

"I didn't either," Cindy confessed.

"Really?" Lori raised her eyebrows showing interest in the conversation for the first time.

"Well, I went because I had to go. But just because I was there I didn't have to enjoy it. Know what I mean?"

The girls laughed and nodded.

"Why didn't *you* want to be there?" Lauren was curious.

"Basically, it seemed so uncool at the time. I just felt like I was above the whole church thing. I had no idea that making foolish choices at sixteen would have such a profound effect on my life. All I wanted was to be cool."

The girls were suddenly mesmerized as Cindy began to explain how she lost touch with God and the church, and then finally found her way back. Stephanie had been right, once the questions started it was hard for Cindy to keep up. As the first bell rang to indicate there were only five minutes left, Cindy gasped.

"We're nowhere close to being through!" she yelped.

"You've got to come back next week," Lori insisted. "Stephanie won't mind."

"I don't know if I could handle the stress of this another week."

"Well, you don't have to teach anything," Lauren told her. "You never even got to my question, and it was really good."

"Please, say you'll come back," Kaleigh pleaded.

Cindy shrugged her shoulders and eventually nodded. The girls cheered, and Cindy almost burst into tears. This morning had gone very well.

She sat in the choir loft and tried her hardest to pay attention to Pastor Jon's sermon, but with Kyle sitting on the front row and Kylla dancing in a pew on the left side of the church with her mother and Barbara Wright letting her do pretty much as she pleased, Cindy was lost to the message. Kylla was active, but quiet, and too adorable for words. Kyle, however, was intent on the sermon, and his serious look made him seem more handsome than ever. Yet the thing that Cindy found most attractive about him this morning was that he was absorbed in the preaching of the Word. It had meant the world to her when he prayed with her before class, and to see him engrossed in what Jonathan was saying made her realize that there were Godly men out there, men completely opposite of those she had dated over the years.

She remembered a youth camp once when a former Miss America contestant was talking with the girls about *love, sex and dating*. At that time, Cindy paid very little attention to what anybody had to say at Christian events, but this woman had managed it. She was a *somebody* and she was taking her time to speak to these girls about something she found important.

"We all have our lists of the perfect man," Miss Alabama told them, "but what are we doing to become the perfect woman to attract him? We want men to be polite and gentlemanly, we want them to think we're special, and we want them to be Godly, but we walk around with our smart mouths, cutting everybody down, gossiping, and so often we do as little as possible to grow in our relationships with the Lord or to protect our purity. I'm here to tell you: if you want a Godly man, you've got to be a Godly woman, and that starts right now by choosing decisions that make you a Godly girl first."

Cindy had been far from Godly, and the result had been men who cared no more for God than she. But now, the thing that drew her to Kyle more than anything else was his commitment to the Lord even though his life had been shattered into a million pieces.

He caught her looking at him and he smiled at her. She felt her face grow warm; she hadn't meant to stare. He winked at her but quickly turned his attention back to the preaching.

After lunch, Cindy and Kyle insisted on cleaning the kitchen and told everyone else to relax. It was more fun than it was work, but a double scream from the great room had them dropping their towels and running.

"Look!" Sue screamed again. "Watch this!"

Barbara was holding a standing Kylla by the fingers and Sue's arms were outstretched.

"Come to Granny Sue," she coaxed the baby. "Come on! Come here!"

It took Kylla a few moments, but she finally stepped out and waddled over to Sue's arms where she was picked up and twirled around immediately.

"She walked!" Cindy exclaimed. "Oh, my gosh, Kyle!"

"I had no idea she was ready to walk!" Kyle said throwing his hands up. "You ladies keep beating me to all the punches! I'm missing all these firsts with her!"

"Well, then, you just need to have more babies," Sue stated. "You're bound to catch some of these moments if you have a houseful."

"I think I'll prefer a wife for the next round, thanks."

"Then get on it!" Sue cried. "You're not getting any younger."

After finishing the kitchen, Kyle and Cindy took Kylla outside so she could walk in the grass. There was no stopping her. Cindy finally pulled off her heels and walked—or ran—around barefooted in her Sunday dress as she chased Kylla all over the backyard. Kyle would occasionally scoop the baby up and nuzzle her for a moment, but she was anxious to get back down and start going again. When the two adults felt they could barely go on from exhaustion, Kylla collapsed in Cindy's arms on the swing and fell fast asleep.

"This is a beautiful sight," Kyle said as he sat down next to Cindy and laid his arm behind her on the swing.

"What? A still Kylla?"

"Well," he laughed gently, "that too. I was talking about you and Kylla. You know, it's strange, because even though in the back of my mind I know that Caryn was her mother, she looks nothing like her. She looks like she should be your daughter, Cindy. Blond hair, blue eyes, dimples …"

She was overcome by the suggestion. She loved Kylla as though she was her own. "Thank you," she whispered softly. "I might have to fight my mother for her though."

"Oh, I think Granny Sue is just fine in the role of grandmother."

She nodded as she brushed her chin across the top of Kylla's head. The baby sighed and Cindy's heart skipped a beat. She had no idea that it was possible to love someone so deeply. She wondered if a man and a woman could love this deeply also. She had never fallen in love before; she had avoided it. And although she knew she loved Kyle, it was *unofficial.* They were not acting on it, talking about it, or attempting to move forward with it. Because of that, she kept her feelings well guarded and tried to be happy with moments like these right now that were few and far between.

"Have you ever wanted to have a child?" Kyle asked her.

"No," she said quickly. "In fact, the whole prospect scared the daylights out of me."

"Why? You're so good with Kylla. It's almost as if you just picked up naturally where Caryn left off."

"I can't explain it. Maybe it was because she was so vulnerable, or so beautiful. I don't know, but when I saw her in that room at Reese and

Alicia's, my heart nearly fell through the floor. It was like love at first sight."

"Just think, if you could love a baby so quickly without having seen her before, imagine feeling one growing inside of you for nine months."

The thought overwhelmed Cindy. The concept of carrying a child and giving birth had never seemed pleasant in any way to her, but after Kyle's statement, she felt herself longing to experience it. Would she be a good mother? Could she handle that responsibility twenty-four hours a day? If it were possible, she would gladly spend every moment of her day with Kylla. She always ached inside whenever she had to leave her to move on with the responsibilities of real life. Could it be that she actually had desires for motherhood? My, she had come farther than she could ever have imagined.

Thirty-Eight

Sometimes Jonathan loved deacons meetings, but Sunday afternoon was one of those that made him wish he had never pastored at all. He should have known the minute John Cramer and David Deaton walked in together that trouble was brewing, but Jonathan was on a ministerial high because everything in the church was *working*. Attendance was up, finances were actually ahead for a change, Cindy had impressed everyone with her work, and Kyle had brought a whole new level to the music ministry—like nothing this church had ever seen before. In fact, Jonathan actually felt sorry somewhat for Harvest Hollow. Had it been a legitimate trade, Dockrey would have been on the winning end. Kyle was a step above any music man he had ever seen, and it was more than just his musical abilities; it was the man himself.

After several rounds of typical business, going over this and that, Jonathan was prepared to adjourn when David Deaton said he had some new business to bring up.

"I've been a little concerned about the situation concerning our *interim* secretary," and he stressed the word *interim*, "and our *interim* music minister. It was my understanding that we were hiring them until we could form committees to begin searching for permanent replacements."

"Your point being?" Jonathan asked carefully.

"My point is very obvious. We have no committees formed as of yet, and people are beginning to act as though … as though everything should go on as it is right now."

"You feel like this is a problem?" Jonathan was still being cautious. He knew exactly what David Deaton wanted to do, and he needed to be careful that this didn't turn into a Jonathan vs. David predicament.

"I feel like our church needs to move on," David was trying to sound earnest and caring. "We're in limbo. Why have no committees been organized? Why haven't we been moving forward?"

"Are you concerned about their quality of service?" Jonathan posed. "As far as I've heard, everyone seems to be pleased with the jobs both Cindy and Kyle are doing. Are you complaining?"

"No, I'm not *complaining*," David cleared his throat. "The issue isn't whether they're adequate or not. The issue is that they were supposed to be temporary, and now they've been here for five months. As I see it, no one is doing anything to follow what we agreed upon."

Jonathan leaned back in his chair and brought his fingers together.

What was the best approach to this? Before he had a chance to answer, Floyd Benson spoke up.

"I'm a little confused, David." Floyd looked at him soberly. "What exactly is the rush?"

"Rush? It's been five months! They're temporaries! I want two committees formed as soon as possible so this church can get back on its feet."

"Back on its feet?" Ricky Tatum joined in this time. "What's wrong with our church? As far as I can see, it's in the best shape of its life. Attendance is at an all time high, giving is actually ahead of our needs for a change, and people seem to be thriving in Sunday School, worship services, and even Discipleship Training."

"David isn't saying there are any problems." John Cramer rose and went to stand behind David. "He's saying that as a deacon board, we had agreed to hire Cindy Marcum, a woman of questionable reputation, as our church secretary with the understanding that a committee would be working on a permanent replacement. Then we agreed to hire Kyle Sarkos, a divorced man, to lead our church in worship, once again with the understanding that a committee would be in the process of finding a legitimate replacement. Yet the fact remains that nothing has been done to move us toward those *legitimate* replacements."

"I like Cindy," Ricky said cheerfully. "In fact, I'll just be honest with you: I used to shake in my shoes whenever I had to call the office for something when Kaye was here. She was like a sergeant, you know? And it never mattered what the reason, by the time I hung up I wished I'd never called."

"Know the feeling," laughed Charles Emerson.

"But with Cindy, she's so cheerful and cordial. In fact, she always asks about my family, my girls and such, as though it mattered who I was."

"And then there's the bulletin each week," Charles added this time. "It looks like we hired it out to some professional printer or something."

"She has an incredible command of the computer," Floyd continued with the praise. "You should've seen the program she made for the Senior Adult Banquet last month. It was marvelous."

"Then there's the financial reports," Ricky came back in again.

This comment brought Charles to life. "Absolutely! I can actually understand them now!"

"Hold on! Hold on!" David Deaton practically yelled as the other ten deacons vocally agreed to the positive changes in the financial statements. "This isn't about the efficiency of Cindy Marcum! This is about her reputation and the fact that she is involved in every intimate detail of our church!"

"Last time I checked, our church was a church that practiced the principles of the Scriptures," Floyd brought up. "I believe forgiveness is one of those principles."

Ricky added, "Foundational, I would think."

"Okay, hang on, everyone," Jonathan said as he sat up and put his hands out for everyone to settle down. "Let's bring this back to the point."

David interrupted by reiterating, "Which is that Cindy Marcum is meant to be an interim!"

"David … John," Jonathan was trying to sound as calm and reasonable as possible. "There's no disagreement about the fact that they were meant to be temporary. When I brought up Cindy's name with the idea of hiring her on here, I believed it was from the Lord. Something told me it was the right thing to do. Now, I don't exactly know why God wanted this. Maybe it was for us? Maybe it was for Cindy? I'm not really sure. But I will tell you something I *am* sure about: I felt God wanted to accomplish something, and as far as I can tell, that something hasn't happened yet."

"For crying out loud, Jonathan!" John Cramer exploded. "What are you waiting for? Lightning?"

"Maybe? I don't know. But my spirit tells me it's not yet time for her to go."

"You aren't the only one who hears from God in this church," David said with a threatening tone.

Ricky jumped to his feet and looked straight at David as he said, "That's right, Deaton. And I think that a lot of us in this room have been hearing the *same* thing as Jonathan: it's not time for Cindy to go … nor Kyle for that matter."

"Now wait just a minute!" John Cramer joined back in. "This Kyle fellow has swung in here and mesmerized just about everybody! Harvest Hollow knew exactly what they were doing when they fired him! We're idiots to think some divorced man who can't even control his own wife should come in here and run a *huge* ministry in our church!"

Charles, normally sedate and easy-going stood to his feet. "Interesting word there, John, that word *huge*. The music ministry is *huge* now, like never before, and that has to do specifically with the talents, organizational skills *and* ministerial skills of Kyle Sarkos."

Floyd followed that with, "We could never afford anyone with the qualities and abilities of Kyle. For heaven's sake! This is Dockrey, Alabama! Population 3,852! If you want to see what the Kyle Sarkoses of this world are doing, you need to tune in your television to Memphis or Nashville; not even Huntsville has anyone like him!"

David Deaton was all over it. "I am *not* questioning his abilities! I am questioning his integrity! He is divorced, and it is our policy not to hire divorced ministers!"

"Is that in the constitution and by-laws, Deaton?" asked Ricky

Tatum who had just finished a revision of them on a committee last fall. "I don't recall that."

"Okay, okay," Jonathan stood this time and ran his fingers through his hair as he walked to the front of the room. "This is getting out of hand gentlemen. The issue here isn't what *we* think or how *we* feel about Kyle or Cindy, adequate or inadequate. The issue is whether God would have us move them out at this time … or wait."

"I think five months has been more than enough time for them to *do* whatever it is you think they should *do*," David griped.

"See, that's the whole point, David," Jonathan tried to clarify. "I have no agenda here; this is about what God has planned … for them … and for our church."

"But five months, Jonathan!" John Cramer complained.

"We're not measuring time in our terms here, men. God told Abraham to go to a place that He would show him. He gave no specifics. It took a lot more time than Abraham would have liked, I'm sure. It was twelve years from the time Joseph had his dreams until God placed him as second in command to Pharaoh. Noah built an ark in his backyard for over a hundred years while the world ridiculed him. He just obeyed God and trusted his timing. That's all I'm trying to do here: obey God and trust *His* timing."

"Amen," said Charles under his breath.

The worship service that evening was exceptionally moving. Kyle had organized a youth led service with lots of Scripture reading and instrumentalists on and off between the congregation's singing of unusual arrangements of hymns and choruses. Jonathan had walked into the service following the deacon meeting feeling as though he were the wrong man for the job—regardless of his twenty-eight years here—but when it came time for him to enter the pulpit, his spirit had been so moved that he felt he could almost touch the gates of heaven. To see teenagers share their talents and be willing to read and lead in worship to this degree was something that had never happened before at First Baptist. And it was interesting to note that neither David Deaton's nor John Cramer's teenagers participated.

Thirty-Nine

"Want to go on a picnic?" Kyle asked Cindy the following Friday morning at work. "The weather is gonna be gorgeous tomorrow, and I'd love to take Kylla out somewhere for a change."

"Do you think that'd be safe?" she asked with concern. They had been careful to keep her behind the fence as much as possible.

"I'll talk to Agent Hall. Maybe they can send some kind of protection, or at least have someone following us."

"Well, if they think it's okay. What'd you have in mind?"

"I don't know, just get out of Dockrey and go somewhere else for a change."

She giggled. "Are you finally starting to get the Dockrey blues?"

"Dockrey blues? What's that?"

"It's what happens when you live in Dockrey for too long. You feel closed in, nothing to do but the same-old same-old. You start itching to get out. It's really bad when you're a teenager."

He laughed and imagined it was. "Maybe that's it. I just want to *do* something different—I want Kylla to see something other than the four walls of the Wrights' house and the inside of the church."

"Call Ben Hall first. If we don't have protection, I don't even want to think about it."

"Agreed."

Kyle leaned against the counter of the office's small, makeshift kitchen and punched in the name of Ben Hall.

"Hello, Kyle," answered Agent Hall. "What's up?"

"I want to get Kylla out of Dockrey for a day, just take her somewhere fun for awhile. Maybe have a picnic, see something a little girl might think is incredible."

"Good idea. Can you take Miss Marcum with you?"

"I can try; she gets rather ornery sometimes." He winked at Cindy.

"This is the kind of stuff we've been wanting from you two. The more time you spend out together, the more convinced those following you will be that Kylla belongs to the two of you."

"It's just hard; we're so busy, and then it's scary taking her away from the security of the house."

"We understand. How about the zoo?"

"There's a zoo? Where?"

"There's a nice one in Memphis. It's big, and we could have agents all over that place keeping an eye on you, and keeping an eye on *them*."

"Is there a place to picnic? I really want Kylla to have a picnic."

"Hang on." Ben Hall called someone over and discussed the zoo for a moment. He got back on the phone and said, "That's a thumbs up; they have a picnic area outside."

"Super! When should we leave?"

"You name it, and we'll have a tail pick you up when you pass Bubba's Gas and Auto."

He put down his phone and asked Cindy, "What time you want to leave?"

"Where are we going?"

"The zoo in Memphis."

"Hmmm, it'll take about two and a half hours … how about nine o'clock?" Kyle lifted the phone "I'll leave around nine o'clock, pick up Cindy, and then head out."

"Got it. Now, I have something I'd like you and Miss Marcum to consider. It's rather involved, but it would answer some questions and maybe even give us some much-needed information. Want to hear it now?"

"Shoot." Kyle winced. That was twice he had told an FBI agent to *shoot*. "I mean, yeah, now is fine."

"We'd like you, Miss Marcum, and Kylla to take a trip to Martha's Vineyard to see Kylla's *supposed* grandparents."

"But we've already determined the Carters didn't live there."

"No, we said the people who *did* live there are named Jackson and Miranda Malone. But we also know—from your identifying them in the photo—that they are Bill and Linda Carter, Caryn's parents. We thought we could send the three of you up there, let you show up for a visit at their house, and then see what happens."

"Wow, okay. That'd be really weird. Do you think they'd tell me something?"

"Who knows, but in the process we might possibly discover who Caryn actually was."

Kyle furrowed his brow and Cindy mouthed a *what is it* at him. "Let me talk it over with Cindy, and then talk to the pastor. I'll get back with you about that."

When he hung up, he looked soberly at her and said, "He wants me and you and Kylla to go to Martha's Vineyard and see Caryn's parents."

She was stunned by the suggestion. "That would be a major trip for Kylla. What do you think?"

"I don't know. We'll see."

***

On Friday evening, Kyle and Cindy sat with Kylla and looked through her book of zoo animals. They pointed out all the different creatures she would see on Saturday, and she squealed in glee every time they saw the monkeys.

"Monk-monk," she would laugh as she pointed at them. Of course, each animal's eye was always touched and pointed out, followed by the declaration, *eye.*

Kyle walked Cindy to her car as they made their final plans.

"Don't forget the stroller," she reminded him. "And are you sure you're up to making lunch? That's a lot of work. We could just do Burger King or something."

"No way! Kylla's first picnic is *not* going to be fast food."

"Whatever you say." She opened her car door. "Do you want me to bring anything?"

"Just your sweet, little, cute self."

"Puh-leeze," she said shaking her head as she got into the car.

***

The next morning went smoothly. Kylla was excited about the monkeys they would see, Kyle had actually fried chicken while Barbara made her famous potato salad, and Cindy braided her hair as she imagined trying to deal with the heat that had been forecasted for the day. Kyle had changed the hard top on his Jeep to the canvas so that if it was warm enough when they reached Memphis, he could put the top down.

As they passed Bubba's Gas, they noticed a non-descript white car pull out behind them. He showed it to Cindy so she would calm down about being out and about with Kylla. As was usual, after about thirty minutes of driving, Kylla fell asleep. If what the neighbors had said about Caryn was true, Kylla never rode in a vehicle except home from the hospital after her birth. Apparently the lull of the motion made her drift.

"Why is First Baptist out in the middle of nowhere?" Kyle asked. "You'd think a First Baptist Church would be stuck smack dab in the middle of town."

"Long story," Cindy yawned. "Do you really want to hear it?"

"Yes. What are you so tired for? Stay up late? I didn't keep you out too long."

"There was a Martin Sartin movie on last night. I couldn't help it; he's so hilarious."

"I love Martin Sartin! Which movie was it?"

"The Blue-Eyed Bumbler."

"Oh, man! One of my favorites! I wish I had known."

"I would've called you," Cindy mumbled as she stretched out in her seat. "I didn't know you were a fan."

"What time was it over?"

"Two thirty."

"Good lands! No wonder you're tired. I like Martin Sartin, but I would have never stayed up that late—I don't think I *could* have stayed up that late."

"I'm beginning to think it was a bad idea myself," she said as she glanced back to check on a peaceful Kylla.

"Forget the church story—go to sleep."

She smiled gratefully as she folded up the picnic blanket to use as a pillow. "Wake me when we get there," she yawned.

When Kyle reached the outskirts of Memphis, he pulled into a gas station to put the top down. Cindy went in to use the restroom, and Kylla laughed in amusement at having no roof above her. The white car drove past him and parked at the store area. Kyle's phone sang its silly tune.

"Hello?"

"You've got a tail all right." Kyle looked over to the white car. Agent Morrow waved his phone as Agent Sparks sat on the passenger's side.

"Yeah, *you* guys are tailing me. I picked up on that before we even left Dockrey," Kyle replied as he snapped the canvas down.

"No, not just us," Morrow said. "There's a black Corvette."

"Corvette, huh?" Kyle grinned. "Bet it makes you guys a little envious, huh? All you got was the white clunker."

Silence.

Cindy returned from the restroom and waved at the white car as she passed. Agent Morrow shook his head soberly. She shrugged.

"Glad I put my hair in this braid," she said as she climbed into her seat with a fresh cup of steaming coffee. She turned back to see Kylla. "Hello, Sweetie. Do you like Daddy's car? Where did the top go?"

"Dadda!" she yelled out. "Monk-monk!"

"Yes, I can believe that," Cindy grinned over at him as he finished with the canvas. "Dadda's a monk-monk."

Kyle just shook his head as he jumped up into the Jeep. He leaned way back to give Kylla a kiss and she poked him in the eye while announcing, "Dadda's eye!"

He rubbed his eye. "Yes. That's Daddy's eye. Nice of you to notice."

Cindy was impressed with Kyle's picnic. Her versions of picnics had always been sandwiches and chips, and in truth, they had been minimal. She never cared for eating with the ants and flies, and in north Alabama, the insect list would include yellow jackets. But as the three of them ate, she found herself enjoying it. She and Kyle alternated giving Kylla bites of chicken and potato salad, but she only wanted to stand up and run around. The picnic area was lush and green and spacious, so they just let her go. She would grab her sippy-cup, run for a little bit, then come back for another bite of food. Her cheeks were getting pink from the heat, but it didn't seem to bother her.

"Are there more agents around here other than the two parked in the white car?" Cindy asked as she lay back on the blanket.

"Probably. I wouldn't even begin to try and pick them out."

"I think I'm gonna let you two go inside the zoo," she yawned as she rolled over on her side. "I'm just gonna park it right here and go to sleep again."

"Oh, no you don't," he said as he leaned over to her. "You've got zoo duty today. I can't help it if you're infatuated with Martin Sartin."

"What if I refuse?"

"I'll have to force you then."

"Good luck," she said with another yawn as she rolled to her back.

"Okay ... just remember you forced me to do this." He inched his way down to her feet—where she had removed her sandals—and began to lightly drag his fingernail across the bottom of one.

"Stop," she said irritated as she jerked her foot up.

He ignored her and grabbed her ankle as he began to tickle her feet even more. She tried not to laugh, but she couldn't stand it.

"Stop it!" she said more forcefully now. Kylla ran over and began to giggle as Cindy continued laughing and protesting.

"Okay! Okay!" she cried, but he wouldn't stop.

Kylla jumped on top of Cindy's tummy and began to bounce up and down as she laughed.

"That's my girl!" Kyle exclaimed as Cindy tried to deal with both the tickling and Kylla's bouncing. "Make her get up, Kylla."

"Mama!" Kylla giggled. "Mama!" Then she poked Cindy in the eye. "Mama eye?"

"I'll get up! I promise!" She could barely breathe, and her eye was now watering from Kylla's finger. Kyle relented and pulled the baby off then stood up and held out his hand to her. She sighed in relief and let him pull her to her feet.

"That was close to torture," she said out of breath.

"Really? It didn't bother me one bit."

"I'll bet."

The zoo was fabulous, and Kylla went from one level of amusement to another. Cindy had been looking for possible agents when they first entered the zoo, but as Kylla's excitement grew, she soon forgot about potential danger and enjoyed the afternoon. Kyle was wonderful also. He reminded Cindy early on that they needed to act married, but he promised he wouldn't be as overt this time. He kept his gestures to simply placing his hand in the small of her back to lead her on, or gently pushing back a strand of loose hair that would occasionally stick to the perspiration on her face. Even with that, however, her heart would race. He had to be the kindest, gentlest man she had ever known, and that included her father.

Watching Kyle with Kylla became her favorite activity. It made her jealous at times because they had a connection with each other that she couldn't have with either of them. She wondered how Caryn could have given all this up so easily. Even if she hadn't truly loved him, she had to know the kind of man he was, and the fact that he had wanted children so badly. How could she have turned her back on him, denying Kyle a child, and denying Kylla a father who would dote and adore her endlessly? Cindy hated to admit it, but there was a part of her that despised Caryn profoundly.

If she could turn back time, knowing what she knew now, life would have been totally different. Her parents had begged her to go to Furman; they wanted her to go to a school that would have some Christian influence. She would have been there the same time as Caryn. Of course, back then Kyle would have just been one of many guys on campus, but surely she would have been drawn to him. He captured her heart now with just a wink or a smile. She could have saved him the humiliation of a divorce, could have stood by his side in the ministry, and Kylla could have been hers. *Hers.* At least she could dream that would have happened. But the truth was that at that time, Cindy's heart was black and her motives were selfish. Even the wonderful Kyle may not have turned her head. It took something deeper than that: the death of her father.

"What's on that pretty mind of yours?" he asked after putting Kylla back into her stroller for the trek to the next animal. "You don't seem happy with the hyenas right now. Bad memories from *The Lion King*?"

She smiled at his never-ending wit. "You and Kylla are lucky. Waking up to each other every morning, knowing you have the rest of your days to spend together—I can't imagine having that kind of connection with someone."

"It's wonderful. It almost seems like a dream sometimes because of all I lost with Caryn. I really thought my chances for happiness were gone. But now, even the divorce doesn't bother me anymore, especially with all this crazy stuff we're finding out about her. Did she ever really love me? That hurts more than anything. But when I look at Kylla, it doesn't matter. She was a product of *my* love, and that's all that counts."

Cindy looped her arm inside his and leaned her head against his shoulder. How was it possible that a man could be so wonderful? Her brother was a complete jerk; every other man she had ever dated was a complete jerk. She wished she could somehow put Kyle out of her head, but her love for Kylla would always connect them, even when they were gone. She knew she would wonder how Kylla was growing and what she would be doing, and as she thought of that, she would have to think of

Kyle. But then, some thoughts of him would stand on their own.

After the zoo, they drove through McDonalds for supper and headed back to Dockrey. The day had been perfect, and Kylla was worn out. They tried to force a few French fries down her, but it soon became obvious that she was going to sleep, empty stomach and all. The trip was relaxing, and the conversation light and easy. By the time Kyle drove into Cindy's driveway, she was ready for sleep herself.

He jumped from the Jeep, and she knew that meant he was coming to open her door. She slipped on her sandals and waited for him to come around. He offered his hand, and she gladly took it as he helped her down from the seat, but he didn't let go as he walked her up to the deck.

"Is this for the benefit of those watching us?" she asked as she squeezed his hand.

"If you want to believe that, then *yes*. But personally, I have wanted to do this all day. I love your braid, by the way."

She was blushing again. He could always say the right thing at the right moment. Pretending to be married to Kyle Sarkos was fun, but it was also scary. One day the game would be over, and Kyle and Kylla would move on with their lives. Cindy, however, was beginning to doubt that she could ever move on again. Yet she had survived her father's death; she would somehow survive losing Kyle and Kylla too.

Forty

Agent Ben Hall sat in the church office with Jonathan, Kyle and Cindy as they discussed the possible trip to Martha's Vineyard. Kyle was nervous; he wasn't a good liar, and the thought of trying to convince the Carters, a.k.a. the Malones, that he was ignorant of their involvement with Caryn's lies made his stomach churn relentlessly. He also dreaded having to bring Kylla. What if something happened?

"The whole island will be crawling with agents," Ben told him. "You'll know where we are this time too. A white van will be monitoring your movements, and you'll be wearing wires. Every conversation will be recorded. There's no way anyone can get to you—or Kylla."

Kyle breathed a deep sigh and glanced over to Cindy. She just shrugged her shoulders.

"I'm willing to do whatever needs to be done," she said. "But I'm like Kyle; I'm nervous."

Agent Hall pulled out a brochure and handed it to her. "This is a bed and breakfast, more like a bed and restaurant. They have a top floor suite where the three of you will be staying."

"Wait a second," Jonathan held up his hand to halt the conversation. "You need to remember they're not actually married. They can't stay together in an inn. That would just be ... well ... wrong. And if the church ever found out ..."

"No problem, pastor. It's a suite with two bedrooms, and a center living area. We thought of that. They're very private ... the bedrooms. In fact, because the bathroom is in a separate hallway, they many times will rent one of the rooms out by itself. Officially, it's a top floor suite. For this case, it can be two separate rooms."

Jonathan leaned back in his chair, folded his arms, and thought for a moment. He finally nodded and said, "That would work."

"Great," Ben continued. "The rest of the rooms will be filled with our agents only; we would reserve the entire house for our staff. No one else can get in—except for the restaurant—and it'll be monitored twenty-four hours a day the entire weekend."

"That sounds safe," Cindy said with relief. "I feel a little better about it now."

"Kyle?" Ben looked over at him.

He was still unsure. The thought of being blatantly deceitful was still weighing on him.

"They'll be all around us, Kyle," Cindy encouraged. "And it might possibly answer some of the questions everybody has about Caryn."

Ben continued his appeal. "You need to understand, Kyle, that at this point in time we have no clue as to Caryn's true identity. As far as we know, the only people who could tell us are the Malones, or the Carters, whoever they are. Our best chance at finding out who Caryn was, and then hopefully why she was murdered, is this trip." He paused. "We really need you to do this for us."

Kyle looked over at Cindy again. If she was for it, somehow he could make himself do this. Her blue eyes looked back with unmeasured compassion, and she nodded her head slightly. She was willing.

"Okay," he finally complied. "When do we leave?"

"As soon as possible," Ben said with more energy than Kyle had seen in him before.

"Wait," Cindy stopped them. "Kylla's birthday is this weekend, June 20. Can we get past that first? Let us celebrate that here, and then you can plan whatever you want."

"The next weekend?" Ben suggested.

Kyle and Cindy looked at each other again and nodded hesitantly. It was settled.

***

"Oh no!" Barbara was frantic as she came running into the dining room, phone in hand. "Andie's in labor! Doug is getting ready to run her up to Helen Keller Hospital right now! Jonathan, you need to get the kids!"

"And they're off!" Jonathan dropped his forkful of Kylla's birthday cake and stood up at once. "So Andie goes first, huh. Annie and Angie should be right behind her."

"Jonathan!" Barbara exclaimed. "This is no time for joking! Go get the kids; I'm going to Helen Keller!"

"I want to go too. It's my grandchild also."

"I'll get the kids and bring them back here, Pastor Jon," Cindy offered. "Kyle and I should be able to handle them pretty well."

"These kids aren't like Kylla, honey," Barbara cautioned. "They're a little more ... adventurous?"

"And just think," Jonathan grinned as he rubbed his hands together, "number five is on the way even as we speak."

"We can handle them," Kyle assured them. "I've got Adam and Arly for music lessons and choir; I've already established some authority with them."

"Yeah, right," Jonathan smirked as he grabbed his keys.

Cindy followed Jonathan and Barbara out the door, but then remembered she needed something more than her two-seater Thunderbird to bring back four kids.

"Mom? Can I have your keys? I'd have to tie most of them to the outside if I took my car ... although that might possibly scare the wildness out of them."

"They're in it," Sue called back to her.

The afternoon with Doug and Andie's kids was beyond merely eventful; it was downright chaotic. Adam, Arly and Ashley all understood that a new baby was on its way. Aimee and Kylla had great fun playing together. But the fact remained that there were five young, creative minds and bodies all in the same house, and things were falling apart quickly. Cindy tried to pick up behind them, and a smile rose to her lips as she remembered Alicia's self-consciousness over her house when they had gone to get Kylla. At least there was plenty of cake and ice cream left over from the party to go around.

"It's a girl!" Kyle called out after a phone call from the hospital around five thirty. "Seven pounds and six ounces!"

"Yea!" Ashley screamed. "We've got more giwls than boys now! We win!"

"Yeah, well what if she's a tomboy?" Arly said snidely.

"She's still a giwl ... so there!"

The phone rang again and Kyle went back into the kitchen. "Hello?"

"Yes," said a frantic male voice. "Is Barbara or Jonathan there?"

"Not at the moment," Kyle replied. "They're at Helen Keller Hospital; Andie just had her baby."

"You're kidding? What was it?"

"A girl."

"Wow! This is unbelievable! This is Stephen; Annie and I are in the limo and on our way to the hospital right now!"

"Stephen?" Kyle nearly fainted at the thought of talking to Stephen Williams.

"Yeah! Isn't this wild? Does Jonathan have his cell with him?"

"Yes," Kyle was trying to gain his composure.

"Okay then, I'll call him there. Let me guess from the noise in the background: you've got Andie's kids."

"Bingo."

"Hang in there. Here's a hint: order pizza and put on a movie. It works like magic with that crew."

"Thanks for the tip. I'll call Mr. P's as soon as we hang up."

"Allright then, good luck."

"You guys too. Let us know what happens."

"I will!"

Kyle walked back into the great room with a dazed look.

"What's wrong?" Cindy asked alarmed.

"That was Stephen Williams. I just talked to Stephen Williams. I'd better sit down."

"Was he calling about Andie?"

"No, he told us to order pizza for the kids and put on a movie," he said still stunned.

She plopped down beside him with an armload of army men and Jeeps she had just picked up. "Stephen called to tell us that?"

"No. He and Annie are headed to the hospital."

"Helen Keller? They're in Alabama?"

He looked over at her and tried to pull his thoughts together. "No. Annie's in labor too ... up there."

"No way!" she exclaimed. "I'm not believing this. If she has it today, that means both of their babies ... well, obviously they'll have the same birthday."

"When's the other baby due—the missionary one?"

"I believe she's still got another month to go."

Kyle found out what the kids liked, and then ordered pizza. They looked through the DVD cabinet and decided on the movie. Cindy smiled when she read it was over two hours long. That should keep them still for a while. The phone rang, and she hurried back to the kitchen to answer it.

"Hello?"

"Barbara?" came a distant voice.

"No, this is Cindy Marcum. Barbara and Jonathan are at the hospital; Andie just had a baby girl."

"Really?" came a laugh. The phone was pulled away and she heard, "It's Cindy Marcum—Andie just had a girl too!" He spoke back into the phone. "Angie's been in labor all night ... we've got a little girl also!"

"What? Is this Michael?"

"Yeah," he was still laughing. "Hang on, Angie wants to talk to you."

Cindy's eyes immediately began to fill with tears. Her best buddy in the whole world had just had a baby. She was so happy for her that she knew she would cry when she heard her voice.

"Cindy?" Angie sounded exhausted.

"Oh," she started sobbing immediately. "Is this really you, Angie?"

"I can't believe I'm talking to you either! I'm a mom, Cindy. I have the most beautiful baby girl you've ever seen."

"I wish I were there with you right now."

"No you don't," Angie laughed. "You would be exhausted. It took all night to get her here."

"I didn't realize you were due right away. I knew it was soon, but not this soon."

"I wasn't; she's a month early, but her lungs are fully developed and she weighs five pounds, three ounces. She's gonna be fine."

"Have you talked with anyone in your family?"

"No," Angie said exhausted. "I was calling Moms and Dad first."

"You're not gonna believe this, then." Cindy began to giggle.

"What's so funny?"

"Michael told you about Andie's baby—but Annie is labor as we speak."

There was dead silence.

"This is impossible," Angie finally uttered. "At least my sisters have been suffering with me through all this."

"Not too much. Andie left around two o'clock and the baby came about five thirty."

"I don't want to hear that," Angie moaned. "I did this for sixteen hours."

"It was her fifth. She knows how to just spit them out now."

Angie laughed again. "I wish I could have just spit this little one out."

"What did you name her?"

"Cassandra," Angie said as the emotion returned to her voice. "She's so beautiful. I wish you could see her."

"I will someday," Cindy tried to hold back the tears again. "You know I will. Just send me some pictures for now."

It was nearly eleven thirty when the Wrights returned from the hospital in Sheffield. They came dragging in exhausted but wore huge smiles.

"Did Angie get in touch with you?" Cindy asked as she pulled herself from the couch where she and Kyle had been watching television.

"Yes," Barbara oozed with grandmotherness. "Can you believe it? Three granddaughters within a few hours, and from three different mothers."

"Did Annie have hers too? Another girl?" Cindy was elated.

"Little Ellen Williams named after Stephen's mother. Where's Sue? I see her car's still here."

"Upstairs with Kylla and Aimee," Cindy nodded toward the apartment. "She insisted she would get them to sleep; we haven't seen her since."

"So, how was your day with the Mason clan?" Barbara grinned almost guiltily.

"Exciting would not even come close to describing our day. I have a whole new respect for Andie."

As if on cue, Adam and Arly came running out from the master bedroom.

"Mimi! Is it really another old girl?" Arly asked in near disgust.

"She's beautiful, boys. You will love her to death," Barbara told them as she knelt down and hugged each in a different arm.

"Boys," Jonathan said sternly, "I'm afraid I've got even more bad news."

"What, Gaga?" Adam asked.

"Aunt Angie had a little girl too. Her name's Cassandra. And Aunt Annie had one named Ellen. You guys started us out right, but I'm afraid after today, girl's definitely rule."

"Aw, man!" Arly said with a huge pout. "Just don't tell Ashley. She's been really obnoxious about this."

Cindy couldn't help but laugh. It was funny to hear such a big word come from such a small boy.

"What's our baby's name, Gaga? Did they name her 'laina like Mama said?" Adam asked.

"Alaina," Barbara corrected him. "It starts with an A, dear."

"Oh yeah. Why did ya'll all do that? Why did we all have to have A names. I wanted a B name."

"B? What name would you liked to have had, sweetie?"

"Brutus!" Adam exclaimed as his eyes lit up.

"Brutus?" Barbara repeated in shock. "Why on earth would you want to be called Brutus?"

"'Cause he's tough and gruff, right Mr. Kyle?"

Barbara looked over to Kyle on the couch, and he stood quickly as if embarrassed.

"Kyle? Who is Brutus?" Barbara asked him.

"You know," Adam jumped in to explain. "Even Gruff Brutus Dusts Furniture … the lines in music, Mimi."

Barbara looked back at Kyle with a puzzled look. "I thought that was Every Good Boy Does Fine?"

Kyle blushed. "Well, they're young boys, nine and seven. I thought something a little more … uh … boyish would be more appealing to them."

Cindy couldn't help it; she burst out in laughter. Jonathan followed, and then eventually Barbara joined in, still shaking her head in amazement.

"Does this mean I won't be tarred and feathered for teaching music unconventionally?" Kyle wondered.

Kyle and Cindy went upstairs to check on Sue and the little girls. They found her asleep on the bed with a girl on either side cradled in her arms.

"How sweet," Cindy whispered. "She's eating this up, you know?"

"She should be. She needs to be a grandmother right now."

Cindy sighed and rolled her eyes. She sure wasn't contributing to that need. "I don't know what she's gonna do when you and Kylla leave. She even has her calling her Granny Sue. I think somewhere in her mind she has adopted her as a granddaughter."

Kyle put his arm around Cindy so he could whisper in her ear, "Then that makes Kylla's life almost complete. If only someone would adopt her as a mother."

Cindy looked up at him bewildered. "Trust me, Kyle, that won't be hard. When the right woman meets the two of you, she'll be smitten."

"I'm hoping so," Kyle said as he gently held a strand of her hair and began to run it between his fingers.

Forty-One

After two days with the Mason kids underfoot, Kyle was thankful to be back in the office again Monday morning. He loved the kids, and had grown closer to them while Andie and Doug stayed at the hospital, but he was ready for a break. Jonathan and Barbara had taken them yesterday after church to see their parents and the new baby, Alaina, thrilling them by a stop at McDonalds for Sunday lunch. Kyle, Cindy and Sue had dinner at the Marcums' for a change. Kyle was struggling more and more with his attachment to both Sue and Cindy. Sue treated him as though he were the son she had always wanted, and Cindy was refreshing, wonderful, intoxicating. There was nothing gloomy or dark about these women. They laughed, they teased, and they enjoyed life wholly. It was even harder that Cindy glowed with beauty. It seemed each time he saw her, her eyes looked bluer, her smile sweeter, and her body even more tempting. He tried not to think about her that way, but it was hard. At this point, he loved her more than he had ever loved Caryn, yet she continued to let him know they had no future together. He tried to push his feelings deep inside, but when she held Kylla and gently kissed her cheeks or rubbed her lips across the top of Kylla's soft hair, all he could imagine was sharing the rest of his life with her. And sharing meant sharing everything.

Get a grip, Sarkos.

He was telling himself the same thing as he left his office to ask Cindy to print out address labels for a choir letter. Her back was to him, and she had propped her head on her hand as she stared out the window by her desk to the breath-taking valley beyond. He stopped for a brief time just to gaze at her. Once again, his heart melted and then sank. Why was she so persistent in avoiding him? Some moments she would open up to him like he was a best friend and then days would go by when she barely spoke.

Get a grip, Sarkos.

"Hey, beautiful," he finally said trying to sound more perky than he was feeling. "Got a minute?"

"For you, yes?" she smiled as she wheeled her chair around to face him.

He caught his heart and shook his head. "You shouldn't smile at me like that. It might make me forget that we're only pretending to be married."

"This weekend should be really fun. And we even get to play house a little."

"Don't let that get out. Officially, we're staying in two rooms."

"Three rooms, if you want to be *really* official." She grinned.

There it was again. She was flirting with him now, but tomorrow she could be as cold as ice demanding they keep their distance. Maybe she was just testing him with all of this—trying to see if he could last through the ups and downs she kept dishing out. He felt like he was in high school again with the biggest crush on the most beautiful girl in class who knew his feelings and would occasionally throw him a smile just to see the effect.

"I need ... uh ..." what was it that he needed? "Labels! Choir labels. I have some letters to go out."

She wheeled her chair back around to face the computer and begin clicking away. "I'll have them for you in a jiffy."

He stayed at his door hoping that somehow the distance would cool his feelings. It didn't seem to matter.

Suddenly she wheeled back around to ask him, "Do you know how to make Alfredo sauce—you know, that white creamy Italian sauce?"

"No, but you can get it at the grocery."

"No, no, no," she said emphatically as she shook her finger at him. "I want the real stuff."

"See if you can find a recipe," he suggested as he walked over. "Look it up online; you can find just about anything on the Internet."

"Ooo, good idea!" She spun back around, pressed print for the labels, exited the file, and then pulled up her search page. *Creamy Alfredo Sauce Recipe*, she typed in. Many came up. "Oh, my! Where do I start?"

He read the list over her shoulder then leaned down to point one out. "I've been to this site before. They have easy recipes, but they're really good."

"Great," she nearly bounced as she clicked the button.

He continued leaning down next to her and found her perfume exhilarating again. It was all he could do not to bury his face in her hair.

"Where do you wear your perfume?" he wondered out loud.

She turned her head up to look at him. "What? My perfume?"

"Yeah," he smiled, her face only inches from his. "I love it, and sometimes I would love a closer smell."

"Hmmm," her smile grew. "Here," she touched the inside of her wrists first. "Here." She touched behind both ears. "And then," she motioned just beneath her neck, "here." They continued to stare at each other, neither trying to break the gaze. "Were you wanting a closer smell at this particular moment?"

"Well, I would love one," he grinned, "but seeing that we're in the church office, and David Deaton and John Cramer would love to find some reason to kick us out of here, I'll just take a rain check."

She let her eyes break as she turned back around to the computer. "I'll hold you to that, Sarkos."

He nodded as he slowly stood up. She was definitely flirting today. Why? What made today different than the other days? He went to the printer and gathered his address labels. As he passed her desk, she glanced up at him and flashed her blue eyes again.

Get a grip, Sarkos.

When closing time rolled around, Kyle turned off the equipment and lights in his office and headed for the main room. Cindy was gathering her things and preparing to leave also.

"Find your recipe?" he asked.

"I sure did. Wanna come over for dinner tonight and see how I do?"

Absolutely! Would love to! You bet! What time? "Let me see what's happening at the Wright house this evening. They might need me to hang around and watch kids again." Was he crazy? *Go!*

"Give me a call, then. Mom's going out to dinner tonight for a Sunday School class outing; I don't want to eat Alfredo alone."

Me either. "Maybe Kylla and I can give you some company then."

***

"Let us keep Kylla," Barbara pleaded when Kyle talked of going to Cindy's. "You were so wonderful to watch the kids on Saturday. This will give you and Cindy a break."

"I don't need a break from Kylla," he said warmly as he scooped his daughter up in his arms for a hug. She hugged him briefly, but then squirmed to get back down and run. "They grow up fast, don't they? Used to be I couldn't hold her enough for her liking, now all she wants to do is run and walk—walk and run."

"Welcome to parenthood," Barbara said sweetly as she put a hand on his shoulder. "It seems like yesterday that mine were that age, and all of sudden here I am with eight grandchildren—three of which came on the same day! It doesn't seem possible."

"I'm not ready for her to grow up; I just got her."

"You've got plenty of time yet, Kyle. It'll still sneak up on you, though. Treasure every moment of every day with her."

"I will."

***

Kyle and Kylla showed up at Cindy's followed by a plain white car and a black Corvette somewhere behind him. He had noticed them both on the way over, and his heart raced just a bit. He reached for his cell and punched in Ben Hall's name.

"It's fine, Kyle," Agent Hall assured him. "You guys are well protected and under constant surveillance. Enjoy your evening. Again, it's this kind of stuff between you and Miss Marcum that keeps them guessing. This weekend ought to set it firmly: a family outing to Martha's Vineyard."

"Thanks."

Cindy grabbed Kylla immediately and began to kiss her all over. Kylla squealed and giggled and then put her arms around Cindy's neck for a tight hug. "Mama!" Kylla said in delight.

"Kylla!" Cindy responded.

"How's the Alfredo coming?" Kyle asked as he walked toward the kitchen. "Smells good."

"You should be highly impressed," she told him as she nuzzled Kylla to her chest. He couldn't believe the baby was content to just keep her head there.

"She only does that with *me* when she's ready to drop," he told her as he reached over to touch Kylla's soft curls. "She really misses you when you're not around."

"And I miss her," she confessed as she sat on the edge of the table at the breakfast nook. "I adore her, Kyle." She was brushing her lips across the top of Kylla's hair again. He melted whenever she did that.

"You know she thinks you're her mom."

"I know," she whispered sadly. "I know."

Kylla ran through the house while Kyle helped Cindy finish supper which was just plain fun. She was becoming a wonderful cook, but she was incredibly messy. He spent more time cleaning up her messes than actually cooking. After supper, they finished restoring order back to the kitchen and then went out to the glassed-in porch to relax. They could close the door off so they didn't have to keep a constant eye on Kylla, and Cindy brought out a basket of various toys she had picked up for her over the past months.

"Monk-monk!" Kylla laughed as she pulled out a stuffed monkey Cindy had gotten her from the zoo. She began to pick out one toy at a time and play quietly. Kyle scooted closer to Cindy on the couch and smiled.

"What are you up to?" she asked suspiciously.

"It's payback time."

"What do I owe you?" she said as she scooted farther away.

"You said I could smell your perfume ... you know ... up close and personal." He laughed softly as she immediately began to blush. He scooted over closer, but she was backed into the corner of the couch by now and had nowhere else to go. "You offered this afternoon, remember?" .

"I did, didn't I? Even showed you my secret spots."

"You did," he nodded as he picked up her hand and slowly brought her wrist up to his nose. He took a deep breath and closed his eyes in rhapsody. "Heavenly."

"Is it that good?" she said with a self-conscious giggle.

"Oh, much better. Words couldn't adequately describe it, but I'll try."

He reached for her other hand and slowly breathed in her wrist. "Rapturous," he said this time. "You know, they say that perfumes smell different on different people; they mingle with each person's unique scent and give off different variations of aromas."

"Is that right?" she almost whispered as he now leaned in toward an ear.

"That's what I've heard," he said softly as he pulled back her hair and moved closer. "I didn't major in science … or aromatherapy … or anything like that though."

He gently touched his nose to the area behind her ear, and she nearly collapsed, squirming slightly and tipping her head into his.

"Euphoric," he said this time as he continued to linger at her ear.

He then pulled back just enough to look into her eyes again. She smiled. He made his way to the other ear, pulling back her hair and breathing deeply.

"As for the last spot," he whispered, "that's a little too personal. I'd better hold right here."

She nodded quietly, as though her strength had been sapped. He wouldn't move, remaining barely an inch from her face, so close to kissing her again that he could almost feel his lips on hers. He looked down her face, but when he came to her lips, he closed his eyes and took a deep breath.

"Kyle," she whispered. "How far is too far? I really don't know anymore. It's been so long since … well … since …"

"This is probably too far," he whispered back. "Cindy, I wish we could … I don't even know how to say it …"

"We don't need to be alone, do we?"

"We're not. Kylla's here."

She smiled slightly, but before she could speak, he leaned in to kiss her. It was pointless fighting it. She put her arms around him and pulled him closer to her. The kiss intensified, and soon his hands were in her hair.

"Dadda!" Kylla yelled out.

Kyle forced himself to pull away and give attention to the little blond now pulling on his pants leg.

"You're ruining the moment," he told her as he released Cindy's hair and reached down for Kylla. He pulled her up onto his lap and tousled her hair.

"Mama!" she now cooed as she climbed over into Cindy's lap. She poked her eye. "Mama eye?"

"That's right. Can't we remember some of our other body parts? Where's my nose? Where's Mama's ear?"

"No'ee?" Kylla said as she pointed to Cindy's nose. "Mama no'ee?"

"There we go," Cindy rubbed her eye. "Let's stick with the nose for awhile."

After getting into Cindy's lap, Kylla didn't want to leave. They played Peek-a-Boo and Patty Cake for awhile, but as Kylla grew sleepier, she laid her head on Cindy's chest and began to drift off.

"Lucky girl," Kyle commented as he picked up the remote and turned on the television.

"Why?" Cindy asked bewildered.

"Because she gets to smell the last spot," he said without looking at her.

"I'm sorry about earlier," he finally spoke again after a while of mindlessly watching TV. "I was out of line ... I guess."

She sighed as she gently rubbed Kylla's back. "I don't know. I'm not sure what we are any more. For a long while, I could label us friends. But now, oh, I don't know. What are we Kyle?"

"I was hoping you could tell me," he said without looking at her. "Love your perfume, by the way."

She began to blush again. "Are we crossing lines, Kyle, or are there lines anymore?"

"Oh, they're there. I don't exactly know why, but they're still there."

They sat quietly for a moment then he shut off the television and turned toward her.

"Why are there lines, Cindy? I know how I feel about you, and I'm ready to move on that, but what you feel tonight and what you might feel tomorrow could be totally opposite. Why do you shut me out? Are you just toying with me, or is there a legitimate reason?"

"I would never toy with you, Kyle. I care too much for you to do that."

"Then why do you push me away?" He was frustrated. "When I'm away from you, all I want is to be with you again. And when I'm with you, all I want is to ... I don't know ... hold you? Care for you? Why is that wrong?"

The question threw Cindy into an agonizing mental search. Any reason she could come up with at the moment seemed lame. She was remembering the kiss, his breath at her ear, his hands in her hair, and all she could think of was why it seemed right. This was literally the man of her dreams practically begging to be with her, and she was forcing herself to say *no*. Why? Then reality came back: her past. No matter what had happened in her life since then, the fact remained: she was little more than a prostitute in many ways. She had never sold her sexuality for money, but she had sure sold it for many other reasons: prestige, popularity, pleasure. Kyle deserved more than that; Kylla deserved more than that.

She knew he was watching her, waiting for an answer. She couldn't control the tiny tear that managed to escape.

"What is it, Cindy? What's wrong?" He put his arm on the couch behind her and gently rubbed her shoulder. "Tell me what hurts you so badly when it comes to me. All I want is to care for you; I never want to hurt you."

She tried to sniff back the tears, biting her lip to control the emotion. How did she tell him she couldn't give herself to someone so good? She knew Kyle; he would swear it made no difference. But even that was because his heart was so good. It would be just like him to be drawn to the most helpless of women. That's what had attracted him to Caryn, and that's probably what a lot of his attraction to her was.

She could try to explain, but she knew he would never agree with her He began to caress her hair again, and then he finally just pulled her close and held her.

"I can wait for you, Cindy. And I will wait. Whatever it is that holds you back, I'll wait until it subsides. And then when you least expect it, I'm gonna reach out and grab your heart just as you've done with mine."

She bit her lip as she let her head rest in his embrace. If only he realized that he already had her heart.

As he prepared to leave, he shifted a still sleeping Kylla up to one shoulder. Cindy gently kissed her little hand goodbye. It was always hard to leave her, but tonight seemed impossible. She didn't want Kyle to go either. They stared at each other for a few moments, and then Kyle reached over to kiss her forehead.

"Good night, beautiful. I'll see you in the morning."

"Good night, handsome. I'll be there."

And he left. Cindy felt warm tears begin to stream her face again as she watched him gently buckle Kylla into her seat.

You have my heart, Kyle—my heart and my soul. I wish I could give you everything, but I'm just not worth it. Someday, some wonderful woman will come along, someone who actually deserves you, and you'll barely remember my name, much less my face ... or my perfume.

***

It had happened again. Cindy barely spoke to him the next day. He tried to remain light and cheery, but her mood was downcast. She must have lied to him. There still must be lines in her mind, and he continually crossed over them. He shook his head in despair as he went into his office and closed the door. Thursday morning would be here soon, and she couldn't avoid him the entire three days they were together at Martha's Vineyard. He somehow had to make her see that he loved her and wanted her in his life. And whatever barriers she had concerning their relationship, he would have to tear them down one at a time, until she could finally see that he adored her. She was worth fighting for, even if it meant he had to fight her in the process.

***

On Wednesday night, Cindy finished packing for the trip the next morning. She was excited about going, and there were many reasons other than Kyle for her light mood. She needed some time away; she had been in Dockrey since the last of December, and a little vacation was in order. There was also the fact of going to Martha's Vineyard, somewhere she had always dreamed of going but had never found the time to visit. Then there was the hope of finding information about Caryn and her true identity. She wouldn't admit it to anyone, but the prospect of working with the FBI, wearing wires and having them follow her around, was rather energizing. And of course, there was Kylla. Just the thought of her little arms around her neck made her smile.

But there were more serious things to consider. After Monday night, she realized it was time to move on. Her mother would have her final check-up a week from Thursday after a series of tests on Monday, and if all went as planned, she would be cancer free. Sue's health was the reason she had moved back, and Sue's health would be the reason for her to move on. When they returned from Martha's Vineyard on Monday, she would sit down with Pastor Jon and have a talk. She would tell him to go ahead and form a committee to begin looking for the permanent secretary. With her mother healthy, there was no reason for her to stay—no reason at all. Yes, it was time to move on.

She packed the stuffed monkey in her carry-on bag so she could bring it out for Kylla on the plane. She had shown her pictures of airplanes and explained how they went up high. She tried to find one in the sky over Dockrey to show her, but all she saw were jet trails. She wondered if Kylla would be able to realize they were flying up in the air when the plane took off. With Kylla's tendency to sleep anytime she was put into a car, however, it was unlikely she would do anything other than sleep on the jet too.

With the last of her bags packed, Cindy took her luggage downstairs and placed it by the door. She grinned as she imagined Kyle's comments about how much she had brought. *Kyle.* Would it be possible to one day erase him from her heart? He had become so intertwined in her life now that leaving him would be one of the hardest things she had ever done. It came close to saying goodbye to her father. But it was time. They would have this last weekend together then she would start the process of leaving. She would enjoy Kyle, she would enjoy Kylla, and then on Monday she would take steps to start over … again.

Forty-Two

It was a beautiful day for traveling, and Kylla was captivated by the planes as they landed and took off.

"Pane!" she would squeal and point.

Cindy picked her up and stood next to the wall of windows explaining how they all were about to fly. Kyle was talking with Agents Hall, Morrow and Sparks concerning what would happen when they reached the island. The agents would be traveling on the plane also and would keep an astute eye for anyone who looked suspicious. Kyle was nervous, but they assured him if anyone attempted anything, they would have their hands on him before he could take a second breath.

"Dadda! Pane!" Kylla cried out as Kyle joined them at the window.

"I see that," he tried to smile, but his brows furled and his lips tightened in a line.

"You okay?" Cindy asked.

"Yeah," he lied. She'd been keeping her distance for days now, and he decided just to let her be. If she wanted to be miserable and alienated for the weekend, he would gladly let her. There were too many other things to worry about than to try and keep a log of Cindy's emotional temperature. He was still trying to figure out how to approach Bill and Linda, and to make matters worse, he was to tell them he and Cindy were married. He kept trying to reason with himself that this was play-acting for the sake of the FBI; he wasn't just outright lying. This was all in hopes that Bill and Linda would offer some kind of confession giving information concerning Caryn. From there, the agency could begin a trace that would hopefully lead them to her killer. He shivered at the thought.

The announcer called their flight, and Kyle motioned for Cindy to follow him. He stayed a step or two ahead of her, but did take her carry-on-bag since she was holding Kylla. Once they boarded, he stowed her bag overhead, helped to get Kylla buckled in, and then sat quietly, taking special note of where the three agents were sitting.

"What is your problem today?" Cindy asked him after the jet was in the air. "You're as nervous as a cat."

"Does this whole thing not make you a little antsy? I mean we're basically going undercover to try and locate a murderer ... one who could possibly be after my daughter. And in one sense, I almost feel like Kylla is being used as bait here."

"We're all being used as bait. But look at it this way, at least we get to be with Kylla. It's not like we're throwing her out there on her own."

"Might as well be," he mumbled.

"Plus, we get a little vacation to boot. Think about it: we're as protected here as we would be at the Wrights' house. We can almost feel like life is normal again."

"You're kidding, right? We've got three agents placed around the plane to make sure no one jumps us, every room at the bed and breakfast will be filled by the FBI, and twenty-four hour surveillance will follow us for the next three days. We'll be wearing wires whenever we leave the inn, followed by a white van that plans to record every conversation we have while not in the room. Yeah, I'm feeling really *normal* right now."

"Okay, you can see the glass as half empty, but I'm choosing to let it be half full," she sighed as she patted his knee. "Personally, I'm banking on us getting some information this weekend. I'm tired of nobody knowing what's going on, and I'm really tired of worrying that some unseen enemy is after Kylla … and we don't even know why. I want answers, and I'm willing to do whatever it takes to get them."

"Hang on," Kyle was alarmed. "You better not pull any pranks like you did at the cemetery. You promised, Cindy."

"What am I gonna pull? I'll be with you, and we'll be monitored!"

"You promised," he said looking straight into her eyes.

She shook her head and reached for the headphones. "I'd rather watch a movie than listen to your nervous banter."

***

The inn was perfect for a getaway. Kyle wondered how the agency managed to book the entire place during the prime of a tourist season. Their upper level suite left them breathless in admiration. The living area was cozy with a couch, a loveseat, and a recliner as well as a small kitchenette. Off the living room was a balcony that overlooked the beach. Kyle was somewhat relieved to see there was nowhere for anyone to hide if they were spying on the room.

The two bedrooms were located on either side of the living area. One was large and spacious, probably the one that was rented out by itself when they split the rooms up. It continued with the beach motif used in the living room, only with a more tropical design.

"Why don't you take this big one," Cindy suggested as they looked through the room. "Since you and Kylla are staying together, you'll need the extra space.

"I thought we could split her up. You can have her one night, then me the next—alternate."

Her eyes grew bright as if she had been handed a grand prize. "For real? You're gonna let Kylla stay with me some?"

"Why not?" he replied, but without much emotion as he was still tense and nervous about the whole setup.

She threw her arms around him and kissed his cheek in delight. "Thank you so much!"

"Wow," he smiled, probably the first time that day. "You can sleep with her all weekend if you want. I didn't realize it meant that much to you."

"Yes!" She hugged him again.

The familiar voice of Ben Hall called to them from the living room. "Miss Marcum? Mr. Sarkos?"

"In the big room on the right," Kyle said.

He entered the room with an electronic device and methodically walked around every inch.

"What are you doing?" Cindy asked.

"Checking for bugs."

"Bugs? Roaches or what?"

Ben actually smiled as he shook his head. "Electronic devices … hidden microphones. It would be disastrous if they knew you were coming, got here ahead of time and wired your room."

"They could do that?" Kyle was nervous again.

"Possibly, but this room and the living area are clean. Let me check the other bedroom and the bathroom."

"Someone would put a microphone in a bathroom!" Cindy said in shock.

"You never know."

They followed him into the other bedroom off to the left of the main area. It was considerably smaller than the Master bedroom, and was obviously decorated with kids in mind. It held a set of twin beds and was covered in primary colors with boats and beach balls.

"Makes me feel ten years younger," Kyle said as he looked around the room. "This ought to be fun … sleeping in here."

"You really want to?" Cindy asked a bit unsure about making him stay there. "I don't mind switching up."

"As long as I have somewhere to drop my body at night, I don't care what it looks like."

Kylla loved the room. She immediately went to the wall and began to point at the pretty pictures. "Boat!" she yelled. "Ball!"

Ben continued with the device until he was finished with the second bedroom. "This one's clear. Let me check out the bathroom, and then I'll be back to talk with you both. We need to get our agendas together."

"Sure," Kyle nodded. *Agenda?* He had no agenda whatsoever.

After a few more minutes, Ben Hall returned with his ever-present file folder and suggested they all take a seat. "First, we need you to make this look like a reconciliation weekend." He ran his finger down the notes in his folder. "We have confirmed that at least three men followed you here."

"And you're not talking FBI, are you?" Kyle asked worried.

"No. Two of them have been posted outside the gate at the pastor's house for over a month, supposedly blending in as one of the crowd. The other one was one of the men who had followed you to the zoo in the corvette. It appears, though, that they had no idea where you would be staying, or why you were coming. Their tickets were purchased last minute. They don't know what's going on. This is good."

"Good?" Kyle twittered. "We're being followed by Caryn's murderers and that's good?"

"It's good, Kyle, because it means they're still in the dark. Remember, they can't get a hold of any legal records or documents at this point in time because we have them all under protection. They can't get into the Wright's house because of the major security that was in place from the beginning, and they can't get into Cindy's house or the church office because of our monitoring."

"You're monitoring *my* house?" Cindy asked astonished.

"Absolutely. They're anxious to know what connection all of you had to Caryn. They've attempted twice to break in, but were thwarted."

"Thwarted?" She was beginning to catch some of Kyle's nervousness. "Is someone there now? Will my mom be okay?"

"As long as this case is open, there'll be someone on your house *and* protecting your mother at all times."

She sighed and leaned back, pulling Kylla even closer. Kylla was thrilled and put her arms around Cindy's neck, giving her a tight hug. "Mama," she said softly and sweetly.

"That's right, sweetheart," she whispered back.

"Now, to the agenda," Ben Hall redirected them. "This is meant to be a reconciliation weekend. In public, be affectionate, like you were at the clinic, *not* the zoo." He raised his eyebrows playfully at them. "This evening, sit out on the balcony for a bit; get a little cozy. You don't have to make out or anything, but give these people something to talk about. When you're in the restaurant, take a hand occasionally or do something. You don't have to be explicit, but give the idea that things are working out between you. And through it all, both of you need to dote on Kylla as much as possible, although you do that on a regular basis anyway. That's what has them confused the most. They're convinced you both are her parents because of your love for the baby and her complete lack of Caryn's features. They don't understand why Kylla stays with Kyle all the time, nor why Caryn had her when she was murdered. Apparently, they had been looking for Caryn a long time, and as soon as they found her, they killed her. The baby was a huge surprise for them. They want to know the connection."

Ben Hall then looked at Cindy and smiled, "She looks like she's your baby, Miss Marcum. She looks nothing like Caryn. Lucky for Kylla that she looked like her father instead of her mother."

"W … wait, wait," Kyle stammered. "How do you know all this? How do you know what *they're* thinking?"

"We have a man inside. He's low on the bottom—no idea yet who the boss is or why Caryn is so important. Now, for tomorrow, when were you planning to visit the Malones … er … the Carters?" Ben flipped a page of his notes.

"I was thinking late morning. I'd like to get it over with."

"Fine. What time?"

"Is ten thirty okay?"

"Perfect," Agent Hall said as he stood. "I'll be here at ten o'clock to get you hooked up, and then we'll get moving."

They both nodded, more overwhelmed than agreeing. Ben Hall left, but Kyle and Cindy just continued to sit silently on the couch. Kylla had closed her eyes and was already drifting off to sleep again. Cindy gently brushed her lips across the loose, soft curls on the top of her head.

"I hope all this is worth it," Kyle commented as he scratched his head. "I've always wondered what a sitting duck felt like."

"Quack, quack," Cindy muttered under her breath.

Forty-Three

As suppertime neared, Kyle came from his bedroom after attempting to nap. It had been worthless. Even if he had fallen asleep, his dreams were sure to have been foreboding and miserable. Seeing Cindy standing out on the balcony leaning her hands on the railing actually lifted his spirit. He still found himself dazzled by her beauty and struggled to understand how someone so lovely had given up on saving herself for the right man. He thought about her story—college guys just weren't interested until she was willing to give her body. Why? Were they crazy? If he had met her in college, he knew she could have turned his eyes from Caryn. There were several girls who had tried, but Caryn was possessive. He remembered once during his senior year that a girl had caught his attention, but Caryn managed to pull him back in; she was good at that.

But Cindy was different. There was something about her that captured his whole imagination. Her beauty, her laugh, her smile especially, her freedom to discuss her mistakes and her past, her love for Kylla, and he couldn't deny the way she made him feel anytime he was with her. What if they had met in college? Surely he would have moved past Caryn. Surely he could have saved Cindy from herself. Surely the attraction they both felt now would have been there minus the emotional baggage they now carried, and surely they would have fallen in love and married.

He walked out on the balcony to join her.

"Sleep well?" she asked as she turned to face him.

"You're kidding, right?"

"I tried too. I laid down with Kylla for about thirty minutes, but I couldn't get my mind to stop no matter what I did. There was consolation in the fact that I could hold her next to me for a little while."

Kyle came up to her and put his hands on her waist. "Don't get defensive. I'm just trying to give *them* something to think about ... remember?"

She smiled and put her arms around his neck as she laid her head on his chest. "I'll try to pretend that I'm enjoying this," she teased as she gave a boring sigh.

"Well, don't enjoy it too much. We're not supposed to *make out*; aren't those the words Ben Hall used?"

She laughed as she pulled back to look at him, arms still around his neck. "Yeah, those were the words exactly. I thought I was gonna die. He is so straight all the time. To hear him actually say *that* was nearly comical."

He leaned down behind her ear and breathed in her perfume again.

"You know, I think Agent Hall is actually starting to loosen up around us."

"You think?"

She squirmed at his breath on her neck. Immediately his mind went back to Monday night.

As if deliberately creating a distraction, she asked, "Did I ever tell you that my parents wanted me to go to Furman?"

His thoughts changed. *What?* He had literally just been considering what would have happened had she gone there. "No, you didn't. Why didn't you go?"

She shook her head sadly. "Because I was stupid. I didn't care about school, especially a school that had a few values and a few rules. I look back now and wished they had made me go. Every single one of the Wright kids went to Clarksville Christian College; they had no choice. Andie, Annie and Angie all received considerable scholarships, but none of them actually wanted to go."

"Why did they go, then?"

Cindy pulled her arms down and Kyle released her waist as they both leaned on the railing this time. "They had no choice. Their parents said they either went to Clarksville or they were on their own. So they all went."

"What would you have done if your parents had insisted you go to Furman?"

"Freaked, to begin with. They never made us do anything … well … except go to church. That was the only thing that was never up for argument. You would think they would've learned from that alone—that there *were* things they could make us do. But they never did. Had they insisted I go to Furman, I would've gone. I sure wouldn't have stayed in Dockrey after graduation, and had Furman been my only door out, I would have grabbed it with gusto … and perhaps a nasty attitude, but I would have gone."

They stood in stillness and both mulled the possibilities of what *might* have happened. There was no way they could ever know, but the regret was deep.

Kyle finally leaned to the side, facing her, and asked, "Do you think you would have been interested in a good-old-boy-music-guy? Or would you not have even given me a second glance?"

He was amused by her smile. She even began to giggle a little as she continued to stare out at the ocean. "I wouldn't have glanced at someone like you; I would have gazed." Her cheeks grew pink. "But what about you? Could I have pulled you away from your beloved Caryn? She appeared to have her hooks in you pretty deep."

"If you would've pulled just a little bit, I'm sure the hooks would have fallen right out."

Regret. It had to be the biggest cause of loss in any life. It was even worse than death. Death was permanent and final, but regret constantly hounded you with the consequences of life. Regret could rear its head at any time and shove its reminders in your face, and they were always tinged with bits and pieces that included failure, lost opportunity, and the ever-present fact that you could never go back and change it. If one was beaten with regret often, its shards could eventually inflict enough pain that even the present seemed hopeless.

"But it didn't happen like that," Kyle finally breathed out. "Not even close."

"Nope. And this is how we turned out."

Suddenly Kylla's little voice broke through the gloom like a ray of welcomed sunshine after a week of storms.

"Mama?" she called out quietly.

"Hey, little one," Cindy said sweetly as she reached down to pick her up. Kylla nestled her head onto her shoulder, and Cindy closed her eyes relishing the moment. "Are you hungry?"

"Hungy," Kylla whispered. "Bites."

"Why don't we head on down to the restaurant?" Kyle suggested as he again melted at the sight of Cindy and Kylla together.

The restaurant was wonderful, and Kyle and Cindy ordered a huge seafood platter with two plates so they could split it. Kylla munched on French fries and chicken fingers that Cindy had cut up into small bite size pieces. It was hard to spot the agents in the room, with the exception of agent Sparks and Morrow, and they wouldn't have recognized them apart from the fact that they knew them. They were both dressed casually and acting as if they had been married for many years, complete with wedding bands.

"Do you think they're actually married?" Cindy asked Kyle at one point.

"I doubt it; they have different last names."

"Well, so do we, but we're practically married in the eyes of the FBI." She grinned.

"Trust me; we're nowhere close to being married."

"Sure we are! We spend all our time together, we share a child, not biologically, but in every other way, and look at us now. We're even in the *same room* at this cozy little bed and breakfast in Martha's Vineyard." She whispered the last statement.

"Yeah, but when we leave here, you go to your house, and I go to mine. That is *not* married. Besides, we're in separate rooms. If we were married …"

"I know, I know," she sighed. "It's weird, but after a while of never *finding* anybody I actually wanted to marry, it seemed hopeless. I came to this point that I didn't want to share my bank account, my mortgage or my life with anyone."

"Why didn't you want to share your life with anyone?"

"Why should I? All the guys I dated were … well … jerks. Kyle, I started dating when I was fourteen."

"Fourteen!" he exclaimed. "Kylla will *not* date when she's fourteen!"

"And I shouldn't have either. It killed Angie Wright that I could date. Her dad was firm about sixteen, and his kids had to stay on the honor roll to be able to date. The Wright teenagers thought that was ridiculous, but once again, they had no choice."

"I like that rule too," Kyle nodded as he looked over at Kylla. "Kylla, no dating until you're sixteen, and you have to stay on the honor roll at that."

"Dadda!" she grinned as she picked up another piece of chicken.

"At fourteen, I was already doing things with guys that were too fast. I wonder what my parents were thinking. By the time I hit college, I just assumed guys would fall all over me like they did in high school, but I was just a *kid* to them … until …"

Kyle hated hearing about this again. He didn't want to believe these things about Cindy. "So, do you still feel like marriage is a bad idea?"

"Actually, no. It started with Angie last year. When she and Michael came back from Padawin, they were so in love I actually was jealous. But they had this mutual respect. It was as though they were made for each other. And the thing about it was they were these Godly people who believed in marriage, believed in love, and believed in making a life together permanently. And that type of attitude meant they had this freedom to share things together that you can't get in a casual relationship. I didn't think I ever wanted that until I was around them. But there was another side to it too." She stopped talking and picked at her food.

"Which was?"

"Like I said, from fourteen on, I never was with a guy that I could imagine spending my life with or giving my life to. There was no real connection."

"Then how could you …" He paused. He didn't want to ask that question.

"Because that's all there was," she said with a deep sigh as she leaned back in her chair. "After a while, I gave up searching for more." She barely lifted her eyes to Kyle. "I never knew there were men out there like you."

Her statement took him by surprise. Was she actually admitting that she cared for him? He knew she did; she knew she did, but she would never own up to it. She only ran from it.

"And I wish like crazy that I had known you first," he said as he reached across the table for her hand. She reached back and took his and closed her eyes in regret. It was written all over her face.

"Cindy, that past is over now. It really is. You don't have to look at it anymore and feel like that's all there is. You can move on."

And that's what I'm going to do, she thought to herself in bed that night, *move on*. As soon as she returned to Dockrey she would put her plan into action—talk with Pastor Jon, get her mother through her last appointment, and then do all that was necessary to leave. Kyle was right; it was time to move on.

Forty-Four

The next morning, Kyle got up, got dressed, and headed for the living room to see if Cindy was ready for breakfast. It had been much harder than he thought having her so close to him at night. He couldn't help but imagine what it would be like if they were *really* married. They could come back here and rent the top floor. The kids—surely they would have more than just Kylla—would sleep in the boat room and on the pullout couch in the living room, and he and Cindy …

Get a grip, Sarkos.

It appeared she wasn't up yet. He glanced at the clock near the television; it was almost nine o'clock. Should he knock on the door and see if she was awake? How long would it take her to get dressed, get breakfast and be ready for their meeting with Ben Hall by ten o'clock? It took Caryn and his mother forever to get ready for anything. He had better wake her.

"Cindy?" he knocked gently on the door. "Are you up?"

"Dadda!"

"Kylla? Is Mama up?" he asked a little louder.

"Just a second," Cindy moaned out. "I'm getting up."

After a little shuffling, she appeared at the door looking exhausted with Kylla in tow.

"Did you sleep okay?" he asked with concern as he took Kylla. She looked beat.

"Yeah," she mumbled as she walked past Kyle and toward the kitchen area. "Got any coffee?"

"Let's head down to the restaurant and get some breakfast *and* coffee."

"I don't do breakfast," she groaned as she peered into cabinets looking for a coffee pot.

He was amused at her sweat pants, overgrown t-shirt, and disheveled hair. It reminded him a little bit of the time he had brought food over after Sue's surgery and found her completely out of sorts.

"What do you mean you *don't do breakfast?*"

"Haven't eaten breakfast since junior high," she grumbled as she continued looking through cabinets. "Haven't missed coffee since my only semester in college."

"You do know that breakfast is the most important meal of the day?"

She glared over at him and looked as though she could take him down with one good whack. "Not if you want to keep a figure like this." She stood still and took a final look around the kitchen. "It's one sacrifice that's easy to make."

He frowned. "It's a *bad* sacrifice. Get dressed and let's go eat."

She stared at him indignantly. "I'm serious; I don't do breakfast."

"And I'm serious; get dressed and let's eat."

Kyle found the stare-down that followed amusing, but her expression was growing more hateful each moment.

"If all you want is coffee, fine. But remember: you didn't used to cook or do kitchens either."

"Give me about ten minutes," she moaned again as she stretched her arms into the air and twisted from side to side.

"Let me get Kylla's clothes and I'll get her dressed while you're getting ready."

He followed her into the room and was caught up again in the scent of her perfume. He could get used to waking up to this every morning.

She was true to her word—she didn't eat breakfast. She had two large cups of coffee, and he continued to chastise her on and off concerning how important breakfast was.

"Promise me that when you get pregnant, you *will* eat breakfast," he said as a last resort.

She glanced up at him with a tired smirk. "So, you see pregnancy in my future, do you?"

"After seeing you with Kylla, there's no way you won't have children."

She put her face down to Kylla's and said, "You're the only baby I love. You're my sweetheart, aren't you?"

"Mama!"

***

The meeting at ten o'clock with Agent Ben Hall was nerve racking. There was much to remember about meeting with the Carters/Malones because there were certain bits of information Kyle was to try and elicit. For now, he wasn't to reveal he knew anything other than the fact that they were Caryn's parents. Cindy was to be his new wife, complete with a set of wedding rings Ben brought in, and they were supposedly there under the guise of letting the *Carters* see their only grandchild … again … allegedly.

They climbed into the cab and gave the driver the address Kyle had written down. He still remembered how to get to the house, but the street name and house number continued to elude him. Ben had told them the Carters/Malones were definitely in, so the visit would happen. As Kyle sat back, his stomach grew tighter. This couldn't be a good idea. He took comfort in the white van that was following close behind and the wire that was taped to his chest, but when he glanced over at Kylla and Cindy, he felt he would throw up. He didn't need to involve them in this. He should have faced the Carters alone and kept his girls out of the way.

When the cab stopped in front of the familiar house, he watched as the white van moved on down the street and even turned the corner.

Come back, guys. I know you're trying to look like you're not following me, but I don't want to go in there until I know I have someone ready to jump out and intercept any strange fellows who try to hurt Kylla.

He took his time getting Kylla out and paying the driver. He held her tightly as he watched the taxi leave, and then he glanced around the streets for a sign of the white van. Nothing. But there were several joggers about, so he took some consolation in knowing that at least they weren't alone. Cindy took his hand, and they walked together up the sidewalk to the sprawling porch of the lovely Cape Cod house. He took a deep breath and rang the doorbell. It took a moment before anyone responded, but when Linda Carter opened it, she nearly fell over in shock.

"Kyle!" she said putting her hand up to her heart. "What a surprise!"

"Hello, Linda," he tried to sound smooth and in control. "We had a little vacation time, and I thought you might like to see your granddaughter. I wanted Cindy to see Martha's Vineyard."

"Cindy?" Linda asked looking over at the gorgeous blond.

"My wife. And here," he turned Kylla around, "is little Kylla. I'm sure you've seen her before."

Linda was obviously confused. She stared at Kyle, then at Kylla, and just stood there.

"May we come in?" he asked.

"Well ... uh ... sure," she finally agreed. What else could she do?

She led them into the den. Cindy took special note of every detail in the house. When Linda excused herself to go find Bill, Cindy immediately began to snoop in every corner imaginable.

"What are you doing?" Kyle asked her.

"Looking for clues or information or something."

"About what?"

"About Caryn, silly. Remember? We're here undercover."

"What are you expecting to find?"

"I don't know. When I see it, I'll tell you. But for now, the only thing I've noticed is the obvious absence of any evidence that these people ever had a daughter."

He looked around and had to agree. "Odd, huh? I hear footsteps. Sit down and act like, I don't know ..."

"Like your wife?" she giggled as she slipped back next to him and looped her arm through his.

"Would you be serious? We don't know what we're getting ourselves into."

This time Linda was followed by Bill, both of whom looked

immeasurably distraught. Kyle stood and offered his hand and Bill shook it firmly.

"I thought while I was here, I'd come by for a visit," Kyle began. "I knew you'd probably want to see Kylla again."

"Kylla?" Bill questioned him.

Linda quickly cut in, "The baby, remember? Caryn's baby."

"Oh! That's right," Bill sort of hit his head as though he got it now. "Well, she's a cute one, isn't she?"

Cindy decided to push things just a bit. "I'm sure you'd love to hold your granddaughter. When's the last time you saw her?" She took Kylla from Kyle's arms and handed her to Linda first. Linda awkwardly took the toddler and held her as if she were fragile as glass.

"Uh, well," Linda looked uncomfortably at Bill, "we've never actually seen her. Caryn was planning on coming up eventually."

"She was bad sick during the pregnancy," Bill offered in explanation. "She couldn't travel. And then she wanted the baby to be bigger before she did the plane trip."

"She was an angel for our trip," Cindy beamed.

"She looks just like you, Kyle." Linda was warming up to Kylla's charm quickly. She then looked at Kyle completely confused. "Is she yours?"

"Yep," he grinned. "Can you believe that after all the testing, I actually ended up the father of a child anyway. I guess she must have known it was mine after Kylla was born, naming her after me and all. She never mentioned that to you?"

Bill rubbed the back of his neck as he told Kyle, "No, she didn't. After she left you, we didn't hear much from her."

"Why didn't you guys claim the body?" Cindy blurted out. She was tired of the chit chat—she wanted some answers.

"What do you mean?" Linda asked shakily. "We had her cremated immediately. Her ashes are in an urn upstairs."

Cindy nudged Kyle. He understood. "Could I see the urn? I haven't seen Caryn since she left, and I'd really like to sort of pay my last respects."

The exchange of glances between the Carters revealed lots. There was no urn.

"Well, Kyle, it's probably best that you put all of this behind you," Bill said knowingly. "You've moved on. You have a beautiful wife, a beautiful child, and we're happy for you. We were worried the divorce might have left you devastated."

"It did—it nearly killed me. I still don't get it all. I'm so thankful for Cindy." He took her hand. "She's made me believe that someone can really love me for who I am. Caryn was ... different ... I guess."

The rest of the visit was forced and strange. Kyle was amazed that

Cindy was so forward with her inquisition, but no matter what was asked, the Carters weren't budging. Kyle finally had Bill call them a cab, and they left.

"That wasn't much fun," Kyle sighed as they drove back to the inn.

"That was pitiful, actually," Cindy said as she thought about the visit. "Do you realize there wasn't a single picture of Caryn anywhere in the house? It's as if they'd erased her presence, if she ever really was present in their life as a daughter."

"They did have her high school graduation picture over the fireplace all those other years. Maybe they couldn't stand staring at her knowing she's dead."

"Baloney! They're lying through their teeth. And the way they handled Kylla! What was that all about? This is their granddaughter ... well, supposedly. Remember how my mother and Barbara greeted Kylla when they first saw her? Shoot ... your mother too!"

"They couldn't wait to get their hands on her."

"Exactly! These people are supposedly her blood relatives, yet they acted like we had given them a werewolf or something. They didn't even want to touch her. I can almost guarantee that Linda Carter, or Miranda Malone, whoever she is, has held very few babies in her life, much less one of her own."

"Why would you say that?"

"Because that's exactly how I held Kylla the first time Alicia handed her to me. I was clueless how to hold her and scared to death she might break. That's what Linda was doing. But when Mom and Barbara Wright got a hold of her, they acted as though they had known her all their lives; it was just experience, something Linda Carter's never had."

He looked at her and grimaced. "You're actually enjoying all this, aren't you?"

"I just want to get to the bottom of everything. I'm tired of watching my back, but I'm especially tired of watching Kylla's."

***

Ben Hall was actually pacing back and forth on the upper floor at the inn. "This was a total wash. We did find out one thing: they are *not* Linda and Bill Carter. Their actual identities are the Malones. So we know for certain that Caryn had used them all those years to bluff you into believing she was who she said she was."

He flipped through the pages of his notes as he read through the transcript of all that had been said at the house. "Another thing was having her cremated. That was good, Cindy. They were quick with that. And it was smart not to push the point of seeing the urn. However, Caryn's body is *still* unclaimed."

"So at least something positive came out of the trip?" Cindy wondered as she removed her sandals.

"Not really. It confirmed a few things, but we would have acted on them anyway. For now, we're really nowhere closer than before."

Forty-Five

After lunch, Kylla was ready for a nap and so was Kyle. Cindy suggested they use her room, but Kylla wanted to sleep with the boats, so Kyle laid her next to the wall while he lay down beside her on one of the twin beds. Cindy turned on the television, but she was antsy. She hadn't come all the way up here to play house with Kyle and Kylla and then leave empty handed. They needed answers—the FBI, Kyle, and Kylla. And since her life was so wrapped up in them right now, she needed answers too. Who was Caryn Carter, and why had she buffaloed Kyle all those years? What was she hiding and why was she murdered? Cindy wanted to know, the FBI wanted to know, and the answers were all here ... in this town ... at the house of Jackson and Miranda Malone.

She got up and peeked inside the cracked door of the boat bedroom. They were both out. She thought for a moment, and then finally grabbed her purse. It was time for somebody to do something.

Sorry about this, Kyle. I know I promised you I wouldn't do anything like this again, but I'm sick of the mystery. I'm getting to the bottom of it now. It may only be the top layer of the bottom, but I'm tired of the whole mess.

Cindy grinned to herself as she walked up the steps to the Malone house: the white van had appeared behind her shortly after she left. She had kept her wire on which served as a tracking device as well as a mic, and she had hoped they would pick up on where she was going. She would have to answer to Kyle for what she was about to do, but at least she could use the excuse that she knew someone would be following her.

"Cindy?" This was the second time today that Miranda Malone had been surprised by an unwanted visitor. "Why are you here?"

"We need to talk, Mrs. Malone," Cindy said sternly. "It is *Malone*, right? There are no Bill and Linda Carter in this house, or for that matter, on this island. There are also a lot of other things we know to be untrue concerning your involvement with Caryn. May I come in?"

Miranda nodded, but her face had turned white, obviously distraught at her return. Cindy followed her back into the den, but rather than sit down, she walked around the room and searched for evidence with an air of confidence this time.

"What are you looking for?" Miranda finally asked her.

"Anything that would indicate you had some kind of natural tie to Caryn Carter. We know you're not her parents, but we can't figure out exactly *what* you are."

"Who are *we?*" Miranda wondered. "You keep saying *we* want to know."

"FBI," Cindy stated as though this was something she did all the time. "Now, Mrs. Malone, I'm sure by now you're starting to put a few things together, the first being that I'm not really Kyle's wife. I'm an undercover agent, and it was our hope that you'd come clean with Kyle since he is so ... *non-threatening.* But that didn't happen, so it's time to just face you with the facts and get down to brass tacks. Are you ready?"

"My husband should be here," she said quickly.

"I doubt that," Cindy said as she finally sat down across from Miranda. "I think we can do this woman to woman and save everyone a lot of trouble. For starters, let me tell you what we *do* know. Then let me tell you what charges will be filed against you and your husband if you choose not to cooperate with us at this point."

The agents in the van outside the Malone home stared at each other in unbelief.

"What is she doing?"

"Getting information. She's good, isn't she?"

"What charges is she talking about? We didn't talk about bringing any charges against them. We don't know anything!"

"She's bluffing," one of the men laughed. "If this works, we need to hire her!"

"Charges?" Miranda was literally shaking now. "What can we be charged with?"

"I'll just start the list with obstructing justice and abetting a murderer."

"We know nothing about who murdered her!"

"Oh, Mrs. Malone," Cindy leaned back on the couch and shook her head, "we can do this the easy way, or we can haul you off to jail right now. What we want is information. We believe Kylla's life is in danger. Come here."

Cindy stood and moved to the window at the front of the house. Miranda followed nervously.

"See that van out there?" she asked her. Miranda nodded. "There are three agents in there waiting to take you and your husband away. Obstruction is an easy ten years a piece, and there's no way you'd get off for less than twenty with abetting a murderer."

"I told you, we don't know who murdered her!"

Cindy walked back to the den and waited for Miranda to sit. "I know you probably don't know the name of who actually pulled the trigger, three times in fact, but I can guarantee you know who's responsible. Because of that, you're hiding information that would help put the killer away. And let's be honest—you know Caryn's true identity. This is baffling us. Kyle was married to the woman for ten years, yet she doesn't exist. She has no social security number, no birth certificate, and as you've confirmed today, no parents. Please, Mrs. Malone, her body is still on ice in the Nashville Morgue; she's not *ashed* out in some urn upstairs. What are you hiding? Who was Caryn Carter?"

Miranda would say nothing. Her face was ashen now, and her knuckles white from squeezing her hands. She just sat on the couch and stared toward the window.

"Okay, Mrs. Malone, if this is how you want it. I'll call the authorities in now. They'll go ahead and arrest you, and when your husband returns, they'll bring him in. Too bad you didn't get a chance to say goodbye now. Prison isn't a pretty place. And thirty years is an awfully long time."

Cindy didn't hesitate as she stood and walked toward the front door.

"Wait!" Miranda called out. Cindy turned around quickly. "Wait," she said more weakly this time.

"Do you have relevant information, Mrs. Malone, or are you about to give me the runaround again."

"I don't know everything you think I know," Miranda began. "I can tell what I *do* know, but I promise, I don't know who killed her."

Cindy nodded as she sat back down. She knew the microphone was actually taped to her chest, but she thought a different method might be more convincing. She picked up her arm and spoke into her wristwatch. "Make sure you're recording this boys, and get these down into transcripts as soon as possible. Start on the leads as they come out of her mouth." She then looked back at Miranda and said, "We're ready."

The woman was close to tears. Cindy couldn't tell if it was fear or tension, but whatever the reason, Miranda was an emotional wreck at the moment. She licked her lips and tried to decide where to start.

"Let's just begin with the easy question," Cindy suggested. "Who was Caryn Carter? What was her real name?"

Miranda took a deep breath, exhaled slowly, and then finally said, "Callista Sartin. She was Callista Sartin."

The look of utter defeat on Miranda's face after years of holding this secret was a stark contrast compared to the look of recognition and complete shock that was now on Cindy's.

Callista Sartin? If only I had seen a picture!

Forty-Six

After close to thirty minutes of intense interrogation, Miranda Malone was deplete of information. Cindy thanked her and let her know that because of her cooperation she had saved both her and her husband the next thirty years in prison.

She left the house and didn't hesitate to go directly to the van. She walked to the passenger's side, opened the door and then climbed up. "Shall we go, boys?" she asked nonchalantly.

The three men just stared at her in utter amazement.

"We don't know whether to kill you or kiss you," said the driver in astonishment.

"Do I get commission for this?" she teased.

"I doubt that, but a good tongue-lashing is in order."

"Oh, please!" she sighed in disdain. "You all know this is exactly what you wanted—this is the information we all needed to begin sorting through the whole mess. Just because I didn't follow the *agenda* means the *agenda* was bad to begin with. If the Malones had kept this stuff from Kyle for over ten years, what made you think they'd suddenly open up? Guilt? Ha."

"Miss Marcum, we would have eventually faced them directly …"

"Sort of like I did just now?"

"Sort of …" he cocked his head to the side uncomfortably, "but with a legitimate badge and proper procedure."

"Blah, blah, blah." She was sick of *procedure*. "Just thank me later, guys, and let's get back to the inn. If Kyle has realized I'm gone, he's probably burning up the carpet by now."

"He has … and he is."

She took a deep breath; the fun was over.

As soon as she opened the door, Kyle ran to her and held her tightly. This wasn't the welcome she had anticipated. She put her arms around him for a moment, but when he pulled away and she saw the look in his eyes, she knew she had figured him right to begin with.

"Before you start," she put her hand up to silence him, "I am a big girl, and I can make my own decisions about what I do with my time."

"You promised me you wouldn't do anything like this again!"

She glanced at the balcony and realized Ben Hall was here also.

"Give me a break, Kyle. I had three agents following me, I was wearing a wire, and our window of opportunity was slammed shut this morning. I wanted answers, and in case you haven't heard, I managed to get a truckload."

"What?" Agent Hall came in on that statement. "What did you find out?"

"They haven't told you yet?" Cindy asked in surprise. "I thought all your information ran on that *super technological highway*."

"When we're set up and prepared for it and everybody's in place! All they said was that you were safely out of the house and they were bringing you back here. You found out something for us?"

"Correction: I found out something for me, for Kyle and especially for Kylla. The fact that *you* will benefit from this information is just a pleasant by-product."

Ben smiled and nodded in understanding as he took a seat in the recliner. "So what did you learn, Miss Marcum?"

"First," she looked over at Kyle who refused to sit because he was still shaking with nervous energy, "why didn't you ever show me a picture of Caryn? Surely you had one somewhere! I would have recognized her immediately."

"What?" Kyle stopped pacing. "You knew her?"

"I know who she is. She's been in every tabloid for the past, I don't know, fifteen years maybe, on and off."

"How?" Ben asked with curiosity. "If she were with Kyle, how could she have been in a tabloid?"

"Apparently, when she told Kyle she was visiting the Carters, she was out with her old boyfriend."

Kyle looked at her in shock and began to grow faint. He eased himself onto the couch and cleared his throat. "Boyfriend?" he said weakly. "Who was she, Cindy?"

"Callista Sartin … or should I say, the *brunette* version."

Kyle just looked blank. Ben Hall, however, knew exactly who she was, and his face actually began to grow pale.

"Callista Sartin!" she exclaimed to Kyle. "Martin Sartin's daughter! Kyle, you were married to Martin Sartin's daughter!"

He leaned back and shook his head. "I didn't even know he had a daughter."

"Yeah, with that Spanish actress, Maria Cruz," Cindy went on to explain. "They were married for several years, but she finally left him because of his intense drug problems. According to the magazines, they still loved each other, and he had tried desperately to get her back, but she wasn't going to expose her daughter or herself to his drug issues anymore. A couple of years later, Martin was arrested and then charged with so many counts of drug related stuff that he was sentenced to prison for something like 250 years."

"The actor," Agent Hall acknowledged. "Real funny guy. White hair, premature gray, with the blue eyes. Did that Saturday night comedy show. So Caryn was Callista Sartin. Amazing what a change in hair color and very little make-up can do."

"But I still think I would have recognized her had I seen a picture," Cindy insisted.

Ben stood up and began pacing where Kyle had left off. "Maria Cruz, his wife ... she was murdered also."

"Right." Cindy knew the story well. She had been a huge Martin Sartin fan and had followed his life for many years. "It was shortly after he was convicted."

A look of concern crossed Ben's face. "Whoever was after Maria must have been after Callista. That would have been right about fourteen years ago. Kyle, when did you meet Caryn?"

"Fourteen years ago," he sounded as if his throat was parched.

"There's more," Cindy told them. Both men gave her their attention. "Bill Malone was a talent agent in Hollywood. He represented Martin when he decided to leave television and start doing movies. They were very close, and Callista had grown up around the Malones. When Martin was arrested, he blew the whistle on everybody in some kind of national drug organization. Because he's been behind bars forever, the organization can't get to him."

"So they went after his family," Ben interrupted.

"Exactly! Sartin gave the Malones control of his estate with the agreement that they would help keep Callista in hiding. They tried to find the most unlikely place for her to go—a hot shot Hollywood debutante with a world famous boyfriend, Philippe DuBois."

"Philippe DuBois?" Kyle exclaimed. "She dated Philippe DuBois?"

Cindy tried to say it gently, "I know I saw a picture of them in a Hollywood magazine not long ago— but her hair was blonde again ..."

"Who's Philippe DuBois?" Ben asked confused.

"A French musician," Kyle said flatly as he scratched his head. "Well, more like a singer who can shake his behind real well ... long blond hair ... very smooth fellow."

"I'm sorry, Kyle," Cindy uttered compassionately. "I know this must hurt."

"Not really. I guess I'm sort of numbed to it by now. It explains a lot of things ... I suppose."

She paused before continuing with Miranda Malone's information. "Callista picked this somewhat religious college in the South, thinking that would be a good hiding place. Apparently it was. The Malones never actually knew where she was; she even kept her whereabouts from them."

"Where did I come in?" Kyle wondered. "Why was I a part of all this?"

Ben stopped pacing and turned to Kyle. "You became the ultimate cover. Nice guy, minister no less, the least suspected person for a wild Hollywood starlet to be with. She was good."

"That's all Miranda could, or *would* tell me. But I figured it was enough to go on. We have a name, we have a motive, and that means we have a place to start. She swore she knew no names as far as who might be the killer. She said you'd have to talk to Martin Sartin himself if you were gonna find any of that out."

Ben Hall walked over to the couch where Cindy was sitting and stuck out his hand. "Congratulations, Miss Marcum. You did an incredible job."

"Thanks," she smiled back. His hand lingered a moment longer than she was comfortable with. She finally pulled it back.

"Should you ever decide to leave secretarial work, I'm sure the agency could find a good place for you."

She laughed. "You couldn't afford me, Mr. Hall."

"Okay," Ben sighed and gathered his composure. "I've got a lot of work to do. I'll leave you two alone so I can begin going over the transcripts from today. I'd hate to be Mrs. Malone when her husband comes home. Can't wait to see how he reacts."

"You have people over there watching?" she was surprised.

"Lots of joggers on the lane today," he winked.

"The joggers are agents?" she was amazed.

"I told you, Miss Marcum, we've got you well-covered." Ben moved toward the door, then turned back for a final word. "You two should probably go out today and do something. At least see the docks. Remember, this is a vacation, and you're trying to put the relationship back together."

"Isn't it all over now?" Kyle asked in near collapse.

"Are you kidding?" Ben replied. "It's only just beginning now. In fact, it's more important than ever that we keep Kylla under the guise of being the spawn of you two."

"Why?" Kyle was obviously tired of the whole thing.

"If these people killed Sartin's wife and daughter, I'm sure his granddaughter would be next on the list, only they don't know she's his granddaughter ... yet."

"Mr. Hall," Cindy said as she stood to her feet, "please don't refer to Kylla as the *spawn* of anything again. I find that a rather repulsive thought."

"My apologies, Miss Marcum. Perhaps I've been in this work too long."

When Ben finally left, Cindy went over to Kyle and kneeled down in front of him. She placed her hands on his knees, but he wouldn't look at her. His head was laid back on the couch, and his eyes were closed. She knew this had to be hard.

"I'm sorry, Kyle," she said tenderly. "I wish the whole story had been different."

Keeping his eyes closed, he simply voiced, "She had a boyfriend the whole time. I at least believed that somehow our marriage was legitimate, but it was a sham—totally."

"You deserved better."

"Apparently not. I should have listened to my parents. My dad told me more than once I shouldn't have anything to do with her. *She's not the right woman for you, Kyle*, he said over and over again. Even my pastor during my college years had reservations. I lost my friends after a while because Caryn was too shy. I just stayed with her. Somewhere down the line, she convinced me that she needed me in her life ... but I never really knew why ... until now. I thought I was doing the right thing by her ... good old Kyle—he always does the right thing."

Thunder began to roll in the background, and Cindy peered out beyond the balcony to size up the weather. The sky was beginning to grow dark and the breeze was picking up.

"I would suggest we take that walk to the pier, but it doesn't look like a good time right now," she told him.

"No," he said faintly. "Besides, I don't feel like keeping up appearances at the moment. You'd think I'd be good at it by now, being married to a total stranger for ten years."

"Kyle," she placed her hand on his face and forced him to look at her. "This wasn't your fault, and this isn't fair for you. Don't get down on yourself because you were taken in by a con artist, a very beautiful con artist. She engineered all of this, and you were just a helpless victim."

He nodded, but he wouldn't respond.

"And always remember: you got Kylla out of the deal. That will be one blessing you can always take with you."

Forty-Seven

Dinner was quiet that night. The restaurant buzzed because it was Friday evening, but Kyle had very little to say. Cindy spent most of her time carrying on with Kylla, and would occasionally try to draw him in, but he was distraught. He had already come to the conclusion that his marriage to Caryn had been created for her convenience, but he had imagined she was some nobody from nowhere. To find out she was a sophisticated Hollywood woman with a famous French boyfriend whom she had obviously been seeing throughout their entire marriage was just too much to fathom. He felt like a complete fool, and in truth, he had no one to blame but himself. Had he listened to those who truly loved him, he would have never married her.

When they returned to their room, Cindy continued playing with Kylla while Kyle turned on the television hoping for some distraction. He eventually found himself watching the girls play together, and for a moment or two, that pleasure was able to take him away for a bit. Kylla was so full of life. He was thankful he had the paternity test before now. Had he discovered Caryn had been with Philippe all those years, he would have probably believed that Kylla belonged to the singer. Caryn obviously knew though because of the name she chose for the baby.

Cindy bathed Kylla, dressed her for bed, and then brought her back into the living room to rock her in the recliner. As she sat down with the baby, Kylla immediately rested her head on Cindy's chest and closed her eyes. She was completely comfortable with Cindy. Kyle felt sorry for the little girl because he knew she needed the constant attachment of a mother. Apparently Caryn had spent all her time locked away with Kylla, and then to have her mother torn away and to have been transplanted into a strange home with complete strangers had to be hard. But you would never know it to be around her.

She reached up and took a strand of Cindy's hair as they rocked, and began to softly knead it between her tiny fingers. He smiled. It must be genetic; they were both obviously taken with Cindy's silky hair. He continued to go back and forth from the television to the recliner with his gaze. Cindy was oblivious. She was completely enthralled with the process of rocking the little one to sleep.

For a moment, he let his mind wander again to the thought of being married to Cindy. This would be his life every night. They would be together after work, care for Kylla, feed her, bathe her, and then get her to sleep. Then when Kylla was down, they could be together themselves. *What a wonderful dream. If only Cindy would dream it too.* They could legitimately be on vacation right now. When Cindy put Kylla down, in his dream world, she would join him on the couch and they could cuddle. He could feel her hair and smell her perfume, but most of all he could finally tell her he loved her with no lines drawn, no regrets, and no uncertainties. They could watch old movies, read a devotion book, or sit on the balcony and hold hands. Then when it came time for bed, they didn't have to say good night. They would just be together.

He heard Cindy snapping her fingers and looked over to see what she needed.

"This recliner is too stuffed," she said softly. "I can't get up. Can you sort of pull me out so I can lay her down?"

He nodded and went over to her. "How?" He surveyed the seat. "This is one puffy chair."

"Should you get behind me and try to sort of push me up?"

"Too high." He continued his examination. "How 'bout I grab your waist and pull you up?"

"Okay. That should do it."

Kyle reached down and took hold of her waist then carefully pulled her to her feet, baby and all. Cindy smiled with relief and then slowly walked to the bedroom. He followed to help get things set up, but she had taken care of that before she even started rocking. She laid her down, gently covered her with a blanket, and then reached over to kiss her goodnight. They turned and left the room.

"Thank you for letting me have her this weekend," Cindy said as she closed the door almost shut, leaving a two inch crack so they could hear her if she awoke. "It's gonna be hard for me to leave her again."

He nodded as he walked out on the balcony and had a seat. The rain had not yet fallen, but the thunder and lightning were putting on quite a show. Cindy joined him and pulled a chair next to his.

"Tell me about Caryn," she requested hesitantly. "You've given bits and pieces of information to me, but I never wanted to intrude into your past."

"And now you do want to intrude?" he asked without looking at her.

"Yeah, I do. I want to help you put all this together so we can figure out the whole crazy mystery. The sooner it's put to rest, the sooner life can settle down for you ... and for Kylla."

"Is it really me you want to help, or is it Mr. Ben Hall and the FBI?"

Cindy gaped at him. "Why on earth would you think that?"

"You seemed to really enjoy pumping Mrs. Miranda Malone for info today."

"What I *enjoyed* was getting some answers to the whole Caryn Carter package of baloney."

He propped his feet up on the railing as another peal of thunder rolled in the background. He ran his hand through his growing hair and was amazed at the sweat from the humidity. Why should he share his past with her? She was just curious about the whole Callista Sartin situation. Besides, she had made it clear, sort of, in a murky manner, that they would have no life together. What was the point of opening up his soul to her anymore? He was already in too deep.

Suddenly she leaned over and kissed him gently on the cheek. That got his attention.

"Just keeping up those appearances," she smiled.

"Feels more like bribery to me."

"Is that what bribery feels like?"

"That's what it feels like tonight. However, for it to really work, it'll cost you more than that. I mean, one little peck on the cheek? That's like giving me a quarter."

"Okay, what will it cost for some real information?"

"What are you willing to give?" he was getting into the game.

"Hmmm, one on the other cheek?"

Kyle shook his head and clicked his tongue. "That's not even close. If you want fifty cents worth of info, that'll do. But you're asking for in-depth information. We're talking 500 dollars worth. And remember, I let you have Kylla to yourself all weekend. You're already behind."

She thought for a bit, and then out of the blue she reached over and grabbed his shirt by the collar. She pulled him to her and planted one smack on the lips. He found himself grinning more than kissing, however.

"You can't kiss me when you're laughing," she grinned back. "If you want 500 dollars worth, you'd better get busy."

He leaned into her and kissed her back this time. She tugged his shirt closer. He then pulled back her hair and began to kiss the side of her neck behind her ear.

"That's a good 200 there," she whispered to him as she squirmed.

He moved to the other side and began to kiss again. Cindy giggled as his lips tickled her skin.

"I guess that's up to 400 now?" he asked.

"Easily," she managed to breathe out. "What's next?"

"Hmmm," he placed his forehead on hers and just smiled. "Let me think." He leaned down and began to kiss her again.

It was Friday night at the bookstore all over again, and Monday night after Alfredo sauce. She unleashed her hand from his shirt and gently moved it to his neck. This time, however, neither of them chose to end the kiss. As it went on, Cindy found herself pulling him closer to her and wishing their chairs didn't separate them. When they finally parted, the twinkle in his eyes almost made her laugh.

"We do that so well," he grinned. "Why is it again that we always make ourselves stop?"

"Because we're *just friends*," she reminded him.

"Oh yeah. And why is that? Just friends?"

"I don't recall at the moment. But if you'll let me get my head together for a bit, I'm sure I can remember."

"Do you kiss all your *friends* that way?" he asked, still close to her face.

"No, only those who I'm pretending to be married to."

He lifted his left hand and stared at the fake wedding band he was wearing. "A lot of power seems to be packed inside this charade, don't you think? If you remember, we were told we didn't have to *make out*."

"That wasn't making out. That was a bribe, if *you* remember. And I'm curious, did it pay the bill?"

"Hmmm." He sat back in his chair, but he kept hold of her hand. "I'm not sure. You're asking an awful lot." He pulled her hand up to his mouth and kissed it then turned it over so he could breathe the perfume from her wrist. "Your hands and wrists are so delicate."

"That's because I don't eat breakfast. Am I paid up yet?"

He now laced his fingers between hers and sighed deeply. "Caryn. Where do I start? I guess I actually first met her while I was sitting in the library."

Cindy sat back and let him keep her hand.

"I was studying something at a table, and she came over there to look at some books beside where I was sitting. She asked if she could sit with me so she could be near the volumes she was using for her paper. At first, I barely even noticed her. I mumbled something about it being fine and then went back to my own work. Next thing I know, her pen doesn't work, and could she borrow mine. When she said thank you, I saw her eyes for the first time. They were beautiful."

"I know," Cindy whispered. "They were her mother's eyes."

"They were so dark and deep. She looked too young, so I didn't bother to get her name or anything, but I did tell her she had the most exquisite eyes I had ever seen. She acted like I had embarrassed her, but I assured her I wasn't coming on to her. She thanked me again, and I had to leave.

"The next day at lunch, she walked by my table and smiled and said hi to me before moving on. The guys I was sitting with made this huge deal about it. *Sarkos! She's got a thing for you!* No she doesn't; she's just some freshmen I helped out in the library. *She's hot! Look how gorgeous she is. Olive skin. Deep brown eyes. Go for it, Sarkos.* I honestly wasn't interested. By the end of the week, we had run into each other several times. She always seemed to need help for something. She'd dropped her books, she'd lost something, she needed directions to a certain building, where would be the best place to buy a lamp for her room. She wanted to thank me for all I had done, so she took me out to dinner."

"She asked you on your first date?" Cindy asked surprised.

"Yeah," he chuckled. "Looking back, I can see how orchestrated the whole thing was, but at the time ..."

"You were just a good man, Kyle."

"Yeah ... too good."

She squeezed his fingers and brought his hand to her lips this time. "There's no such thing as *too good*."

"Anyway, within a month we were really dating. I tried to get her to sit with my friends, but she was so dog-goned shy."

"Nobody recognized her as Callista Sartin?" Cindy asked in unbelief. "I can't figure that out."

"Well, she wore these somewhat dark glasses, always wore a hat, and wore frumpy sort of clothes."

"Frumpy?"

"Yeah, you know," he gestured with his free hand, "loose, baggy, non-descript. I knew she was this beautiful girl underneath, and I guess I sort of took on this challenge to turn the caterpillar into the butterfly."

"By the end of my senior year, we'd been together a long time. I really did think about seeing other girls, but truthfully, I just wanted to get married. I would be leaving for seminary in June, and I wanted to take a wife with me. Don't ask me why, it was just sort of a personal goal. She was beautiful, but not loads of fun. She was devoted to me, but hard to get to know. I decided to have a serious talk with her about the future. The truth is, I really hoped I would scare her off—but I didn't. When she realized I wanted to get married, she threw her arms around me and swore she would treat me right all the days of our lives. She promised she would see me through my education, take care of me, and then stand by my side as the perfect minister's wife when I finally started my career. She said our life together would be an adventure that went on and on."

He sighed and stood up, walking to the edge of the balcony. The thunder was closer, and the wind was gusty and cool. Cindy stood up beside him and put her arm around his waist.

"She was so ... intriguing," he confessed. "I guess I didn't understand what love was supposed to be. The thought of being with her my whole life was almost prideful, I guess. She was an enigma, and she could be mine. My dad told me no. My pastor told me no, and my roommate told me no. But everyone else thought it was the greatest thing. So I married her."

As Kyle leaned down on the railing, Cindy rested her chin on his shoulder.

"What was she like after you were married?"

"Devoted, but distant. We didn't really *talk*, you know, about deep things. She would get me talking about myself, and I suppose I rattled on so much that she never had to talk. I tried to get her to tell me about her life growing up, but she would just give little bits and pieces and then act like she was all embarrassed. *My life was so plain compared to yours*, she would always say. *Traveling around the world and visiting all those fascinating places, when I just stayed in Martha's Vineyard most all the time.*" He shook his head. "I totally believed her."

"Why shouldn't you?"

"I don't know, but it sure seems like I should have been suspicious. She never worked. She said she wanted to stay home and take care of me, and she did. We managed to live on a really tight budget, but she was incredible with stretching meals and clothes and material needs. I told her she was welcome to work so she could have finer things, but she insisted she only wanted to meet my needs. And did she ever."

Cindy nodded and then leaned down on the railing with him. She hesitated before she asked her next question, one that had burned in her mind from the day they first discovered that Caryn Carter may have not been Caryn Carter.

"Curious," she started. "How were things … well …"

"I know what you're asking," he stopped her. "I was actually one of the few guys in the entire world who waited to have sex until I was married. That was the best part of our marriage. Apparently she understood guys really well. I talked with other men who would complain like crazy about their sex lives—mine was great. I don't know how she managed all that if she didn't really love me, but I guess desperate times call for desperate measures."

"She may have loved you, Kyle. You don't know for certain that it was all a scam. I mean, I can't imagine how someone could live with you, know you for thirteen years, and not think you're the most incredible person on earth. I'd be willing to bet that somewhere down the road she fell in love with you."

"Me *and* Philippe DuBois," he mumbled.

She began to feel small sprays of mist blowing onto the balcony. Surely Caryn had loved him at some point. How could someone be married to him for ten years and not care deeply for him? He was too wonderful, too perfect—and then to have shared a child with him but never let him know. How could she? Was she so hardened and so scared that it always remained as it had begun: a sham?

"So," he leaned on one side and looked at her intensely, "you say no one could live with me and not love me. You really believe that?"

She smiled at him and nodded. "Completely. You're too amazing, Kyle Sarkos. Someone would have to be blind."

He took her hand again and pulled her to him. "So what about you? This is day number two of living with me. Do you love me?"

She tried not to look at him, but she could feel his eyes searching for the truth. She glanced up, hoping to just briefly catch his expression, but he held her gaze.

"Do you love me Cindy Marcum?"

She tried to smile and be light. "Do you mean as a friend?"

"At this moment, I would accept love from you in any capacity. Just to know that I'm truly loved and not being used would be a welcomed relief."

She swallowed hard and then looked out as the rain began to grow harder. "I love you, Kyle. I don't know how or in what manner, but I definitely love you. Next to my mother, you and Kylla are the most important people in my life. I don't know what that makes us, but if it's my love you question—don't."

He said nothing more but pulled her close into a warm embrace. She was so confused at the moment, feeling sorry for him, feeling deeply for him, but not wanting to act on any of it. If he were to kiss her now, it would scare her to death. But Kyle, as always, seemed tactful and wise. He merely held her, resting his chin on her head as the rain became steady.

Forty-Eight

On Tuesday morning, shortly after Jonathan came into the office, Cindy asked to speak with him. He motioned her in and sat behind his desk with his typical warm smile.

"What can I do for you?" he asked in a way that reminded her of her father.

"I want to begin by saying how much I appreciate being able to work here while my mother has been recovering." This was harder than she thought it would be. "Just being in this office has been wonderful. Working with you and Kyle, doing the things I've been doing, it's all been like a dream ... that's the only way I can think to describe it."

"We've been glad to let you do it, and you've done an excellent job."

"I've really tried to." She shifted in her seat. "I think it's time, however, for you to form a committee and begin looking for someone permanent. Mother is healthy—she had her scans yesterday, and when we go Thursday, I'm sure she'll get a clean bill of health. That's the only reason I took this job ... to care for her. I think it's time to move on."

His expression changed to concern. She could tell he was thinking before he spoke. If only she could learn to develop that quality.

"Why do you want to leave?"

"I just think it's time." She was nervous. Did he not agree?

"But why? Do you not feel like you're doing a good job?"

"No, that's not it. I just need to get on with my life. I can't stay here forever and live in this, well, this bliss ... practically."

He chuckled as he ran his fingers through his hair. "So, bliss is not good?"

She rolled her eyes and shook her head. "I know it sounds crazy, but I almost feel like I'm hiding here. I feel like I'm in this wonderful little place with all these wonderful people, but I know I can't stay. I'd rather begin moving on and getting back to *real life* than prolonging the inevitable."

"And what is the inevitable, Cindy? Misery? That's what you make it sound like."

"I don't want it to be, but all this is temporary! Sometimes, Pastor Jon, I'm afraid to breathe, because I might wake up and realize all of this has been a dream."

"All of what?"

"Working here. Being back in Dockrey. Having a simple life again with good people around me."

"Do these people include Kyle and Kylla?" he raised an eyebrow.

"Sure," she tried to sound detached. "They're a part of my life right now. I've gotten close to both of them, but they'll be moving on soon too. I'm tired of trying to convince myself that ... oh ... I don't even know how to say it!"

"You're afraid to believe that life can be this good?"

"I don't know if that's exactly it." Well, yes, that was it exactly—but when he said it, it almost sounded inane.

"Let me try and help you put all of this into perspective." He stood up and came to sit on the front of the desk. "Your father died last year, and it began the process of tearing your world apart. And what a world it was! Then your mother got diagnosed with cancer several months later, and a few more bricks fell away. God got your attention. So you made some drastic changes. You moved back here, took a low paying job, and suddenly found that there was more to life than money, sex and alcohol. Now your life is completely wrapped up in your mother, your church, and a man of God who has a daughter who's absolutely captured your heart. But now you're ready to leave all that, because of why?"

"It's not as simple as you make it sound. I'm not the permanent secretary; Kyle's not the permanent music man. Mother isn't going to need me anymore. I'm not needed here; it's time to move on."

He nodded and pursed his lips as he crossed his arms and sighed deeply. "You may believe that *you* are not needed, but have you ever considered that maybe you still have *needs* that should be met here? Maybe you still need this church, this job, your mother, Kyle."

She began to feel tears forming in her eyes. "Of course I need them. I need everything I've found here. I need to know you're just inside this door so I can talk when I have a spiritual struggle or miss my father and need some advice. I need to walk into church every time the doors open and see people who embrace me with love, acceptance and forgiveness. I need to hear my mother tell me she loves me and she's proud of me and the changes I've made." A tear began to trail. "And yes, I *need* to know what it's like to be with a man who thinks I'm just as beautiful inside as outside, a man who respects me and cares for me as though I was someone truly special—a man who shares his life and his child with me." She felt more tears begin to fall. "But all this is temporary! My heart will break, Pastor Jon, when I have to leave."

"So, you're ready to just pick up and leave right now? Cindy, God isn't through with you yet. When it's time for you to leave, you'll know."

"I already know," she said resolutely. "I can't stay here forever; please do as I've asked." She stood and went to the door.

"Cindy?"

She turned around. She owed him that respect.

"If this is really what you want, I'll get started on it, but not until after your mother's Thursday appointment."

"Thank you." She left.

***

This was the third night in a row Kyle couldn't get Kylla to sleep.

"Mama," she said with lips quivering as she was about to cry. "Mama."

"Kylla," he said tenderly as he tried to cradle her to his chest. "Mama is at her home. This is where Kylla and Daddy live."

"Mama rock," she said in a choked little voice.

"No, Daddy rock," he tried to be calming.

She wouldn't lay her head on his chest for long. She pulled up and stared at him with alligator tears brimming beneath her lids. His heart broke. Cindy had rocked her to sleep each night and then awakened with her each morning at Martha's Vineyard. Something in that had cemented itself into Kylla's mind, and she felt a loss without Cindy being here. He had called Cindy last night hoping that when Kylla heard her voice it would settle her, but it only got worse. She had finally cried herself to sleep, something he had never seen her do before. He dialed Cindy again this night.

"Is it Kylla again?" she asked as soon as she answered.

"Yeah. Cindy, if you could see her eyes right now, it would break your heart."

"Oh, Kyle, I had no idea our little weekend in Massachusetts would affect her like this. I feel horrible."

"Don't." Was he going to have to reassure Cindy as well? She had avoided him entirely since they had returned just as he had expected. That was becoming vintage Cindy behavior—they would get close, and then she would pull away.

"Do you want me to talk to her again?" she finally asked.

"No, I want you to come over here and rock her to sleep for me."

"Kyle, you know I can't do that."

"Why not? She sees you as her mother. She's lost one already, and I have no idea how much of Caryn she remembers. But the bond you two share is close, probably even deeper than the one I have with her."

"That's not true. She adores you, Kyle."

"I'm not doubting that. But to her, you're her mother. She needs *you*, Cindy."

"Kyle, the fact is, I am *not* her mother ... and I never will be. I'm sorry. I love her so much, but I can't be a surrogate anymore. I have to move on; you have to move on."

Kyle bit his bottom lip and tried to pull Kylla back down to his chest, but she began to say *no* and started to cry.

"I'm sorry, Kyle," Cindy whispered as she clicked off her phone.

She fell across her bed and began to weep. Just to hear Kylla's whimper through the receiver tore her to pieces. She loved her so much, and she knew it must seem selfish to not go over there, but it was time to stop all the pretending.

There is nothing pretend about love, a voice came inside her head. *Love is patient and kind—it's never selfish. You are selfish, Cindy Marcum. You're trying to save your own emotions and attachments, and you're hurting everyone you love in the process. What more will it take for you to begin thinking of others instead of yourself. What more?*

Forty-Nine

Cindy and Sue sat expectantly in Dr. Ashton's office late Thursday morning. At least this would be a bright spot in Cindy's week. Since her discussion with Kyle on Tuesday evening, he hadn't spoken a word to her, and Jonathan hadn't been much better. At least her mother had been sweet, but she didn't know of Cindy's rejection of Kyle and Kylla, nor her plan to leave the secretarial position as soon as possible.

Dr. Ashton finally walked in with a folder full of charts and information. "Good morning, ladies," she said soberly as she looked up.

She must have had a bad morning, Cindy thought to herself. *Maybe Mom's report will cheer her up.*

"How are you feeling, Mrs. Marcum?" Kate asked as she sat down and crossed her arms.

"Well, I'm still pretty tired and worn out from all the treatments, but I'm happy and life is good," Sue replied with a smile.

"Mrs. Marcum," Kate was still serious, "you're not tired because of the treatments. You should be pulling out of that by now."

"What are you saying?" Cindy asked cautiously as an alarm began to go off in her head.

"I'm saying," the doctor picked up the folder again and turned to the top page, "that it appears your cancer has returned."

"What?" Sue gasped as she put her hand up to her heart. "How can that be? I thought we had *aggressively* attacked this thing. I thought after the major surgery and the chemo treatments I was supposed to be fine."

"That's what we *hoped,*" Kate said as she handed a piece of paper to Sue. "According to your scans, the cancer has spread into your left lung and the uppermost part of your liver."

Cindy dropped into a chair.

"Are you okay, Cindy?" Kate asked a bit distressed. "Are you gonna pass out again?"

"No," Cindy shook her head. "This isn't what I expected."

"It's not what I expected either," Kate shook her head. "I'm just gonna be honest with you: the fact that the cancer spread in the midst of all these treatments isn't a good sign."

"And now what does *that* mean?" Cindy wondered as the fear grew higher.

"It means we need to get started right away on diagnosing this fully, and then deciding how we want to attack it."

"No!" Sue practically screamed. "I am *not* doing this again. I'm not having surgery, and I'm not going back on chemo!"

"Mother!" Cindy cried as tears began form. "You can't be serious!"

"Dead serious."

"Mrs. Marcum, your options are extremely limited, and time is literally life threatening. I can't let you put this off like you did last time."

"I'm not putting anything off," Sue said calmly. "I'm not doing it. Final answer."

Kate Ashton went on as though Sue had said nothing. When she gave Sue her slip for the receptionist, Kate motioned for Cindy to stay behind.

"You can't let her ignore this," Kate was firm. "You need to find another rabbit to pull out of your hat like you did last time."

"I don't have any more rabbits. Angie Wright was my only hope last time; she's on some Pacific Island right now with a new baby."

"Look, we can't put this off. I'm having her make another appointment for Monday so we can begin more diagnostics."

"What if she won't come?"

"That's not *my* job. You get her here, and I'll do my part."

The ride home was miserably tense. They had be so positive on the way to Tupelo earlier that morning, but after meeting with Dr. Ashton, it was the worst possible let down imaginable. Cindy kept trying to think of a way to convince her mother to try it all again, but when she remembered the struggle after the surgery and the weakness after the chemo, she couldn't blame her.

"Mother," Cindy began gently, "please give it another try."

"Why?"

"You told me you felt like life was good again. It's the first time you've felt alive since Daddy's death. With me being home again, and Kyle and Kylla around, we've had fun, Mother. We've had a good time."

"But all that's about to change, isn't it, Cindy?" Sue asked her as she looked over with a sarcastic smile.

"What do you mean?" What was her mother talking about?

"I hear that you're ready to go," Sue said looking back toward the front of the car. "You want a committee formed, and you're ready to get out of here—ready to go back to your old life."

"First, I don't want to return to my *old life*." Cindy was slightly humiliated. Why hadn't her mother told her she knew about her plans? "I came back to Dockrey to help you through your treatments and recovery. My job at the church is only temporary, and that's all it ever was. At some point I'm gonna have to leave. I figured this was as good a time as any."

"And what about Kyle and Kylla?"

"What about them? Mother, my life isn't tied to them! They're a family; I'm not a part of their family. I'm a friend. What am I supposed to do? File for joint custody or something?"

"Kylla needs you right now." Sue sighed. "And so does Kyle."

"Mother, I know where you're headed with this; I can't just link myself up with Kyle. It would be wrong to do that to him."

"Can you *please* explain that statement to me? It would be *wrong* for you to link yourself with Kyle?"

"He's a minister!" Cindy said dumbfounded, unable to comprehend why her mother couldn't understand that. "What kind of ... woman ... would I be for his life?"

"For crying out loud, Cindy! A forgiven woman, a woman who loves his child as much as he does, a woman who's capable of supporting him and standing beside him when he faces inquiries about his divorce and his ex-wife's death, and as seems obvious to everyone but you, a woman that he adores."

Cindy would have screamed in frustration had she not been an emotional wreck from discovering the cancer again. The situation was not as simple as all that.

"It's not that easy. How can Kyle be with someone like me?"

"Did I not just explain that?"

"It would be ridiculous, ludicrous! As much as it may seem like a good idea, it would never work. I would be the millstone around his neck, and I would be this *woman of reputation* as Kylla's mother. How could I do that to them?"

"You're an idiot!" Sue spat out. "Do you know who the only person is who would ever have a problem with that?"

Cindy shook her head.

"You! You're bound and determined to pull yourself away from the best things that have ever happened to you because you're afraid it might require a little too much effort to make it work! Well, here's a news flash, Cindy: anything worth having requires a huge amount of work. Living alone, committing to no one, sailing through life with no stresses or worries—yes, that's way easier, but in the end, you wind up lonely, sad, with nothing worthwhile to show for your life. Your father's legacy isn't insurance. Nobody cares that he sold insurance! He's remembered for the warm-hearted, compassionate, and giving man that he was. Not one person came to me during his viewing or funeral and said, *He was such a wonderful insurance man. I bet you're proud he left you so well off.*"

"I get the point, Mother." Cindy gritted her teeth.

"Do you? I doubt it. The thing about all of this that makes me so sad is that one day you're going to wake up and realize you messed up. You'll see that you walked away from the perfect life, but it'll be too late. And there you'll be: sitting in your fluffy oversized bed, surrounded by pretty things, with no one beside you or squealing in delight in the next room. And I'll tell you this: I have no intention of being alive when that happens."

"Mother!" Cindy nearly slammed on the breaks. "Is that why you won't have any more treatments? You're pinning this on me?"

Sue sat still, her face and will resolute. "I have a no-good son who doesn't even have the decency to pretend he cares by showing up more than two or three times a year. I have a daughter who never cared about anyone but herself, yet turned her life around in order to help me overcome cancer, only to turn back around and live in her selfishness all over again."

"I'm not gonna be like I was before! My life's gonna be different; it's just not going to be in Dockrey."

"Make yourself believe that, if you can, but it doesn't matter what you do on the outside. The truth is, you're running away because inside of you dwells a selfishness that's afraid to step out and love, step out and commit, step out and *give* of yourself for a change, instead of just soaking up what other people have to offer. Ruin your life, Cindy, just like your brother, but for heaven's sake, please don't expect me to go through those horrible treatments again just so I can watch it all with my own eyes."

That pretty much summed it up. What could Cindy say? She certainly didn't see it that way; she was thinking of Kyle and Kylla. Her mother was sick, upset, and irrational. Maybe as the days passed, her thinking would become clearer and Cindy could better explain why it was so important that she leave … soon.

Fifty

On Friday morning, Cindy was thankful to be in the office by herself. Her hours began at eight, but Kyle and Jonathan didn't have to be in until nine. She stared out the window to the valley below, but her heart wasn't warmed as it had been in the past. How could things have been so wonderful and perfect the past few months, and now have fallen apart again? She knew she should pray and ask God what was going on and what she should do next, but she couldn't find the inner strength to even do that.

When Jonathan and Kyle came in together, Kylla was with them. As soon as she saw Cindy, she screamed in delight. "Mama! Mama!"

Kyle tried to hold her, but Kylla squirmed and held her arms out to Cindy so much that he nearly dropped her. He had no choice but to let her go. The look on his face tore Cindy's heart on an even deeper level. Kylla rushed to her and threw her arms around her legs. There was no way Cindy could ignore her. She picked the toddler up and cradled her to her chest.

"Mama," Kylla said in a voice that sounded more like relief than affection.

"Hey, sweetheart." Cindy stroked her soft curls. "How's my girl?"

"Mama," was all Kylla would say as she grabbed a strand of Cindy's hair and began to rub it between her fingers.

She looked up at the men and noticed their sober faces.

"Why isn't your mother answering the phone?" Jonathan asked with great concern. "What happened yesterday? Barbara had to go to a meeting today and couldn't keep Kylla. We were trying to get Sue, but she's not picking up. What's going on, Cindy?"

She felt tears forming. She bit her lip as she gently rubbed Kylla's back and told them, "The cancer is back."

"No," Kyle whispered in utter shock. "That can't be."

"How bad?" Jonathan asked.

"Pretty bad." She pulled Kylla closer as a tear found its way out. "It's spread into one of her lungs and the top of her liver."

Jonathan actually had to brace himself against the wall to keep from falling.

Kyle looked at Cindy with a pained expression and asked, "How are *you* doing?"

She buried her face in Kylla's hair as she tried to keep herself from the sobs that were close to surfacing. Leave it to Kyle to be concerned about *her* at a time like this. "I'm dealing with it," she managed to get out.

"Cindy," Jonathan said firmly, "go to my office, please."

She nodded. Kyle came to take Kylla, but she refused to let go. "It's okay. She can come in with me."

"Answer the phones, Kyle," Jonathan told him just before shutting the door.

Jonathan didn't sit; he paced slowly around his office and ran his hand through his hair several times. She continued to cradle Kylla who was completely still except for her hand in Cindy's hair.

He finally paused and turned to her. "How many people have to die, Cindy, before God gets your attention?"

"What? Are you saying this is *my* fault?"

He sat on the edge of his desk and crossed his arms. "God works through need. Remember Joseph in the Bible?"

She nodded.

"God's plan was to make him a great leader. God even gave him dreams to let him know, but it took twelve years and a lot of pain and suffering before Joseph was ready for that call."

He stood again and went behind his desk to the chair. He sat down and propped his elbows up then stared at Cindy for the longest time. "I told you God wasn't yet finished with you here, but you were determined to move on anyway. Let me ask you, Cindy—did God just find another way to make you stay? Did He do one more thing to get your attention?"

She was astonished. He *was* blaming her. "I thought God was a God of love," she said totally confused.

"He is, and He loves you too much to watch you walk away from here before He's finished with what He needs to accomplish."

"But my mother! Why her? Why doesn't He strike me with cancer?"

"Don't tempt Him," he said sternly. "I think right now you'd better get on your knees and ask God what He's up to … and what it is you need to do."

Kylla sat up at last and gazed deep into her eyes, but she wouldn't smile. She seemed to be searching for some reason why Cindy had been gone from her life.

"Mama," she said softly again. "Mama."

The emotional overload she was facing at this moment was almost too much to bear. Between her mother's cancer, Jonathan's accusations, and Kylla's hopeless eyes, she felt like she should simply crawl under a rock and stay there until all the storms had passed. That's when she realized what everyone was saying was true. Her nature had always been to run away from trouble. When a problem arose, especially with people, she simply walked away. But right now, walking away would hurt those she cared about the most.

"What do *you* think I should do?" she asked Jonathan feebly. "I need some guidance. Obviously I'm in no condition to try and figure out what's the right thing to do."

He finally smiled. "That's why God puts people in churches. He wants to surround us with those who care about our lives and see the directions we need to heed. Cindy, I'm not only your pastor, but I'm a man who deeply loves your family. If you seriously want my advice, I've definitely got some."

She nodded at him. "I want your advice, Pastor Jon. I'm lost right now."

He leaned back in his chair and gave a sigh of relief. "First, stay here. Don't plan on leaving."

"But the position is temporary."

"Don't you think I know that? I also happen to know that you've done an exceptional job and that people are talking about hiring you permanently."

She looked up at him in surprise. She wasn't sure if she was delighted about it or not, but it felt good to know that people in the church believed in her.

"That's number one. Number two—you're holding her there in your lap." He paused as he watched Kylla with Cindy. "Whether you like it or not, you're her mother. You didn't ask for that, and you probably didn't even want it, but the fact is this: God placed *you* in her life at a very critical time. God chose *you* to be her mother. I don't know which is worse for that little girl—having her first mother murdered, or having her second mother ignore her."

Those words stung Cindy deeper than anything ever had. She bit her lip in humiliation.

"I don't know how you're gonna work this out with Kyle, but I'm sure he's more than willing to do whatever it takes to ensure you and Kylla are together. I've watched him come down in tears this past week trying to comfort a distraught little angel because you were sitting at home drowning in selfishness. God's given Kylla to you, and I know you love her … it's written all over your face and in the way you hold her and care for her. You need to come to terms with that."

She didn't want to accept it, but she knew it was true. Kylla lay back down on her chest and grabbed another strand of hair.

"As for your mother, your duty isn't over there yet either. I don't know if God did this to keep you around, or if indeed it's getting close to the time He takes her also."

She winced at the thought.

"Whatever the reason, she most certainly doesn't need to be alone. Would you agree to that?"

She merely nodded. There was no way she could form words at the moment.

"Then I suggest you begin to give some permanence to your thoughts about Dockrey."

She sat there with Kylla and wondered what to do next. He was right—her mother was right. She was running away because somewhere in the midst of all of this she had found herself losing bits and pieces of her heart to other people, and it scared her. Love wasn't easy, and somewhere in her past she had decided to stop giving her true self away. God indeed was love, and it was time Cindy began to be more like the God who gave His life to save her from herself.

"Pastor Jon, the bulletin's done," she said softly. "Would you mind if I took Kylla home with me so I can talk to my mother ... and make up a little time I've lost with this ... angel ... the past few days?"

"That's the smartest thing I've heard come out of your mouth in a long time."

***

"Cindy? Kylla!" Sue was stunned when they walked into the house. "What are you doing here?"

"We need to talk, Mother," Cindy said firmly. "Let's sit down."

Fifty-One

On Friday evening, Cindy took Kylla back to the Wrights' house, followed by the white car and the black Corvette. Kyle had gone to visit his parents for the afternoon. She spent some time talking with Barbara and Jonathan and explained that she would be staying at her mother's indefinitely, and if the church indeed wanted to hire her permanently, she would be more than willing. When Kylla began to rub her eyes, Cindy took her upstairs, bathed her, clothed her, and then rocked her to sleep. She waited for Kyle to return before she left.

"I need to apologize to you," she said to him quietly not wanting to disturb Kylla.

"You've had a lot on your plate." He was always so kind to her.

"No more than you. Only you didn't have the luxury of shirking your responsibilities to Kylla."

"I didn't want to shirk them." So, he did harbor some resentment after all.

"I don't know what God's doing in my life right now. I do know that Kylla needs me, so I plan to be here for her as long as you're here. When you leave, I'll just deal with that then. My heart will break, but I've learned now that I can live with a broken heart."

"I'm not leaving, Cindy."

She looked at him in surprise.

"When my position is done here, I plan to start giving private lessons. I talked with the principal at the school this week. He said I could have a room in the band hall to give lessons during school. I won't be a millionaire, but it should be enough to get Kylla and me a place to stay and put food on the table. If I ever need some extra cash, I can always sit in with a few recording sessions at the studio."

"You're not leaving Dockrey?" She was still stunned.

"I'm comfortable here; I feel like I belong here … more than any place I've ever been. Hard to believe, isn't it? That someone would actually run *to* here instead of run away."

She smiled. Hope was slowly returning.

He continued, "And you're welcome to see Kylla anytime you want. In fact, I was thinking maybe you could take her home a few nights a week. Martha's Vineyard really impacted her relationship with you. She needs you, Cindy."

***

Cindy needed some time alone, so she decided to go to Florence on Saturday. She shopped at a few of her favorite stores but eventually wound up at the mall. She really wasn't hungry but was slightly nauseous from the intensity of her last couple of days, so she ordered a Chic-Fil-A and sat out in the mall hoping it would help calm her churning stomach.

"Cindy, the gorgeous babe," came a voice from behind her. She didn't have to turn around to know who it was. In fact she wanted to hide. Evan Clark.

Sure enough. He pulled up a seat, turned it backwards, and straddled it as he sat down with her. "What have you been up to?" he said with a charming smile.

"A lot," was all she would reply. She really didn't want to get into her life with Evan.

"How's your mom?"

"Not doing too well." *None of your business.* "We just found out on Thursday that her cancer's returned." *Like you care.*

"Wow, sorry to hear that." He sounded sincere, but she knew Evan had only one thing on his mind, and she knew if she lingered long enough, he would eventually suggest it. "I bet all this has been tough on you."

"I'm making it." She didn't need to appear weak or needy. He would try to reel her in if she did—and the thought sickened her. "It's been tough at times, but my mother and I have gotten really close. I've been glad for the time together."

"Becoming a regular old family gal, huh?" His gray eyes were like ice, so different from the warmth and sparkle of Kyle's.

"Looks that way." *Leave, Evan. Leave.*

"How's the job?" he continued with the small talk.

"Working out great. They're talking about hiring me permanently."

He laughed at this. "I know you're thrilled about that! Cindy Marcum as a church secretary! There's a vision."

"I am thrilled," she said seriously. "I love working there. I love the values that being back in Dockrey has created for me."

"Values? I like *your* kind of values."

"I'm not like that anymore, Evan. I really do have values … and standards now, morals if you like."

His face grew serious. "Is that possible? Don't get me wrong; I personally loved your *lack* of morals. But come on, Cindy, you're not the picture of scruples."

"Believe me, I know. My past haunts me on a regular basis."

"Why?" he shook his head and reached for her hand. "Your past had a lot of great moments. I was part of quite a few of them."

She pulled her hand back and stared at him in disgust. "Yes, you were. And in the process we destroyed your marriage, your wife's life, and the normal life your children should have had with Daddy coming home every night as they grew up. I'm not proud of that, Evan, and I don't ever want to be that way again."

He laughed at her again. "Don't tell me *you* want to grow up, get married, have kids, and live happily ever after?"

She stood up quickly and grabbed what was left of her sandwich. "If I could be so blessed to find someone who could look beyond my past, yes … in a minute! What we had Evan, was stupid! It was selfish and shallow and nothing more than animal behavior."

"Whatever, but it was still great."

"No, it wasn't. It was what happens to people when they decide that the only person that matters is yourself. My life affects other people now. I have more to be responsible for than just what pleases me."

Evan's furrowed brow slowly changed into a smile. "Oh … my … gosh," he exclaimed. "You're in love."

"That's not it."

"Yes, it is! I can't believe this. I really thought I could make you fall in love with me, but you were one cold chick. I was willing to settle for just sleeping with you. Man, you're so beautiful. I wanted you forever, but I didn't think you had what it took to actually love anyone. Who is he?"

She crumpled her food up in the foil and tossed it in the garbage beside her. She then picked up her things to leave. He stood quickly and gently held her arm.

"Cindy, I'm not trying to be calloused," he said as he stood next to her. "I just always cared for you. Before you move on with this guy, give me another chance. I can give you anything you want. You want us to get your apartment back? I can do that. You want to travel around the world? I can do that too. I can give you anything your heart desires; you know that." He then leaned down to her ear. "Have dinner with me tonight. Let's talk."

She jerked her arm away but smiled as she faced him. It thrilled her to know that she wasn't even tempted. "I'm not interested, Evan. Besides, my heart doesn't desire those things anymore."

"That's right. You've got *values* now."

"Goodbye, Evan." She stepped away from him. "If I were you, I'd work on getting my wife and kids back. That would be the smartest investment you could make."

He shook his head. "I don't want them back. You, however, I'd gladly welcome."

She was sickened even more. She finally turned and left. As she walked down the mall and out to her car, the nausea grew thicker. Was she ever really like that? Her heart was so far from that lifestyle now. At times, it even seemed like it had never been her, but just some disgusting imagination. Yes, she had values and morals now, and yes, she wanted a life that was good and honest and right. She threw her packages inside her car and climbed down into her seat.

Thank you, heavenly Father, for saving me. How did I live that way? How did you forgive me for all those things I did ... all those men? But more importantly, where do I go from here? Please, make it clear. I've ruined lives and families in the past—show me how to bring healing to others now. My mom. Kyle. Kylla. What do I do?

***

When she returned from her shopping trip, she stopped by the Wrights to see Kylla. The baby was thrilled. She ran into Cindy's arms and clung to her tightly. She found herself eating dinner there again, and for the first time since Friday morning, Kylla stopped clinging. She wouldn't leave a room where Cindy was, but she was at last content to play quietly by herself as long as she was near.

"Want to take her home tonight?" Kyle asked her as they sat upstairs on the couch in his apartment.

"I've been thinking about that," she said seriously. "As tempting as it is, do you think that'd be good? She's your child, Kyle. She lives with you. It would almost be like joint custody or something. I've never liked that. It was so ... unnatural."

"It's okay. It was just a suggestion."

"Maybe when she gets older and she realizes that I'm not really her mom, then we can have some sleepovers."

He chuckled. "How will you tell her that you're not her mother? What will you do? Tell her she has to start calling you Indee again ... or what? If you'll remember, she started calling you Mama all on her own."

"Well, you planted the suggestion."

"Just a word in passing. I didn't think she knew what we were talking about."

"You know what? I'm not gonna worry about it right now," she said firmly. "What she needs at the present is for me to be here for her. So that's what I'm gonna do. The day may come when we all have to say goodbye, but it won't be anytime soon. Until then, I'll just keep being Mama I guess."

He breathed a huge sigh. "I can't tell you how glad I am to hear that. You don't know how hard it's been this week with her. I've never seen Kylla inconsolable, but I couldn't do anything with her. She would finally cry herself to sleep, and then she would heave a sob on and off for thirty minutes after I laid her down." He smiled at Cindy. "She loves you, you know."

"The feeling's mutual."

"Book, Mama," Kylla interrupted them with her zoo book in hand. Kyle grabbed her up and placed her on Cindy's lap. She gave her cheek a kiss and then turned her around so they could read together. It took an incredibly long time to get through pointing out all the animals, their eyes, their noses, and their ears. When they neared the end of the book, Kylla began to rub her eyes.

"Somebody's sleepy," Cindy said softly as she put down the book and turned the baby back around. Right away Kylla laid her head on Cindy's chest and grabbed a piece of hair. "Should I give her a bath? Church is tomorrow."

"I'll go start the water," Kyle nodded.

As he walked toward the bathroom, he turned back to take in the vision. As much as he wanted to resent Cindy and chastise her again for her on and off emotions, his resentment dissolved at her beauty. He could see her profile as she talked with Kylla to keep her awake. Part of him wished it was just her beauty that had captured his heart, but it was so much more. Everything about her drew him to her. Even her emotional wreckage had pulled him in also. He wished more than anything that he could help bind up the wounds that seemed to still bleed in her heart. He wanted to help her, not punish her. And above all, he longed to be the man that finally broke down the walls she had built for so many years.

Fifty-Two

July Fourth had been a wash for Cindy since it came on the heels of her mother's latest diagnosis. Even the Wrights had not celebrated this year the holiday that had always been a huge family get together. On the following Monday, Cindy had driven Sue back to Tupelo for extensive testing. The day was tense, exhausting, and somber. On Tuesday morning, when Cindy walked into the church office, she felt a huge sense of relief. There was nothing better than a busy routine to take one's mind off of stress.

As she worked on things that had been put off from yesterday, she glanced occasionally out the window and into the valley. The sun was bright and the air was clear. Even in the midst of all the struggles she was facing, there was a peace today knowing that she had chosen to do the right thing. Cindy had seldom done anything simply because it was *right*. Angie Wright had to talk her, or guilt her, into staying with her mother. This time, however, Cindy knew that her decision was permanent. But more than that, she knew she had made this choice not because it was best for her, but because it was best for everyone else in her life. There was nothing to tie her to Florence except a group of wild friends, a few old flames, and a job that paid six times more than what she was making now. She smiled. She never realized that making right choices, regardless of the sacrifice, could bring such peace. She took comfort in knowing that for the first time in her life she had sown some good seeds. She had certainly reaped the fruit of her bad choices, and it was reassuring to know that somewhere down the road she would reap the benefits of the choices she was now making.

Being caught up in her thoughts, she was startled when Ben Hall walked into the office.

"Good morning, Miss Marcum," he said in his usual straight tone. But then a little gleam sparked his dark eyes. "Been doing any FBI snooping lately?"

"No, sir," she grinned at him, slightly embarrassed. "I'm leaving that up to the big boys."

"You did an excellent job, by the way. Did I ever tell you that?"

"In so many words, I think so."

He looked around the office, surveying various areas, then asked her, "How are things between you and Mr. Sarkos?"

Cindy thought that was a strange question. "In what capacity?"

He avoided her eyes and continued his surveying. "I'm never really sure how much of what you do is acting and how much is real."

"Oh." What did it matter?

Ben Hall glanced down at his watch. "Eight fifty-seven. They should be here shortly."

"They?"

"Reverend Wright and Mr. Sarkos. We've had some interesting developments in the case."

"Really?" Cindy came to life at that statement. "Are you any closer to finding Caryn's killer?"

"That's actually classified, Miss Marcum. If Mr. Sarkos doesn't mind you hearing, you can be present at the briefing."

She decided to tease him a bit just to see if he could loosen up. "Oh, come on, Agent Hall. I'm practically a part of the agency now. You can share classified stuff with me."

He actually winked at her as he said, "Not until you hold a badge, Miss Marcum, although I'll confess that when you smile like that it's hard to refuse you anything."

Was he flirting with her? Ben Hall? Her face grew warm and she turned back to her computer. She sighed with relief when the door opened and in walked the two ministers.

"Ben!" Kyle said as he stuck out his hand. "What brings you here for a personal visit? Good news, I hope."

"Well, it *is* news," Ben affirmed, "but whether it's good or not will depend on how you look at it."

"Wo, sounds serious." Kyle stopped smiling.

Ben opened his folder and said, "I think you may want Reverend Wright with you as I reveal this. It might need some moral interpretation. Do you want to go somewhere private, or do you mind Miss Marcum snooping around in your business?" He winked at Cindy again. Kyle saw it.

"No. Cindy can stay. She's as deep into this as I am."

"Very well," Ben mumbled as he walked over and sat on the edge of her desk. Kyle raised his eyebrows at her and she gave a slight shrug. "Those documents you gave me, the marriage license and the divorce papers, remember those?"

"Sure," Kyle nodded. "You've had them a long time."

"Yep. Couldn't get a run on them. Caryn, or Callista as we now know she was called, never put a social security number on any of them. Come to find out, they're both frauds."

Ben was quiet as he let the essence of his discovery sink in.

"What exactly does that mean?" Kyle asked slowly and deliberately.

"Well, the good news, Mr. Sarkos, is that you're not divorced any more. I know that bothered you."

Kyle rubbed his chin as another realization dawned. "Wait. That means, then, that I was never married either doesn't it?"

"That's what it means. Which leads me to a question that has puzzled me all morning: who did your taxes?"

Kyle's face grew red. "Caryn." He closed his eyes in embarrassment. "Unbelievable. She told me she loved math and that this would give her something to do. Why? What's wrong with my taxes?"

"Nothing, except for the fact that they were filed as though you were a single man all those years."

Kyle pulled up a chair and plopped down.

"Where were you married, Kyle?" Ben asked him.

"At her parents' house in Martha's Vineyard. My parents didn't want us to get married, so she suggested we fly up there and just take care of it one weekend. Why not? If I was gonna marry her, I wanted it done before I went to seminary, and I was starting in two weeks. So I just did it."

"The guy who officiated doesn't exist either," Ben sighed.

Everyone sat quietly as they considered the ramifications.

"One good thing about it, Kyle," Jonathan laughed lightly, "you're not a divorced minister anymore!"

"No, I only lived in adultery for ten years, that's all … while I served churches, by the way."

"I'll disagree with you there," Jonathan countered. "You *personally* weren't living in adultery. As far as you knew, you had obeyed all the laws, and I'll have to say that in the eyes of God, you were married."

"Nice perspective," Kyle said sarcastically. "I wonder how many churches would agree with you."

Ben interrupted. "Another thing to consider also is that it could be called a common-law marriage. Some states will hold to that."

Kyle stood and began to pace. "This is ridiculous! I lived with a woman for ten years, thinking she was my wife. She filed all my taxes, cooked my meals, washed my clothes, and shared my bed, and in all that time it never occurred to me that she was the daughter of a convicted celebrity who was running for her life! Is there a name for men like me? Is there a word with a deeper word than *stupid*? How could this happen?"

"Now we know why she wanted nothing from you or the house: it would have required you getting a lawyer," Ben stated.

"Why? She knew she was pregnant with my child! Why did she leave? Why did she decide to end the charade then? Why didn't we just go on like we had? None of this makes any sense!"

Cindy felt something prick her heart when he talked about Caryn that way. Was she still jealous of his dead wife?

"We're not sure," Agent Hall said as he closed his folder. "But it does explain why no one thinks the baby is hers. To those on the other side, they can't figure how you fit in. I've got a couple of theories about Caryn's behavior, but I'm guessing, based on her actions over the years, that a legal birth in a hospital would have ruined her cover. There's no way she could have gotten out of not having a legitimate social security number had you been there with her."

"But doesn't Kylla have a birth certificate?" Cindy remembered. "That's how you knew that Kyle was listed as her father."

"Yes, but there's no number for Caryn. And then there's that whole mess too: Kylla's birth mother is listed as Caryn Carter Sarkos. We know the truth; we have to change it."

"That can't be good," Jonathan jumped in. "Then whoever was after Callista would know that Kylla was her baby … and that Kyle was the father."

"For now," Ben explained, "that document is still tied up in red tape. The only way anybody could get a hold of it would be if they had someone working on the inside. That's unlikely."

Kyle stopped pacing and lowered his head in surrender. "This can't be happening. Is there any way any of this can ever be cleared up?"

"Glad you asked," Ben said as he stood up and dropped his folder on the edge of Cindy's desk. "We've got another plan."

Kyle rolled his eyes as he looked over at Cindy. "Please tell me it does *not* include Cindy prying information from people."

Ben laughed much to the surprise of the other three. "No. This will not involve Miss Marcum. However, we're going to need *you* to pry some information."

"Surely you've figured out I'm pitiful at that. Who is it?"

"Our best offense at this point is to go straight to the horse's mouth, so to speak."

Kyle looked over at him and asked, "And who would this horse be?"

"Martin Sartin."

Kyle plopped down into the chair, crossing his arms in frustration. "You can't be serious. You want me to talk with Martin Sartin?"

"He's in prison in California, serving several life sentences," Ben reached for his folder and pulled out the paper at the top of the stack. He handed it to Kyle. "We should have everything in place by July 18. What do you say?"

Kyle chuckled nervously. "I say this is crazy. You want *me* to talk to Martin Sartin? What am I supposed to say?"

Ben scrunched up his nose at Kyle's question. "Are there not things you want to ask him concerning Callista? Don't you have this burning need to know some answers about what she did to you and to Kylla?"

"He won't know me from Adam!"

"I'd bet you ten-to-one he knows exactly who you are. He's probably the one who suggested she pull the whole deal off to begin with. I'm inclined to believe that on some of those weeks when she was supposed to be in Martha's Vineyard, she was probably out visiting her real dad a bit."

Kyle looked at the schedule on the paper. "July 18, huh? If this thing isn't settled soon, I'm going to develop an ulcer."

"Welcome to *my* world," Ben grinned.

When Ben Hall exited, Jonathan had to leave for the Shoals to make some hospital visits. Kyle just sat in the chair rubbing the back of his neck and reading over the itinerary for his visit to California. He didn't want to do this.

"Want me to go to California for you?" Cindy asked mischievously as she grinned over at him. "I'm good at this kind of stuff."

He kept his head down but glanced up at her with raised eyebrows. "No, you get to keep Kylla while I'm gone."

"Oh, goody. I'll have way more fun, then."

"Yeah, you will," he said weakly as he began to roll his head around on his neck.

"Tense?"

"Why on earth would you think that?" He was being sarcastic again.

She shook her head and went over to him. She put her hands on his shoulders and began to rub her thumbs into his neck.

"Oh, man," he sighed. "That feels incredibly good."

"Try to relax, will you. Maybe I can work some of this tension out for you."

"No problem." He sat still as she kneaded his muscles with her thin fingers. "That feels really good. Could I hire you to do this on a regular basis?"

"Sorry, I only do it on a *need* basis, and right now you look like you really need this."

"I don't know if it's possible to be any needier than I am right now."

Fifty-Three

Wednesday evening church groups all met in the sanctuary so that the focus could be a prayer meeting for Sue Marcum. She hadn't wanted to tell people about her cancer again, but with the support and concern the church had shown during her first bout, she agreed with the Wrights to let them in on it this time from the beginning. Jonathan began with a few words about God being in control, being all-powerful and all-wise. He then had Sue sit in a chair at the front of the sanctuary. Various people came up and prayed for her individually, then near the end, the entire church gathered around her, as many touching her as possible, and all the rest touching each other. Jonathan led in a prayer for healing and restoration, and Cindy felt her knees grow weak.

Father, she prayed silently, *please don't make my mother suffer for my mistakes. If Jonathan was right about You needing to keep me here, don't punish Mother because I was too blind to see that. I know You have the power to guide Dr. Ashton in a way that can bring my mother complete healing. Please guide her, give her wisdom, help her to see the whole problem ... and please don't let my mother have to suffer anymore for my inadequacies. I can't change my past, but I am wholeheartedly giving You my present and my future.*

After church, many expressed to Cindy and Sue how they would be praying earnestly the next day during the appointment. Everyone was believing God to bring full healing this time around.

Jonathan took Kyle off to the side before choir rehearsal. "I want you to go with them to the doctor tomorrow."

"Why? If anyone goes shouldn't it be you?"

"Bill Nabors is having by-pass surgery in Birmingham. I'll be up and gone before the sun rises. I feel like the Marcums need someone there for them during this. You're as close to them as I am; please do this, okay?"

"No problem." Then he frowned. "What about Kylla?"

"Barbara will watch her."

"Then who'll answer the phone at the church?"

Jonathan chuckled and shook his head. "No one, Kyle. This isn't Harvest Hollow. The church won't fall apart simply because we have a day now and then when no one can be in the office."

"David Deaton really gripes about it when that happens."

Jonathan laughed heartily this time. "Gee, what a surprise!"

***

Kyle drove Sue and Cindy to Tupelo in Sue's car the following morning. The worry was thick. Kyle wished he could be light and fun, but between Sue's impending diagnosis and his upcoming trip to California, he was probably in worse shape than the ladies.

After they arrived, they sat quietly in the waiting room thumbing through various magazines lying around on tables. When they were finally called into the back, Kyle hesitated. Was he supposed to go in too? Would Mrs. Marcum be changing clothes or getting examined? He just sat there.

"Come on, Kyle," Sue reached out her hand. "This meeting will be in Dr. Ashton's office. This is why you're here: moral support."

"Ashton?" Kyle swallowed. He had forgotten all about Sue's doctor being Kate Ashton. His face began to flush.

"That's right," Sue nodded as she pulled Kyle to the back of the building.

Cindy grinned and then teased, "Kyle knows Dr. Ashton really well. They had lunch together the day of your surgery."

"Not really," Kyle replied quickly. "We just sat together in the cafeteria."

He was uncomfortable waiting with the Marcums in Kate's office. She was very vocal and tended to say exactly what was on her mind. He hoped she would have enough professional tact to not say anything to Sue or Cindy about their date. He began to chew on a thumbnail, something he hadn't done in years.

When Dr. Ashton came in, she was shocked to see Kyle with them. "Mrs. and Miss Marcum," she smiled as she shook their hands. "Kyle." She smiled up at him. "Here in a ministerial capacity this morning?" she asked him.

"No," Cindy replied before he had a chance to speak. "He's a good friend. Let's call him moral support."

Kyle suppressed his smile. *Go Cindy*, he thought to himself.

Kate opened the chart and shook her head as though she didn't know what to say. "This is difficult, ladies," she began. Cindy's heart fell. "I don't exactly know how to explain all of this to you."

"Just shoot with us straight, Dr. Ashton," Sue said soberly. "Whatever it is, we want to know the bottom line up front."

"Okay." Kate folded her hands on her desk and looked directly at Sue. "The cancer is gone. Whatever was there last week has totally vanished now."

No one said anything. Cindy's mind began to race with a million thoughts. She literally felt her head begin to go black like when she had passed out after her mother's surgery months before.

"Cindy?" Dr. Ashton asked in concern. "Are you all right? You face is very pale."

Kyle went to her immediately, took her hand, and knelt down beside her at the chair. "Do you need something?" he asked quickly. "Are you gonna be okay?"

She swallowed and nodded. "I'll be fine. Dr. Ashton, please explain what you just said."

Kate glanced down at Kyle holding Cindy's hand, but went right back to her charts. She pulled out two x-rays and hung them on the display. Turning on the light she pointed to the first one. "This was from last Monday. If you'll look here you'll notice the cloudy areas." She now pointed to the second x-ray taken from a different angle. "And here it is again. My natural assumption was that the cancer had returned."

She then pulled up an image on her computer. This is one of the tests we ran this past Monday—a much clearer and more detailed diagnostic. It should have shown specifically what the cloudy areas were. Instead, we see a completely clear picture. Mrs. Marcum, there's nothing there." Kate was shaking her head in unbelief.

Kyle stood up and stared at the picture. "How do you explain that?"

"I'm not sure," Kate said as she crossed her arms. "It's possible the machine could have had a smudge on it."

"But look at this," Kyle pointed to the other angle. "It's still there in this picture, same place. Would a smudge have done that?"

Kate shrugged her shoulders. "Frankly, I don't know what to say. I'm actually embarrassed. From the first pictures, even knowing what we know after the second ones, I would still say that this was definitely cancerous tissue."

Everyone stared in astonishment.

"In your professional opinion, what's going on?" Kyle finally asked.

"My professional opinion?" Kate raised her eyebrows. "There was a glitch in the machine and the cloudy areas weren't actually there. Something went wrong with the tests."

Kyle sighed as he looked back at the pictures. "Okay, how about your unprofessional, off-the-record opinion?"

Kate shook her head. "I've never seen anything like this before. Off-the-record I would say it's some sort of miracle, I guess. I will tell you this—my first hunch when I saw the second test results was that there was a big problem with the x-ray machine on the first tests. I compared Mrs. Marcum's pictures with others taken before and after hers; theirs were fine."

Sue finally spoke. "I don't know what everyone is so confused about. We prayed for healing; we prayed for a miracle. God did it. I can promise you, Dr. Ashton, I did nothing on my own to bring this about. I ate no mangos, drank no castor oil, and didn't comb my hair any different ... what little there is of it. If there was cancer there last Monday, and it disappeared this Monday, I had nothing to do with it personally … and neither did your machine."

"I believe you," Kate smiled. "If it was cancer, it was quite a bit. If it disappeared, it was more than a mango."

Suddenly Kyle gave a loud whoop. Everyone jumped. "I'm sorry! But this is flat out supernatural! Y'all can wallow around in shock if you want to, but I'm just a little too excited to stand around quietly."

Sue gave out a whoop herself. "I'm with you, Kyle!"

Kate continued to shake her head. "Mrs. Marcum, I'm giving you a clean bill of health. Every test we ran indicates that you're just fine. I'd like to see you again in six months, but until then, just keep doing what you're doing."

***

To celebrate, they went to Olive Garden for lunch. This was the happiest any of them had been in months. It had seemed as though nothing in life was working out, but for the first time, things were looking up. With her cancer behind her, Sue began to make some plans.

"I'm going to have a deck built out back," she began. "I've always wanted a deck out there so I could go and sit and read outside. I'm going to get right on that. And I want to put a swing set up for Kylla. Someday, she should be able to play outside at my house. If I have to, I'll put up a twelve foot fence too!"

Cindy felt a peace she couldn't possibly express. Only she and Jonathan Wright truly understood what had happened today. She wondered how many miracles she had missed before simply because she had made wrong decisions and lost the possibilities that God had planned. As she watched her mother's animated conversation, and felt Kyle moving next to her with excitement as well, she nearly burst into tears of joy. The only thing missing from this moment was Kylla who had become the light of her life.

***

Sue called Barbara to let her know about the appointment, and the delight was beyond fantastic. Barbara said she would call Jonathan immediately and plan a big celebration dinner that night. As an added bonus, she put Kylla on to say she loved Granny Sue. Sue's heart flip-flopped at her little voice. If she never had grandchildren, just having Kylla call her *Granny Sue* would help to make up for it.

On the way home, Sue thanked Kyle for coming with them, and tried to explain to him what he had come to mean to her the past six months. "I know that Billy is pretty much a worthless piece of flesh. The only time I've seen him through all of this was the day of my surgery. That's pretty pathetic."

Kyle tried to reason with her. "He's just searching, Sue. He hasn't come to the end of himself yet."

She laughed sarcastically. "Oh, that's an understatement. It's been an indescribable blessing having Cindy with me and knowing that she's living for the Lord. I take a lot of solace in that. And Kyle, to be honest with you, in so many areas you've stepped up to the plate like a son in my life. You've filled in the gaps left by Billy's absence, and you've made all of this wonderfully tolerable. I don't know if I could ever thank you enough."

"Sue, you've meant a lot to me too. The Lord has bonded us together because of our hurts, and in many ways, I do feel like I'm your son. Now I'm hoping that just as your cancer is gone, so will all my problems concerning Caryn and Kylla. I so long for the day when I can function again without having to look over my shoulder for some sinister person ready to snatch my happiness. I want the freedom to bring Kylla over to your house and let her play in your backyard ... with no fences or agents nearby."

"It will come, Kyle. I know it will. If God can do what He just did in my life, He can certainly take care of little Kylla."

Fifty-Four

The celebration was just what Kyle needed to take his mind off of California and Martin Sartin. He felt comfort in how Kylla had settled down again since Cindy was spending more time with her. In reality, Cindy was her mother, and Kylla had chosen her to be that. She had actually spent more time with Barbara and Sue, but it was Cindy she had bonded with. She adored the other ladies, but Cindy was something she needed. He wished she could feel a freedom in that role, but she always emitted a slight hesitancy about it ever being permanent.

The evening was unusually cool as a storm was beginning to roll in, so the group ended up on the screened-in back porch. Kylla played quietly as the adults talked, and she would occasionally walk over to Cindy just to hug her.

"She's an angel," Sue said after one such incidence.

"I know," Cindy said warmly. "Are all children like that?"

The entire group gave her a resounding *no* in unison.

"You must not remember keeping my grandchildren last month!" Barbara exclaimed.

Sue jumped in to say, "Now they're angels too."

"Not like Kylla," Barbara responded quickly. "In fact, I can't recall watching a child so young play by herself this quietly. She demands practically no attention at all ..."

"... unless Cindy is around," Jonathan put in.

"...or isn't around," Kyle added. "It makes me wonder: what was her life like before she came here? Did Caryn give her much attention, or maybe she smothered her with love. I find that hard to believe, but it could be possible—Caryn wasn't the smothering type."

"Who knows?" Barbara said. "I had four totally different children."

Jonathan sighed and said, "At least they were different when they were young. Those three girls of yours all pretty much turned out the same way: stubborn-headed and opinionated."

"Three girls of *mine*?" Barbara laughed. "They certainly didn't get those traits from me, Mr. I-know-a-lot-about-everything! You brought them up well!"

Sue laughed out loud and slapped her knees. "She's got you there, Jonathan! They're all clones of you!"

"I don't know," Cindy interrupted. "Angie's changed. In high school, she was definitely like that. And even through college and all her medical training."

"Add seminary in there too," Barbara said glumly. "I was scared to death the mission board would fire her before they hired her."

"But she's not like that anymore," Cindy continued. "When she came back from Padawin, she was this big-hearted, calm, collected island lady or something. It was like she had nothing to fight for anymore, but not in a bad way. It seemed as though she was finally at peace with her life."

Barbara nodded in agreement. "All her life she had pursued one thing: a medical degree for the mission field. It was a long, hard quest. And I suppose that when it finally happened, she truly was at peace. And then there was Michael to add to all of that. Their marriage was like the cherry on the top of her life."

"Actually, I would say he's more like the ice cream, and Baby Cassie would be the cherry," Jonathan corrected her.

They smiled, but then Sue spoke up again. "I've seen the same thing in you, Cindy."

Cindy was caught off guard and her expression showed it.

"It's true. Last year this time, you were a mess. Your father's death only drove you deeper into that miserable life you had. You were headed down the same path as Billy, but then something stopped you. And when you came back to Dockrey, you began to change immediately. I didn't expect the change, to be frank. I expected you to do your duty by me, so to speak. But working at the church, caring for me, and eventually for Kylla … all those things softened you, and the Cindy I knew as a little girl began to emerge again. The sweet, sensitive, and sometimes silly little blond that used to be the light of her daddy's life reappeared. I'm so thankful to have you back."

Cindy was nearly in tears, but a peal of thunder brought Kylla to her feet and running to Cindy for assurance. She picked her up and cradled her to her chest.

"Oh no," Kyle grinned. "If you let her do that, she'll be out for sure in a few minutes."

She needed to get away for a moment. "I'll go up and change her. Then she can fall asleep whenever her heart desires." Cindy left with Kyle following close behind.

After changing Kylla and getting her dressed for bed, Cindy sat in the gliding rocker Jonathan had put up in the apartment from his own bedroom. Kylla immediately nestled in her arms and began to gently twist a strand of hair with her little fingers.

"Mama," Kylla said sleepily. "Night, night?"

"Night, night, sweetheart."

Within five minutes she had fallen asleep, but Cindy wasn't ready to put her down. She just kept rocking and holding her, gently caressing her hair, her face, her little arms, her feet.

"When I go to California, why don't you stay here with her?" Kyle suggested. "She doesn't need to sleep outside of this security until the case is solved."

Cindy rocked gently and thought. "That might be good. But then, it might be bad too."

"How could it be bad?"

"To have her all to myself, even sleeping with her again, I don't know how I could pull away. It's getting harder and harder for me to leave her, Kyle. I think it's hard on her too."

"Well, hopefully this whole mess will be cleared up soon, and then Kylla can spend as much time with you as she wants. You can take her for whole weekends."

"Do you think that would be good for her? You would let me do that?"

"She adores you, Cindy. You fill something in her life that I never will. She knows I'm her Dadda, but there's something about you that she needs desperately. I want her to have that."

She reached out her hand to him. He took it and softly squeezed it, then released it.

"You're an incredible man, Kyle Sarkos," she said tiredly. "I've never known anyone so unselfish. I think you're the thing that's rubbed off on me the most. Just watching your life, your integrity—it's made me believe that choosing God's path is really the best way to live. I'll be honest, before you, I never really saw anyone live Christianity so faithfully. I knew good Christians, starting with the Wrights, but I never experienced life with them like I have with you. Even Angie, she was gone during most of her turnaround years. She wrote me and called me, but it wasn't the same as being around her. I grew farther away from the Lord, and she wasn't near enough to be an influence." She paused. "But you are."

"I'm not this strong person that you think I am," he said weakly.

"That's just it. You're strength is in your humility and in your willingness to follow the Lord no matter what. What's happened to you could have torn many men apart. The whole Kylla thing would have been too much. But you picked her up, took her in, and loved her more than anyone could. And yet you know all along that she's Callista's child, and you know what that represents."

"But that's not Kylla's fault. I can't hold her mother's mistakes over her innocent head."

"No, you couldn't. But many men would, Kyle. That's what I'm saying."

"Besides … somehow … I guess because I never saw Caryn with her, I don't see Caryn as her mother. I only see you. It's like she belongs to us and Caryn was never even in the picture."

Cindy was warmed by that thought. She found herself feeling more and more envious of the elusive Caryn/Callista. She was the woman Kyle had committed himself to forever, yet she used him, lied to him, and even apparently cheated on him throughout their entire marriage. Maybe someday Kyle could start over again. Maybe he would find someone who would be the perfect compliment for his life. Yes—she longed to fill that part—but if Caryn was blight number one on his life, a woman with Cindy's reputation and past would merely be blight number two. She couldn't bear that.

Fifty-Five

Kyle was frantic as he finished packing for the trip. He still didn't want to go to California, didn't want to talk to Martin Sartin, and didn't want to pursue anything again with the FBI that directly involved him.

"Isn't the whole point of the FBI to do the investigating?" he grumbled as he pulled out a red polo shirt from his closet. "Why do they have us normal people running around with all kinds of wires hooked to our bodies doing dangerous things?" He took the red back into the closet and came out with a brown one.

"Take the red shirt," Cindy told him as she balanced Kylla on a hip. "It looks nice with your complexion."

"Oh, there's something I haven't thought of! Yes, how should I look in the midst of all this undercover mumbo-jumbo? Red is nice, isn't it? If I'm gunned down sometime during the process, the blood should blend in well with the shirt and not cause too much discomfort for those watching me die!"

"That's not what I was thinking. You look dashing in red." She reached up to touch his face. "Calm down, Kyle. No one's going to shoot you."

He stopped and closed his eyes for a moment. "I *almost* wish you were going." He then stared at her soberly. "Almost, but not quite. At least I can rest at ease knowing you won't be sneaking into the prison through a dumpster or something."

She smiled and tweaked his nose.

"Oww! Why did you do that?" he whined as he rubbed the end of his nose.

"To take your mind off your nerves. This is going to be a good thing, Kyle. You'll be talking to Martin Sartin tomorrow, Callista's father, Kylla's grandfather. You'll have the opportunity to find out who's responsible for Caryn's death, and why they're so interested in finding out about Kylla. This may be what we need to settle down to a normal life again. Just imagine, we can take her to McDonalds, to movies, to the park. We can all be together without knowing we've got several sets of eyes watching everything we do."

He nodded and then looked at her pensively. "And you won't leave Kylla? You'll stay in Dockrey … watch her grow up … help me raise her?"

She smiled her warmest smile. "I promise."

***

Ben Hall met Kyle at the Tupelo Airport. It was a small terminal with no major commercial flights. A private jet had been ordered for the trip, and what a jet it was. There was so much electronic equipment that Kyle barely had room to sit. He wasn't sure what the purpose of all the paraphernalia was, but from the looks of it, they were expecting something major from this journey.

He sat in one of the seats, buckled up, and held his breath as it took off. He had ridden in a small jet before and remembered hating it. The ride was fast and bumpy, and every little jolt or noise gave him the creeps. His usual entourage sat around him, agents Hall, Morrow and Sparks, and all were quietly looking over various pieces of papers in marked folders. After close to thirty minutes of total silence, Ben Hall finally spoke.

"Are we ready to brief him now?"

"Just about," Morrow replied. "Did you see the rap sheet listed on Sartin?"

"Unbelievable, isn't it?" Ben chuckled. "He'd have to live to be 350 to even get a chance at parole."

Great, Kyle thought to himself. *I'm about to talk to a guy who is so bad he can't even dream of being released from prison in over three lifetimes. What am I doing?*

"Mr. Sarkos," Ben was addressing him now. "I'm sure there are many things you'd like to ask Mr. Sartin, and feel free to do so. You'll have all the time you need. But there are certain pieces of information that we need you to push. We want to go over these with you now … and then a couple of more times. You don't need to be bringing in any kind of paper as a reminder—people might think you're working for us."

Very reassuring, Kyle thought. *I'm an idiot to do this!*

"First, we need to know as much as possible about the people who are responsible for Callista's death," Agent Sparks began. "We need names and locations."

Morrow spoke up to add, "And if he thinks they're also connected to his ex-wife's death, that would be helpful."

"Great," Kyle said sarcastically. "I'll be lucky if *he* doesn't murder *me*. He probably thinks I should have seen through it all and somehow protected his daughter in the process." He could feel a drop of sweat begin to stream down the side of his face. "How many years did you say he was in for?"

"Relax, Kyle," Ben Hall told him. "Sartin may not be as bad as your imagination is creating. He was a man caught in all the wrong places at all the wrong times."

"Well," Kyle sighed, "that's one thing, other than Caryn … uh … Callista, that we seem to have in common."

The list went on and on, and Kyle started to feel overwhelmed with what they were asking. There was no way he could remember all this. Even after the briefings to come, his best bet would be to just hit the high spots. He tried to tell them so, but they insisted it would all come back to him, and no one seemed worried in the least.

***

Cindy enjoyed her day with Kylla. They baked cupcakes, watched a cartoon, played with her blocks, and read a few books. When she went down for a nap, Cindy took the time to straighten up the messes they had created in the Wrights' house. By the time she had finished, she collapsed on the couch next to the portable crib where Kylla was sleeping. When Jonathan Wright walked in, she was nearly asleep herself.

"A bit tiring, is it? All this home stuff," he teased her.

"Tiring, but wonderful," she smiled as she sat up. "I can't imagine being able to be with her all day long. It's actually … well … fun."

"I know the feeling." He sat in a recliner next to the couch. "So tell me, Cindy, how do you feel about your life right now? You've made some big decisions that have required some big changes. What do you think?"

She considered it all. "I feel at peace, Pastor Jon. I certainly don't know why, but I do. My life is one total turnaround, and I can hardly believe where I've landed."

"You need to know that you've done the right thing. In the end, you'll understand why these choices were best. This is why God gives us guidelines. As humans, so many things cloud our vision and our judgment. But His Word shows us that when we choose the side of agape love, choosing to benefit others above ourselves, we've chosen the right side. God will honor your choices."

"You know what, Pastor Jon? I don't really care or expect it. I'm already honored that God has allowed me a second chance, or shoot, a third chance now, to care for those He's given me. That's honor enough."

He stood, walked over to the crib and glanced down at the sleeping baby. "You've still got more choices to make, Cindy. You know that, don't you?"

She frowned. "About what?"

"Kylla." He nodded towards the baby. Then he looked over at her and raised his eyebrows. "And Kyle."

"I've made my decisions about Kyle," she said swiftly.

"Ah, yes," he ran his hand through his hair. "My hair keeps getting thinner and thinner. I'm beginning to think you're contributing to a lot of that."

"Me?"

"Yes … you. It's like I'm having to raise a fourth daughter all over again. You're not all that opinionated, but you are definitely stubborn-headed."

He waved and left the living room for his bedroom. She just shook her head. No one seemed to understand her feelings about Kyle. She wasn't trying to hurt him, only help him. At least Kyle finally seemed to be aware of it.

***

Kyle checked into the hotel and dropped his bag to the floor. This place was plush. If the FBI could afford to waste money on things like this, surely they could afford to hire a professional person to go into prisons and question convicted felons about possible murderers after innocent people. He glanced out the window to the California skyline and was thankful for a place like Dockrey. He would miss serving the church there, but he already had many interested kids, along with a few adults, who would fill up his teaching schedule quickly.

Immediately his thoughts went to Kylla and Cindy. He reached for his phone and punched her name.

"Hey," she answered. "How was your flight?"

"Stressful. Tense. Nerve-racking. Need I go on?"

"How's California today?"

"Sunny."

"Imagine that. Seen the beach yet?"

"You're kidding, right?"

"No! While you're in California, you should at least go to the beach."

He sighed. "The last beach I went to was Martha's Vineyard with you and Kylla. I think that's the memory I'd like to keep. Speaking of Kylla, I imagine she's on top of the world today having you all to herself."

"I can't answer for her, but I'm doing terrific. We made cupcakes today."

He smiled at that thought. "Save me one?"

"Absolutely. In fact, Kylla made one especially for you. We set it aside for when Dadda comes home."

He stared out the window and wished he was there with them.

"What's your schedule tomorrow?" she asked him.

"You know the FBI, ten o'clock briefing, then off to prison. They're consistent."

"I'll be thinking about you ... and praying for you."

"And I'll appreciate it."

There was silence, but Kyle hung on. He couldn't bring himself to hang up. "I miss you," he confessed softly. "I wish I'd been kinder to you before I left. I wish I'd have hugged you goodbye and told you that I couldn't wait to get back. I wish you were here with me now and going into that prison tomorrow to talk with Martin Sartin. You could have remembered all this stuff I'm supposed to find out." He paused. "You've become my right arm. I can't even function at church when you're not there. I need a name or an address or a former bulletin ... I can't find anything. I ask you, and I have it in five minutes."

"You're tired, Kyle, and you appear to have the blues. Get some rest."

"You're kidding, right? I have another briefing over dinner about important things I can never seem to remember."

"Then remember this—we'll be one step closer to the truth when you're done there."

Fifty-Six

As the white van pulled inside the fence at the prison gate, Kyle's stomach did a few more somersaults. He slid out another peanut butter cracker from his package of Nabs and tried to wash it down with Diet Mountain Dew. Churn, churn, churn. If he didn't get a grip, this was going to be a disaster.

The guards walked him through a metal detector. Beep, beep! The sound of the machine's alarm caused him to jump.

"What?" he held up his hands innocently.

"Do you have keys?" the guard asked severely.

Kyle reached into his pocket, pulled out his keys and dumped them into a plastic container. Fearing he might set off the alarm again, he went ahead and emptied all his pockets and dumped the contents into the tray. When he stepped through this time, the alarm went off again.

"Do you have any metal plates in your body?"

"Metal plates?"

"Replacement parts in your head, legs, anywhere?"

"No! I swear." He felt like he was about to be admitted himself.

"Any metal in your shoes?" the guard looked down towards Kyle's feet.

"I have no idea."

"Take them off, please."

Kyle removed his shoes and handed them out to the guard.

"Just drop them and walk through the detector again," the man said with folded arms.

Kyle literally dropped his shoes and braced himself for another trip through the device. He squinted his eyes and held his breath as he walked in. No alarm. Exhale.

"Here are your belongings," the guard said flatly as he handed the container and shoes back to Kyle. "Have a seat against the wall, and we'll have you in the visiting area as soon as your social security number clears."

Clears? Clears? What are they looking for? Wait! I've never done anything! Get a grip, Sarkos! Pull yourself together.

After nearly twenty minutes, he was allowed to go. He was shocked to see people visiting all over. There was a long table divided into speaking booths, with glass fronts and telephones used for communication. The room was loud and reeked of cigarettes and body odor. He coughed a few times as the stench and smoke permeated his nose.

"Over there," the guard pointed to one of three empty booths. "Sartin will be out in a minute."

Kyle walked slowly to the booth as he wiped his sweaty hands on his khakis. A child ran in front of him screaming as another child chased him. He nearly screamed himself from the startle. He finally got to the booth and eased down onto the edge the metal chair. The glass before him was smeared with many handprints, and a few other smudges he didn't want to try and figure out. The table was covered with graffiti and felt greasy to his touch. He removed his elbows and leaned back in his chair. He glanced up at the telephone and wondered how many germs were crawling all over it. He assumed it would also be oily when he finally picked it up.

A loud clang caused him to jump again, and as he looked to the back of the room, he saw a huge iron-barred gate sliding open, and on the other side was Martin Sartin. Kyle swallowed as the man in the orange jumpsuit stood there in handcuffs waiting for the door to stop. Once inside the room, the guards frisked Martin before unlocking his wrists. Kyle tried to breathe normally. This was definitely Sartin. His hair was completely gray, but his body was very thin. He could already make out his blue eyes even from the distance. When Martin was pointed to Kyle's booth, the man nodded and walked over slowly. His stomach began to churn again, only at a whole new level. Martin sat down without a smile and just stared at Kyle for a moment. Finally, the man reached for the phone; Kyle followed and pulled his receiver from the wall. It was greasy.

"You're an idiot, you know?" were Martin's first words.

"Excuse me?" Kyle replied.

"I can guarantee you there are spies in this room right now shuffling their minds trying to figure out why the ... why you're here."

"I brought spies? What?"

"No, you brought the FBI. They don't concern me. It's those on the *dark side*, if you will, that will now pin Kylla to me."

"So, you know about Kylla?"

"Of course I know about Kylla. And she was well-protected ... until now."

"She's still well-protected. She's behind a twelve foot fence with high security all around it."

"Right, what a fluke that you ended up living at Stephen Williams' father-in-law's house. Be thankful."

"Would you like to see a picture?" Kyle asked him.

"No," Martin said firmly.

"You're kidding? She's gorgeous." Kyle stood up to reach for his wallet.

Martin yelled several expletives and told him to sit down.

Kyle was stunned. "Are you some kind of hard-hearted ..."

"Shut up, Kyle," he said sternly. "I'd love to see her, but if you whip out a picture and show me, you'll reveal to anyone watching that I have an interest in the child. And then she becomes number three on the hit list! Does that make any sense to you?"

Kyle swallowed again and nodded.

"Look, this was the worst possible thing you could've done. Until now, Kylla was linked to you, not to me. But now, everyone is gonna wonder why you came. They're gonna want to know what connection we have. See, no one knew that you were married to Callista."

"I wasn't, or so I found out."

"Exactly! But look, here you are, and you're now a link to her … thus linking Kylla. Why did you have to come?"

"It was the FBI's idea," Kyle confessed. "I'm even wired right now."

"Duh," Martin laughed. "Look, what do you need to know? The quicker we do this, the less suspicious anyone will be."

"Who murdered Caryn?"

"I have no idea who actually pulled the trigger. But the ultimate man behind it is Jimmy Thornton. And trust me, the chances of finding him are extremely slim."

"Why did he kill her?"

"Because I blew the whistle on his operation. Thirty-eight of his guys were arrested because of my testimony. He had to start all over again, and trust me—he lost millions in the process. He's out for revenge."

"So, he's killing off your family one by one?"

"He's not a very nice guy, Kyle." Martin paused, then added, "He's not like you."

"And so you think he's after Kylla now?"

"Of course he is, but only if he can prove that Kylla is my descendant. Listen, you're a good man. Callista talked highly of you, and believe me, she hated having to use you like she did. But you saved her life for at least ten years. Then she got careless and got pregnant."

"What was the deal with that? All the phony tests and the doctor? Why didn't she just say she didn't want to have children?"

"Because you wanted a family so bad! You pushed and pushed. She had to play the part of the *supportive minister's wife*, remember? It was the best way to get your mind somewhere else."

"Well, she played the part well. I had no idea the whole thing was … well … a sham."

"Look, Kyle," Martin's voice was softer now. "I'm sorry that you were the pawn in all of this. After Maria was murdered, and she was *supposed* to be under protection, I knew we had to take drastic measures to guarantee Callista's safety. She staked you out for quite a while, not even telling me where she was. You were the perfect candidate."

"Yeah, yeah, yeah," Kyle groaned. "But explain something to me: why couldn't she stay with me and have the baby? Why did she have to leave?"

"Complicated, isn't it? As long as Callista was playing this out on her own, it could work. As you obviously have figured out, the marriage was a fraud. She could be tracked if it were legal."

"Social security number, right?"

"Yep. And a birth of a child would be a nightmare."

"She didn't put her number on Kylla's birth certificate."

"I know, and Kylla never went back to the doctor, never had an immunization, never left her apartment. From the time Kylla was born, Callista stayed locked up and lived off the money wired to her by the Malones ... whom you've met, I understand, as the Malones, I mean."

"If she were so bent on not having a baby, and she had no problem lying about everything else, why didn't she just have an abortion?"

"Ah," Martin chuckled a little at that. "Because of *you.*"

"Me? She lied to me about every other aspect of our life! Our marriage was a complete fraud! What was wrong with adding abortion to the list?" Kyle regretted that statement as soon as he said it, but when tears begin to track down the side of Martin's face, he cringed.

The man looked up at him. "Because it was *your* child. You had an effect on her. Because *you* loved children and hated abortion, she couldn't bring herself to terminate *your* child. You had convinced her that abortion was another form of murder, and she just couldn't do it. It would've solved everything, but she just ... couldn't ... do it."

Kyle's jaw dropped. So ten years had meant something after all.

"She did everything she could to hide the baby and herself," Martin continued. "She could call me by cell phone, and so we talked once a week. She had no idea they had found her. I don't think it was traced from the baby; there's no way. Someone somewhere must have recognized her. But see, Kylla was with her."

"How do you know all this?"

"I have spies too. I get bits and pieces of information. And my hope for Kylla was that you could protect her."

"Why didn't they think she belonged to Caryn?"

"Look at your baby, Kyle. She's blond-headed and blue-eyed!"

"But everyone says Caryn ... Callista ... was blonde too."

Martin smiled. "Not naturally. She looked like her mother. They knew that. Then there's the fact that Caryn's name, not Callista's, is on the birth certificate. That will help."

"They got the birth certificate?"

"No, not yet. Thanks to your friends at the FBI, they can't. But it can't stay protected forever. And see, Callista was never the motherly type. Their first assumption was that she was a babysitter and this was how she made a living."

"They don't assume that anymore?"

"Well, they *didn't* know. But your little trip here today may change all that."

Kyle's heart began to pound with fear. "So, what do I do?"

"I don't know exactly. You can't be followed and protected by the FBI forever, and you can't keep Kylla behind those walls all her life. My best advice would be for you to get someone else's name on her birth certificate."

"You want me to give her up for adoption?"

"No, not *your* name, Caryn's name. Get someone to legitimately adopt her. Get a real name with a real number, address and existence on Kylla's records. Then when Jimmy finally gets a hold of them, it looks like Callista never was her mother to begin with."

"Do you think that'll stop him?"

"I don't know; you just asked my advice. That's the best I can offer."

Kyle considered the option. Could it work? Could it take Kylla out of the spotlight?

"I have a question for you," Kyle said as he looked directly into Martin's eyes. "Was Caryn seeing Philippe DuBois during our marriage?"

The look on Martin's face answered it before he opened his mouth. "It was only meant to be a publicity stunt. Callista needed to be seen in public so that Jimmy would think she was still *Callista* and not actually hiding out. She kept in touch with Philippe, and yes, their relationship more or less continued throughout your marriage. I'm sorry, Kyle. You became a rather unaware victim in all of this."

"Tell me about it."

"I really am sorry. You were a good influence on her. You made her think about things she'd never considered before. She was always a spoiled little rich girl, but you showed her another side of life. There were even moments when she considered coming clean with you, but Philippe and the Malones always talked her out of it."

"You didn't?" Kyle was surprised.

"She made sense to me. I hated seeing her live out her life in a lie. I also felt for you. She cared for you, Kyle. I don't know that she actually ever loved you because you were so different from her, but she respected you and admired you. And I have to tell you, when Kylla looked so much like you, she would often cry over the phone as she talked about how she had hurt you, and in turn hurt Kylla because she would never know what a wonderful father she had."

"I would have tried to protect her," he told Martin. "I would have changed my life ... at least for Kylla ... had she ever told me."

"And Callista knew that, but she couldn't ask that from you. It killed her when she left you."

"You wouldn't know it."

"She would have been a wonderful actress had she had the chance. That's what she wanted to do. When she concocted the whole plan about her going into hiding, she saw it as the role of a lifetime, and that's how she approached it. But you got to her, Kyle. You were good, honest, moral. It blew her away that you were a virgin when you got married."

Kyle blushed, both in anger and embarrassment. "I thought she was too."

"Look, this whole thing has been one big mess, and it'll only get messier if Jimmy Thornton ever realizes who Kylla is. He suspects, that's why he has guys tailing you all the time, but there's a blond that keeps him confused."

"Cindy," Kyle whispered.

"They think she's the mother."

Kyle nodded. "Kylla looks a lot like her—blue eyes, blond hair."

"Could you get her name on the birth certificate?"

Kyle shook his head. "No. That wouldn't be good for Cindy."

"But it might save Kylla's life."

"No. I won't ask her to do that." Kyle stared at a greenish smudge on the glass. This visit was almost worthless. There were a few tidbits of information that had been given out, but for the most part, he could have stayed home and avoided the suspicions that would now connect him with Martin.

"If it matters, I'm glad to know that my granddaughter is in your hands. If you ever need anything for her, you can contact the Malones; they're in charge of my estate. I'll tell them you have full access to everything I own."

"I appreciate it, but no thanks. I can take care of her."

"I know you can, Kyle. Callista may have done a lot of stupid things in her life, and that's mainly because of me, the stupidest of all men. But when she picked you, she did the only smart thing she's ever done. Thank you for ten more years with her."

Kyle was emotionally and physically at the end. He nodded, thanked Martin for his time, and then hung up the phone. Martin remained in his seat and waved to Kyle as he turned back one last time at the door. He moved numbly as the agents escorted him to the van. No one said anything as he was seated and they pulled away.

They went directly to the jet from the prison. He was thankful for their silence. He knew the questions would come eventually, but at least they respected his need to be alone for a little while.

Fifty-Seven

Cindy tried not to be nervous after Kyle's call from the Tupelo Airport, but he sounded horrible. He seemed tired, defeated, and refused to say anything until he got back home. She attempted to play with Kylla, but her thoughts were distracted. When Sue and Barbara came walking in with big smiles and glowing faces, her attention was immediately diverted.

"Guess what we got?" Sue said bursting with excitement.

"I'm almost afraid to ask," she replied cautiously.

"Ganny Sue!" Kylla yelled as she ran over to her.

"Granny Sue got Kylla a pretty new bed!" Sue clapped her hands and reached down to pick up the little girl.

"You got her a what?" Cindy was astonished.

"It's so adorable," Barbara was gushing now too. "It's all pink and pretty, with little shelves at the top. It's still crib-sized, but it's lower to the floor and will be a wonderful transition bed."

"A bed, huh?" Cindy laughed. "I thought this shopping trip was for the two of you?"

Barbara grinned from ear to ear as she said, "And what better for two grandmothers to do than shop for their grandchildren!"

"Let's bring it in and put it together," Sue suggested as she started for the door with Kylla.

"What is this?" Jonathan called out as he came in the door with a huge box. "What did you ladies buy today? My van is packed full, and I found this thing tied to the top. Next time you go shopping, we're gonna have to rent a U-Haul."

Cindy knelt down by the box. "Kylla, come look. Granny Sue got you a pretty new bed."

Kylla hobbled over and pointed at the bed. "Bed? Pretty!"

"Sue," Jonathan said, "come show me what's yours and I'll transfer it to your car. I'll bring everything else in."

Sue laughed and even blushed a little. "Oh, it all stays here. I felt Kylla needed a few things."

"Mother!" Cindy exclaimed. "What did you do?"

"I had a ball!"

Everyone had forgotten about Kyle as they looked through all the packages. There were clothes, toys, animals and an adorable set of flowered linens for Kylla's new bed. Sue had even found a hat with attached sunglasses that Kylla took to immediately. She put on the glasses and pulled the hat down over her ears.

"I pretty!" Kylla grinned, showing her six teeth proudly. She then looked up at the door. "Dadda!"

Everyone turned to see an ashen Kyle standing there. Cindy jumped up immediately, and without thinking, ran to him and threw her arms around him.

"Are you okay?" she asked softly in his ear.

He held her tightly, but wouldn't answer. Kylla's tugging at his pants leg finally pulled him away. As he leaned back, his blue eyes pierced through Cindy. She needed to know what was on his mind. This had something to do with her; she could tell. Kyle picked up Kylla and held her close, eyes shut tightly as though he could possibly lock out the harsh reality of the world for a moment.

"How did it go?" Jonathan finally asked.

Kyle sighed, his face still pale. "We all need to sit down."

Kylla was content to sit on her Daddy's lap as Kyle explained his discussion with Martin Sartin.

"Were the FBI familiar with this Jimmy Thornton?" Jonathan asked him at one point.

"Oh, yeah. They knew exactly who he was. And where Martin Sartin was dismayed at our meeting, the agency felt hopeful. They believe Jimmy Thornton will somehow make a move to do something ... most probably by looking for documents. If they can find someone digging into her records and then trace them down the line, they should eventually catch up with Thornton. If that happens, they have enough evidence to put him away even longer than Martin Sartin."

"So they won't come after Kylla, then?" Cindy asked hopefully.

"Martin thinks they will. He thinks my trip there was extremely dangerous, and that Jimmy will now make a connection between Kylla and Martin."

"Oh, no!" Sue gasped. "He's going to try and kill Kylla too?"

"Nobody knows," Kyle said hopelessly.

"How do we protect her?" Barbara asked in near panic. "Do we just keep her here ... inside this fence? I mean, at some point, will Kylla be able to live a normal life?"

"I don't know!" Kyle said in exasperation. "If they can catch Thornton, they can cut off the head of the organization, and then Kylla will be safe."

"What are their chances of finding him?" Jonathan asked soberly.

"Very slim."

Sue jumped back in. "So what do we do in the mean time? How do we ensure Kylla's safety? I'm not going to just sit here and let her be a target for some drug lord. There's got to be some way to protect her ... protect her life, her identity. Surely the FBI gave you some tips."

Kyle leaned back on the couch and rubbed his chin. "Martin suggested something, and the agency agreed with him."

"Well, what is it?" Barbara wanted to know. "We'll do anything!"

"Absolutely!" Sue agreed.

Kyle glanced over at Cindy who had been silent for the most part. He tried to smile at her, but it was obvious his emotions were in complete turmoil. He looked at her as he explained, "They suggested we get someone's name other than Caryn's on Kylla's birth certificate. If Kylla is officially another lady's daughter, then they can release that information, set a trap for Thornton hoping he will hunt it down, and then kill two birds with one stone. If Thornton is told by his man that Kylla isn't Callista's child after all, and they can possibly track the informant back to Thornton, those two possibilities might bring a permanent solution."

Everyone was silent, and no one looked around. They all knew the answer was simple. Cindy was as much a mother to Kylla as anyone ever could be. The natural step could only be to legalize it.

"I'll do it," Cindy said weakly. "You know I'll adopt her."

Kyle nodded, but his expression became even more pained. "I can't let you do that"

"What!" Sue burst out. "You're kidding right?"

"She already calls her Mama!" Barbara added. "If this is the chance we need to help bring all of this together … Kyle, you've got to let her!"

"I'm sorry," he said as he shook his head again. "I can't do that to Cindy."

Everyone sat stunned and exchanged confused glances with each other.

"What's the problem, Kyle?" Jonathan asked. "From the outside, this looks like a perfect solution, but I trust your judgment. What do you see wrong with this?"

Cindy looked at Kyle completely perplexed. Perhaps her fears that he could never accept her past were relevant now. He toyed with her romantically when it fit the bill, but the thought of having her adopt his child was asking too much.

His expression became tender as he explained, "Cindy's worked so hard to put her life back together. She's borne the brunt of comments about her reputation and working in the church. She's dealt with the stares and the *misplaced concern* of those who struggle to believe she's changed. People are finally beginning to see that she's for real; it took courage and commitment on her part for that to happen. If she adopts Kylla, then it all starts over again. The suspicions, the comments, and then everyone will begin to think that something improper has been going on between the two of us. I can't do that to Cindy."

"You're nuts!" Sue yelled out in unbelief. "We're talking about a child's life and you're concerned with Cindy's reputation?"

Cindy just stared at him. She was amazed again at how large his heart was. He knew she would volunteer without thinking of the ramifications it might cause her, and he had already come to her rescue.

"It's okay, Kyle," she assured him. "I can handle the problems. I love Kylla. I'll do anything for her."

"There you go!" Sue retorted. "It's settled. Who do we call, Jonathan?"

"Wait!" Kyle put his hand up. "It is *not* settled."

"Kyle ..." Cindy tried to protest.

"No," he shook his head firmly. "I won't let you lose your reputation again. Not for me, and not for Kylla. This isn't the right answer to this problem."

"Don't be an idiot!" Sue proclaimed.

"Mother, would you pipe down!" Cindy finally cried. This was awkward, and she could feel her face flushing. It all seemed logical, but Kyle's obvious desire to protect her reputation was now overwhelming her.

"Hang on a minute," Kyle said putting up his hands in surrender. "May I talk with Cindy alone?"

Everyone nodded anxiously.

"Let's go upstairs," he suggested as he pulled her from the chair.

Fifty-Eight

Kyle led Cindy toward the stairs while he placed his hand on the small of her back. As her hair swooshed back and forth, he closed his eyes and breathed a prayer at what he was about to put forth.

"Mama!" Kylla called out as soon as Cindy hit the stairs.

Jonathan intercepted her and placed her on his shoulders. "Wanna see the flowers, Kylla?"

"Flowers!" The distraction worked.

Once in the apartment, Kyle closed the door and tried to breathe normally. His heart was pounding again and his palms were even sweatier than when he had walked inside the prison that morning.

"What's this about, Kyle? What's wrong? I really don't care about my reputation. I'll gladly adopt Kylla and help put an end to all of this."

"I know, but I care, Cindy."

He went over to the couch and she followed. When he sat down, he placed his elbows on his knees and rested his face in his hands. She sat beside him and gently began to rub his back.

"What is it, Kyle?"

He sat up and laced his fingers together. "Cindy, I've watched you beat yourself up over your mistakes time and time again."

"But this wouldn't be a mistake," she assured him. "This would actually be doing something right for a change."

"Not for a change," he said as he looked at her intently. "You've been making right decisions for some time now, but you keep letting your past wash over you like muddy slime from some stagnant swamp. You almost believe in yourself, and then your faith drops out from beneath you."

"This wouldn't do that to me."

"Yes, it would. Somebody would make some off-color reference to you, and it would start all over again."

"I promise it won't, Kyle."

"And what happens when Kylla starts school?" he continued. "She gets registered, and there's Cindy Marcum's name on the birth certificate. You've never been married, you're the mom, people put two and two together, and the whole process starts over again."

"I'll deal with it," she said as she threw her hands up in the air. "This isn't about me! This about Kylla!"

"No, Cindy," he shook his head. "This is very much about you. I've tried for nearly six months to break down the walls that you've put up because you don't think you're good enough to be with me. I get glimpses of light now and then, pieces of hope that maybe you could love me back, but as soon as I get close to you, you throw up a barrier again, and I have to start over."

"Kyle! You're a minister! How can I be with you when everybody here knows what I've done?"

"Exactly! That's what I'm saying! I don't care about your past or your reputation or anything that had to do with your life before the second week in January! I know who you are *now*, and people here know who you are *now*. If only *you* could see who you are now, then you could open up your heart to me. Sometimes we're so close to being there, but you stop. And it happens over and over and over again. As much as I love Kylla, that's how much I love you. And I can't sacrifice one for the other."

She stood up and folded her arms as she walked over to the window. He got up and began to pace.

"What do you want me to do, Kyle?" she asked hopelessly. "Admit that I love you? It doesn't change the fact that you're a minister ... and I'm as far from a minister's wife than anyone could be ... than anyone should be."

He walked over to her. "But I won't be a minister much longer. I'm only a temporary here. When the position's up, I'll simply be a music teacher. You can be a music teacher's wife, can't you?"

"That is so wrong," Cindy bit her lip with tears. "You should be a minister! You're a good man, Kyle! You're a Godly man! Your reputation was soiled because somebody else played you for a fool. That shouldn't be held against you!"

"Well, that's what I get for being a fool, then." He looked down at the fence that was Kylla's only protection now. "We can solve this easily if you'll agree to it."

"I've already told you: I'll adopt her. What more do you want?"

He paused and refused to even look at her as he mustered up the courage to say, "Marry me." He could barely whisper it out.

She turned to him in shock. "What?"

"If you'll marry me, I'll let you adopt Kylla. It'll be legal, and it'll save your reputation. Shoot, it'll save mine for that matter. We'll catch Jimmy Thornton, build a house, I'll teach music, and we'll all live happily ever after."

She stared at him in astonishment. "You can't be serious."

"Why not? Look, I never loved Caryn the way I love you already, and I was married to her for ten years. I didn't even know what love was. I was a twenty-one-year old virgin with raging hormones and a gorgeous girlfriend who was more than willing to follow me to Seminary. I didn't know if I loved her or not. But with you, Cindy, I can barely breathe sometimes when

I look at you. You walk into a room, and it's like my life becomes a little sweeter. Yesterday, all day long, I only thought about you. Last night, like every night, you were the last thing on my mind before I drifted off to sleep. I've tried to be what you need, but you won't let me. So now, let me care for you the way you want to care for Kylla. Let me build my life around you, build a life with you, share myself with you. You ... be a *real* mother for Kylla. Be there for her when she wakes up, not just when she goes to sleep."

Kyle took her hands and looked deeper into her eyes than he ever had before. "We can do this, Cindy. If you'll just admit that we can move beyond *your* past, we can do this. And it's not just for Kylla; it's for me, and it's for you."

She gazed at him, blue pools forming in her eyes. "I don't deserve you, Kyle."

"But I deserve you," he pleaded. "Don't I deserve to be with someone that I adore? Don't I deserve a marriage this time that's based on truth? I know who you are, Cindy, and I want a chance to make all that up to you. I want the privilege of showing you what love can be too. Look, I know all this is crazy, and even sudden, but let's just go for it. For me, for you, and for Kylla."

She looked away then tightly shut her eyes.

"Cindy," Kyle forced her to look back at him. "Do you love me?"

She rolled her eyes.

"Answer me," he said more firmly. "Do you love me? It's a simple question."

"Just because the question's simple doesn't mean the answer is. It's too ..."

"No, answer the simple question with a simple *yes* or *no*. Don't make this complicated."

"But it *is* complicated!" she was protesting again.

"No! Just tell me if you love me or not!" He calmed down and took her hands again. "That part isn't hard, Cindy. Just tell me from your heart."

He pulled her close until his forehead was touching hers.

"You know that I love you." She barely breathed it out.

He kissed the top of her head and then pulled her into an embrace. "We don't have a whole lot of time to hash this out. We need your name on Kylla's birth certificate. I won't put it there unless you're my wife."

"I'm not exactly ready to be *married*. We haven't even dated. I need ... time ... I guess."

"We'll take the relationship part slow, but we can't wait on the marriage. We have to do it now. I'll sleep on the couch; you can have the bed."

"I can't let you do that!"

"Fine! Whatever you want!" he threw his hands up in surrender. "You can sleep on the couch and I'll sleep on the floor!"

"The floor? Why would you sleep on the floor?"

"Well, if you're on the couch, I'm certainly not sleeping in the bed. It goes against everything I am. The least I can do is be a gentleman."

She shook her head and grinned nervously. "This is crazy, you know? This almost beats what Angie Wright did."

"Not quite. And this is different because we do love each other. We do, Cindy. We'll take our time, and we'll ease into this relationship. But I won't sacrifice your reputation by doing it any other way. People will simply believe that we fell in love, got married, and then you adopted Kylla. There'll be no talk, no rumors, just people happy for us. And when you think about it, that's really how it happened anyway. We're just rushing into the marriage a little quicker because of Kylla's situation."

She bit her lip again as she continued to weigh the decision. Kyle hoped he had gotten through.

"We can make this work, Cindy. You know we can. Just let go of your past, and let's move on."

She looked back up at him. He knew the weights and balances, pros and cons, were ping-ponging back and forth, over and over inside her head … and her heart. She closed her eyes and finally nodded her head in agreement.

"Yes," he whispered excitedly. "Let's go tell the folks downstairs before they form a lynching party and drag me through the streets of Dockrey on a rope."

"Wait," Cindy hesitated. "When do we do this? How do we do this?"

"We get a license tomorrow and get started on the papers immediately. I'm sure Ben Hall can expedite all of this."

Cindy took a deep breath and shook her head. "This is crazy."

"Perhaps. But then, isn't love supposed to be?"

"I wouldn't know. I've never been in love before."

"Neither have I. It feels good, doesn't it?"

"In a scary sort of way."

When they stepped out on the balcony, the ladies' eyes turned upstairs immediately. Kyle wanted to grab Cindy's hand and yell at the top of his lungs that she had just agreed to marry him, but his wisdom got the best of him. Instead, he followed behind her as she made her way down the stairs.

"Have we worked this out?" Sue wondered nervously. "Are we thinking of Kylla now and what's best for her?"

"Where's Jonathan?" Kyle asked. "He needs to be here for this."

"He's out back with Kylla," Barbara said as she got up and headed for the back porch door. "I'll call him in."

Barbara called for Jonathan while Sue stared at the couple still reeling with emotion at both Kyle and Cindy's stubbornness.

When they were all seated in the great room again, Kyle began his explanation. "For Cindy to just up and adopt Kylla, it would cause many questions to be passed around as the years go by. I can't do that to her."

"But …" Sue started to complain.

"Mother!" Cindy interrupted. "Let Kyle finish! I think you'll be pleased with his solution. Okay?"

Sue nodded and sat back in her chair, giving Kyle her full attention.

"I want Cindy to be Kylla's official mother, but I want it done in a way that's proper and right and benefits Cindy. Because of that, I've asked her to marry me … and she's accepted."

The stunned look on the faces of Sue, Barbara and Jonathan, caused Kyle to laugh out loud for the first time in days.

"Are you serious?" Sue asked as she put her hand up to her heart.

"Guess what, Mother?" Cindy smiled. "You're really going to be a grandmother."

"And a mother-in-law!" Sue cried out. "Kyle will be my son!" She jumped up from her chair and ran over to hug him.

"Well, I'll be," Jonathan was still in shock. "How did you manage to talk her into it?"

"I believe it was divine intervention," Kyle confessed.

"We've been seeing a lot of that lately," Barbara stated as she shook her head in complete amazement.

Fifty-Nine

After a call to Ben Hall, the wedding was set for the next afternoon, with the adoption following immediately. Jonathan could perform the ceremony, and the FBI would furnish the papers and the judge to make it all legal. Cindy stayed long enough to get Kylla to sleep, and then Kyle walked her out to her car.

"Don't be nervous about this," he tried to assure her.

"I sure hope you know what you're doing," she said doubtfully. "I don't want to mess up your life, Kyle."

"I think I pretty much accomplished that already. We can only go up from here."

She nodded, but still felt unsure. If only it hadn't happened so fast.

"May I kiss you goodbye? For the last time?" he asked her.

"I thought we were taking this slow," she said cautiously.

"We are. Ben Hall said if we get married we really need to keep up appearances for those standing at the gate. I'm not asking you to kiss me in the privacy of our bedroom."

She could see his raised eyebrows in the darkness, and nearly giggled with giddiness. "I guess I have no choice then if agent Hall suggested it."

"At least act like you enjoy it," he said in mock hurt as he put his hands around her waist.

"I'm very good at acting."

He gently brushed her lips and then pulled her head to his chest.

"That wasn't much of a kiss," she complained as she ran her fingers through his growing hair.

"I wasn't finished." He leaned back and faced her with a smile. This time he kissed her warmly and let his lips linger on hers. She wished it could go on and on. At that moment it felt good to know she had admitted her love to him and that the barriers were gone. No matter what, she would be his from now on, and her excuses and past decisions no longer carried any weight. She pulled him closer to her and let herself go for the first time ever without guilt or hesitancy. He might as well know how she really felt.

"And you want to keep it slow?" he asked her when he finally broke away.

"It was only a kiss."

"No it wasn't," he said as he took her hand and walked her to her car. "That was way more than a kiss. That was ... well ... a lifetime experience."

She giggled again. "Hey, you're the one who wanted to get married.

I'm just following your lead."

He leaned down and kissed her again. She lifted her arms to his neck without hesitation and pulled him close as she kissed him back. How could she have settled for cheap imitations time and time again? Had she just given up on love at some point in her past?

"Wow," he breathed as he kissed her forehead. "Slow, huh?"

"Appearances, remember?"

***

The next day, Cindy loaded up her some of her clothes and a few personal belongings to carry over to the Wrights' apartment. The whole situation still seemed unreal to her. She was marrying Kyle Sarkos today, and then adopting Kylla afterwards. Tonight she would be a married woman and an official mother. She only *thought* her life had changed before.

Kyle helped her carry her clothes up to the room and showed her where he had made space in the closet for them. She was polite, but in the light of day, the reality of the situation was a little hard to swallow. She tried to make small talk and asked where Kylla had gone. She was at the church with Jonathan to get cups and plates for the reception.

"Reception?" Cindy asked in surprise. "Who's coming to a reception?"

"Well, as soon as Jonathan told Andie, she insisted there needed to be at least a few people here," Kyle explained. "The list sort of grew."

"Grew? To how many? I thought it was just gonna be us, Mom and the Wrights."

"Well, not a bunch. Maybe thirty or forty."

"Thirty or forty!"

"People are happy for us. Apparently ... this love we tried to keep hidden was obvious to a lot more people than we imagined. Folks are thrilled and they want to be a part of our *blessed event.*"

She leaned against the wall and closed her eyes with a sigh.

"You know what this means," he grinned as he put his hands on her waist.

"Tell me," she said as her head began to spin with all that was happening.

"You have to kiss me at the ceremony ... for appearances' sake, of course." His hands went farther around her back as he moved in closer.

"Are you looking for a practice session right now?"

"I pronounce you husband and wife," he said somberly. "You may kiss your bride."

***

"What on earth are you doing here?" Cindy asked in complete shock at her brother's sudden appearance in the Wright house.

"I think that's the question I should be asking you!" Billy nearly yelled. "The last time I see you, you're passing out on a hospital floor, next thing I know, Mother calls and says you're getting married and adopting a kid! Are you nuts?"

"No, Billy, I'm in love," she said tersely. "You should try it sometime." She headed back up the stairs with a box load of her things.

"I did try it! Twice."

"That wasn't love, Billy. That was your poor attempt at marriage."

He grabbed her arm. "And that's exactly what you're about to do too." He looked fiercely at her. "Cindy, we're too much alike. Trust me when I say this won't work for you either."

She jerked her arm away. "You don't have a clue what I'm like. Do you realize how much has happened in Mother's life and mine since her surgery? Life has changed for us, Billy, and I'll never be the same. Kyle has been a big part of that."

"But marriage!" he exclaimed again as she went toward the apartment door. "And adoption! These are huge steps! Couldn't you just live with him for awhile to see if it works?"

"You don't *see* if a marriage works. You make it work. But you wouldn't know anything about that, would you?"

"This guy's divorced with a kid! Have you totally flipped out?"

Cindy spun around and stuck her finger up in his face. "Don't waltz in here and try to act noble. It doesn't suit you well at all. Kyle is the most amazing man I've ever known. He's good, kind, Godly, and believe it or not, he actually loves me, faults and all."

Billy gave a sinister laugh. "He obviously doesn't know *all* of your faults then."

Cindy slapped his face as hard as she could. "I'm no fool! Do you think I'd marry a minister without telling him my past and my mistakes? Do you think I'd marry anybody without laying it all on the line? If you want to play the *knight to the rescue* here, go talk to Mother. You haven't seen her since she had surgery. You don't even know how her last check-up went, if she's still sick or if she's healthy."

"Look, I have a life away from here. Don't get high and mighty on me. I chose to leave Dockrey and never look back. Is it my fault that you came sliding back in here when things got rough?"

"Rough!" Cindy couldn't believe his gall. "Things got rough for Mother, not me! My life was coasting along just fine. I chose to see *our* mother through a horrible time, and in the process, I got the chance to start over."

"In Dockrey," he was laughing again. "That's like going back to the primordial ooze, isn't it?"

She was sick of the insults. "Why exactly are you here?"

"To talk you out of the biggest mistake you'll ever make. You're not marriage material, Cindy," he said soberly. "And you're definitely not mother material."

She scrunched her nose in disgust as Kyle and Kylla walked in.

"Mama!" Kylla squealed as she held out her arms. Kyle brought her over and Cindy took the baby. Billy stared in near distress.

"That's right," Kyle smiled. "And tonight, Mama stays with us. And in the morning, she cooks eggs."

Cindy giggled despite Billy's brooding presence. "Don't tell me you heard about my eggs."

"Well, Kylla wasn't complaining, but Jonathan said he'd never seen anything like it before."

Kyle then reached out for Billy's hand. "I'm Kyle. I remember you from the hospital."

Billy shook his hand, but he was baffled as he watched Cindy nuzzle Kylla beneath her chin.

"Beautiful sight, isn't it?" Kyle smiled adoringly.

"It's weird," Billy confessed.

Cindy blew a strand of hair from her face and moaned, "Don't be morbid, Billy. Is she not adorable? And imagine, you're gonna be her uncle."

"I can swallow that, but you being a mother? That's not natural."

***

As the afternoon drew on, people came to set tables and chairs outside, to bring flowers and arrangements from their personal gardens, and to provide lovely linens and table decorations as well as loads of food. What was meant to be a small private ceremony had obviously turned into a church-wide affair.

"We should've just done it at the church," Andie said as she passed by Cindy carrying another plate of food. "But it's a beautiful day; I suppose it was special ordered. Just curious, who's giving you away? Or are you just walking down the aisle alone?"

Cindy caught her breath. "I'm walking down an aisle? I was just gonna show up in the living room when all of this started."

"Billy could do it," Andie suggested.

"Over my dead body," Cindy said under her breath.

"I heard that," Andie smiled as she reached up and put her hand on Cindy's shoulder. "Don't let Billy ruin any of this for you. This is a good thing that's happening here. Billy's clueless about life or love in general. Be happy for yourself, for Kyle and for Kylla."

"Agreed."

"So what are you wearing?" Andie wondered as she arranged the plate on one of the tables.

"Definitely *not* white. I can hear the remarks now."

"Listen—the people coming here today are not people who want to criticize or judge you for what you wear. Everyone here today supports you and Kyle. Come out in your slip, for all I care!"

"Oh, that would be perfect! I guarantee they would talk then!"

Sixty

At four o'clock, Cindy stood nervously inside the great room. She had chosen a long pastel formal she had bought last year for a real estate conference. It was powder blue and looked springy and cheerful. She was more nervous than she would have been had the wedding remained small and simple, but as she glanced through the small window on the door that led to the back porch, she realized there were way more than forty people out there. In fact, half had to stand because there weren't enough chairs.

"Are you ready?" Jonathan asked as he came out from the bedroom in his suit.

"I'm not sure," she confessed honestly.

He raised his eyebrows. "If you're not sure, this is the time to bow out."

She looked back out the window. It truly was a beautiful day.

"Want some advice?" he asked warmly.

"I would certainly welcome some at the moment."

"I feel good about this. I've felt good about this for a long time. And it's more than just you and Kyle. I do believe you belong together and that God orchestrated all of this so that you two could complete each other. But what developed between you and Kylla is amazing. This marriage is as much about her as it is the two of you. My advice," he reached up and gently stroked her cheek, "is that you do this right now ... no qualms, no fears ... and then all three of you put your lives back together—together."

She tried to smile, but one thought continued to plague her mind. "Pastor Jon, do you really think I'll be a good wife for Kyle? Am I good enough for him? Will he have doubts later on down the road, but just stick with me because he's a good man at heart?"

Jonathan took her in his arms and held her tightly just as her own father would have done had he been here. "You will be the best wife he could ever have. Your heart and your life have been transformed, and as the years go by, Kyle will grow to treasure you even more than he does right now."

"I hope so."

He placed his arms on her shoulders and looked her eye to eye. "Your dad is thrilled right now."

She glanced up at him and furrowed her brow. "Do you think he knows?"

"I can't help but believe that the Father would somehow let him see this."

She gently wiped her eyes and sincerely said, "Thank you, Pastor Jon."

"Ready?"

She nodded as she took his arm. They walked onto the back porch, and Cindy could hear Andie playing *Autumn Sunset* from the electric piano on the lawn. When they walked outside, Doug nodded to Andie and she began *Canon in D*. Everyone stood as Cindy and Jonathan walked down the midst of the chairs. Andie had been right: the only people there were those that Cindy knew loved and supported her. She received smiles, waves, winks and nods as she made her way slowly. Down at the front stood her mother holding Kylla, pointing Cindy out, and smiling brightly. Cindy stopped to hug them both.

"You're blessed, Cindy," her mother said tearfully.

"I know," she whispered back.

"Mama," Kylla whispered as she joined in. "Pretty."

"Thank you, sweetheart. Kylla's pretty too."

Jonathan led her to Kyle who looked more handsome than Cindy had ever remembered. His smile and sparkling blue eyes melted her heart as Jonathan placed her hand in Kyle's and then had them turn toward the audience to face him so that all could see them exchange their vows. Jonathan turned to the people and made a few comments, then turned back to Kyle and Cindy.

"Let's do this," he winked.

After the ceremony, the fellowship was sublime. Person after person came up to Kyle and Cindy and handed them envelopes that were usually reserved for love offerings at the church. They didn't bother to open them, but would thank the people, and then Kyle would stuff the envelopes into his coat pocket. Kylla was thrilled to have Andie's children there to play with her, along with a couple of other children she knew from the church nursery. Cindy made a mental note: *invite children over to play with Kylla.*

As eight o'clock approached, people finally began to disperse. What would normally have been a wedding reception ended up more like a church picnic. People laughed, ate, played, talked and relaxed in the Wrights' backyard and then began to help clean up and put away as the evening went on. By nine o'clock all was back to normal and the last stragglers said their goodbyes.

Kylla walked over to Cindy and rubbed her eyes. "Mama, night night," she said softly.

Cindy picked her up and cradled her tightly to her chest. She walked over to Barbara, Jonathan and Andie and thanked them whole-heartedly for the work and effort they had gone to so that this simple occasion could be memorable. As she walked into the great room, there sat Kyle, Ben Hall, and a judge at the dining table.

"Cindy," Kyle's eyes still sparkled as he looked up at her, "are you ready to sign all of this?"

She walked over with Kylla and sat next to him.

Agent Hall asked her, "Do you need me to go through all of these papers with you, or do you want to take our word for it that they're legitimate and proper."

"Take your word for it," she said tiredly. "Where do I sign?"

As Ben placed paper after paper before them, they signed each one and moved on to the next. Kylla fell asleep in the middle of the signing, and Cindy could only smile at her sweet face. Her body warmed at the thought that at this moment she was legally becoming her mother. When all this was through, she would take her upstairs, change her for bed, and then get the privilege of knowing she was near all night long.

***

"So … you're really gonna do this?" Cindy asked Kyle as he made a bed for himself on the couch.

"Either I sleep on the couch or on the floor."

"I feel guilty; this is your house—you should be sleeping where you normally sleep."

"Cindy, right now I'm so high from all that's happened I could sleep on a bed of rocks and it wouldn't matter. You're my wife, Kylla has a mother, and we have the rest of our lives to build together. This time last year, I thought my life had fallen apart. I had no hope, no future, no family, and nothing to look forward to. Look at me now." He leaned against the back of the couch and spread out his arms. "I have the whole world, and I owe it all to you. I don't know how to thank you."

"You want to thank *me*?" She laughed softly. "I'm so afraid right now that none of this is real. It's like I'm dreaming and when I wake up I'll still be back at my apartment in Florence and have to drudge through another day of that dreary life again."

"Just curious," he said as he gave her a mischievous look. "Is it still *winter midnight* in your life?"

"What?" She had no idea what he was talking about.

"You told me that day when I helped you clean up your kitchen that you felt like your life was a winter midnight … it was the darkest and coldest possible moment imaginable."

"I don't remember that. I must have been really down. What a description."

"That's what I thought too. It was at that moment that I realized how much I wanted to take care of you … wanted to help you find some light and hope again."

She smiled thoughtfully as she shook her head in amazement. "I still say you're too good for me."

He grimaced as he stood and reached out to take her hands. "You've got to stop thinking that. I've made so many mistakes in my life, and Caryn was the biggest. The fact that you're willing to look beyond my *damaged goods* and commit to this with me is like a miracle. I'm determined to make this work. We'll take our time, we'll build on what we've got right now, and as we face the future, we'll do it together. But you need to know that I'm gonna make big mistakes over the years when it comes to a lot of things. But we'll work through them, okay? We'll get through everything ... together."

She squeezed his hands and stepped closer to him. It scared her to feel like she did about him. Old habits were screaming at her to protect herself and run away. To love this deeply meant there was the chance to hurt just as deeply, but as she gazed into his eyes, she knew Kyle was not a man who would leave her or hurt her intentionally. God had brought him into her life, and she would trust God from now on with whatever happened.

"Good night," he whispered as he kissed her forehead. "See you in the morning."

"G'night," she whispered back as she laid her head on his chest. "Please don't make me cook eggs in the morning."

"No problem."

Sixty-One

Kyle woke up early the next morning. He was still on top of the world from marrying Cindy, but his meeting with Martin Sartin left a dull ache inside. He tried to grasp that Caryn was really Callista, and Callista was Martin's daughter, and Martin was Kylla's grandfather. He thought about his own parents and how thrilled they would be to discover he had married Cindy. They had missed his first wedding, and now his second, but this one was understandable. They were near Greece on a Mediterranean cruise, and since time was of the essence, the marriage and adoption needed to happen as soon as possible.

Kylla was still sleeping, snuggled beneath the soft sheets in her new bed. He carefully pulled up the blanket and ran his hand over the top of her soft locks. He then looked at Cindy. She was curled up, sleeping on her side, and her long hair flowed out on the pillow behind her. His heart stopped. He had seldom seen her without make-up, but her beauty was still incredible. He tried to imagine Caryn lying there, but Cindy had erased all memories of her. The two women were contrasts, not only in looks, but in every aspect. The only thing he could not compare them in was their relationship to Kylla. He was glad. Cindy was everything Kylla needed, and that was enough.

He went downstairs to the kitchen determined to furnish the one in the apartment later today with groceries so they could at least have coffee and breakfast together as a family. He knew it would be impossible to keep Sue away any other time, so they might as well continue eating with the Wrights. Perhaps he and Cindy could do some of the cooking for everyone now.

He poured himself a cup of coffee and pulled out the mental note of how thrilled Cindy had been when he poured her a cup at Martha's Vineyard. He also knew now how she liked it: two spoons of creamer, and one of sugar. He fixed them both a mug and carried them upstairs. The girls were still sleeping. Did he dare wake Cindy? Was he pushing his luck? He placed his own mug on the small kitchen counter and tiptoed with Cindy's coffee over to the bed. He sat down gently beside her so as not to cause any sudden movement.

"Good morning, Cindy Sarkos," he said softly. "I've got coffee."

She stirred slightly and then rolled over on her back ... still asleep.

"Cindy-Cindy," he said again. "Coffee's ready."

She still slept on. Her coffee would get cold if she didn't get moving.

Also, it was Sunday morning. Kylla didn't get a bath last night, so she would have to be bathed in addition to Cindy and Kyle. She needed to get up. He reached over and gently ran his hand down the side of her face.

"Morning, beautiful," he said a little louder. "Want some coffee?"

She slowly opened her eyes and tried to focus. At first she was disoriented.

"Kyle?" she asked sleepily.

"Hey, welcome to Sunday morning."

"What are you doing here?" She closed her eyes again.

"I've brought you coffee."

She smiled this time. "That's wonderful, but what are you doing here?"

He chuckled. She still thought she was at her Mom's.

"No, the question should be, what are *you* doing *here*?" he said as he held up the coffee mug for her to see.

She opened her eyes again and then shot up in the bed. "Kyle! What *am* I doing here?" There was panic in her eyes.

"You're fixing to have coffee," he grinned as he handed her the cup.

"Mama! Dadda!" came Kylla's voice from her little bed. "Bites?"

"Hey, little bit," he said excited as he went over to pick her up. "Look who's here … Mama!"

He carried Kylla back to Cindy's bed and sat her down.

"We got married yesterday, didn't we?" Cindy nodded as she finally began to wake up.

"Yep. And you became an official mom."

"I sure did," she said as she took a big swallow of coffee. "Mmmm. Perfect. How did you know how I liked my coffee?"

"I take notes. I was hoping some day I could bring you coffee in bed." He leaned over to Kylla and gave her a big kiss on the cheek. "What does little Kylla want for breakfast?"

"Eggs!" Kylla answered immediately. "Mama, eggs?"

"No! Mama shower. Dadda makes the eggs."

"Should I make *you* some?" he asked hopefully.

She grimaced and shook her head. "I don't do breakfast."

He sighed.

"I don't," she defended.

"I remember. Just promise me one thing. If later on down the road you end up pregnant, please tell me you will eat breakfast for the sake of our baby."

"I promise. Are you planning this any time soon?"

"Not as long as I'm sleeping on the couch."

She blushed. Kylla grabbed Kyle's hand and demanded eggs, and Cindy was thankful for the rescue. He picked her up and tossed her into the air as she squealed and laughed. She took another drink from her coffee and closed her eyes in delight. Had she died and gone to heaven? No, if this were heaven, her father would be here too. A sense of peace flooded over her as she realized at this time last year she hadn't wanted to go on with her life. Her father had died, she was completely miserable, and she couldn't imagine ever feeling a reason to keep going. But as Kylla squealed on her way down the stairs—and as she held a cup of coffee brought to her by Kyle—the loss of her father seemed like only a passage in life.

***

When Kyle grabbed his coat from the closet for church, he remembered all the envelopes he had stuffed in there. He pulled them out; there had to be close to forty in various pockets.

"Cindy!" he called out as he began to drop the envelopes on the bed.

She peeked out from the bathroom where she was finishing her make-up. "What is it?"

"All these envelopes—we should probably open a couple before going to church. It would be nice to see what people wrote to us."

She came out with a tube of lipstick and began to apply it as she joined him on the bed. He was smitten all over again. She wore a spring skirt and blouse full of bright flowers and her perfume had been freshly applied. He couldn't help but smile.

"So you think these are notes?" she asked him, apparently oblivious to his adoration.

"I'm just assuming," he said as he handed her one. "This is from the Freemans, Danny and Stephanie. People are probably well-wishing us or something."

"How sweet. I guess normally we would have had a shower or something," she said as she opened the small white envelope. "Oh, my gosh!"

"What is it?"

"Fifty dollars!" she exclaimed. She looked up at him with her mouth open in surprise. "Surely all of this isn't money?"

"Why would the Freemans give us money? They barely have anything themselves." He picked up another envelope. "This is from the Tatums. Open it."

"You open it. I'll get another one."

"No way!" Kyle yelled in astonishment. "$150. The Tatums gave us $150! What's going on here?"

"$100," Cindy said as her jaw dropped.

"Who's that from?" He leaned over to see the envelope.

"It's a check from the Humphres. This is unreal."

"Do you think somebody suggested this?"

"I have no idea. This is so sweet. Why would they do this?"

"Well, we don't have time to open the rest right now." He looked at his watch. "After lunch today we can finish."

"Put these three back in the envelopes. We need to make a list of who gave us everything so we can send out thank-you notes."

"Good idea." He was overwhelmed.

They put the money and checks back inside and then he held out his hand to pull her up from the bed. "Ready for church, Mrs. Sarkos?"

She giggled as he pulled her up to him. "Ready as I'll ever be."

***

Sunday dinner at the Wrights was festive and fun. Sue was there as well as Andie's family. Kylla played and ran with Ashley and Aimee, and Cindy held baby Alaina for the longest time as the adults talked. She was tiny compared to Kylla, and her features were so adorable and petite.

"Sweet, isn't she?" Kyle whispered in her ear at one point.

"Very," she nodded in awe. "How can something so tiny be so ... I don't even know how to say it ... so ..."

"Perfect?" he suggested.

"That will do. She is perfect." Her spirit grew sad as she thought out loud, "I wonder what Kylla was like at this age."

He reached up and gently rubbed his finger across Alaina's little hand. "I've thought about that more than I should. Was Caryn attentive to her? Did she cradle her to her chest like you do when you rock her? Did she hold her when she cried? Did she talk to her and play with her? I wish I could know. I just want to be assured that Kylla was loved before she came to us."

"You never told me," Cindy grinned at him, "how many kids you want?"

"At one time I dreamed of a house full, but now I'm happy with one child and one wife. We'll see what happens as time goes by. It's hard to imagine God could bless me any more than this."

Kylla came running up and stopped abruptly at the sight of her mama holding another baby. She walked over and tried to look into Cindy's lap. Kyle picked her up and sat her on his knee, and then she leaned over and kissed baby Alaina very softly on the cheek.

"Baby," she said so faintly she could barely be heard. "Mama love baby?"

"Mama loves Kylla," Cindy said earnestly.

Kylla looked up at Cindy with a satisfied smile, and then bounced down from Kyle's lap. She ran off to find her playmates.

"I wish I could know what she was thinking at times," Cindy said wistfully. "It seems as though her thoughts are so deep. What was that about? Was she jealous? Was she curious? Or was it all as innocent as it appeared?"

"If she's like most women, we'll know exactly what she's thinking in a year or two when her vocabulary increases."

When Kylla went down for her nap, they opened the remainder of the envelopes. It was overwhelming what the people in the church had done. When they finished counting, they had over $3,000 dollars in cash and checks. They were humbled, awed and amazed.

"I don't exactly know what to do with all of this?" Kyle said as he lay back on the bed.

"I have an idea," Cindy told him as she lay down on her side and propped her head on her palm.

"Tell me. Give me some direction here."

"It could be a down payment on some land for that house you wanted to build for you and Kylla."

He raised his eyebrows and glanced over at her. "We can add your name to that house too now, you know?"

She smiled. "Just checking. I was curious if you regretted the whole thing or not."

"Surely you're kidding."

Sixty-Two

Jonathan carried his notebook into the deacons' meeting and tried to check his attitude outside the door. Charles Emerson would be recommending the permanent hiring of Cindy Marcum Sarkos this afternoon. There would be a war, and Jonathan's job would be to referee. That in itself would be close to impossible because a referee was supposed to be a neutral party—he was far from neutral where Cindy was concerned. It would be as if the entire discussion was about one of his own daughters, and he knew there would be a struggle for him to keep his mouth and opinions to himself. As long as David Deaton and John Cramer kept it clean, he should be fine. But if accusations began to fly, he feared his temper.

As usual, the first part of the meeting was routine. Nobody really cared about the budget or the upcoming events because all had been well for some time now. The youth were doing great, no problems. Vacation Bible School had been super—okay ... good. All was fine ... blah, blah, blah. But as Charles stood, Jonathan felt the muscles in his neck tighten, and he couldn't help but glance at David and John—he knew their reactions to the suggestion would be severe.

"I'd like to bring up something that many in the church have been recommending," Charles began in his slow, drawn out, southern drawl. Nice, sterile, mundane ... so far. "The church feels it's time to consider the permanent position of secretary."

"Amen," David Deaton practically yelled out.

"It's no secret that Cindy has handled the temporary assignment with proficiency and even excellence," Charles continued. "I've been approached by many, many people, even have a list of at least 200 names in my pocket here," he patted his shirt, "of those who've asked me to recommend Cindy for the full-time position."

David's naturally pink face began to grow red.

"Because of that, as a deacon representing the desires of this church, I'd like to recommend to this group that we present Cindy before the church for the position of permanent church secretary."

"Second!" exclaimed Ricky Tatum before anyone else had a chance to speak.

"Now hold on just a minute!" David was starting. If possible, smoke would have fumed from his ears. "I cannot believe what I'm hearing right now!"

"This was recommended from the church," Charles reminded him. "I'm just telling you what the people have suggested." He pulled the list of signatures from his pocket and laid it on the table.

"I don't care what people have *suggested*," David said with gritted teeth. "We hired Cindy Marcum for a temporary position, and that's all she was meant to be."

Ricky glared at David. "And she's done a job above and beyond what anyone could have imagined."

"That's really beside the point!" David slammed his hand on the table. He was giving both barrels right up front "This *woman* of reputation comes waltzing back here because she has a sick mother, and she needs a job. I can take that, but I won't sit here and watch the moral standing of this church be demised because we want to compromise now on the staff that we hire. This church has been a pillar of the community for over 100 years, and we owe it to ourselves and to this town to keep our standards high. Absolutely not! We won't even consider this recommendation."

Floyd Benson stood slowly. "If I'm correct, there are twelve deacons in this room. That means there are twelve opinions concerning Cindy. You don't have the power, David, to tell the rest of us what we will or will not consider."

"I have the power to tell this group what's right and what's wrong with this whole mess. Cindy Marcum ..."

"Cindy Sarkos," Ricky reminded him.

"Yeah, there you go!" David exclaimed in disgust. "Let's bring up Mr. Sarkos, the divorced music man, while we're at it!"

"He's widowed, David," Floyd said with control.

"Widowed? Ha! He's divorced! She left him before she died! What does that tell you about this man? Huh?" David was starting to rant.

Charles answered this time. "He never wanted the divorce, did everything he could to heal the marriage, but the woman was killed, and now he has no chance *nor* obligation to put it back together."

Ricky came to his feet and added, "And God sees fit in His plan to bring a beautiful young woman into his life to love him, honor him, and become a mother to his child."

"You people are unbelievable!" David started it up again. "Next thing you know you'll be telling me we need to hire him full-time too. Let's just make the whole church a house of ill repute rather than a house of prayer!"

"I'd recommend him," Floyd raised his hand. Several other deacons nodded.

"I can't believe this!" David now left his place at the table and began to rant full force as he walked around the room. "Where did your sense of morality go? I'm sorry, but I won't sit here quietly and watch you men destroy the character of this church by suggesting we hire some ... some ...

hussy on staff!"

Jonathan came to his feet; David had gone too far. "That's enough, David," he said sternly. "We won't resort to character assassination during this meeting. If you have a problem with Cindy, you'll discuss it without name-calling or derogatory remarks. As you may recall, Cindy has turned her life around, so much so, that she's a testimony to the saving grace and power of our Lord. If you want to refer to her again with the name that you just alleged, you'd better start on your knees and take it up with the Lord first—the one who shed His blood to purchase her pardon. Because if His sacrifice wasn't adequate for Cindy, then it's not adequate for any of us."

The deacons glared; Ricky Tatum applauded.

"Don't make this religious, Jonathan," David warned. "I've stood by and watched you weave your misconstruing of Scriptures for over twenty-five years. I won't sit by and let it happen again."

"Did I mention there are twelve of us?" Floyd stuck in.

"Shut up, Benson!" David yelled out. "This is *not* about the majority. This is about a pastor who continually deceives this church into doing whatever he wants!"

Charles reminded him, "This didn't come from the pastor; this *came* from the church." He pointed to the list. "Do you need me to read the list out loud?"

"This church has been wiled by a man who knows how to sneak his will inside! And if you all would open your eyes, you'd see the results!" A vein was beginning to throb in David's forehead. "We agreed to *temporarily* hire a *loose* woman to take care of our church records, and then we *temporarily* hired a *divorced* man to lead our worship! What are you people thinking?"

"Enough!" Jonathan stood to his feet. "I told you, David, to keep your character assassinations out of this!"

"I've sat by all these years and let you do whatever you wanted," David started to say, but Ricky wouldn't let him finish.

"You've never let him do what he's wanted!" Ricky countered. "I've served on this board for eight years and never seen you agree with him on any point—even as to how much we should spend on VBS! It's ridiculous! Why are you in this church, Deaton?"

"Aha!" David threw his finger into the air. "There's the bottom line! I'm in this church because someone has got to keep a lid on this man's issues!" He pointed toward Jonathan. "A church isn't run by the pastor; it's run by the members!"

Charles now picked up the list and tossed it toward David Deaton. "Then let the church run it!"

David was glaring around the room, then his gaze stopped on John Cramer. "Are you leaving me in this all alone, John? I can't believe you're just sitting there keeping your trap shut! Would you back me up here?"

All eyes went to John Cramer. It was unusual; he always agreed with every word and idea David had. But at this moment, he looked like a man who had lost everything. He barely raised his head. Slowly he put his hands on the table and lifted himself from his chair as though he were about to be read a verdict of *guilty*. Once on his feet, his lip quivered.

"Debby called us last night," John began. She was his nineteen-year-old daughter, a sophomore at Auburn University. "She's pregnant."

David gasped, but no one else made a move or sound.

"She'll be leaving school at the end of the summer term so she can come back here to have the baby," John practically mourned. He was fighting tears. "It won't be long before she walks into this church on Sunday mornings and it's obvious to everyone why she's not in college." He now looked up at the men who were on the verge of deciding the fate of a young lady who had messed up but been transformed. "I would take great comfort in knowing this is a church that chooses grace over law, a church that can forgive a girl's mistakes and help her get past them in the process. What better testimony or example is there for my daughter than Cindy Marcum ... Sarkos? She was the wildest, and we all knew it. But God changed her, and He gave her a wonderful Godly man to care for her and complete her life." John was now choking. "I can only pray that God will be so gracious to my Debby."

He sat down and put his face in his hands and wept. The men, one by one, stood up and put their arms on him, everyone but David Deaton.

"I will *not* give credence to this," David said as he grinded his teeth together. "I resign from this board, and I resign from this church. And I hope it goes to ..."

"Enough!" Jonathan said soberly as he held up his hand. "You've made your point well. And right now the issue is no longer Cindy; it's John and his family. We'll deal with Cindy later. Are you walking out on *this* ministry also ... ministry to a hurting friend?"

"I've said all I'm going to say." David slammed the door behind him.

The men prayed for John Cramer, one after another, asking God for wisdom and grace to get through this situation. As each one prayed, John found strength to pull himself together for a little while. The deacons assured him they would do everything they could to help him and his family through this crisis. But before they left, John wanted to speak.

"I don't know about the rest of you," he said with swollen, red eyes, "but I would like to vote that the deacons recommend Cindy Marcum Sarkos for the position of permanent secretary in this church."

Jonathan smiled and looked to Charles, the chairman of the deacon board.

"All in favor?" Charles asked. Every man raised his hand. "I believe, pastor, that's a pass for us," he said with relief. "Do we recommend her at Wednesday's business meeting?"

"I would say so," Jonathan nodded.

"Pastor Jon," John raised his hand. "I know it goes against procedure, but if the board wouldn't mind, I'd like to make the recommendation."

Jonathan raised his eyebrows in question to Charles.

"No problem," Charles said quickly. "It's all yours."

***

"I can't believe it," Cindy said later that night as Jonathan relayed the fact that the deacons had unanimously voted to hire her. "I didn't believe it would actually happen."

"I told you the church was talking it up," Jonathan reminded her.

"The church is one thing. The deacons are another."

Jonathan hadn't bothered to tell her about David Deaton, his arguments nor his storming out of the meeting. The board had agreed to keep that to themselves. David would tell his select few followers who would most probably tag along wherever he chose to go next, but the issue of John Cramer would even put a dent into that. Jonathan actually smiled at the possibilities. For twenty-nine years he had fought John and David on every single issue, and God had blessed the church in spite of their attitudes and sabotages. He tried to calm his mind as he thought of the possibilities for this church now that David was gone and John was broken.

Sixty-Three

During Wednesday evening's business meeting, Cindy sat nervously on the front row. She had wanted to sit in the back, but since she was now married to Kyle, it would only be appropriate to sit with him. He sensed her mood and reached over to take her hand. She jumped.

"Sorry," she said apprehensively. "I forget we're married. It's only been four days."

"Time will take care of that. Don't be nervous. These people adore you," he paused until she looked at him, "and so do I."

She appreciated his support, but that didn't stop the knots pulling her stomach tighter and tighter. She remembered a few church business meetings in the past, and they could get nasty. She hoped this wouldn't be one of those. If it got too bad, she would just leave, or even withdraw her name. But she loved this job. It was challenging, creative, and just plain fun at times. If it were anything other than a church position, she would fight for it, but that all seemed improper here.

Lord, You've done so much in my life that I can't even imagine right now that this position is another possibility. You've given me Kyle and Kylla; You don't have to do this. If You do, I'll mark it up as another miracle for this year, but if not, I'll accept it as from Your hand, and I'll spend my time caring for Kyle and Kylla. She laughed out loud at that thought. She was actually telling God she would be a happy housewife if He would let her.

"What's so funny?" Kyle asked as he leaned into her.

"Life."

Jonathan stepped up to the pulpit and made a few announcements then he called the meeting to order. Some preliminary reports were given, and then each person in charge of a ministry discussed what was happening in the church. Several committees talked about the progress they were making, but everyone knew what was coming, and everyone was ready. Finally, Charles stood for his report.

"As most of you know, we're going to be discussing the position of church secretary this evening, so I would like to turn the meeting over now to John Cramer."

The gasps of surprise in the church were loud. Cindy felt like crawling under the seat. If John were starting the whole thing off that meant it was going to be a tense and conflict-filled evening. She leaned back against Kyle's arm and tried to look calm. He gently patted her shoulder in support, but it didn't ease the rising apprehension.

John came to the platform and then stood with both hands on the pulpit, almost as if he were bracing himself. He glanced down at Cindy for just a moment, which nearly made her jump out of her skin, and then looked out at the congregation.

"The deacon board would like to unanimously recommend Cindy Sarkos for the permanent position of secretary at our church. This recommendation is now open for discussion."

"Amen!" was the first comment made. There was some gentle laughter that followed.

Charles came back to the pulpit. "Is there any discussion or question? Let's bring it up now and get it all out if there is." He looked around the room, but all he saw were smiling faces.

"All right, you had your chance." He grinned with relief. "Pastor?"

Jonathan went back to the pulpit. "The deacons didn't put this out as a motion, only a recommendation. Would someone like to do the honors?"

Sue Marcum jumped to her feet. "I move we hire Cindy Marcum Sarkos as the permanent secretary for this church."

"Second," yelled a man from the back. There was real laughter now.

"Very well," Jonathan said as he winked at Cindy. "I have a motion and a second. We'll start with a count by hands. If it's too close, we'll go to secret ballot. All those in favor let it be known by the uplifted hand." As far as Jonathan could see, every possible hand was raised. "Thank you. Those opposed by the same." He looked over the group, but not a single had was raised against her. "There are none. The motion is carried."

The crowd now applauded, and Cindy could feel her eyes growing thick with tears. Kyle's arm pulled her into a hug, and he whispered in her ear, "Congratulations. This makes you the official breadwinner of the family right now."

"Cindy?" Jonathan called to her. "Would you like to say anything?"

Her heart began to pound. No, she didn't want to speak in front of anybody, but when the congregation began to applaud again, she felt she had no choice.

"Just share your heart," Kyle spoke into her ear. "These people love you."

She walked slowly up to the platform trying to collect her thoughts as she approached the pulpit. This was a first, not just speaking in church, but speaking in public period. Jonathan patted her on the back as he stepped away, but it didn't inject her with confidence. She saw her mother beaming with pride and gratefulness, and then she saw Kyle nodding his head gently. She could do this. They deserved her thankfulness.

She gripped the sides of the pulpit as John Cramer had. She

understood the need to hold on to something.

"First, let me say that I'm completely humbled by this vote of confidence," she began shakily. "But I know it's not because of me that you've done this. What you've admitted to tonight is that our God is a God of complete forgiveness and total grace. I have no problem admitting to you that I feel like the woman caught in the act of adultery when Jesus picked her up and said, *Go and sin no more.* I could try and pretend that all has been well with my world—but you know and I know that's not the case." She paused and swallowed. "The truth is that God, in His unmatchable love, has reached down and touched my life in a miraculous way. I have no answers for why He chose to bless me after so many years of rebellion, but I'm thankful that He did."

Tears began to slide down her cheeks. She reached up to wipe them and continued her speech. "What you've done for me is not only a testimony to the greatness of God; it's also a testimony to how big the heart of this church is. I love this job. It's the best thing I've ever done with my life, and to know that you trust me with every aspect and detail of your church means that you believe in the complete transforming power of God in my life. To simply say *thank you* is nowhere near adequate."

She bit her lip and put her hand up to the congregation as she tried to gain her composure. "But it's all become so much more than that. Because you allowed me here to begin with, you put me in the position to meet the most amazing man and little girl I've ever known." She was about to choke up. She took a deep breath and went on. "I can't thank you enough for that. Sometimes obeying God means taking someone who totally blew her life and putting her in a place where God cannot only change her, but bless her and grow her up. I know," she sniffed, "that if my daddy could speak to you right now," another sniff, "he would say, *thank you for embracing my little girl after I was gone.*"

She had to pause now. When she looked at her mother, she saw tears. And when she looked at Kyle, she saw compassion and adoration.

"I know you let me come here out of honor for my father. I pray that as the years go by I will not only uphold the honor of my earthly father, but also honor and glorify my heavenly Father Who can truly make all things new." She wiped her face again. "Thank you, so much."

As she turned to leave, Jonathan reached out and took her in his arms. Now she began to sob. Kyle and Sue joined them on the platform and each added to the hug. Pretty soon, the entire congregation gathered around them, some on the platform, some in the choir loft, and some on the base floor of the church. Jonathan began to lead a prayer, not only for Cindy, but for the future of a church which chose to believe God and His power to perform miracles in a day that could seem dark and despairing at times.

Sixty-Four

Cindy awoke Thursday morning to wonderful sounds and smells. Kyle had finally been able to get to the stores and get enough things to make their little kitchen in the apartment usable. She rolled over in bed and saw that he was cooking away over the two-burner stove. Each morning he had awakened her with a cup of coffee from downstairs. Was it possible there was a pot brewing up here right now?

She slowly lifted herself up to a seated position and stretched and yawned. She hated mornings—getting up was the worst part of the day. But at this moment, she could see Kylla sitting on the counter beside Kyle babbling away about eggs, and her heart was full. She let her feet hit the floor and then she shuffled over to the kitchen area.

"Morning, beautiful!" Kyle said cheerfully. "You're up early today."

"Mama!" Kylla called out as she reached her hands toward Cindy. She grabbed her and held her tightly.

"What's that wonderful smell?" Cindy asked as she looked into the pan.

"It's called breakfast. I thought I'd introduce you two."

"I don't do ..." Cindy began, but Kyle interrupted her.

"I know—you don't do breakfast. I thought we might give it a try. It would be a great *family* thing for us."

"Family thing?"

"Yes, families eat breakfast together. Now look, before you start griping about calories and such, let me explain. This is turkey bacon. It's very good, tastes just like regular bacon, but is less in saturated fats. And over here," he pointed toward a loaf of bread, "is whole grain, no sugar bread. This is all very healthy and a good part of a balanced diet."

Cindy smiled as she headed to the coffee pot. "I don't suppose those are turkey eggs?"

"No, they're chicken eggs, and they're a great source of protein. I'll only cook you one. How would you like it prepared?"

She couldn't remember the last time she had eaten an egg. She poured her coffee, added two spoonfuls of cream and one of sugar and stirred pensively. "I don't really know. How do you like your eggs?"

Kylla jumped in with a response. "Scwamble!"

"There you go!" Cindy laughed. "Why not?"

"Two scwambles comin' up."

She didn't want to admit the breakfast was wonderful, but Kyle deserved the compliment for going to all the trouble. "Breakfast was good."

"Glad you approve," he said as he took her plate. "Can we make this a date every morning now?"

"And what about my schoolgirl figure?" she teased.

"You're too skinny anyway," he frowned as he placed the dishes on the counter next to the sink. "A little fattening up would do you good."

"I work hard to be this skinny!"

"Then I'll just have to work hard to pull you out of it."

"You don't like my figure?"

He came out behind her and leaned down to put his arms around her. "I *love* your figure, at least what I've seen of it so far." She could feel herself blushing. "But you're gonna need more to your constitution now that you're a mom ... full time ... and a working mom at that."

***

Morning at the office went by quickly. Cindy took the opportunity to do some rearranging now that she had been officially voted in as secretary. She wanted to pinch herself to believe it was real. Within one week she had become a wife, a mother, and a church secretary. If her old friends could see her now. Speaking of old friends, she hadn't written Angie in weeks. She had fifteen minutes before lunch; it was time for a little break.

She first wrote of how adorable the pictures were on Facebook of the new baby as well as Angie herself. She scolded her for being too tanned from spending much time in the sun. She then attempted to explain her marriage to Kyle, her adoption of Kylla and her full time hiring as secretary. Even with her personal newfound life in Christ, Billy seemed unmovable. He wasn't impressed or even convinced that Cindy had changed. He believed time would tell.

"Ready for lunch?" Kyle asked as he stepped out of his office.

"Just a second. I'm writing Angie. Let me close it up."

She attached a couple of pictures taken at the wedding of her and Kyle and Kylla, but most of all she thanked Angie for caring enough about her to be bold and frank. Had she not, Cindy wouldn't be living the blessed life she was now privileged to call hers.

She pressed *send* and then pushed back her chair. "Let's go eat!"

***

Lunch was what it always was: a time of gentle laughter and easy conversation shared over the simplest of meals. It was probably one of the most relaxing hours of the day. Kylla was usually content to be held by her mother or father because it was getting close to naptime, and since the wedding on Saturday, everyone practically felt related. Sue and Barbara had always been close, and James Marcum had been Jonathan's biggest supporter in the church. Angie and Cindy had been like sisters growing up, and then Kyle had nearly become a son to both the Wrights and Sue. They all laid claim to Kylla.

"Kyle?" Sue asked as they sat back in their chairs lingering over the meal. "How on earth did you end up in Dockrey? Why did you even visit our church to begin with?"

Kyle smiled sheepishly as he looked over at Jonathan. "Stephen Williams," was all he said.

"Stephen invited you?" Sue asked in surprise. "You know Stephen?"

"No," he shook his head. "I was in mourning over my life, and I had all but given up on my home church in the Shoals because everyone knew my story and wouldn't let it lie. If I didn't find someplace else, I'd struggle to stay in church at all. I knew Stephen had married the daughter of a pastor in Dockrey. I looked it up and was thrilled to see it was a Baptist church … at least I wouldn't have to change denominations. So I came to visit, and Jonathan brought me here for lunch that very first Sunday."

"What a story." Sue thought over the situation. She had seen many miracles this year, and Kyle stumbling upon Dockrey would just add to the list. "Have you told Stephen?"

"Oh, no," Kyle replied immediately. "I've never even seen the guy."

"You will next week," Jonathan spoke up. "He and Annie are coming for a visit."

Kyle was stunned. "No way! They're coming here?"

"She's my daughter; of course they're coming."

"Should we move out of the apartment. With two kids they'll need plenty of room."

"Forget about it," Barbara said with a sigh. "Annie absolutely insists on staying in *her* room when she comes. She's very sentimental *and* adamant about that."

"But with two kids?" Kyle protested slightly.

"You'd think," Jonathan shook his head. "She wants her room. Period. No questions asked."

Cindy chuckled and added, "And if you knew Annie, you'd know that means it's pretty much written in stone."

"Wow," he whispered. "How do I act?"

Everyone looked at him in surprise.

"You were raised around famous musicians," Sue exclaimed. "What's the deal?"

"Average, famous musicians," he corrected her. "Stephen and Annie are … oh man … the best I can come up with is *exceptional*."

***

Back at the office Kyle did everything clumsily and Cindy couldn't help noticing his agitation. She would tease with him when she got the chance, but his distraction wouldn't ease.

"What's wrong with you this afternoon?" she finally asked. "You're so jumpy."

He sighed and sat down on the edge of her desk. "Stephen Williams is coming *here*. How am I supposed to act?"

She smiled. "I guess to me he's just Annie's husband."

"Well, then there's Annie too. When I saw them in concert, I couldn't believe this girl was from Alabama. She's probably more talented than he is."

"He says she is … but then, he's in love. Annie's just … well … Annie to those of us around here. She was quite a character in high school."

"What's your age difference?"

"She was two years behind me and Angie. But what she lacked in age, she made up for in mouth and attitude."

"I saw a little bit of that on stage. I'll never forget the first concert when they did a piano duel. She was so smug and sure of herself when it came to her ability. I was sitting there thinking what a pompous little girl she was—then she started playing."

"Did you know that song was a commercial in Florence? Some Ford place, I think."

"You're kidding?" Kyle was astonished. "That's an awesome song. Now I really feel intimidated."

Cindy laughed as she reached up and patted his arm. "Trust me; they're down-to-earth and easy to know people. By the time they leave, you'll be best friends."

"I doubt that."

Sixty-Five

On Friday afternoon, Cindy took the bulletins over to the sanctuary for the Sunday services, and when she returned, she was startled to find Debby Cramer sitting in the church office.

"Can I help you?" she asked her.

"Daddy thinks you can," Debby said grimly.

"Really? What does he think I can do?"

"Work miracles," Debby sighed.

Cindy nodded, still puzzled. "So how's college?" Perhaps a different approach would be better.

"Fun. Hard. Troubling."

She sat down at her desk. If she was supposed to work a miracle, she needed to know what she was working with and for. Debby wasn't being very cooperative.

"I finished one semester," Cindy nearly mourned. "Did you know that?"

"No. Why not more?"

She gave a small laugh and replied, "Because I obviously didn't think it was as much fun as you do."

Debby leaned back in the chair and crossed her arms. Cindy knew what that meant from a few body language lessons while selling real estate. She was saying she was closed to anything and didn't want to be here. Okay. What next? Perhaps she should be direct. It was apparent Debby didn't care to share the real topic.

"Why are you here, Debby? What exactly am I supposed to do?"

The girl shifted in her chair, unfolded her arms and then rubbed her hands along the tops of her legs. "I'm pregnant."

Cindy caught her breath and hoped the gasp was silent. Now things made sense. No wonder John Cramer had supported her as secretary; he was raising one just like her. "I see," she tried to sound undisturbed. "Want to tell me a little more about the situation?"

Debby looked up toward the ceiling and crossed her arms again. "Not really. It was an accident."

"Accident?" Cindy found herself saying before she thought.

"Yeah. It was an accident. I've always been careful, but this one guy kinda pushed a little harder than I was used to, and we were out camping, and nothing was available ..."

"I get the picture," Cindy stopped her. What a situation. The girl didn't seem the least upset about what she had done, only that she was pregnant from it. "So what are you gonna do?"

"I don't have much of a choice. My parents insist I have the baby, so I have to drop out of school for a year. That wasn't *my* plan."

I can imagine, Cindy thought to herself. "I suppose your dad sent you over so I could tell you how wild I was and then how God turned my life around."

"I suppose," Debby drew out with a breath. "Why?"

"Why what?"

"Why did you turn your life around? You had it all."

"I thought I had it all, but I had nothing."

"That's a joke, right?" Debby looked at her hard.

"No. I had everything I thought I ever wanted, but once I got it, I found out it was all empty. When my father died, I would've traded everything I'd gained to have him back. That hurt badly because I'd even alienated my father in order to pursue all that stuff. And as I sat in that apartment I'd worked so hard to acquire, I felt empty. Drinking, sex, work … nothing filled the void."

"But God did?" Debby asked sarcastically.

"Not at first." She tried to head off the pessimistic direction. At first, I just thought I hadn't found the right connection … or combination. Then when my mother got cancer, and I realized that I needed to be here with her, I miserably and grudgingly gave it all up because I didn't want to regret losing my mother like I had my father. It was then that God began to work in my life."

"Did lightning strike?" She was still doubtful and sarcastic.

"No, but cancer was worse. Lightning would have been quick and pretty painless. A double mastectomy and chemo treatments were miserably long and drawn out. It was hard not to run away, but my mother had nobody else—I owed it to her to be there for her."

Debby nodded, and her face lightened up slightly. "So," she finally said, "now you're this really good girl, working at the church, and you've married a minister. Sounds exciting."

Cindy smiled and shook her head at the rebellion in Debby's voice. This was easily her ten years ago. "It is exciting. It's the best thing that's ever happened to me. I know you can't fathom that right now, but it's the truth."

"So, do you mean to tell me that married sex is better than before?" Debby nearly blurted out. "I mean, it's all so predictable! Same guy, same bed, same routine. I know it's only been a week for you guys, but please, you can't tell me it's better."

This question made Cindy blush. Of course, she had no real answer since she and Kyle weren't sleeping together … yet … but she couldn't tell that to Debby Cramer. *Grant me wisdom, Lord. You let her come here today; you need to give me the words to say.*

Cindy thought for a bit, then an idea crossed her mind. "What if I woke up pregnant tomorrow morning? How do you think I'd feel about that?"

"That's not the point," Debby responded firmly.

"It's very much the point. Part of God's design in creating sex was for children. It's a wonderful bond between a man and wife, and it's an awesome way to reproduce. The natural by-product of a sexual union is children. If you're not ready for children, you're not ready for sex."

"So are you telling me that when two people get married, they should only sleep together in order to have kids?"

"You know that's not what I'm saying," Cindy was starting to get flustered. She was arguing with herself ten years earlier. "All I'm saying is that when you decide to take on the responsibility of intimacy, there are natural consequences with it. This idea of sex with no strings attached is baloney. Every partner you have takes a string with him, a string you can never get back. And you may try to convince yourself that you're free and not bound down by traditions or rules, but it doesn't stop the fact that it was all created by God for one man and one woman in the context of marriage."

"It's easy for you to say that *now*," Debby said sardonically. "You've had all your fun. Now you get a great guy on top of all that."

"Shut up!" Cindy finally yelled out. "Do you have any idea what you're saying? That's like saying, *Oh, Cindy, now that you've served twenty years in prison for murder, you're out and everything is okay. And besides, that witch you murdered, at least she's not around anymore. You're free and all the consequences are over!*"

Debby glared at her. "Really ... random ... analogy."

"I know, but it's the only thing that makes sense. You're trying to say that my sexual promiscuity was this great thing, and that now I have a marriage on top of it. My exploits will always remind me that I didn't wait for God's best. And every time I look at Kyle, there's this part of me, well many parts of me—all those strings I never thought were attached—that are hanging on to all those men I never really cared about." She hung her head and felt like crying. Kyle deserved so much better than her. "Kyle deserves better than me, but I have to trust his love and God's forgiveness to make this marriage work."

Debby had a glimmer of remorse in her eyes at last, but her arms remained folded and her expression like stone. Cindy knew it would take more than one conversation to change a heart like Debby's, and she prayed that perhaps God would grant her the opportunity and wisdom to help turn Debby around before it was too late.

"Are you gonna keep the baby?" Cindy asked her.

"Who knows?" Debby replied slightly deflated. "I don't want to raise a baby. Mom and Dad might. I just want to go back to school and pick up where I left off."

Maybe a year off and a baby will change that attitude some.

***

Kyle had spent his entire afternoon in the choir room, and when closing time rolled around, he still hadn't come back to the office. Cindy had spent her entire afternoon after Debby's visit thinking about the conversation. It had gotten to her. Debby was asking her to compare her relationship with Kyle to her relationships with all the other men in her past, yet she couldn't make the comparison because she still let her past come between them. Cindy had married Kyle, and he deserved her trust, and some of that trust meant believing him when he said he could get beyond her past. He had given his vow: 'til death do us part ... and so had she. Why then, when Kyle had sworn his allegiance to her, did she still want him on the couch? It was time for some changes.

She finished straightening the office, locked it up, and then headed for the choir room to find Kyle alone before heading home. He was sitting at the piano pecking out notes from a chorus book. She stood quietly in the doorway for a moment and just watched him. He was animated and intent as he tried to learn the song. She loved the intensity in his face when he concentrated on something single-mindedly. His hair had grown out again; it wasn't long, but it wasn't the neat, stylish cut he had gotten when he first came to Dockrey. She smiled as she thought of how soft it felt in her hands, then her smile grew as she thought of how much he loved to touch her hair. It was the first place his hands often went when he was near her.

"Hello, handsome," she said as she walked on in the room.

She caught him by surprise and he jumped from the sound of her voice. "Wo! Where did you come from?"

"It's time to leave, did you know that?"

He glanced down at his watch. "I had no idea. I was going through some new music."

She walked over to the bench and took a seat next to him. He looked at her with pleasure, and rather than pull back or blush or feel uncomfortable, she stared right back at him.

"What is going on in that pretty head of yours?" he wondered.

She didn't answer; instead, she leaned over and tenderly kissed him.

"Good answer," he grinned. "I like the way you think."

She reached up and ran her hand through his hair. He just kept staring and smiling at her. He had no idea what she was up to.

"I have a suggestion," she said as she moved her hand toward his face. "It's Friday, you know. We've been married a whole week now."

He frowned. "You're not having second thoughts, are you?"

327

She gazed into his blue eyes and gave him a mischievous grin. "Not about the wedding."

"About what, then?"

"Our ... *arrangement.*"

"You're gonna have to do better than that. Remember, I'm only a musician, not a rocket scientist."

She moved in closer and kissed him again. "Since it's Friday, I was thinking maybe you and I needed to take a brief honeymoon."

His eyebrows flew up. "A honeymoon? How so?"

"Maybe we could get Mom to come over and keep Kylla for the night at the apartment. I'm sure Jonathan and Barbara would be glad to help. And you and I could go somewhere away from Dockrey, see a movie, eat out some place nice, and then ... perhaps ... get a room somewhere." At that suggestion, she felt her cheeks warm, so she turned her head away.

Kyle's jaw dropped. "Are you serious?" he nearly whispered. "A room?"

"After the movie and the meal. This is ridiculous ... what I've been trying to do here with the couch and the bed and ... all of it."

"What *are* you trying to do?" His question was more compassionate than curious.

She leaned her head back and stared up at the ceiling. How did she explain it best? "I love you, Kyle, but I still struggle with not being good enough for you."

"Cindy, don't ..."

"Let me finish," she put her hand to his lips. "But at this place in time, all of that is pointless. I married you; you married me. We gave each other our vows. I meant them, Kyle."

"So did I."

"I know. You wouldn't have done something like that without taking it seriously." She took his hand and held it up to her heart. "Waiting until I feel ... legitimate ... isn't going to change anything. The thing that will make this marriage begin to feel like a marriage is if we live and act like it is. We're not posing for the FBI anymore; we're genuine. I want to be your wife, Kyle, because you want me to be. I don't want to spend the next who knows how long trying to dodge issues and situations. I'm ready to move on."

She leaned in to kiss him again—no barriers or restraints. He wrapped his arms around her pulling her closer and reached up to take a strand of her hair. She couldn't help smiling.

"Are you sure?" he asked her again.

She could barely speak from the emotion, but she softly confirmed, "If I wasn't before, I certainly am now."

She kissed him again, and for the first time Cindy believed that she could be what Kyle wanted, what he needed. She never imagined that someone could really love her the way he did, but she believed him because he was a good man. And with everything within her, she would devote herself to becoming a good woman, a godly woman, a woman that would bring honor to him for the rest of his days.

***

Sue was thrilled. She threw a few things in her overnight bag and zipped over to the Wrights as quickly as possible. She didn't know which thrilled her most. Was it keeping Kylla, her granddaughter, for an entire night, or was it the fact that her daughter was now married to a wonderful man. Sue had wondered about the marriage, if it were real, genuine, even consummated, but she would never ask. She knew it had happened because of Kylla, but in time they would settle into it. She just didn't imagine it would be so quick.

When she arrived at the Wrights, only an hour after leaving Kylla from babysitting that afternoon, the toddler was thrilled to have her back. Sue's heart melted when Kylla dropped her toy to run into her arms. Cindy and Kyle came downstairs with Kyle carrying a small piece of luggage and both of them dressed up for the evening.

"My, but don't you two look nice," Sue said with admiration. "Where are you going?"

"Huntsville," Kyle told her. "We've reserved a room at the Hyatt and made reservations at Shogun. Hopefully we'll catch a movie somewhere in between."

"Mother, her pajamas are laid out on her bed," Cindy began explaining. "She has a snack around 8:00, then her bath, and usually she is out within a few minutes."

Sue just glared at Cindy.

"What?" Cindy asked defensively.

"I *am* the grandmother," Sue reminded her with a pointed finger. "Grandmothers do *not* follow the rules or routines."

Barbara walked in and agreed. "She's right, you know? You do all the raising; we do all the spoiling."

Cindy looked up at Kyle. He merely shrugged his shoulders.

"In fact," Sue said as she kissed Kylla's cheek, "little Kylla just might sleep with Granny Sue. How would you like that? Want to sleep with Granny Sue?"

Kylla clapped and nodded. That settled that.

Sixty-Six

The drive to Huntsville was long enough to give them a chance to talk about their relationship and their future. Neither would be making much money, and when music lessons began and the church job ended for Kyle, consistent income for him would be over. If a kid were sick or absent or had a test, or any number of things, there would be a drop in pay for the week. At least Cindy's job would provide insurance. He could always go to his father's studio and sit in for a couple of sessions if things got really tight. She had some money put away that could serve as a down payment for the house, but he didn't want to touch that. He preferred to leave it alone and let it grow so there would always be a cushion to fall back on in case of emergencies. Of course, they both knew their parents would help if a financial bind ever presented itself, but that was a road Kyle had never walked before, and never intended to if he could help it.

They went to the Hyatt first and found their room.

"You actually got the honeymoon suite?" Cindy asked in surprise as they walked in.

He blushed at his extravagance. "I wanted it to be special. You deserve something more than just a second rate room with a bed and a table."

She smiled at him in adoration. How could he be so thoughtful of her? She walked over to him, slid her arms around his neck and drew him to her.

"I thought we had to do dinner and a movie first," he winked.

"This is only a foreshadowing of what's to come," she whispered as she kissed him warmly.

Kyle placed his hands on her waist and pulled her closer. She was driving him crazy. For so long she had put him off about everything, and now she was so eager to love him. Who cared about the money, the job, or even his loss of ministry when he finally had Cindy at long last? He leaned down to her ear and smelled her perfume, then kissed her neck. He felt her squirm. He kissed the other side and got the same response. He then pulled one of her hands from behind his neck and smelled and kissed her wrist, then the other.

"And now," he grinned as he leaned down beneath her chin. He finally kissed the front of her neck and top of her chest as he smelled the last place where she dabbed her perfume. "Divine," he whispered.

"You should be on this side," she giggled as she pulled his lips back to hers.

***

Shogun was packed. Kyle was thankful he had made a reservation. They had to park across a back street far from the entrance. He was uncomfortable with the spot, but he held Cindy's hand tightly as they walked toward the restaurant. He was her protector, and he would give his life if someone ever tried to hurt her. As they came to the door, the place was crowded with people waiting outside. They had to maneuver themselves through the tight space.

"Sarkos," Kyle said to the petite Asian woman. "Reservations for two."

She glanced down her list and nodded in delight. "Yes. Come with me. We are ready for you now."

They followed her to the table where they were seated with four other couples. The evening was wonderful. Normally when coming to Shogun, Cindy would have chatted and gotten to know everyone at her table, but with Kyle beside her, she found herself totally wrapped up in him. They talked even more about their plans, what kind of house they needed, and wondered how long it would be before Kylla would be safe enough to move there.

"It's always this black cloud hanging over my head," Cindy confessed to him after the chef had finished cooking and left their table. "All these wonderful things are happening in my life," she reached for his hand and squeezed it tightly, "but Jimmy Thornton is back there somewhere threatening to steal it all away. Sometimes, Kyle, I feel like I'm suffocating because of it."

"I understand, believe me." He kissed her hand and reached up to caress her hair. "I wish there were some way all of this could be resolved. Who could've imagined that two people in Dockrey, Alabama, would be so intertwined in a mess like this?" He leaned over to kiss her. "At least we've got each other to lean on now."

"Hey, buddy," called out one of the men at their table. "You guys need to get a room!" The other couples laughed. Most of them were pretty well wasted from the alcohol.

Kyle smiled unashamedly and said, "You're right. We're on our honeymoon. I think it's time to head to the room right now."

They stood to leave, and he felt like a king as her took his hand. This was what his father had meant. Caryn never made him feel this way. He had felt like a father, a protector, a friend, and a number of other things with her, but he had never felt like a king. Once outside, he reached for two coins to throw into the fountain. He handed one to Cindy.

"Make a wish," he whispered in her ear.

"I don't need to," she whispered back. "Wait!" She remembered one thing. She tossed the penny into the water and said, "I wish Jimmy Thornton and all his little thugs were out of the way once and for all so all I had to do was love you and Kylla for the rest of my life."

Kyle smiled and tossed his own coin. "Ditto," he said as he pulled her to him. She kissed him again and all he could think about was how incredible it felt to hold her like this in his arms. Her lips were warm and inviting, and he could taste the gloss she had put on after the meal. Her perfume still got to him, and as the kiss went on, the idea of a movie seemed less and less appealing.

"Do you really want to go to a movie?" he asked with slight hesitation.

She looked up at him and giggled. "What are you proposing?"

He yawned a fake yawn and stretched his arms out behind her. "I'm tired. I was thinking that maybe ... maybe ... we might just go on back to the room. If you really want to see a movie that badly, we could go tomorrow sometime."

She closed her eyes in contentment and threw her head back. "A movie doesn't even sound enticing in the least right now." She yawned too. "I vote for the hotel."

Kyle bent down to kiss her again. "Let's go then."

He took her hand and led her through the back lot and across the street. On the way to her little red car, they discussed the possibility of house colors, the inside decor, and the fact that Kyle would still have to teach her more about cooking. When they reached her car, they barely noticed the man standing next to a tree just feet away from them. As she waited for him to find the keys, Kyle heard her gasp.

"What is it?" he asked as he followed her stare.

"Mr. and Mrs. Sarkos," said the man as he stepped away from the tree and toward them.

"Who are you?" Kyle asked as he immediately put himself in front of Cindy.

"An old friend of your wife," he replied amused in a distinct northern accent. "We had a conversation once at da cemetery, didn't we?"

Kyle's body tensed. This was the man who had followed Cindy the day she went to visit her father's grave. "What do you want?" Kyle tried to be firm and calm.

"I need yous to come wid me," he said matter-of-factly. "Jimmy Thornton t'inks it's time we all had a little talk."

"Listen," Kyle began to reason with him. "I don't know who you are or why this Jimmy Thornton is so interested in me and my family, but I can guarantee you that we don't have anything he wants."

"Dat's a matter of opinion."

"Leave Cindy alone," Kyle insisted. "You can take me if you want, but I won't let you hurt her."

"Don't be noble, Mr. Sarkos," the man laughed sinisterly. "You don't really have a say-so in any of dis." The man whistled and five others stepped from the shadows. "We can do dis da easy way, or we can do it da … well … da bloody way."

"Bloody?" Cindy asked in horror.

"Don't listen to him, Cindy," Kyle tried to move her back toward the car.

"Mr. Sarkos, surely you don't think you can escape? Dere's six of us, and dere's two of yous." The man took a step toward Kyle.

Why didn't I call Ben Hall and tell him what we were doing? Kyle thought to himself. *How stupid. The FBI should be here!* He was going to have to fight these men himself. He had a black belt, but he hadn't used it or practiced it in years. He would give his life to defend Cindy, but with six men probably holding six guns, it would be a pointless match. Maybe he could give her enough distraction to run.

"Cindy," he whispered to her. "When I jump this guy, you run."

"Are you crazy?" she looked at him with fear.

Kyle didn't answer. Instead he lifted his right leg into the air, jumped and kicked the chin of the man. "Run!" he yelled to her. She started toward the restaurant, but two of the men intercepted her immediately. Kyle turned to face the next man he knew would be upon him any moment, but before he could think about what to do next, the butt of a gun hit the back of his head. He felt consciousness leaving him, but he looked for Cindy. When he saw her face, she was screaming in terror and trying to reach her arms out to him. "Kyle," she shouted as he felt himself fall to the ground. He tried to look up at her. He could see her legs. He put his arms to the ground to push himself up, but the gun hit him again and finished the job. He was out.

Sixty-Seven

Kyle tried to open his eyes and change his position, but the pain in his head was paralyzing. He struggled to find consciousness, yet the unfamiliar sounds and smells were confusing. Was he not at home? He finally managed to open his eyes and discovered he was in a strange, dimly lit bedroom. Lying beside him on the bed was Cindy. Then he remembered—Huntsville, their date, honeymoon, Shogun—then he really remembered. He tried to reach over to her but realized his hands were bound.

"Cindy," he said softly. Augh ... it killed his head to move in any way.

Cindy immediately opened her eyes. "Kyle!" she said in a panic. "Are you all right?" She tried to reach up to his face, but her hands were bound too. Instead, she just grabbed his fingers.

"Where are we?" he could barely speak.

"I have no idea," she said looking with deep concern. "We drove several hours to get here."

He tried to smile as he asked, "You mean we're not at the Hyatt?"

"Very funny. I think we're in big trouble, Kyle. They keep coming in to check on you to see if you're awake yet."

He suddenly became alarmed. These people were responsible for Caryn's death; would they attempt to hurt Cindy too? "Have they harmed you in any way?"

"They don't seem to care that I'm even here. It's you they want. How's your head?"

He closed his eyes and groaned, "I don't think I've ever known pain like this before. What happened?"

"You got whacked on the back of the head ... twice. At least they let you lay with your head in my lap for the trip here. I tried to keep you turned so there would be no pressure on the wounds."

"Sorry I missed the ride, especially the part with my head in your lap," he smiled as he kept his eyes closed. "Is there anything to drink? I'm dying of thirst."

She sat up. "There's a pitcher of ice water over here." As she left the bed, he got a glimpse of what was binding their hands: thick plastic ties. He tried to watch as she maneuvered herself awkwardly to pour him some water, but his head hurt too much. There would be plenty of time in the future to admire Cindy. Right now, he had to figure a way out of here, and muster up the strength to do it with a throbbing head.

"Here," she said as she sat down gently on the bed. "I'm afraid you're gonna have to sit up. There are no straws."

He tried to move, but his headache practically threw him back down. He moaned as he tried to reach up to grab his head, but his bound hands made it even harder and more painful.

"Tell you what," she said as she put the glass down on a bedside table. "Let me try to get you propped up."

"Ooooh," he groaned as he thought about having to move again. "I don't know if I can."

"Which is worse? Your thirst or your pain?" She was looking at him tearfully. He could tell she was trying to be brave for his sake. He must look awful.

"Okay, help me up."

She gently pulled him up, but it was hard with the plastic tightly binding their wrists. He moaned and even yelped once, but she managed to get him upright and then put his and her pillows behind his head and back. She held the glass to his mouth and helped him to drink. At last there was relief for his thirst.

"Thank you," he said as he eased his head back against the pillow. "At least something feels better."

She leaned up and kissed his cheek as gently as she could. "This isn't how I imagined our evening turning out."

"You and me both. What time is it?"

She glanced down at his watch; it was easier to read than hers at the moment. "Almost five forty-five."

"Is that in the morning?"

"Yep," she sighed as she placed the glass back on the table.

"You didn't see where they were taking us?"

"Nothing. We were in this big industrial type van. The only windows were out the front, and these guys wouldn't let me see anything. I sat on a carpeted floor facing the back with your head in my lap. They blindfolded me before they let me back out."

"Hmmm," Kyle thought for a bit. "That might be good."

"How so?"

"If they don't want you to remember where you are, that might mean they intend to let you go at some point."

"I hope so," she mumbled as she shifted her wrist in the plastic tie. "I've been here too long already."

Suddenly the door burst open and in came the man from the Shogun fiasco.

"At last, da dead arises," he said with a smirk. "You up to talking, Sarkos?"

"No, he's not!" Cindy answered right away. "His head is killing him from the knots you guys gave him."

335

"Hey!" the guy protested, "he nearly broke my jaw wid dat kick! We had ta disable him before he tried anything else."

"You can't fault me for self-preservation," Kyle said as his head continued to throb.

The man laughed obnoxiously. "You can when you're dealing wid Jimmy Thornton. You don't even know what yous got yourself into, Sarkos."

"You're right," Kyle agreed. "I don't know why I'm here, who Jimmy is, or why on earth he thinks I've got anything he wants. I'm a minister, for crying out loud!" The yell made his head begin to spin. "Ahhh," he moaned and fell back onto the pillows.

Cindy came to her knees and tried to think of something she could do to ease his pain.

"Might as well relax," the man relayed. "Jimmy will explain it all when he talks to yous."

Kyle swallowed hard. So Jimmy Thornton was here ... within driving distance of Huntsville, thus Dockrey. How foolish he had been to let his guard down.

"Can I get yous anything while you're waiting?"

"Advil? Tylenol? Aspirin?" Cindy suggested. "Anything that will help take the edge off his pain."

"I'll see what I can do."

He left the room and Cindy sat facing Kyle. She reached for his hand and gently ran her fingers over his. "Do you really think we'll make it out of here ... alive? These men don't appear to be the real tender and caring type. I'm taking a huge guess that their boss is a lot like them."

"We'll make it out," Kyle assured her. "God has moved heaven and earth to bring us together; this is *not* the end of our story."

"I wish my faith were as strong as yours."

"Then let's pray."

Sixty-Eight

At nine-thirty a.m., the cemetery man came back into the room along with two other guys. The new men brought in wooden dining chairs and placed them next to each other in the center of the room. They then proceeded to move toward the bed. One man helped Cindy off the bed, but the other jerked Kyle up. He yelled in pain.

"Can you not be gentle with him!" she screamed. "He's hurting badly!"

"Shut up, Blondie," said the man with Kyle. "I'm not up for the *Mr. Nice Guy* award."

Not only is he ugly, he's remarkably stupid, she thought.

Cindy was seated on one of the wooden chairs, and then Kyle was practically thrown into his. She grimaced as she knew he was trying to stifle his groans. She wished she could hold him and care for him, but at the moment she was as helpless as he.

A couple of minutes later, a well-groomed man entered the room. The three men immediately stood straighter and oozed with respect.

"You two, out," he told all but the cemetery man. "Amos, you stay in here with me. I can't imagine them getting ... *restless* ... but just in case."

"Right, boss," Amos replied. "I'll keep an eye out." His accent was really grating on Cindy.

Jimmy Thornton was a handsome man, and he appeared to be much younger than he probably was. If he had been responsible for Martin Sartin's struggle over thirteen years ago, the man had to be older than he looked. Cindy had imagined Jimmy Thornton, drug king, to be your typical mafia, Italian type guy, but he was far from it. His hair was bleached blond, his skin fair, but well tanned, and his eyes a chilling gray. He was short, but obviously well built and fit. He paced back and forth in front of Kyle and Cindy for the longest time. Finally he paused, stood before them, and crossed his arms almost defiantly.

"Anything you want to confess?" he began by asking Kyle. "You could make this very easy for all of us, Mr. Sarkos, if you would just come clean."

"About what?" Kyle asked him as he tried to focus his eyes on Jimmy. "I don't know what you want with me."

Jimmy gave an amused laugh. "Okay, we'll play your way for a little while." Jimmy began to pace again. "What is your relationship to Callista Sartin for starters?"

"I don't know a Callista Sartin," Kyle said honestly. "I know who you're talking about, though. I knew her as Caryn Carter. I never knew her by that other name."

"But you know who she is now?"

"Yes," Kyle admitted. "But I promise you I had no idea who she was until just a couple of months ago ... after she was killed."

"Why did she have your baby?" Jimmy asked pointedly.

Kyle was silent. Cindy looked over at him and bit her lip nervously.

"Now, Mr. Sarkos, if there's one thing I know about you, it's that you're a good man ... you're an honest man. You won't lie to me." Jimmy came over and stopped in front of him. "Your silence is not very reassuring. It would lead me to believe that you're hiding something."

Kyle closed his eyes. The truth was, he was scared to open his mouth. His head was killing him, and he wasn't sure if he was thinking clearly. Thoughts were scrambling themselves inside his brain, and who knew what might come out if he tried to talk.

"Would you like me to paint a little picture for you, Mr. Sarkos?" Jimmy said in a rather sing-song way. He knelt down in front of the chair so Kyle wouldn't have to lean his head up to see him. "For a while now we've tried to find out the identity of your little ... Killa?" He pronounced it with a short *i*.

"Kylla," Cindy corrected him immediately.

"Oh, how cute," Jimmy smiled patronizingly. "Named after her Daddy, I presume. Would you believe that no records were available on her until Monday morning ... conveniently after you and Miss Marcum here tied the knot?"

"Mrs. Sarkos," Cindy grumbled out.

Kyle tried to breathe normally as he explained. "There was a lot of investigating after Caryn's death. The FBI was holding things up."

"Hmmm, I see." Jimmy stood back up and started his pacing again. "Why would little Kylla be tied up in Callista's murder investigation? That's what I kept wondering. Could you give me any hint as to why that might be, Mr. Sarkos?"

Kyle said nothing. Jimmy stepped in front of Kyle again, and Kyle did his best to lift his head and focus on the man. But as soon as Kyle rested his head, Jimmy backhanded him so hard on the right side of his face that it drew blood.

"No!" Cindy screamed as she jumped up from the chair to reach for Kyle.

"Sit down, *Ms. Sarkos*," Jimmy said as he pushed her back into the chair. "I said I would do this your way if Mr. Sarkos would cooperate, but I'm getting nowhere."

Kyle was moaning now as his face contorted and blood trickled from the right side of his mouth. The pain had just doubled.

"Now, let's try it again," Jimmy knelt back down in front of Kyle. "Why did she have your baby?"

"She was caring for Kylla," he managed to answer.

"Uh-huh," Jimmy responded unconvinced. "That just doesn't seem to wash with everything else. For example, why the visit to a California penitentiary to see Callista's father? If you didn't know who she was, why did you visit him."

Kyle wished he could spit out the blood. He needed to spit, but he was helpless. He finally swallowed it so he could answer. His stomach was getting nauseous. "I had found out who Caryn really was. I had been close to her. I just wanted to talk to her father. I had been a fan."

"Right," Jimmy wasn't convinced. "Okay, let's go with another question. What exactly was your relationship with Callista? In what capacity did you know her?"

Kyle thought and then answered, "I didn't know she was Callista."

"Okay, all right," Jimmy was now getting exasperated with Kyle's runaround. "Then what was your relationship with Caryn? How did you know her?"

"We went to college together," he said groggily. "We became friends there."

Jimmy nodded and stood back to his feet. He was rubbing his chin again. "Mr. Sarkos, I know that you're choosing to be vague right now, but I *will* get the truth out of you one way or another. I know that I'm not phrasing these questions right in order to get that information. Forgive me. I normally use a gun pointed at someone's head to elicit what I need to know. Call me loveable, but I just have a soft spot for ministers. I'm trying to do this the nice way." He stepped back in front of Kyle. "What was your relationship to Callista—or Caryn—whoever you want to call her? We're talking about the same person here, just so you know."

Kyle hung his head. The pain had so permeated his face that he wondered if he could stay conscious much longer. "College," he breathed out. "Friends in college."

"And ten years later she's watching your kid?" Jimmy chuckled. "Fill in the blanks for me, Kyle. That's not good enough."

He sat motionless. Jimmy this time took his fist and struck Kyle on the left side of his face close to his eye.

"Would you stop!" Cindy cried out. "Can't you see he's hardly able to speak already? Leave him alone! Let him rest!" She got softer. "Please."

"I said for you to fill in the blanks, Mr. Sarkos," Jimmy said more firmly. "Your answers aren't adequate."

Kyle's head was practically bobbing now, and he felt his left eye beginning to swell. He tried to speak, but he was teetering at consciousness.

"For a minister you sure are one tough egg to crack," Jimmy sighed. "I really didn't want to drag Ms. Sarkos into this," Jimmy began to threaten. Kyle looked up as quickly as he could manage. "I actually believe she's an innocent party here. I also believe that her name was not on that birth certificate until sometime last week."

Jimmy reached over and gently ran the back of his hand down Cindy's face. "You are one gorgeous creature," he whispered. "Perhaps we could do a little role playing here for Mr. Sarkos. I could pretend that you are *my* wife. I don't have a problem with that, seeing that I'm not near the moral man that you are, Mr. Sarkos."

Kyle tried to speak. "No. Please. Not Cindy."

"Well, I agree with you there," Jimmy remarked as he stepped back in front of Kyle. "I'm not actually that type of guy. But at this point, I've been given such a runaround that I'm at my wit's end. Tell me about Callista, your relationship with her, and why your baby was in her apartment when she was killed."

Kyle was slumped in his seat now. Every part of his face and head was throbbing with excruciating pain. "First," Kyle practically panted, "answer me something."

Jimmy actually gave a genuine laugh this time. "Sure! Why not? What do you want know, Mt. Sarkos? What possibly could you want to know?"

Kyle focused his eyes on Jimmy and squinted as he asked, "Who actually pulled the trigger? Was it you or one of your thugs?"

Jimmy sighed and smiled as he knelt back down in front of him. "Oh, it was me. The whole point of killing her was for my pleasure."

"You are sick," Cindy muttered. "How could you just …"

"Shut up!" Jimmy told her tersely. "You're starting to get on my nerves." He turned back to Kyle. "I told you, now quid-pro-quo, Kyle."

He was silent again. He clamped his jaw as tightly as he could in hopes that his mouth wouldn't overrule his brain.

"You're just not being fair to me," Jimmy sounded as though he were chastising him. "Amos, take Ms. Sarkos to the bed. It's time to force the issue, I believe."

"Sure, boss," Amos said a little too eagerly. He walked over to Cindy, but as he reached down to grab her arm, Kyle came out of the chair, twisted his body around and landed a kick first at Jimmy Thornton, and then at Amos. He lost his balance right away and fell to the floor. Unable to brace his fall because of his bound hands, he once again fell on his face.

"Kyle!" Cindy screamed.

Amos reached out to grab Cindy, but Jimmy put his hand up to halt him. Jimmy stood up, rolled Kyle to his back, and then literally lifted him up by the shirt collar. He threw him back into the chair, and then brushed himself off.

"I'll give you an *A* for effort, Mr. Sarkos, but that wasn't the wisest play in the book," Jimmy said calmly. "I understand your passion. Ms. Sarkos is a beautiful woman. I would really rather not have to violate her in your presence. In fact, I would just as soon let Amos do the honors."

"Thanks, boss," Amos grinned big.

"However, like I said, if you'll just spit out the truth, we can settle all of this now. Nobody gets hurt anymore."

Kyle was barely conscious, but he knew enough to know that Cindy was in danger of some kind of assault if he didn't act quickly. "What?" was all he could ask. "What do you want to know?" He couldn't even remember at this point.

"Callista, Kyle," Jimmy was beginning to lose his patience. "Your relationship to Callista, and why she had your baby at her apartment the night I deliciously ended her life."

The phrase turned Kyle's stomach. Jimmy motioned for Amos to get Cindy again. As he walked back toward her, Kyle began. "I married her. I thought she was Caryn. I married her. But it was fake … just found that out too. She used me."

"She was one smart cookie, I'll hand that to her," Jimmy shook his head. "How long were you married?"

Cindy answered for him. She was obviously sick of watching him struggle. "Ten years."

"And the baby?" Jimmy pushed.

Kyle managed to look over at Cindy. Her face was wet with tears, and he could now see pure horror in her eyes. If he didn't tell Jimmy the truth, he would hurt Cindy. If he did tell the truth, Jimmy would kill Kylla. Was he actually going to have to choose between one or the other? He loved them both deeper than any kind of love he had ever imagined. This was an impossible decision.

"I'm waiting, Kyle," Jimmy motioned for Amos to lift Cindy from the chair. He obeyed.

"She was ours," Kyle finally gasped as a sob escaped his mouth. "Caryn was pregnant. I didn't know it was mine. She left." He began to cry pitifully through his unending pain.

"Let her go," Jimmy told Amos as he straightened himself up.

"But boss?" Amos began to protest.

"I said to let her go," Jimmy raised his voice. "We'll decide what to do with them later. Right now, I've got to deal with Martin Sartin's granddaughter. "

"Please!" Cindy began to cry. "She's innocent! Why does this have to go on? Can't it just stop?"

"It will," Jimmy said in an almost assuring manner. "Kylla will end it all. She is the last of Sartin's family. When I kill her, all will go back to normal."

"You would kill a child?" Cindy was screaming in panic. "There's no sense in it! She'll never even know who her mother or grandfather was!"

Jimmy leaned down into her face and gritted his teeth as he said, "But *I* will. And it's time to pay my final respects to the Sartin family. I took care of Maria, Callista, and now sweet little Kylla. The cycle will at last be complete."

He turned to leave, but Cindy jumped from the chair and threw her bound arms around his neck from the back. "Leave her alone! She's innocent in all of this!"

Jimmy threw her arms off of him and tossed her to the floor like dead weight. But a sudden gunshot from somewhere in the house grabbed all of their attention.

"What the ... what was that?" Jimmy asked Amos.

"I don't know, boss," Amos shrugged. "Someone with itchy fingers maybe?"

"That's exactly what we need here—some moron making gunshots to give us away."

Another shot fired and then some yelling began to ensue.

"Is Garner drunk again?" Jimmy began to show some panic for the first time. "Get down there and shut them up, will you?"

Amos immediately ran for the door, but as soon as he opened it, three familiar faces burst into the room.

"Ben Hall!" Cindy screamed from relief this time.

Agent Sparks ran to Cindy, cut her plastic band, and then helped her to her feet.

"Forget me!" Cindy was crying out. "Get an ambulance for Kyle! He's hurt really bad!"

Cindy ran to Kyle while Ben Hall handcuffed Jimmy Thornton. The look on Jimmy's face was one of complete astonishment.

"You little trickster," Jimmy said as he shook his head toward Kyle. "You had a tracking device, didn't you? Where was it? On your watch? On your body? I can't believe I didn't think to check you."

"Wrong, Thornton," Ben Hall said as he threw him to the bed. "He had a tail ... several in fact. We've been with him from Dockrey all the way here to Nashville. We managed to listen in up here ... we've got some incredible equipment, the FBI does. We were just waiting to make our move."

Cindy wasn't listening to anything. Agent Sparks had managed to get Kyle on the floor and his feet elevated. Cindy was now leaning over him trying to get him to respond to her.

"Kyle, please wake up," she was crying. "It's over, Kyle. It's over. The FBI is here and Jimmy Thornton is in custody. Kyle, please." She cried as she dropped her head to his chest. "Kyle please be okay."

Agent Sparks spoke into her communicator, "Get three ambulances here pronto. We've got three in critical condition."

Static crackled and a voice responded over the speaker, "Gunshot wounds?"

"Two of them—but the third has a severe amount of head injury and trauma."

More static and then, "Ambulances are on their way."

Cindy looked up to see Ben Hall grabbing Jimmy from the bed and pushing him toward the door. Jimmy looked back at her and smiled. It was a defeated smile as he shook his head again in disbelief.

"It's almost unbelievable, isn't it?" Jimmy chuckled. "I had everything, but I've just lost it a second time around because I wanted to get back at Sartin. My mama always did tell me that I couldn't leave well enough alone."

"Shut up, Thornton," Agent Hall shot out. "You do realize you're completely caught, don't you? You've confessed to murder in the presence of two witnesses. There's no way out of this."

"Ironic, isn't it?" Jimmy chuckled again as he walked out the door and into the custody of two more agents. "So, how many of you guys are here? Just curious. At least I could brag about the fact that it took a whole team to bring me in."

Ben walked over to Cindy and knelt down beside her and Kyle. "We'll make sure he gets the best help."

"Why didn't you come in sooner?" she wondered as tears continued to flow. "You could have prevented this?"

"It was a hard decision." Ben was shaking his head. "Until he admitted to killing Callista, all we could have done was book him on kidnapping a couple of adults … and trust me, he could have gotten out on that. He would still be after Kylla, you guys would never have peace, and this case would go on and on." He rubbed the stubble on his cheek and squinted his eyes shut. "I hated to hear it happen, but as soon as he confessed, we began to move." He looked into her eyes and honestly said, "I'm really sorry. Very sorry."

Cindy looked back down at Kyle. His face was so swollen now that it was almost unrecognizable. She leaned down and gently kissed his forehead as a tear dropped from her eye onto his cheek. "It's over, Kyle. It's really over."

He moaned and then barely acknowledged, "It's over."

Sixty-Nine

Jonathan literally dropped to the couch as he turned off the phone.

"Well, tell us!" Barbara cried frantically as she and Sue stood in the great room.

"They're all okay," he said in a choked tone. "Kyle's been beat up pretty badly and he's on his way to the hospital, but Cindy was untouched."

Sue broke into sobs of relief and turned to embrace Barbara.

"Jimmy Thornton confessed to Callista's murder and also his intent to kill Kylla. He made it known that he was responsible for Maria's death too."

"What kind of man is he?" Barbara exclaimed in sheer disgust.

"A man in custody of the federal law," Jonathan said smugly.

They all absorbed the meaning of that statement.

"Is it finished?" Sue asked as she went over to Kylla who was asleep in the portable crib at the edge of the room. "Is Kylla free?"

"Seems so," Jonathan nodded. "With Thornton out of the picture, life goes back to normal."

"Normal?" Barbara nearly laughed. "Kyle and Cindy and Kylla have never seen normal together. They won't know what to think!"

Jonathan sighed as he ran his hand through his hair. "They said Kyle held out on the truth to the very end. It wasn't until they threatened Cindy that he gave in and told them Kylla was Caryn's daughter."

"How badly is he hurt?" Sue wondered.

Jonathan shook his head. "They don't know. He was fairly beaten up—took two whacks from a gun handle in the back of the head outside of Shogun. Then Thornton got him a couple of more times at the house in Nashville. Some kind of neuro doctor is on standby at the ER waiting for him. They'll call as soon as they know anything."

***

Cindy was exhausted, but she couldn't fall asleep. She stared at Kyle as he slept—wires hooked to his head, tubes running into his arm. She had sat with him for a long time, holding his hand and talking to him, but there was no response. Finally, out of utter frustration to be near him, but also needing to rest, she climbed up in the bed next to him and curled beside his resting body. She put his arm on his abdomen and draped hers over his, gently lacing her fingers between his. At some point she dozed off as his rhythmic breathing finally lulled her to sleep.

She awoke when a nurse came into the room to check his blood pressure.

"How's he doing?" Cindy asked as she tried to focus her eyes.

"His vitals are excellent," the nurse smiled at her. "I'm not sure if you're allowed up there with him."

"Take it to the FBI," she said with a yawn. "We were married one week ago today. You'll have to get a court order to move me."

"I think we can overlook this minor infraction," the nurse said tenderly. "He took quite a beating."

"I had to watch it all. When do you think he can leave?"

"Depends. As long as nothing develops, maybe a couple of days."

"What do you mean *develops?* What might develop?"

"Swelling, blood clots, bleeding—any number of things that often accompany head trauma, but for the moment, everything looks fine." Then the nurse added, "Surprisingly fine."

***

Between the medication being pumped into his body and the draining events of the past 24 hours, it was late in the afternoon before Kyle awoke. When he did, he saw Cindy's smiling face directly in front of him.

"How's the head?" she asked him caringly.

"Not as bad, but still not good. So, it took something as dramatic as all this to finally get you in bed with me?"

"I was just playing hard to get," she joked back as she reached up to gently caress his face.

They lay still for a bit and relished the moment. After months of tension, unwanted surprises, and possible danger lurking after them, to know that it was all finally in the past seemed unbelievable.

"I bet I look wonderful right now," Kyle said with a hint of a grin.

"Let's see, you tried to save my life twice, I'm thinking you look more handsome than ever at the moment. Where did the Karate stuff come from? I didn't know it was possible for a man to lift his leg that high."

He tried to smile, but between a busted right lip and a swollen left eye, it was hard to manage. He knew he must be on some pretty powerful pain medicine for his head not to ache so badly. "I was pulling every trick out of the hat I could." He stared into her eyes and was overcome with the thought that he could possibly have lost her. "I was scared, Cindy. I struggled with telling him the truth. When it came down to it, I couldn't ... couldn't ... watch him hurt you ... in any way. I just couldn't."

"I understand," she assured him as she took his hand. "I don't know how you lasted as long as you did."

He closed his eyes and relaxed. The medicine was doing its job well. Right now more than anything he wanted to hold her and kiss her and pull her as close to him as possible, but he felt washed up.

"Sleep, Kyle," she said tenderly as she gently kissed his swollen lip.

"Will you still be here when I wake up?"

"I'm not leaving your side until we go home."

"Home," he said longingly. "We can really get our home now. We don't have to stay at Jonathan's; we don't have to hide behind that fence. We can take Kylla to the park, to MacDonald's ..."

"To Chuck E. Cheese," she added.

"Do we have to?" he grimaced.

"Yes, I'm afraid so."

"Hmmm," he breathed out suspiciously.

"What's the *hmmm* about?

"I can see right now that I'm gonna have to keep an eye on you. And I mean that literally seeing as I can only open one eye at the moment."

She giggled and gently kissed his forehead. They were going to pull through this.

His eyes rolled, but he hung on to consciousness. Nothing else mattered anymore. Not the ministry, not his past, not her past, not finances ... nothing. All that mattered was that he was alive, Cindy was alive, and no one was coming after Kylla ever again. They could be a normal family and they could live their lives in peace and simplicity at last.

"Have you talked to Kylla?" he asked her.

She shook her head. "My focus is on you right now. Mother said Kylla is doing just fine. Occasionally she'll ask about us, but Mother assures her we'll be back soon. In the meantime, she's enjoying ice cream, Jell-O, macaroni and cheese, and sugar sweetened Kool-Aid."

Kyle let a gentle smile creep across his lips. "She's being spoiled then."

"A-one spoiling, I think."

"Good. She deserves it."

Cindy reached up to push back several strands of hair that had fallen across his face. He couldn't fight the sleep any longer. As he drifted, however, he could feel her beside him, and his sleep would be sweet because of it.

Seventy

On Tuesday morning, Kyle was released from the hospital in Nashville. Ben Hall thought this would be a great time to have a debriefing of the case, so he managed a comfortable conversion van. He sat in the back with Cindy and Kyle as they hashed through all that had happened, all that would be happening, and all that would be required of them when the court date approached.

"You won't have to be at any of the proceedings except when it comes time to testify about his confession to Callista's murder, and his intent to kill Kylla," Ben explained. "You're free to come to any you want, but this will be a long process. Jimmy Thornton has been wanted for a long time. He's got a list of felonies that will make Martin Sartin look like a saint."

"When will all this be?" Cindy asked.

"No time soon. He won't be allowed to post bail, so you don't have to worry about any repercussions happening. He'll sit in jail for awhile, then a court date will be set ... several months most probably."

"Will we be hounded by his lawyers in court like they always are on television?" Kyle wondered.

Agent Hill smiled at the question. "Yeah, but all you have to do is stick with your story. When they ask you if you heard Jimmy say he killed Callista himself, you just say *yes*. When they ask if he made known his intent to go after Kylla, you say *yes*. When they try to divert you in some other direction, or accuse you of something yourself, you don't go there. You just stick with what you know."

Kyle sighed and rubbed the back of his head. The knots from being knocked with the gun were huge and sore. At least his head wasn't killing him anymore. His eye and face were still aching, and he had three small stitches inside the right corner of his mouth. He couldn't believe this was all the damage that had been done.

"Need a pain pill?" Cindy asked as he winced while touching a tender spot.

"Yeah, I do. I would try to appear brave and resist it, but I'm through with bravery. Hand me one."

She opened her purse, pulled out the bottle, and gave him a pill. After swallowing it, he reached over and took her hand and she scooted next to him. She leaned her head on his shoulder, and before he knew it, she was asleep. Three days in the hospital had worn her out too. He gently kissed the top of her head and soaked up the glory of having her near him with no lines, boundaries or fears still hanging on. He had won, and what a prize she had become.

As the van approached the Wright house, hundreds of people stood outside the gate. Kyle was floored. Were they here for him? Surely not! Then he noticed the press. Were they going to push for an interview with him? Had this whole Jimmy Thornton thing gotten out of hand?

"Why are they here?" he asked in near shock.

"Stephen and Annie came in yesterday," she explained.

"No way. They're here right now?"

"I'm pretty sure of it."

He heaved a heavy sigh. "I look horrible. I haven't even had a shower since ... when did we go out? Friday?"

Cindy grinned and kissed his cheek. "They know what you've been through. In fact, they offered to send a limo to pick you up, but Agent Hall thought a nice van would be more appropriate."

Ben Hall turned around and smiled.

"I would have preferred the limo," Kyle teased.

"The FBI has a tight budget, you know? That's why we always drive around in these ugly vehicles."

The van was cleared to move through, and Kyle watched behind them as several security officers pushed people back and away from the gate. He rubbed his stomach as it began to feel queasy at the thought of meeting Stephen and Annie. What should he do? How should he respond? One thing was sure; he would excuse himself right away and head up to take a shower. Yuck, he felt dirty and greasy all over.

The van stopped and Agent Hall stepped out first. Cindy followed and Ben gave her a hand stepping down. Kyle maneuvered through the van and finally outside. He turned to Ben and shook his hand firmly.

"I don't know how to thank you for all you've done," he told him sincerely. "If you hadn't shown up when you did ... well ... I doubt things would have turned out as good."

Cindy protested saying, "You call this good?" and she pointed to his eye.

"I wish we could have gone in sooner," Ben admitted. "But you did good to get that confession ... both of them in fact. I was afraid it might not happen. If things would've gotten out of hand, we would've moved on in. But we had an agenda to complete."

Cindy chuckled. "Yes, I'm familiar with your ever-present agenda."

"Take care of yourselves," Ben told them as he moved back to the van. "Enjoy your newfound freedom. I'll be in touch as time passes." He started to step up to the door, but turned back around. "And by the way—congratulations. You guys should make a happy family."

Kyle nodded as Ben stepped inside, closed the door, and the van pulled away. Suddenly a yell caused both of them to turn to the house.

"You're back!" Sue was screaming as she came running down the sidewalk. "I can't believe you're back!"

"Mother!" Cindy called as tears filled her eyes. She ran to her mother and embraced her snugly.

"Kyle!" Sue motioned for him to join them. He came up and put his arms around them both. They just clung to one another for a bit and held on to the relief they felt at that moment.

"Let me see you," Sue said to Kyle with a huge frown across her face. "Oh, my." She reached up and touched his swollen, black eye. "I can't believe this happened to you."

"But it's all over," he told her. "And Kylla can live like a normal little girl for the first time in her life."

"That's right," Cindy smiled at the realization. "She has no idea what life is like outside the walls of a home. She stayed inside with Caryn almost her entire first year, and with the exception of church and a brief trip out occasionally, she's remained inside these walls too. Just think … she gets to enjoy all these new aspects of life."

"Well," Sue began with a very guilty grin, "she already knows what a *Happy Meal* is. When Agent Hall told us she no longer had to stay behind the fence … well … Saturday evening we went to McDonald's. Then we went again Sunday evening before church. And I took her there for eggs this morning; she wondered where the toy was—they didn't have a breakfast *Happy Meal*. So I just bought her one anyway."

"Mother!" Cindy laughed. "You *have* been spoiling her, haven't you?"

"You bet I have!"

They walked up the walk and into the front door of the house. Immediately Kylla spotted them.

"Mama! Dadda!" she called out as she jumped up from the floor where she was playing with a little curly headed blond boy. She ran to them as fast as she could.

"Hey, sweetheart!" Cindy said emotionally as she picked the toddler up and held her close.

Kylla pulled back and looked into Cindy's eyes for reassurance. Cindy smiled at her and kissed her nose.

"Mama's back," Cindy affirmed.

Then Kylla turned to Kyle. "Dadda eye?" She pointed to his swollen face.

"Dadda has an ouch on his eye," he told her.

"Dadda eye hurt?" she asked.

"Just a little," he said as he showed her how little with his fingers.

Kylla reached out for him and he took her in his arms. She placed her little arms around his neck and clung tightly to him. As Kyle closed his eyes, he felt Cindy put her arm around his waist. This was what he had always dreamed of: a wonderful wife, and children. Kylla leaned up and kissed him on the lips.

"That's Daddy's girl," he grinned.

The back porch door opened, and Jonathan and Barbara came inside followed by Stephen and Annie.

"What's all the commotion?" Jonathan asked as he walked over to Kyle and Cindy. He stared at Kyle's eye and then asked, "So, what did the other guy look like?"

"He fared much better than I did," Kyle confessed. "But then, my hands were tied and some thug with a gun was standing too close to Cindy for my comfort. I thought I'd just let him beat me up a little bit."

Cindy jumped in, "But he did this Karate kick thing two times! You should have seen him. Jimmy Thornton had already smacked him around several times, but when Kyle got the chance—whack! He jumped up and knocked Jimmy to the floor … along with the cemetery guy."

Stephen walked over and offered his hand to Kyle. "And to think, *we* hired extra security for *you*. I guess you could have taken care of things yourself had we known."

"Hi," Kyle said shyly as he shook Stephen's hand. "Kyle Sarkos."

"Sarkos?" Annie said with a grin as she walked up holding a sleeping baby girl. "Of Sarkos Music?"

"My dad owns it."

"Unbelievable," she grinned. "I spent a lot of money at that store over the years. In fact, that's where I bought most of my equipment when I used to write commercial jingles."

"You probably helped put me through college then," Kyle chuckled. "I thank you."

Annie turned to Cindy and reached over to put her free arm around her. "It's so good to see you. I can't believe what God has done in your life this past year. Let's talk some time while I'm here."

"Be glad to. And let me see this baby." Cindy peeked down at the tiny being with curly blond locks. "How can something so small be so adorable and endearing?"

"You ought to know … *Mom*," Annie smiled at her.

"Yeah. I became a wife and a mom on the same day. That's sort of rare."

"Daddy would have killed me if I would have done that," Annie said smugly as she glanced over at her father.

"Always the smart aleck," Jonathan shook his head.

Seventy-One

Kyle finally got into the shower, lingering long after the actual bathing. He let the warm water pour over his body as he relived the memories of the last few days. It reminded him of his tonsillectomy at nineteen. He had struggled with throat infections and ear infections for so many years, and at last the doctor insisted they remove the tonsils. He was told it would be a miserable experience, that at his age it would seem unbearable after the surgery, but when things were finally healed, his quality of life and his health would be much better. That was his life right now.

He had lost Caryn to divorce. He had lost the ministry because of his failed marriage. He had lost his hopes, his dreams, and his future. He came to Dockrey as a last-ditch effort to put his life back together, and suddenly things began to turn around. But there was more recovery to come, and after this past weekend, the last of the wounds were gone. Kylla was safe, he and Cindy were ready to move forward, and he had regained his hope, his dreams, and his future.

His body was still chronically sore. It was all he could do to shampoo his hair, but he finally managed if he moved slowly and deliberately. When he stepped out of the shower, he dried off and gingerly put on a pair of gym shorts and t-shirt. He brushed through his hair, but his arms were aching. He didn't think he had it in him to actually use the hair dryer. He cracked open the door and found Cindy sitting next to a sleeping Kylla on the little bed. She was rubbing Kylla's back, but the baby was sound asleep. The touching was strictly for her benefit.

"Hey," Cindy looked up at him from the bed. "Feel better?"

"Feel cleaner," he half smiled. "Do you think ... well ... would you mind ... I'm really sore." He hesitated to ask her for help.

She gently got up from the bed and walked to him. "What is it you need, Kyle? Just ask."

"Could you just run the dryer over my hair until most of the moisture is out?" he asked. "You don't have to do anything fancy, it's just that my arm is killing me."

She pushed open the bathroom door and reached up on her tiptoes to give him a tiny kiss. "Go to the couch; I'll bring the dryer."

"We can do it in here," he told her. "I don't want to wake up Kylla."

"Oh, please," she said with a moan. "That child can sleep through anything. Go to the couch, Mr. Sarkos. I'll be right there."

351

He literally shuffled to the couch. He was aching worse now; it must be time for more medicine. She came over and tousled his hair with her hand. After turning on the dryer she began to run her hand through his hair moving it back and forth.

"It's amazing how fast shorter hair dries," she noted. "Don't let me hurt you. I'm trying to be gentle, but I can feel the knots from where that thug knocked you."

"You're doing fine."

"All done," she said as she unplugged the dryer.

"Thanks. Is it time for me to have another pain pill yet?"

She turned to look at him and her expression was full of compassion. She sat down next to him and gently ran her hand over his face. "Yes. You may have one up to every four hours." She took his hand and helped to pull him up from the couch.

"Are we going back downstairs?"

"No," she said as she led him to the other side of the room. "You're going to bed. I'll get you a glass of water and your pill in a second."

She pulled back the cover and helped him to sit. "Let me get your pillow out of the closet."

Because he had been sleeping on the couch, he had kept his sleeping things on a shelf in the roomy closet. Cindy retrieved his pillow and came back to the bed to help him lie down. When he was finally in a position where he could rest, she covered him and then went to their tiny kitchen for a glass of water, a straw, and the prescription from her purse. When she came back to the bed, he had closed his eyes for relief.

"Kyle," she said softly. "Here's your medicine." He started to sit. "Don't get up; I've got one of Kylla's straws."

She put the pill to his lips along with the straw. When he had swallowed, he smiled a thank you, and glanced into her eyes just briefly. It felt good to be back in his own home and in his own bed, but it felt even better to see Cindy there with him.

"I'm gonna run over to the church office and try to catch up on some work. Just rest. I'll have Mother check in on Kylla," she whispered.

"Okay," was all he could get out.

***

At the office, Cindy turned on the computer and the air-conditioning and started a pot of coffee. She watered the two plants she had brought in several weeks back, and made a quick list of things she needed to accomplish that afternoon. She sat down and logged onto Facebook. Yes! Angie had replied.

Dear Cindy, Pardon my writing if it seems a little "off base" today, but I hit my head from falling to the floor after reading your letter. First, let me say that Daddy said nothing about any type of relationship between you and Kyle, and he hadn't told me about the wedding or the adoption, so your news was extremely newsy ... even shocking if you want the truth. When did all this happen? I mean ... suddenly deciding to get married? What's up with that? The last thing you wrote was that you knew you had feelings for Kyle, believed he could do much better than some wild girl like you, and that you were doing your best to discourage him even though you had fallen in love with his DAUGHTER—not him. You have freaked me out to the highest degree!

Now that you're a wife and a mom, do you cook? Ha! I would love to see that! Seriously, though, I'm so proud of you and how you've allowed God to work in your life in such a short time. Deep down I always knew you were a person much more noble than you ever believed. (Your brother? I'm still not sure about him.) I know you, and that you'll try to hide your past to keep from bringing shame on Kyle and Kylla, but remember this: God can use your past in a mighty way to reach those who have been in similar circumstances. You don't need to embellish your life, but you need to be willing to share it with those who need direction and healing just like you did—once—long ago. I'm so happy for you, Cindy. The only regret I have about being here in Padawin is that I miss out on sharing my life with those I love back home. I'm thankful for the Internet, but it doesn't replace looking into your eyes and seeing the emotion and reality of all you are living. I miss that horribly.

Keep me updated on your life, as it seems to be on an ever-changing track right now. And a hearty congratulations is in order for landing the secretary job full-time. Who would've ever thought that??! Take care and KEEP IN TOUCH! Much Love, Angie

Cindy's heart was heavy as she ached for Angie to be here so they could talk in person. There were so many things Cindy needed to know about her new life. Angie had become strong in her convictions once she turned her life over to Christ, and Cindy could use her years of dedication and experience to spur her on in the Lord. Also, just to talk with her about being married and raising a child would be wonderful. She and Angie had shared everything over the years, even after long periods of separation. Whenever they were together, it was as though time had stood still for them, and they picked up exactly where they had left off. Cindy wondered if it would be that way again now that their lives had changed so much.

She replied to Angie's message and then began to tell of the events that had unfolded this past weekend. As she relived them, she found herself emotional again over all that had happened. Kyle could have been killed, she could have been hurt, Kylla could have been murdered, and things could have turned out so differently. Yet once again she found that God was always in control. How easily things could have taken a turn for the worse, but miraculously, again, those she loved were spared.

She thought about Kyle and what he had endured for the sake of his little girl. She considered the way he had held out as long as he could to keep from telling Jimmy Thornton that Kylla was Caryn's child, and then how he did his best to give information that was misleading, yet not a lie. She admired him for his courage and his integrity, and felt overwhelmed that God had blessed her with such an incredible man. She whispered a prayer that God would transform her into the kind of woman that would complete his life in every way possible, and that she would learn how to be a mother that would meet all the needs Kylla would have in the years to come. She prayed she would raise her and train her so she could grow up and fulfill the purpose for which God had created her. What a heavy thought. She had never considered the fact that Kylla would one day grow up and move out on her own, and what Cindy did during these early years would have a major impact on the woman Kylla would become.

Dear Father, please help me be the kind of mother that will encourage and inspire her to be Godly and honoring to you all the days of her life. Don't let her choose the path that I walked for so many years. And don't let my indiscretions become an excuse for her to do the same.

Seventy-Two

Cindy left the office near five o'clock. She had caught up on everything and would be ready to work on the prayer list the next morning. When she got back to the house, she was surprised to see Kyle up and on the couch with Kylla. She had imagined he would sleep all afternoon. She had asked her mother to keep a check on the baby so that when she awoke, Sue could take her downstairs and let Kyle sleep. Annie was sitting in one of the recliners with Ellie, and Stephen was holding little Stevie, and the conversation was rather animated between them all.

"It looks like I'm missing out on something," Cindy said as she walked over to the couch to join Kyle.

"Mama!" Kylla called out. When Cindy sat down, Kylla immediately crawled onto her lap.

Stephen laughed and remarked, "I believe Cindy may have you outranked, Kyle!"

"She does, believe me," Kyle affirmed. "When we got back from Martha's Vineyard, Kylla wouldn't even think of going to sleep without Cindy being here."

"Being married sort of fixes that little problem, I imagine," Annie winked to Cindy.

"Completely." Kyle reached over and took Cindy's hand. It was almost as though electricity shot through her body whenever he touched her.

"How do you feel?" she asked him. "I was surprised to see you up and about."

"That medicine does wonders. Besides, when Kylla started stirring, I wanted to spend some time with her."

"She's a beautiful child," Annie said as she rocked her own. "I don't know if I've ever personally seen a baby so pretty. And she looks just like Kyle. He told us all about the situation and when you went up to get her. I bet there were no doubts after seeing her who the father was."

"I saw her first," Cindy explained. "I could've fainted from shock."

Kyle chuckled and noted to Stephen and Annie, "She looks like she could be one of yours ... the blonde hair, the blue eyes."

"Nope," Stephen shook his head. "She may have the features, but she looks too much like you."

"Gee, Kyle," Annie teased him, "she's so pretty, but she looks like you—does that make you *pretty* too?"

"At this moment in time? No way! My eye sort of takes away from looking *pretty* at present."

Cindy leaned over and kissed his cheek. "I think you're beautiful."

"Awww," Annie said with a smile. "How sweet. And you guys are officially still on your honeymoon. You should go off somewhere for a weekend." Kyle and Cindy both looked at her in dismay. "What?" Annie wondered at their expressions.

"That's what we *were* doing when we got kidnapped and beaten up!" Cindy exclaimed.

***

Sue made baked beans and Barbara fixed her famous potato salad for supper, while Jonathan grilled ribs out back. Kylla and Stevie played in the yard as the men sat around the grill and watched their children. Kyle's pain was beginning to come back a little, but he hated how the medicine dulled his senses. There was so much going on in his life right now that was good, and he didn't want to miss a beat of it.

"Stephen," he said hesitantly as he looked over at the man he had admired musically for so many years. "I wouldn't normally be as bold as I'm about to be, but this is something that has hounded me for months now."

"Sure, what is it?" Stephen asked eagerly as he tossed a little ball back to Stevie.

"Shortly after Cindy and I first met, she made a statement that stuck with me for a long time. She said that her life felt like a *winter midnight*; it was the coldest and darkest point that it had ever been."

"Wow, that's quite an emotional image."

"I know ... that's what I thought too," Kyle continued. "And I couldn't help but correlate that to your song *Autumn Sunset*. The more I thought about it, the more I thought that it could be a great song."

Stephen nodded. "Did you write it?"

Kyle laughed and shook his head. "No way! I'm *not* a songwriter. But the thoughts and feelings that are conjured up when I remember her telling me that are very strong."

"What was happening when she said it?"

"Her mother was recovering from surgery. The house was a wreck; every dish in the kitchen was dirty and piled up on the counters and the table. Her mom was miserable, and Cindy, who had just left a life of luxury, was doing her best to take care of her. She was tired, she was worn, and she was in a huge mess. I offered to help her get things back together, and she looked at me with the most pitiful expression and said, *I feel like my life is a winter midnight ... the darkest and coldest time possible.*"

"She had sacrificed a lot to be there."

"Yeah. It was a hard time for both her and Sue. And my life wasn't much better, except for the fact that I was healthy."

"You should write that song." Stephen looked over at him soberly.

"I'm not a songwriter, but you and Annie are."

Stephen leaned back and crossed his arms. He finally shook his head and said, "You're a musician, Kyle—and you're a deep thinker. This idea has impacted you profoundly; you're the one who needs to write the song."

Kyle shook his head in disagreement. "I'm not a songwriter, Stephen. I wouldn't even know where to start. Do you do the words first? Do you do the music first? I want it to be meaningful and ... well ... good. Not something thrown together."

"Then don't throw it together. You start with whatever comes first. If you hear the music first, then you go with that and add the words eventually. But if the words start forming, you put them down and then add music later." He sighed and said, "Then sometimes they both start coming at the same time."

"So you're not gonna do this for me? You're gonna make me hash it out on my own."

"It's in you—you need to write it. Besides, I think it's been *winter midnight* for both you and Cindy a long time now. You're the only one who can really do it honestly."

"Hmmm," Kyle was a little disappointed. He had never even considered writing music. "I was really looking forward to getting you to do it."

"Tell you what, you write it, you send it to me, and I'll put it together for you in the studio."

"You've got to be kidding," Kyle laughed as he shook his head. "No way! I wouldn't write a song and then send it off to Stephen Williams! That'd be like creating a math formula and asking Einstein to have a look at it."

Stephen laughed. "You know the only thing that makes me a better a songwriter than you?"

"Millions of dollars?"

"Nothing! It's all subjective! There are people in the world who think I'm the biggest quack musician ever born, but there are others who think I hung the moon. Whenever I put out an album, the critics are always mixed. When Annie joined the team, some said that at last there would be some quality music coming out of my studios, while others mourned the loss of my independent stylings. There's no such thing as *good* music or *bad* music, especially if it comes from the heart." Stephen looked at him seriously this time. "You write that song, and even if it only has two chords, it'll be a good song. Even if the words don't rhyme, it'll be a good song. If it stands for something and means something, it'll be significant. It doesn't matter what anybody thinks about it; the polls will always be conflicting. It amazes me how people feel they have a right to tell me their opinions on *Autumn Sunset* since it was the song that catapulted my fame. Some will say it's the most incredible song ever written, that it changed their life, that it did this or that. Then I'll have others tell me that it's the sappiest, most drawn out pile of blubbery whining they've ever heard."

"No way," Kyle was astonished. "People tell you that?"

"All the time."

"And how do you feel?"

"At first, I was floored. But on this side of it all, who cares? Everybody's a critic, and everybody's different. My goal as a musician is to be true to myself and to write what's inside. There will always be people who will connect with me because of that. And those who don't, who cares? There are thousands of others out there who would disagree."

"Church work is kind of like that too," Kyle agreed. "There are some who think you do an awesome job, and there are others who think you're just some pompous, pretentious guy who couldn't make a career of music doing anything else—so he got stuck with music in a church."

"They don't think that about you here ... at least from what I've heard. According to Jonathan, Barbara, Sue and Andie you're the most incredible music man this church has ever known—and they believe you are *called* to it, not settling for it."

"I am called—or at least, I *was*." Kyle's expression dropped as he thought of that. He loved music ministry, and he loved it at this church more than anywhere he had ever been. He loved the way Jonathan referred to it as *exhaling*. That had given him a completely different focus on the music he chose and the way it was presented. He loved Jonathan, he loved the church, he loved how they had rallied behind Cindy and embraced her new choices, and he loved how they had supported his getting a daughter suddenly out of nowhere. He was humbled at the wedding when an impromptu reception was created because the people of the church wanted to celebrate his and Cindy's marriage. One consolation was that even if he wasn't working at the church, Cindy would be, and he would still be in Dockrey.

***

During supper Kyle's pain became intense again. He didn't have to ask for medicine; Cindy went upstairs and got a pill then placed it in his hand at the table when she returned.

"Thank you," he whispered in her ear as she sat back down by him.

"I think you're trying to do too much too soon. After supper, why don't you lie down?"

"Are you kidding? Stephen and Annie Williams are here in this house. That's like practically unbelievable."

"And they'll still be here tomorrow ... and the next day ... and the next."

Kyle reached beneath the table and took her hand. He would be so glad when he was back to normal and they could move on with their lives.

As if she could read his mind, she leaned over and said, "This won't last forever. One day, we'll be in our own home running our lives on a regular schedule."

"I can't wait." He squeezed her hand.

After supper, Cindy practically dragged him up the stairs. Kylla was playing contentedly with Stevie again, so Cindy took the moment to see to it that he rested. She pulled off his shoes and fluffed up his pillow before letting him lie down.

"Are you trying to spoil me?" he asked as he finally rested his body.

"As much as I can," she grinned, sitting down beside him on the bed.

"I haven't been spoiled in a long time. I almost feel guilty about it."

She climbed over him and lay down next to him, draping her arm over his chest.

"As soon as I get better, I need to talk with the school about getting lessons set up," he mumbled as the medicine began to take effect. "I don't know how long the job at the church is gonna last, but if we're gonna get a house on our own, I need to get a steady income."

"Kyle, I've got plenty put away that we can use for awhile."

"I know, but we don't need to mess with that. And there's no sense in it anyway. The sooner I get established as a private music teacher, the sooner people will begin to sign up. Since I can work during school hours, it'll be ideal for us. You'll get off at three, and so will I." He turned toward her and grinned. "We'll be together as much as possible."

"I look forward to it," she said softly as she reached up to stroke his hair.

Seventy-Three

By Saturday afternoon, Kyle was beginning to feel normal again. The swelling around his eye had subsided, but the inside was bright red, and the outside was now turning green. When he awoke that morning, he was determined not to take any medication except for Tylenol or Advil. So far, so good. He had struck up a friendship with Stephen and Annie, and found himself really impressed with Annie. Having known Jonathan and Barbara, and having heard about their children often, it was interesting to finally meet one other than Andie. He also enjoyed being able to hold little Ellie now and then. He had completely missed Kylla's baby months, and he found himself longing to know what those times were like. He wondered if Caryn had taken any pictures. He wished he could have some kind of information on his daughter before the time that he got her.

Saturday evening, the Wrights hosted an outside barbecue and picnic, and Andie and Doug and their clan joined the feast. The noise of children playing and screaming and the chatter of adults sitting around fellowshipping were wonderful reminders to Kyle that his life had found meaning again. This time last year he was dark and hopeless, but here he was with a family that had practically become his own. He thanked God for the healing and for the restoration that he had desperately longed for and needed.

As Cindy and Annie played a game of chase with Kylla, Stevie and Aimee, he watched his wife with admiration. She was the most beautiful woman he had ever seen, and she seemed to genuinely love him now. Everything about her appeared perfect at the moment. He knew her past— she had clearly described it to him several times, reminding him that she was not the woman he should fall for. But as he watched her play and laugh with Kylla, he could only marvel at the transforming power of God. This was not the girl she had described herself as. She was humble, gentle, sweet, a wonderful, caring, attentive mother, and she had been an incredible tender and compassionate wife this past week. It was still hard for him to believe he would be spending the rest of his life with her.

"Kyle!" Barbara called to him as she came outside waving his phone. "It's your father! You really need to stop leaving your cell laying around all over the place. One of these kids is gonna pick it up and call Moscow someday!"

Kyle snapped out of his thoughts and immediately stood and went for the phone. His parents knew nothing about what had happened in his life the past couple of weeks—from his marriage to Cindy to the abduction, and finally the arrest of Jimmy Thornton. He took the phone and headed back inside the house. This would be a long conversation.

"Dad?"

"Hey, son!" Bradley Sarkos was obviously refreshed and revived after his vacation. "How are things going?"

"Great on this end. How was your trip?"

"The best we've ever had, but I'll confess it's great to be back home again."

"I can remember." Kyle's vacations while married to Caryn had been relegated strictly to visits to Martha's Vineyard. "Maybe someday I can get away and go somewhere for a little relaxation again too."

"You should've come with us. It would've been just like old times, well, except that you could've brought along that cute little blond with you."

"Which blond are you referring to? Kylla or Cindy?"

"Well, I was thinking of my granddaughter, but I would've been thrilled to have had Cindy along too. Are things looking … uh … more positive in that area?"

"Very," Kyle found himself grinning. "In fact, you guys have missed quite a bit being out of the country and all."

"Is that so? Catch me up, then."

As Kyle gave out the details of all that had happened—from California with Martin Sartin to the kidnapping—his father was floored. With each new development, Bradley would gasp even more.

"Well, that settles it," Bradley said firmly. "Next time we leave the country, you're going with us!"

"Gladly," Kyle smiled still overcome with relief that Kylla was no longer in danger.

"Look, since you can all get out again, why don't you come over for dinner tomorrow? We'd love to see you … and of course, your girls too."

"I'll talk to Cindy about it and let you know."

***

"Of course, we'll go!" Cindy said in delight that night as she laid Kylla down in her little bed. "I'd love to see your parents again. And I'm sure they're dying to see this little sweetie." She covered Kylla with her comforter, and gently kissed her forehead. "Night-night, sweetheart," she said tenderly.

"Let me call them," Kyle said as he started for the phone.

"Hang on just a minute." She his arm and pulled him to her. "You seem to be feeling much better this evening." She put her arms around his neck and stared up into his face.

He smiled at her beauty and admitted, "I'm feeling much better.

Thank you for noticing."

She pulled his head down to hers and softly kissed him. "Make that phone call quickly, okay?"

Kyle caught his breath and realized what she was suggesting. "Real quick," he told her as his pulse began to race. He kissed her back, but this time there was less gentleness and more passion.

He found his phone on the couch, punched in his parents' number, and impatiently counted the rings. Cindy had gone into the bathroom, and all he could think of was the kiss still tingling his lips.

"Hello?" It was his mother.

"Mom, it's Kyle."

"Hey, baby. I'm so happy for you! I can't believe you went through all of this and we were totally out of the picture!"

"It's been an interesting couple of weeks to say the least. I was just calling to tell you that we'll be over for dinner after the morning service tomorrow."

"Oh, wonderful! I just can't wait!"

"Okay, then. I'll see you tomorrow." He was trying to get off the phone, but his mother wouldn't think of it. She went on and on about every little thing that came to her mind. He kept trying to cut her off, but nothing seemed to work—his mother wanted to talk. He finally fell back on the couch and settled in for the duration. He wouldn't be getting off the phone until his mother was good and ready.

He heard the bathroom door open, so he turned around to let Cindy know he was still on the phone. His mouth fell open. She was wearing a beautiful piece of turquoise lingerie with a sheer matching robe. Whatever his mother was saying at that moment was lost. Cindy simply smiled and walked over to the couch. She sat down beside him and began to gently kiss his neck, his ear, his cheek. Was his mother still talking?

"Mom," he said weakly. "Cindy's calling. I need to go. We'll see you tomorrow."

"Okay, honey. You go tend to that wife of yours."

"I'll do just that," he said with a smile.

"Okay. Bye-bye."

As soon as he said goodbye, Cindy took the phone from him, turned it off, and then placed it on the table beside the couch. He wrapped his arms around her waist and pulled her down on the couch with him.

"My mother told me I needed to *tend to my wife*," he said with a grin as she leaned in for a real kiss.

"It's about time," she whispered as she found his lips.

"Nice outfit," he said, barely able to breathe.

"Glad you like it," she smiled at him. "I bought it just for you."

"Thank you … very, very much."

Seventy-Four

When the alarm went off the next morning, Cindy rolled over without her typical groan. This was a new day, not only literally, but also in every other way. After Kyle shut off the alarm, he turned to her and reached for her body beneath the covers.

"Good morning, Mrs. Sarkos," he smiled at her. "Did you sleep well?"

"Not for awhile," she said as she slid to him. "But once I fell asleep, it was the best night's sleep of my life. In fact, it was the best night of my life … Mr. Sarkos."

"Are you ready for church?" he asked as he kissed her forehead.

"Not yet," she said with a longing grin. "Is Kylla still asleep?"

He looked back at the little bed on the other side of the room. "Sound asleep."

"Good," she whispered as she began to kiss him again.

"We've got to get a house with our own room," Kyle told her as he wrapped his arms all the way around her.

"Agreed. Tomorrow, we start looking."

***

The trip to Kyle's parents was liberating. He had put the top down and Kylla squealed as the wind blew through her hair. He put on a Stephen Williams CD, and he and Cindy sang each song at the top of their lungs over the noise of the air rushing past. When they pulled up to the front of the house, he reached over for her hand and pulled her to him for a kiss.

"Careful, cowboy," she grinned. "The baby is watching."

"Let her watch," he breathed. "It's time she realized what true love really is."

Cindy laughed and kissed him back. She couldn't believe this was real. She wished she could talk to Debby Cramer now and explain that being married was a totally different experience. Her life before today was nothing in comparison. To have Kyle all to herself and to have a child with him was beyond description. Even though biologically Kylla wasn't hers, in every other way she was their child, hers and Kyle's. They hadn't known her before Caryn's death—all they knew was Kylla had been theirs since the moment they did get her. One day they would hopefully have children of their own, but they would never usurp the love and attachment they had to her. They had endured much and gone through many personal changes to have this little girl. That would be a bond with them that none of their other children would have.

"Let me see my baby!" Emma called out as she walked down the porch toward the Jeep.

Kyle unbuckled Kylla from her car seat while Cindy went over to greet Emma.

"And my new daughter-in-law," Emma smiled as she wrapped her arms around Cindy first. "I knew you were the one the first time I met you."

"I wish I had somehow known," Cindy told her. "It would've saved a lot of time."

"No," Emma shook her head. "You have to grow into love. Part of the process is the discovery. You and Kyle had to realize how much you needed each other before you could really love each other. Your lives will be so much different now."

"I know, and I can't wait. So far it's been heavenly—with the exception of being kidnapped and having Kyle slapped around a bit."

Emma laughed and hugged her again, but then she went for her granddaughter.

***

Jonathan took the opportunity of Kyle being away to call an impromptu deacons' meeting that Sunday afternoon. As the men came in, they each asked what was going on; why the meeting? Jonathan was nervous, not because he thought they would disagree with his suggestion, but because for the past twenty-eight years, John Cramer and David Deaton had made sure that every deacons' meeting was filled with stress, turmoil and dissension. David Deaton wouldn't be here; that was one consolation. And when John walked in with a smile and a handshake and a compliment on the morning's message, Jonathan felt a rare peace.

"What's up, pastor?" Ricky Tatum asked in anticipation. "We're all curious."

Jonathan ran his hand through his hair and decided to just throw it out. It wouldn't matter how he presented the idea. Either they would be for it or against it; he didn't want to attempt any manipulation in any way. He believed it was from God, but if the deacons didn't, he would let it rest.

"Kyle Sarkos," Jonathan finally replied. They looked at him in confusion. "It's time we decided what to do about him."

"I agree," Floyd nodded. "This temporary thing has lasted a long time. I kind of feel sorry for him. He works hard to do what he does all the while knowing he could be up and out at a moment's notice."

"So what are you saying?" Charles asked. "Are you saying we need to form a committee and start looking for someone?"

Everyone stared up at Jonathan. Kyle was way beyond what their church would ever have again. No one really wanted to see him go.

"I'd like to make another suggestion first," Jonathan said as he stood and went to the dry erase board. He picked up a red marker, removed the lid, and then wrote Kyle's name at the top. He drew a line down the middle and turned back to the deacons. "I don't want to see him go."

"Agreed," Ricky Tatum said right away.

"But," Jonathan stopped any more conversation, "we need to weigh this heavily before we come to any conclusions." He wrote at the top of the left column the word *pros*, and at the top of the right, *cons*. "Let's be honest about Kyle, and let's determine if he's really the man God wants for our church." In his heart, he wanted to believe that Kyle should stay, but he knew his personal feelings about Kyle were too strong for him to be discerning about the position.

"Here's a pro for you," Charles began. "Write this down first, Jonathan: he's a man of God."

Everyone agreed, and Jonathan wrote *obvious man of God* at the top of the left column.

"He has an unusual gift for leading and teaching music," another man said.

"That's the truth," Floyd added. "Put that next."

Jonathan wrote, *extremely gifted in teaching and leading music.*

"The man has an undeniable call to what he does," Ricky said next. Everyone agreed again.

Called to this ministry Jonathan wrote in red. He turned back around for more suggestions. The left list went on and on. Jonathan finally put up his hand to stop the discussion. "We need to be realistic about this." He turned back to the board and added the first of the cons—*divorced.*

"Hang on right there, Jonathan," John Cramer stood as he said this. "That's not fair at this point. I think in reality, after most of us in this room have come to know the situation, the proper word is not that he was *divorced*, but that he is *widowed*." Every deacon expressed agreement.

"I feel that way too, men," Jonathan told them. "But to be fair about this assessment, we need to say that at one point in time he indeed was divorced."

"Fine," John said, "but put *widowed* on the other side then."

"Why? Do you consider that a pro?" Jonathan asked.

"I consider it a *balance* for the word *divorced* that you insist on keeping up there," John said soberly.

"Very well." Jonathan wrote *widowed* in the left column.

"Draw a line from *divorced* to *widowed*," John told him.

Jonathan grinned to himself as he drew the line. This was going to be easier than he thought. It seemed as though Kyle Sarkos had endeared himself to the rest of the church also.

"I do have a problem, though, with one thing," Charles brought up.

Oh, boy, Jonathan thought. *Not you, Charles. You're one of the good guys.*

"Sure. What is it?"

"There's got to be some way," Charles began, "that we can raise his salary."

Jonathan sighed with relief. This was a *good* problem. "Well, let's first discuss the possibility of hiring him permanently. We can deal with the details later. The church has to agree to this too, remember?"

"That won't be a problem," Ricky said convinced. "All I hear from people is how wonderful he is. I think when you bring it up, you're gonna hear nothing but whoops of delight."

"Okay," Jonathan needed to do something to make all of this seem more official. "Do we have any more cons? I mean … this whole list is rather lopsided."

The men looked around the table at each other and shrugged.

"I can't think of a thing," Floyd finally voiced. "Why don't you call for a vote, Jonathan?"

He looked each deacon in the eye as he voted to make sure no one could accuse him of railroading anything through. Each man gave him a positive response. "All right, then, it seems all are in favor of pursuing Kyle Sarkos for the permanent position of Music Minister in this church. That makes it unanimous." Jonathan couldn't help but grin at all of them. "Do you realize that for the first time in twenty-eight years we're going to present a unanimous decision to this church? Well, Cindy's vote was unanimous, but it was somewhat tainted by David's resignation." Jonathan tried to look grim. "Somewhat …" his grin returned.

Ricky Tatum began to laugh, and soon the others joined. Even John Cramer was enjoying being a *part* of this group rather than the loose segment he had been for so many years.

Seventy-Five

Monday morning at the office, Kyle and Cindy tried to concentrate on their work, but they kept finding reasons to be in one another's presence. That afternoon they were going house shopping. They had bought a Dockrey paper hoping to find some good possibilities before they left.

"Look at this one," Cindy said as she walked back into his office for probably the twentieth time. "Four bedrooms, two and a half baths. It sits on two acres."

"Where is it? In Dockrey?"

"No," she said sadly. "It's about thirty miles away. But it's in our price range."

"We need to be close to here. Dockrey is our home."

She nodded, closed up the paper and leaned down to kiss him. He pulled her to his lap and began to kiss behind her neck. She giggled from the tickling sensation.

"Mr. and Mrs. Sarkos?" came a faintly familiar voice from the front office.

They looked at each other and grinned. "I'd better get up," she whispered to him. "What if it's a deacon? I could get both of us fired."

"Don't worry about it," he whispered back. "I'll be out of here anyway soon."

Cindy gave him a quick kiss and then popped up. "Be right there," she said as she straightened her skirt on the way out. She was shocked. "Ben Hall? What brings you here?"

"Is Mr. Sarkos in?" he asked in his typical no-nonsense, just the facts manner.

"Kyle," she called back to his office. "Agent Hall to see you."

"How are you doing since marriage, abduction and freedom have all overtaken you?" he asked her.

"Rather well, I must confess."

"I can imagine."

Kyle walked into the front office with a puzzling look. "Agent Hall? Is there a problem?"

"No, not at all," Ben reassured him. "I brought some things I thought you might want to have." He held out a small canvas bag. "These items were found in a locked box in Callista's apartment during the investigation. I think you'll be interested in having them."

"What are they?" Kyle wondered as he took the bag.

367

"Personal things mainly. There are a few CD's with some digital photos, a couple of old photographs and her jewelry."

Cindy's heart thudded. She had to remember that he did have a past with this woman, Kylla's real mother. They had a new life together, but it would never erase what had happened before. All they could do now was begin building their own life together, their own memories, and their own future.

After Ben left, Kyle just stood there looking at the bag. He didn't really know what to do with it.

"I'll leave you alone, if you want," Cindy told him. "You can look through it in your office."

"No. I don't want to face this alone. You're my present; she's my past. The only reason I can even deal with this is because I have you here with me."

He unzipped the bag and reached in. The first thing he pulled out were photos.

"You know what's funny, I didn't realize she took any with her," Kyle mused as he looked at their wedding portrait, a shot of them in college, and a picture taken at a Valentine's banquet at Harvest Hollow. "I didn't think she took anything as a reminder of our life. I guess it takes the edge off a little bit to know she didn't absolutely hate me."

"She didn't hate you at all," Cindy said quickly. "She was protecting herself ... and your child."

"Well, even though she might not have hated me, she definitely didn't love me."

Cindy stood behind him as he sat in a chair, and she put her arms around his chest. "I hope you know that I *definitely* love you."

He took her arm and pulled her back down onto his lap. "What we have is so different," he told her from his heart. "Saturday night, last night ... Cindy, I don't even know how to tell you what they meant."

"You don't have to," she said as she touched his face. "I know how different it is. I didn't know that life could be this sweet."

"Me either," he said as he pulled her closer. "At least not for me."

As Kyle reached up to kiss her, Jonathan came into the office.

"Good morning, you two," Jonathan bellowed as he walked inside. "Maybe you need to reconsider that honeymoon."

Cindy blushed, but Kyle just laughed.

"What did the FBI want today? More news or something?"

"This bag," Kyle lifted it up. "It contains Caryn's belongings."

"Oh," Jonathan said soberly. He glanced at Cindy. She smiled. "Kyle, when you get a free moment, I'd like to talk to you privately." He then winked at them. "I hate to force you two to separate, but I need to discuss this with Kyle alone at first."

"Okay," Cindy drew out slowly. She slowly got off of Kyle's lap and walked back toward her chair. "I'll just sit here and answer the phones … or something secretarial like that."

Kyle put the photos back into the bag and zipped it up. "I'm ready now if you are."

"Let's go to my office then."

Kyle followed Jonathan into the pastor's office and closed the door. Jonathan motioned for him to take a seat in front of his desk, and then Jonathan sat on the edge.

"What's up?" Kyle asked him, curious about the private conversation.

"Your job."

"Oh," Kyle nodded. He had known this day was coming.

"The deacons are ready to end the temporary position."

"I was expecting it. I have an appointment with the principal of the school tomorrow to discuss how music lessons are going to work."

"Well," Jonathan ran his hand through his hair and gazed out the window. "There might be a problem with all that."

"The music lessons?"

"Yeah. I don't know if the church would approve of you giving lessons at the school and then working full-time in the music ministry at this church. I don't imagine there would be a problem if you gave private lessons to church members … especially my grandsons."

Kyle looked up at him confused, but there was a shining twinkle in Jonathan's light green eyes.

"I'm not sure what you're saying to me," Kyle said slowly.

"The deacons feel like us trying to find someone to replace you would be a futile effort. They're hoping like crazy that you'll agree to stay on permanently."

Cindy heard a sudden yell from Jonathan's office. She knew it was Kyle, and she knew it was a good yell, but what on earth did it mean? Suddenly the office door flew open and Kyle jumped out with his arms spread wide.

"They want me to stay on permanently!" he screamed to Cindy. "They want me to stay in the ministry!"

Cindy's hands came up to her mouth as tears began to well in her eyes. "No way!"

"Yes! Can you believe it? This can't be happening!" Kyle put his hands up to his head. "I get to stay in ministry! This is too much."

Cindy ran to him and wrapped her arms around his waist. He embraced her back. Jonathan walked out and put his arm on Kyle's shoulder. "They're going to take a look at the budget and see if we can add to the salary some. We've never paid our secondary staff too much. We always knew we were just a stepping stone for most to bigger and better things."

"Stepping stone?" Kyle said in unbelief. "Why would anybody ever want to leave here?"

"That's what I've always said," Jonathan admitted.

"I don't care about the money. What I get now is just fine. It's a better prospect than teaching music. Here I get insurance and benefits. Teaching private lessons means I have to pay everything out of pocket … and hope that the pocket is good for the month."

"Well, the deacons feel like you deserve more than a second rate salary," Jonathan said pretending to be serious. "If I were you, I wouldn't try to fight them on this. As your official mentor now, I would suggest there will be other battles you'll want to take up with them, so don't start off with something as mundane as this."

Kyle laughed and then reached out to hug Jonathan. "Whatever you say, boss. Whatever you say."

Seventy-Six

Friday evening Kyle, Kylla and Cindy ate at Sue's. They wanted to give the Wright family some time alone before Stephen and Annie left on Monday. Sue had prepared a wonderful dish of chicken and dumplings, and they laughed with a freedom that had evaded them for many months.

"How's the house shopping coming?" Sue asked them as they reclined on the back deck while Kylla played in the huge playhouse she had bought.

"Slow," Cindy confessed.

"It's hard trying to find something big enough, but not too big, for the right price ... in a good neighborhood," Kyle elaborated.

Sue nodded as she watched Kylla carry a doll out of the miniature house. "What exactly are you looking for?"

"We'd like to have at least three bedrooms," Cindy told her. "One for us, one for Kylla, and then an extra one."

"More children?" Sue asked expectantly.

Kyle laughed and said, "Eventually. Maybe we need to think bigger, Cindy. Three rooms may not be enough if your mom has anything to do with it."

"I want to run something by you guys," Sue said seriously. She glanced back and forth at them, gazing at Cindy, and then at Kyle. "I'm it for this house. One middle-aged grandmother—compliments of Kylla—living all alone in this massive house. I don't really want to move, but I'm ready for a change. This place holds wonderful memories for me, but it's a waste for me to just stay here."

"You're thinking of moving, Mother?" Cindy asked in disbelief.

"Well ... no. But I'm thinking of some changes?"

"How so?" Kyle leaned into the conversation.

"That garage hasn't held a car for over ten years," Sue said disdainfully. "It holds junk. Nice junk, junk nobody wants to part with, but nevertheless ... junk. It's huge—made for three cars." Sue pointed out to an area of the yard behind the garage. "I could get one of those big metal sheds out there ... maybe one of those maroon ones that looks like a barn—I think they're so cute. We could lug all our *junk* out there to the shed, and then hire Doug to come over and put me in a bathroom, a little kitchen, and a great big closet—finish out and close in the garage."

"You want to live in the garage?" Cindy was a bit shocked. "What are you gonna do with the house? Rent it out? That'd be weird, Mother. You living in the garage while some strange family lives in our big house?"

"I agree," Sue laughed at the description. "That would be awfully weird!"

"Well, then what are you proposing?"

"Simple," Sue grinned now. "Your inheritance."

Cindy just stared at her. "What inheritance?"

"I don't want to sell this place or let it go for any reason, but I'm really tired of living in this massive house all alone. It's paid for, it's mine, and I would like to offer it to the two of you."

Kyle jumped in this time. "Sue, that's a wonderful gesture, but there's no way we can afford a house like this."

"Mother, it's a sweet thought, but we can't handle the payments on this place. We'd have to finance it for 100 years."

"Are you not listening?" Sue chided them. "I said this would be Cindy's inheritance. I have no intentions of *selling* it to you! I'm giving it to you. We'll even sign the papers. All I want is my new huge three-car room with a really big walk-in closet. The rest of the house is yours."

"You can't do that," Kyle said as he shook his head. "That's just ... well, not right."

"Why?" Sue insisted on knowing. "Go ahead and try to reason yourselves out of this! I knew you would. But think of how simple it would make everything."

"But mother ..."

"Let me finish," Sue said as she put her hand up to hush Cindy. "I want my own place, and I want a new place. But how foolish when I have this beautiful house? I don't want to lose this house; I raised my children here and lived most of my life here. It's beautiful. But I don't want to care for it anymore. I want to downsize. I'm not asking you to move in *with* me; please understand that. I want my own kitchen, and I want to take care of myself. But I still get the best of both worlds. My granddaughter is just next door. And when you two go off to work each morning, you don't have to worry about Kylla. I'm here and she's here."

"But Mother, this is a huge house ... it would be a huge gift," Cindy protested again.

"And what happens to this house when I die?"

"Mother! You're not close to death!"

"I was," Sue reminded them soberly. "God has granted me more time, and I want to live it fully. But answer my question, Cindy: what's happens to this house when I die?"

Cindy sighed and acknowledged, "It goes to me and Billy."

"No," Sue corrected her right away. "It goes to *you*. Your father and I put it in your name several years back. Billy squanders; you don't. This house would be yours to do with whatever you wanted. Why wait? That's all I'm suggesting."

Cindy and Kyle were stunned by the suggestion. They stared blankly at each other and shrugged their shoulders.

"You'll have your privacy," Sue insisted. "I want that for you as a family. But I'll just be in the next room in my *own apartment* if you need me for anything. Now, things like Sunday dinner and all, we can do that together if you like. But you'll be in your own house and I'll be in mine, and we'll all live happily ever after." Sue gave a huge grin. "What do you think?"

The couple remained speechless. It was a big offer and not at all what they had been planning.

"Think about it," Sue finally said. "Go talk about it and decide if it's something you would like to do. Just remember, Cindy, the house will be yours one day anyway. It just seems sort of foolish to wait until then for you to actually receive it. Take it now and use it well."

***

Kyle and Cindy lay in bed discussing the prospects of the house. Sue was right: they were trying to reason out why it would not be good even though everything within them was screaming to do it.

"I can't imagine Mother just suddenly moving into her own little room after so many years in the big house."

"It won't be little. That garage is huge. *We* could actually close in the garage and live in there just fine."

"She won't go for that. She's more or less got her mind made up."

They lay quietly for a bit, still trying to determine the best choice.

"Cindy, why shouldn't we do it?" he finally asked honestly. "Let's think about it from a different perspective for a moment. We keep thinking that it's taking advantage of your mother. We agree that we need a home of our own, and that we need a place big enough to raise a family. We said from the beginning we didn't want to have to move in a few years because of outgrowing the house. Your mom's house is … big … very big. How many bedrooms?"

"Five. One downstairs and four up."

"That is big," he continued to think. "Your mom is tired of being there alone. You've only been gone three weeks, and she's feeling the loneliness again. She loves Kylla and watches her while we're at work. We're trying to be unselfish by *not* taking it, forcing ourselves to find something on our own rather than accept something that's being dropped in our lap."

"You think we should do it?" Cindy leaned up on one elbow.

"I think your mom is offering this as much for her as for us. We're looking at it from our angle, and from our angle we're the beneficiaries. If we look at it from your mom's angle, she gains a family back … her daughter, her granddaughter …" Kyle grinned, "… and me!"

"She loves you like a son," she said as she laid her head on his chest. "Maybe even more than a son."

"The feeling's mutual."

"You love her like a son too?"

"Smarty." He reached his hand over and began to tickle her ribs.

"Stop!"

"Ticklish, are you? Have I found a weapon here?"

She managed to grab his hand and hold it away. "You just caught me off guard. Now, stop, because we have a very serious decision to make here."

He pulled her closer to him and sighed as he continued to work through the situation. "What do you want to do, Cindy? What's your gut feeling?"

"I don't have *gut* feelings," she continued to tease. "I am a woman; I have *intuition*."

"Okay, okay … give me your *intuitive perspective* on the matter."

She lay back on her pillow and tried to pull her thoughts together. "It was a little shocking to find that they only put my name down as heir to the house. I can just imagine the fussing and fuming Billy would display in finding that out at her death. However, he wouldn't think twice about the house becoming mine because I choose to live in Dockrey and make my home here. That would simplify some things."

"But other than that. Forget your brother. What about us?"

"It's a beautiful house."

"It's a gorgeous house."

"There's plenty of room for a family."

"Are you expecting to have a big family?"

"I already have a big family, and I've only been married a month. At this rate, we could end up like Andie and Doug. But that's beside the point. The point is that Mother is offering us her house … free and clear. Do we take it?"

Kyle sighed deeply again. "Cindy, this is really your decision."

"No, it's not," she countered quickly. "It's our decision. This has to be something we both want to do."

"Want to sleep on it and decide in the morning?"

"No," she said firmly. "I'll toss and turn all night if I have to *think on it* anymore."

"Okay, then, do we flip a coin?"

"Kyle!" She slapped his arm. "We don't flip a coin over a decision like this."

"Then how do we decide?" he asked her. "We both know it's the best possible thing we could ever dream of, but we're scared to death that everyone is gonna think we're taking advantage of your poor mother."

"… whose granddaughter would be staying near her twenty-four-seven if we moved in."

"Yep … that's another point. People couldn't fault her for that."

"So, you think we should do it?" She sat up this time. "The more we talk the more I feel we'd be stupid not to."

"I don't want to be considered stupid. And I agree: we'd be stupid."

Cindy looked down at him and could see his eyes dancing from the reflection of the moonlight through the window. "Done then. We tell Mother tomorrow."

"Whew," he said with relief. "A load is lifted."

Cindy leaned down over him and asked, "Were you stressed over this?"

"Only a little."

"You really need to learn how to lighten up some," she teased.

"Show me how that's done, will you?"

"Gladly."

Seventy-Seven

Church on Sunday morning was wonderful. Even though nothing had been presented to the church officially concerning Kyle staying on permanently, the word had spread quickly. Apparently the deacons felt it would be a good idea to *feel* the congregation out concerning the possible appointment. So many people came up to Kyle and Cindy begging them to stay that Kyle was humbled knowing God could actually work another miracle and keep him in the ministry.

Stephen and Annie sang a song for the special music. Kyle couldn't believe these two were actually singing in his church. Of all the things he thought he had accomplished by serving at Harvest Hollow, this surpassed them all. Of course, the security inside and outside the building was a bit daunting, but nevertheless, their duet was moving. And when Jonathan stood up to preach, there was a warmth that flooded Kyle because he knew the man well and respected him mightily as a man of God ... and as a friend. He couldn't say that of all the other churches.

He then glanced up into the choir where Cindy sat. She was flipping through her Bible to find the passage Jonathan would be speaking from. She was so beautiful. He couldn't believe God had granted him a second chance for love. His marriage to Caryn was a mistake, and Kyle took full credit for that. He knew things weren't fully right, he was warned that she wasn't the one, but he caved in to his desires and began a downhill journey that only God could correct. Now, all was made right.

He then glanced back over his shoulder to the section of the church where Barbara and Sue sat with their granddaughters. Neither lady was listening to Jonathan. Sue was occupied with drawing pictures for Kylla, and Barbara was handling Aimee who insisted she could dance on the pew. Life was good—no, life was perfect.

***

"We've decided to take you up on your deal," Cindy told Sue that Sunday afternoon as they sat again on the back deck of the Marcum house.

"Yes!" Sue yelled as she jumped up to her feet and did a little jig. "Wonderful!"

"But we need to make all of this legal," Cindy continued. "Billy could care less at this point, but sometime in the future he may try to fight it."

"It will be no problem," Sue assured her. "I've already talked to my lawyer. We can have it all handled by the end of the week."

"Busy little bee, aren't you?" Kyle chuckled.

"I've thought about this for quite a while, but knew we couldn't even dream about doing it until Kylla was safe. I've talked to Doug, and …"

Cindy cut in, "You've already talked to Doug?"

"Of course!" Sue laughed. "I'm ready to get going. Doug says it will take him about a month to complete it, but I see no reason why we should wait for me to get out before you move in. You can have the entire upstairs for now. All I need is my bedroom. But as soon as the room is finished, we start living like two families."

"Are you serious?" Cindy asked incredulously. "You want us to go ahead and move in?"

"Why not? You're living with the Wrights and doing the same thing. Breakfast is the only meal you eat on your own. Come on over here so Kyle can start cooking for me too."

"What makes you think Kyle is going to be the cook?" Cindy pretended to be offended.

Kyle grinned as he shook his head. "You ladies better not put me between a rock and a hard place here." He looked over to Sue. "You're on top of all of this, aren't you? You've thought through every detail."

Sue looked at them both, and her expression became more serious. "Last year, I thought my life had ended. I lost my husband, and my two kids were as far from me as they could possibly be. Then I got cancer, and I really believed my life was over. Yet here I am with a daughter that gave up everything to make sure I regained my health. She has a husband who's a wonderful man of God and who I know I can trust to take care of her and make her happy for the rest of her life. And the icing on the cake?"

"Kylla," Cindy said tenderly.

"Kylla," Sue affirmed. "What a precious jewel. And she belongs to *me*. I promise you I couldn't love her any more if she were Cindy's blood child."

"Me either," Cindy agreed.

They sat and rested in the moment of decision and finality. For three people who had had their lives turned upside down, order and restoration were beginning to prevail. It was comforting to know that a new *normal* would now take over, and that they no longer had to live with the uncertainty of what tomorrow might bring.

"So," Sue broke the silence, "are you moving in next week?"

"I just moved out," Cindy groaned a little.

"Where will *we* sleep?" Kyle asked Cindy. "Which room?"

"Mine, I guess."

Kyle just grinned mischievously.

"What?" she asked him.

"I'll never forget the first time I saw that room," he mused. "I thought to myself that this was the room you had grown up in, and that someday some lucky guy would whisk you off your feet and get the chance to stay there with you when you visited your mom."

"I looked horrible that day!" Cindy said in shock. "You were actually thinking positive things about me?"

"Always," he smiled as he took her hand.

***

Jonathan called the church to order that Sunday evening as the worship service began. "As you were told this morning, the deacons wanted to have a special business meeting to settle an issue they feel needs to be addressed." The smiles and nods in the congregation were comforting to Jonathan. "I'd like to recognize Charles Emerson, our chairman, who will present the recommendation."

Charles came to the platform, unfolded his notes and placed them carefully on the pulpit. He leaned into the microphone and began in his strong southern drawl, "As most of you know, Kyle Sarkos was hired at this church in January as our interim music minister. He was to serve until the church chose to move on and search out a full-time person to fill the position.

"Over the months people found themselves admiring Kyle for more than just his exceptional music ability. They realized he was a man of character, integrity, that he possessed a good sense of humor ... which is important if you have to work with Jonathan," the people laughed, "and that he truly desired to honor God with his life. The truth is, we've never had anyone in his position that ever did a finer job or ever was a finer man. And that little bug was put into the ears of the deacons over and over and over again." Charles grinned at the crowd. "You people are persistent." Smiles broke out.

Charles placed one hand in his pocket as he began to get emotional. "When Kyle first came here, he was a broken and shattered man, but he gave his all to the ministry in this church because that's the kind of man he is. He is a man with a call, a call from God that drives him above and beyond any unfavorable circumstance that might pull other men away from the focus. His former church, for all practical purposes, fired him because they were more concerned with the circumstances than they were with the man." Charles paused and looked down at Kyle and Cindy on the front row. "That ... was *their* loss." The church agreed with nods and amen's. "And their loss was most assuredly *our* gain. I don't honestly believe that this church could ever replace Kyle. And besides, since he's married to our secretary, it would probably help all the way around if we just let those two stay together as much as possible." This time gentle laughter rose.

"So, as chairman of the deacons of this church, I would like to present a recommendation from the deacons, who, I suppose, are actually serving as the committee in this case, that we hire Kyle Sarkos full time as our

Minister of Music."

Charles stepped back and Jonathan took the pulpit again. "Thank you, Charles. Is there any discussion?"

To Jonathan's surprise, several people stood up. His heart fell, but he soon learned that people only wanted to speak on Kyle's behalf; no one spoke against him.

"Kyle belongs with us," one elderly lady began. "He's a part of us, and has been from day one. To disagree with this would be like cutting off a part of the body ... and that's just how I feel about it."

Another lady stood. "I've never been so moved in my entire life through worship like I have since Kyle's been here. I'm amazed at how we can move from one of those fancy, new, syncopated choruses into a hymn and have it mean so much."

A teenager stood this time. "We like Kyle too. He makes youth choir pretty cool, and then he comes to all our fellowships and things. Our other music minister got put out with us. I know we're not the easiest group in the world to tolerate, but Kyle just rolls with us." He paused. "He cares about us, and we know that."

***

"Congratulations, Mr. Sarkos," Cindy said as she crawled into bed next to him that night. "It would appear that you have captured the heart of this church."

Kyle pulled her to him and wrapped his arms around her waist. "The only heart I'm interested in right now is yours."

She kissed him gently and smiled as she reached up to turn out the light. "You've got mine."

"Then I'm good."

"Can you believe all of this?" she asked as she remembered all that had happened to the both of them over the past few months. "Any *one* of these things would have been wonderful, but when you start combining them all, it almost seems implausible."

"I know." He leaned up on his elbow. "You getting a temporary job so you can care for your mother. Me getting a temporary job because Jonathan had a big heart. That put us together ... even though you were adamant about refusing me."

"I got over it," she said as she reached up to tweak his nose.

"Then Kylla comes into the picture, but with mega baggage along. Then we get married, you adopt Kylla, and one week later Jimmy Thornton is arrested."

"He ruined our honeymoon," she pouted. "I was so looking forward to that night."

"Me too, but you've made it up to me ... many times." He sighed in contentment. "Then tomorrow, we move back into your house which will become *our* house by the end of the week. Our very own house. What more could we want?"

"I have a request," she said as she traced her finger over his chest. "What about another child?"

Kyle's eyes popped open. "Really? You want to have another one so soon?"

"When I was growing up, I had Billy. It was fun to always have somebody with you wherever you went. We stayed close, even through high school. It wasn't until he married the first time that we began to grow apart."

"I grew up all alone," Kyle said sadly. "It was very lonely. I never wanted to do that to my children."

"Then we're agreed?" Cindy looked up at his face glowing from the moonlight.

"Are you sure? I mean … I love the idea of a houseful of kids, but you're the one who carries them and has them. You've gone from being this free and easy single girl to mom and wife in just a short time."

"And I've adjusted rather well, don't you think?"

"Very well." He reached up and took a handful of hair and brought it to his face. "I do wonder what *our* child would look like."

"It wouldn't have much choice," she giggled. "Blond hair, blue eyes."

Seventy-Eight

It still felt strange but wonderful to be free again. As Kyle carried boxes into the Marcum house and up the stairs to Cindy's bedroom, he kept reminding himself that there was no need to look over his shoulder for some shady person who might be watching his every move. He read the top of the box: *books*. He hauled this one to a spare bedroom and turned back around to the stairs. He heard Cindy telling her mom as she started up not to worry about supper; they would pick something up and just make it easy tonight. He snuck into her room and hid behind the door to wait for her.

When she walked in, she took an armful of clothes to the closet and hung them back in their usual places. She moved her shirts to the same side as her pants and dresses to make space for Kyle's things and was in deep thought when she started for the hallway. Kyle jumped out from behind the door, grabbed her by the waist, and pulled her down onto the bed with him.

"What on earth do you think you're doing?" she screamed out. "You could have given me cardiac arrest!"

"I'll keep that in mind ... weak-hearted," he grinned as he pushed her hair behind her ears. He rolled back on the bed and stared around at the various mementos of Cindy's life that were displayed on the walls and shelves of her room. "Did you live here all your life?"

"I was four when we moved in. I remember when it was being built—Billy and I thought it was great fun running through all the rooms after they were studded off. Mother showed us which rooms would be ours, and we would imagine how they would look when the house was complete."

"Did your room meet your expectations?"

"Oh, yeah. Mother made sure they were decorated just like we wanted." Cindy stood up and pointed to a shelf high up on one of the walls. "See that shelf up there? It used to be full of every princess doll you could imagine. Mine was a princess room. It was all pink with a beautiful canopy bed having a white net hanging from the four posts."

"What happened to all the pink?"

"Thirteen," she said almost sadly. "I grew out of the innocence of make-believe and went straight into adolescence."

"Billy too?"

"Not yet." She dropped down onto the bed. "He was a little behind in his growing up, at least until Angie Wright caught his imagination. She pulled him out of boyhood really fast."

"The preacher's daughter, huh?" he said with a mischievous smile.

"I've heard about them."

She chuckled a little, but her expression became serious again right away. "She didn't start out all that wild; she always had a heart for what was right and noble ... and always had a hunger for missions. I sometimes think Billy and I were responsible for pulling her in the wrong direction. But we had always been such good friends. I think she tried to break off our friendship several times, but the bond was too tight. She might as well have been another twin."

"Wouldn't that make you triplets?" he smiled as he pulled her to him.

"I guess. The three of us were inseparable after awhile. I can't help but wonder how different we might have all turned out if Angie had been the influencer all those years instead of Billy and me."

Kyle took her hand and gently kissed it as he looked into her blue eyes with deep compassion. "Cindy, stop beating yourself up over your past. You can't change it."

"But when I think of ..."

"Shh ..." he put his finger up to her lips and shook his head. "Stop." He leaned over and kissed her forehead. "We could both lie here and bemoan all the mistakes of our pasts, and if we wanted, we could carry the guilt with us to our graves." He placed his hand on her waist and then smiled. "Or ... we could let go of them all, embrace what we have right now ... at this very moment ... and plan on making new memories in this very room. I would really rather choose the latter."

She finally smiled a genuine smile as she leaned over her husband. "I want to, Kyle, but sometimes the hold of the past is strong. Keep reminding me of the here and now. Help me to let go of all that ... and to move on with you."

"So glad you asked." He pulled her down and kissed her with a kiss to make her forget everything, including the fact that they were moving at the moment.

"Okay, you two," came Sue's voice at the door. "I have nothing against physical expressions of love and passion, but in the middle of the day with Jonathan's pickup loaded down with boxes of *your* stuff ... I say let's use our time a little more wisely." She winked at them and dropped a box on the floor. "I'm glad Kylla's getting her own room," she mumbled as she turned back toward the stairs.

"Ugh," Cindy moaned as she rolled to her back. "I hate moving. This is my third time in seven months. I'm ready to stay put for a while."

"How do the next 50 years sound?" he asked as he sat up slowly.

"Heavenly."

***

"Look at Kylla's pretty bed in her pretty new room," Cindy said enthusiastically as she walked Kylla into her upstairs bedroom right next to

382

theirs. Little blue eyes stared in delight at all the dolls and toys that Granny Sue had pulled from the attic that had once belonged to Cindy.

"Pretty," she breathed out in wonder. Then she pointed to her small pink bed that had been transported from their apartment at the Wrights. "Kylla's bed?"

"That's right," Cindy told her as she sat on the bed and pulled the blond bundle up beside her. "Sit here for a moment. I want to show you something."

Kylla remained obediently as Cindy went over to the wall and turned out the light. Next to the head of the bed was a large nightlight with Cinderella dressed for the ball. She came back and pointed out the nightlight.

"See how pretty the light is?" she said pulling Kylla up on her lap.

"That Mama? That Mama light?"

"Yes. When you wake up at night, Mama's light will always be on for you. You can just close your eyes and go back to sleep."

Kylla smiled with sleepy eyes and then let a huge yawn escape from her mouth.

"Is Kylla sleepy already?" She pulled her close and brushed the top of her fine hair with her lips.

"Kylla bed," she affirmed.

Kyle stood quietly in the hallway taking in the whole scene. Kylla had never slept alone in a room before, and everyone was concerned with how she would adjust. Since Cindy seemed to be her lifeline, they all decided she should be the one to introduce the little one to the new arrangement. He stared in total adoration. He couldn't be any more blessed. From this moment on it no longer mattered what kind of mother Caryn had been because Cindy had stepped into the role with her whole heart. Kylla would never remember Caryn, and it would be a matter of much prayer over the next several years as to how much of this information she should eventually know.

"Mama's bed is in that room," Cindy said as she pointed next door. "I can hear Kylla all night long. And if you need Mama, you just call for me … okay?"

Kylla stared up at her, barely able to keep her eyes open. "Night, night, Mama," she said softly as she leaned into Cindy's chest.

"Night, night, baby," Cindy whispered.

Suddenly Kylla's eyes opened wide as she stared up at Cindy in practical defiance. "I not a baby!" she said determinedly. "Ellie a baby. I a big girl."

Cindy giggled as she pulled back the covers and tucked Kylla in. "Absolutely. How silly of me! Kylla is a big girl; Ellie is a baby."

"Stevie a big boy," Kylla informed Cindy also.

"That's right. And Stevie has his own bed and his own room too."

Kylla's eyes grew heavy again, but she leaned over just enough to point at the nightlight. "Mama light," she said wistfully.

Cindy reached down to kiss her cheek, and Kylla placed her little arms around her mother's neck. She hugged her tightly and then released her. When she rolled over to settle in for the night, Cindy kissed her once again and rubbed her back for just a bit.

When she finally emerged from the room, Kyle greeted her with open arms.

"I feel like that was too easy," he said hesitantly.

"Everything with her has been too easy," Cindy yawned as she took his hand and led him to their room. "I'm sure that's purely the grace of God. He'll make it up to us when we have the next few."

When she opened the door to her bedroom, she was astounded with the amount of lit candles and soft music playing. "Kyle Sarkos, what have you done?"

He smiled softly as he placed his arms around her waist and drew up behind her. "I wanted our first night in here, our own home, your old room, to be exceptionally special."

She ran her hands over his arms and felt herself beginning to tear up. "You didn't have to go to all this trouble to make it special." She turned around in his arms and looked up into his handsome face. "Anywhere I am with you is wonderful."

"Well ..." he grimaced slightly, "... except Jimmy Thornton's Nashville abode."

She chuckled as she ran her fingers through his flowing hair. "I'll say this: I would rather have been there *with* you than *without* you."

"I'd rather you hadn't been there at all."

She closed her eyes and shook her head. "We're not regretting the past anymore, remember?"

"Remind me," he grinned as he leaned down to kiss her. Cindy wrapped her arms around him and pulled her body as close to his as possible. "I'm remembering ..." he said as he reached back to close the door with his foot.

Seventy-Nine

On Thursday afternoon following work, Cindy had promised to take Kylla grocery shopping with her. The image Kyle concocted was one of complete chaos based on his observances of one-year olds in stores with their moms. However, he had to remember Kylla was different. Not only was she an extremely compliant child, she could probably never remember being in a store before. She was thrilled to be going off with Cindy on her own, so as they pulled out of the driveway in his Jeep, he suddenly felt alone. It had been ages since he had been by himself.

He walked up the stairs to their bedroom and stared for just a moment. He still struggled to grasp that this house now belonged to him and Cindy. Another blessing he could have never dreamed up this time last year.

God, you're outdoing me here, he whispered with a smile. *You're really making me regret all those things I felt and said toward You when I was down in the pits of despair. I wondered if perhaps You were mocking me at times … but now I understand. You knew all along what my future held, and you were just waiting for the right time to unveil it.*

He glanced over at the computer, still sporting the picture of his new family on their wedding day. His smile grew bigger. But the cases of Caryn's CDs laying beside it brought back memories of a part of his life that still hurt on occasion. He had yet to see what was on them. While Cindy was away, he decided to check them out. He popped in the first disc, and as the images began to unfold, tears began to burn his eyes.

***

When Kyle heard the girls come in, he hurried down the stairs to see how the shopping venture had fared. Kylla was babbling about something, and her face was covered with chocolate. Cindy was carrying in several bags and grinning from ear to ear, nodding as though she understood every syllable that came out of the little mouth.

"Any more bags?" Kyle asked as he joined them in the kitchen.

"Many," Cindy confirmed. "You want to get them while I start putting these away?"

"No problem," he said as he reached down and scooped Kylla up in his arms. She giggled with glee as she grabbed his nose.

"Dadda!" she called out.

"Yes, and what have you been eating? Did Mommy decide to give you a snack just before mealtime?"

"She was so good. I only got her this little tube of M&M's. Look at them, Kyle. They're so cute and tiny."

"I thought these things melted in your mouth, not in your hands, not on your face, man, it looks like she's got chocolate up her nose too."

"Mmmm," Cindy smiled as she leaned up to kiss his cheek. "I bet that smells nice."

"That's bordering on gross. I think this little girl has thrown some of your common sense out the window."

He brought in the rest of the bags and began to help put away the groceries. He looked in confusion at several of the items he pulled out.

"What is this?" He held up three blue packages. "I don't recall putting anything like this on my list."

Cindy grabbed the blue boxes. "These are so cute! I had no idea they had anything like this. They're little frozen dinners for children."

"Why does she need a frozen dinner? We cook plenty of *good* food around here for her to eat, and eat healthily."

She ignored him and described each dinner. "Look at this: pizza, macaroni and cheese, chicken nuggets. These are like smorgasbords for little kids. Look Kylla," Cindy held up a box for her. "Yummy, yummy!"

"Yummy!" Kylla responded as she popped in another M&M.

Kyle shook his head and looked back inside the bag. "What are these?" He pulled out another box.

"These are unbelievable!" Cindy said with excitement again. "It's like real fruit pressed into this gummy stuff that rolls up. Very nutritious."

"What's wrong with regular fruit?"

Cindy looked at him in exasperation and shook her head. "They're just meant to add a little excitement to the eating end of life, Kyle! Simmer down, would you?"

He chuckled and went back to unpacking his first full set of groceries since being married to Cindy. Even this was fun.

"And for the record," she shot out, "I don't only have to buy what's on *your* list. I'm free to purchase things *I* want too."

"Yes, ma'am," he grinned as he shook his head and continued unloading.

When they finished, Kyle took Cindy by the hand and turned her to him.

"What is on your mind?" she asked cautiously as the look on his face was unusual.

"Come with me," he responded. "I have something to show you."

She nodded as he headed toward the stairs, picking up Kylla on the way and toting her to their bedroom. Cindy followed and watched curiously as he sat down at the computer.

"Look at this," he said as he pulled up a file and opened it. Suddenly an array of pictures began to unfold on the screen.

"Who is it, Kyle?"

He looked up at her and smiled warmly. "Kylla."

"Oh, my gosh," she whispered as she sat down on the bed behind him. "Kyle, they're baby pictures."

"This isn't the only disc. There are two more … all filled with pictures of Kylla … and Caryn."

Cindy swallowed hard as a lump hit her throat. Would she ever stop feeling jealous of Caryn? "Can I see one of Caryn?"

"Sure," Kyle complied as he scrolled through the images. He finally stopped on one photo taken when Kylla appeared to be about six months. Caryn was nuzzling her close. Cindy could tell from the expression that Kylla was giggling in the picture. Caryn was beautiful. She had seen many tabloid pictures of a blond Callista, but to see her here with Kylla, her beauty was only magnified. Her long, now dark, shiny hair flowed down her shoulders, and her deep brown eyes almost looked like a drawing they were so … *exquisite* … that was the word Kyle had used.

"She's beautiful," Cindy breathed out in awe.

"Isn't she?" Kyle said in a way that made Cindy wince. "Even as a little tyke she was absolutely gorgeous."

She smiled; he was talking about Kylla, not Caryn. "I meant that Caryn was beautiful."

"She looks happy," Kyle remarked. "I don't know that she ever looked like that in all the years I knew her. Maybe Kylla changed her life like she did ours."

As they scrolled through the pictures, it took them a while to notice that Kylla was staring at them with great interest. When one would come up of Caryn, she would always furrow her brow.

Finally Cindy asked her, "Do you know who that is, Kylla?" Cindy pointed to a pose of Caryn.

"Who that?" Kylla asked with wide blue eyes.

"Man, what do you tell her?" Kyle wondered. "Who is that, Kylla?" He posed the question to her again.

"Who that?" was all Kylla would answer.

"That's Caryn," he finally offered. "Do you know Caryn?"

Kylla just continued to stare at the picture. She looked for a long time, then asked, "More baby?"

Kyle scrolled to the next image. It was Kylla sleeping in a crib.

"Baby," Kylla said sweetly with a big grin. "Lainey?" she asked, wondering if it was Andie's baby, Alaina.

"That's baby Kylla," Cindy tried to explain.

"I not a baby," Kylla said firmly.

Eighty

It was a miserably hot August afternoon, and since it was Saturday, Kyle and Cindy took the opportunity to sit out on the back deck under the fan and watch Kylla play in her wading pool. The iced tea was going fast, and so was Sue's room. Doug and his crew were finishing up the painting at the moment.

"I don't know why your mom insisted on the kitchen area," Kyle sighed as he pushed his sunglasses up on his nose as the sweat kept causing them to droop. "You know she's not gonna cook and eat in there."

"I think she's just trying to be noble," Cindy replied, swirling the tea around in her glass. "She has this plan to give us as much alone time as possible." Cindy then giggled.

"What's so funny?"

"She wants more grandchildren."

He shook his head. "Then why the need for our own kitchen? She doesn't think we're gonna make babies in the kitchen, does she?"

"I have no idea. But I can confirm there will be *no* baby making in the kitchen."

The back door opened and a slightly distraught Sue appeared.

"Mother? Are you okay?"

"That FBI guy is here again," she frowned. "I thought all this was over."

"Me too," Kyle said standing immediately.

"Let me watch Kylla," Sue offered. "You two go in and find out what he wants. I don't want to hear anything more. I want it all finished … now."

"I understand," Kyle nodded as he gently patted her shoulder, "Me too."

Cindy and Kyle stepped through the door and made their way toward the living room where a huge surprise awaited them.

"Mr. and Mrs. Sarkos," Ben Hall said warmly as they entered the room. "I believe you're familiar with Martin Sartin."

Martin offered his hand and Kyle shook it gingerly, followed by Cindy. As if Martin Sartin wasn't confusing enough, also with the group was the thug that had been with Jimmy Thornton the night they had been kidnapped, the one Cindy had talked to at the cemetery, the one who had posed as a pharmaceutical salesman at the clinic where Kyle had undergone the paternity testing.

388

"I think you remember Amos," Ben said a bit more soberly.

"Met him," Kyle said with furrowed brow. "Met the butt of his gun too ... on the back of my head."

"Sorry about that," Amos said sincerely with no accent whatsoever. "I had to do what I had to do."

"What on earth is *he* doing here?" Cindy asked a bit perturbed. "Do you mean to tell me he's working for you now?"

Ben Hall smiled slightly and nodded as he explained, "He always worked for us. If you two want to sit down, we have a lot of ... uh ... clearing up to do with you."

They went into the living room, and everyone took a seat. Kyle was reeling over Martin Sartin sitting here in his living room rather than pining away in the California penitentiary. Cindy was openly fuming about the fact that Amos was an agent who had knocked Kyle over the head with his gun. The accent he had used at the cemetery and at the house in Nashville was obviously fake, because he now sounded as normal as the rest of them.

"I imagine you have a lot of questions at the moment," Ben began.

"Understatement of the year," Cindy said crossly.

"Yes, I'm sure," Agent Hall continued. "If you'll just hear us out, I'm sure most of your questions will be answered within a matter of minutes."

Kyle interrupted, "Like why Martin Sartin is out of prison?"

Cindy added, "And why one of your men bashed Kyle on the head?"

Amos winced.

"Everything," Ben continued. "We'll start with Mr. Sartin. We had bargained with him and he gave us a lot of information concerning Jimmy and his organization when he was busted—years ago. We literally tore the whole ring apart, but we never got Jimmy. We don't know where he went or how he managed to start over, but when Maria was killed, Martin's wife, he left a nice little note explaining that he was back and he was out for blood."

"You knew he was after Caryn all this time?" Kyle asked.

"We knew, but she didn't trust the agency," Ben shook his head. "We wanted to protect her like we tried to protect her mother ... but, well ... you can understand."

Kyle and Cindy nodded.

"Martin's sentence was actually up after 18 months."

"What?" Kyle exclaimed. "You said he had so many years he would never get out!"

"Yes, and that was our public stance and statement," Ben acknowledged. "We had to have the public believe, as well as Jimmy Thornton, that Martin would be behind bars for the rest of his life. If not, Jimmy would have hunted him down like a dog and slaughtered him beyond recognition ... at least, that's what his note said."

Kyle frowned and looked over at Martin. "So you just choose to stay in prison."

"Well ... that's a stretch too," Martin sort of smiled.

"He was supposedly in a guarded cell," Ben went on. "He was actually in a Beverly Hills hotel suite most of the time. We would haul him back to the prison now and again just for appearances sake because Jimmy definitely had plants there. But as far as they knew, Martin stayed locked up in his cell, fed privately, exercised privately, no intrusions because of his fame ... a real loner with special treatment."

"So when I met him at the prison," Kyle asked, "he had just been bussed in from his plush quarters downtown?"

Ben nodded. Kyle reached up to rub his chin. "Why the deception?"

"We had to try and keep up with Jimmy. We knew he was after Martin and anyone close to Martin, and he knew we knew he was after them. All we could do was try to set a trap. If he knew that Martin was free, he would have found him immediately."

Cindy interrupted this time. "Where does Caryn fit into all of this? Why couldn't you protect her too?"

"Well, that's the bad part," Ben explained. "Callista didn't trust us. When Maria was murdered, she fled."

"But didn't Martin know where she was?" Kyle asked.

"No," Martin informed him immediately. "I knew what she was doing and I knew about you, but she never gave me full names or places. I didn't know your last name, and I never knew that she had used *Carter* as her maiden name before marrying you."

"But I thought her hiding on her own without the FBI and all was your idea," Kyle told Martin.

"It was, but then I decided against it. I said she could move in with me. She couldn't handle that. Callista was a free spirit ... she couldn't be confined like that, so she just left one day. After about three months, she called to say she was in college somewhere and wouldn't tell me anything else."

"We tried to trace her calls," Ben sighed, "but she was too smart for that. In fact, we hadn't seen her in so long, that when we were called in to investigate Caryn's murder because there were no records for her, it never occurred to us that this was Callista Sartin. Of course, we had only known her as a blond at that time."

"Why didn't you try fingerprints or something?" Cindy asked.

Ben Hall shook his head and smiled, "She was too smart. I don't know how she did it, but she managed to get them erased from our files ... every file."

"You're kidding," Kyle was astounded. "How? How did she know how to do all that?"

"Survival," Martin broke in. "Callista was a survivor. She would do anything to save herself."

"Obviously," Kyle mumbled.

"Amos here," Ben motioned toward the notoriously familiar figure, "infiltrated Jimmy's organization about two years ago, but Jimmy was real secretive about his vendetta with Martin, at least until he found Callista. After he murdered her, he became curious about the child. Amos had no idea about Callista's murder or who Kylla was, but was assigned to watch you all. It wasn't until Cindy's little escapade in Martha's Vineyard that we were able to put it all together." Ben looked over at Cindy and smiled. "Thank you for that little daring tirade."

"Don't encourage her," Kyle said soberly.

"At that point, Amos was able to edge his way into the operation more, volunteering for this and that when Jimmy would organize. Within a couple of weeks, he had become Jimmy's lead man on your case."

Cindy frowned at Amos and asked, "So when you whacked him on the head with your gun, it was purely doing your job? Couldn't you have done something else ... like one of those sleeper holds they do in wrestling ... or something?"

Amos still didn't answer for himself; Ben Hall did all the talking. "There were greater evils at stake, namely, the safety of your daughter."

Cindy calmed down at that statement.

"We were taking risks, but at the same time, you need to understand there were two agents directly involved with your kidnapping. Amos and Pete were both working with Jimmy, plus there were seven other agents all around at all times. Even while you and Kyle were at the Nashville house, it was surrounded on the outside, and Amos was wearing a bug on the inside. Had anything gotten out of hand, Amos was ordered to take Thornton down."

Kyle leaned back on his couch. Would this story never end?

"Meanwhile," Cindy countered again, "Jimmy gets to beat up on Kyle. Was there no concern that he might actually hurt him ... say ... give him another concussion to join the one that Agent Amos had already pounded on his head?"

"Not really," Ben said sheepishly.

Kyle and Cindy both looked at him bewildered.

"Jimmy has a soft spot for preachers," Ben clarified. "His father had been a priest and had fallen in love with a woman in his congregation. In order to marry her, he had to leave the ministry. It left a huge impact on Jimmy because his father always talked of how much he loved the ministry and how hard it had been to leave his call. Jimmy had mentioned several times to Amos and Pete that he was cornered because Kyle was a minister ... and not only a minister ... but a persecuted one at that. He wanted to see Kyle restored, something that never happened to his father, but in the process, he wanted to murder his child, if indeed it was also Callista's child. Kyle's ministerial status was the biggest reason Jimmy didn't just go ahead and kill Kylla. He wanted to be 100 percent sure ... and he never was ... thus, the kidnapping and subsequent interrogation."

"A bit sick," Cindy muttered. "Why couldn't he just leave her alone?"

"Apparently his hate for Martin overrode his compassion for ministers," Ben assumed.

"How did he finally find out Kylla was Caryn's child?" Kyle wanted to know. Pieces still didn't fit.

"Well, he never really was sure. The eye-opener appeared to be a little investigation he held at the Harvest Hollow area. When people began to open up about Kyle's wife who had left him, he learned quickly it wasn't the beautiful Miss Marcum ... no blonde or fair features. Jimmy produced a picture for someone, and Caryn/Callista was at last identified, but not without question. The picture Jimmy produced was of a blond Callista. But once the person studied it, she admitted it could easily be Caryn with a change of hair color. That was two days before your trip to Huntsville."

Kyle nodded in understanding at last. "If he knew, why did he keep asking me about Kylla during the kidnapping?"

For the first time Amos spoke up. "It went back to his respect for ministers. No one at Harvest Hollow, or anywhere else for that matter, had ever seen Caryn pregnant. Only the hospital, and they had absolutely no information whatsoever ... no positive I.D. ... she was in and out really fast. Callista had been smart about that. She traveled to an obscure small town on the other side of Nashville so no one could trace the place down. Jimmy had no way of knowing where the baby was born. But he had to make sure that his suspicions about Kylla were real before he could actually ... well ... you know."

"How decent of him," Cindy mumbled.

"Actually, that is decent for Jimmy Thornton," Ben told her. "He's not a nice man. Kyle's ministerial standing was ... how should I phrase it ... the salvation of everybody in this case ... everybody but Callista."

Kyle and Cindy took in all the information and tried to process it. Many things finally made sense, but the web of deception and danger that had surrounded the whole case left them both feeling off balance and a bit unsure.

"Is it over?" Kyle finally asked. "I mean ... really, really over?"

"Everything is over," Agent Hall affirmed. "Even for Martin. He's officially a free man now."

"Why the whole California trip to see Mr. Sartin?" Kyle suddenly wondered. "You didn't need any info at all. He was basically under your protection ... you knew everything you needed to know already."

Agent Hall squirmed uncomfortably and nodded. "Yeah ... well ... that was a deceptive little scheme on our part." He squinted slightly in embarrassment as he continued. "We were hoping to find a lead on where Thornton might be ... trying to catch one of his spies transferring info about your visit."

"Then the whole adoption and marriage thing was pointless?" Cindy asked in shock.

"Not completely," Ben explained. "We ... uh ... sort of planted that too."

"Why?" Kyle questioned as his confusion only grew.

"So we could release Kylla's records and hope someone would request them. By the way, it worked." Ben smiled with a guilty looking grin. "That was the big key in finding Thornton. We knew where he was prior to your kidnapping."

"Then why didn't you arrest him?" Kyle practically yelled out this time.

"Sorry, Kyle," Ben Hall bemoaned, "but it would have been pointless. We had to have that confession."

Kyle sighed and looked over at Martin. This wasn't the cocky actor/comedian he had watched on television all those years. This was a man who had lived through hell for fourteen years which Kyle had only experienced for a few months.

"So, what are your plans?" Kyle asked Martin. "Gonna go back into entertainment?"

Martin shook his head sadly. "I don't think so. My job was to make people laugh. It's hard to laugh anymore ... I've lost everything."

Cindy suddenly stood up. "Not everything," she said soberly. "I'll be right back." Within a minute she returned carrying a wet Kylla wrapped up in a large beach towel. "Martin Sartin," she said as she walked over to him, "this is your flesh and blood ... Maria's grandchild, Callista's baby ... your granddaughter."

Martin stood slowly and tears began to drop from his eyes. It was strange. There was no sobbing or crying, but the tears just poured as though a faucet had been turned on. Despite his designer suit, Martin reached out for the wet little girl, and she promptly went to him in typical Kylla fashion.

"Hey, Kylla," he said tenderly.

Kylla pointed at his nose and grinned as she said, "No'ee?"

Cindy came up next to them and pointed Kylla's finger to Martin and said, "Granddaddy."

Martin looked back at Cindy and then over to Kyle.

"That's who you are," Kyle affirmed.

"You'll let me in her life?" Martin was astounded. "After all you've been through because of me?"

"She's your grandchild," Kyle nodded. "You're as much a part of her as the rest of us. Besides, I think you've been through enough pain and loss all these years—your sentence has been served."

The look of gratefulness on Martin's face was beyond description. He turned back to Kylla and gently caressed her soft hair, damp from the water. "You sure do look like your Daddy," he grinned.

"Dadda!" she called out and pointed toward Kyle.

"Should I try and set up some kind of schedule to see her?" Martin asked.

Kyle laughed as he walked over and put his hand on his shoulder. "This isn't California, Mr. Sartin. If you want to see Kylla, just drop in. We've got plenty of room, and you're always welcome here."

Tears began to flow from Martin again. "Thank you," was all he could say this time.

***

"Is it just me, or does this whole thing seem even more bizarre than before?" Cindy asked as she rubbed lotion on her arms while climbing into bed.

"Does bizarre even cover it?" Kyle pulled the sheets back for her.

"What's Martin gonna do? You talked to him for quite a while when I went to put Kylla down for a nap."

"He's not sure. He's thinking about packing everything up and moving close to Dockrey. Kylla's all he's got left in this world."

"How weird. Martin Sartin may become a normal part of our lives."

"This does complicate things a little now, though … you know … telling Kylla someday about Caryn and all that goes along with that. She's gonna figure out that her Granddaddy Martin is not your dad … nor Granny Sue's husband."

"Kyle," she said with a knowing grin as she reached over to pull him to her, "stop borrowing trouble. Remember the worst is behind us, and God took care of us through all of it. He's the one who brought Martin here, and as time goes by, He'll be the one to give us wisdom about dealing with Kylla."

"When did you get so smart about spiritual matters?"

She gently kissed him and said, "My father's death, mother's cancer, kidnapping … surviving things like that tends to give you an edge on faith."

"So, it doesn't bother you that Kylla may have to find out that you aren't her birth mother?"

"Right now, that isn't even in the picture," Cindy whispered as she ran her fingers through his hair. "I'll raise her, I'll care for her, I'll be her mother. Just because my blood doesn't flow through her veins will never change what she and I share."

"Whew," he whispered back. "I always knew you were beautiful, but I never realized how strong you were until now."

"Find me a little intimidating, do you?"

"Very," he grinned as he reached up to turn out the lamp.

Eighty-One

"Could you print me out a set of address labels for the choir?" Kyle asked as he walked into the main office. "I've got a letter about special practices for the Christmas program."

"Starting early with the special practices, aren't you? Late October?" Cindy replied as she wheeled around in her chair.

"You're joking, right? Doesn't the Christmas season start in like July or something now? When did Wal-Mart have their decorations out?"

"You started rehearsals in August. Surely we'll be ready for the program by December."

"Look," he showed her a copy of the letter and the special rehearsals. "All I'm trying to do is get a jump on everyone's Christmas schedule."

"Efficient little fellow, you are."

"And why are you talking like Yoda today?" he knelt down beside her as she pulled up the choir's addresses.

"Feeling giddy, I am," she continued. "Love this weather, I do."

"Mmmm," Kyle responded in his best Yoda impression. "And very beautiful this morning you look. Told you, have I?"

She giggled as she pressed the button to print and then leaned over to put her arms around him. "Love you, I do."

The door opened and in came Debby Cramer, definitely beginning to show in her pregnancy. Kyle and Cindy immediately assumed more respectful positions.

"Good morning, Debby," Cindy said clearing her throat. "What's up?"

"Daddy has a donation for the new van fund," she explained as she walked to Cindy's desk and handed her an envelope. "It's in memory of his father."

"Great," Cindy took the envelope. "We should be able to purchase that new van soon. Sorry about your grandfather. I'm sure that's a huge loss for your family."

"Thanks," Debby said glumly. "Grandad was a neat guy."

There was that awkward silence that always seems to accompany conversations with people you don't know well. The three of them just smiled politely for a bit.

"You look really cute," Cindy finally told her. "A pregnant lady is always so … oh, I don't know … winsome looking, I suppose. Happy. Healthy."

Debby smiled genuinely now. "Thank you." She shook her head.

"Would you believe that you're the first person outside of my family that has even acknowledged I'm pregnant? Everyone else just tries to ignore it."

"How?" Cindy laughed. "It's a bit obvious, don't you think?"

"My friends are the worse," Debby told her as she leaned against the counter. "It's like everyone is trying not to notice the elephant in the room, you know?"

Kyle jumped in quickly to assure her, "You certainly are *no* elephant. And I agree with Cindy, you look adorable."

Debby's cheeks flushed. "Thank you, both. I know it's very awkward, but I appreciate you acknowledging it. I am most definitely *with child* ... kind of consumes my every thought right now ... and it's nice to talk about it with someone for a change."

"Have you made any plans?" Cindy wondered, remembering that a few months ago she had no clue as to what she would do.

"It's still hard to decide. I didn't think I'd want the baby; I thought she would complicate my world in a major uncomfortable way."

"You know it's a girl?" Kyle asked with a smile.

She nodded. "I couldn't help it; I had to know. It's almost as if she's already a part of my life. I can't walk through a store without looking at baby things, even if it's only the grocery and I see baby food. We've talked about adoption, talked about Mom and Dad raising her, and then the possibility of me keeping her." Debby's expression became sober. "I don't see how I could let her go after carrying her all this time. I almost feel guilty, though, because I know she'd have a better life with someone else— a mature couple with a stable marriage who want a baby so badly. But then again, it would feel like I was tearing away a part of myself." She looked at them both with tears forming in her eyes. "I'm really torn ... severely torn."

Cindy stood and embraced her for a moment then pulled back, put her hand on her shoulders, and told her, "We'll be praying for you. God gives us the desires of our hearts; He places them in there. If your desire to keep this baby is that strong, then perhaps that's what God wants."

Debby wiped an escaped tear. "I'll keep that in mind. I don't want to be selfish. I know I need to finish school ... she would need a father—all is not going to be perfect in her little world if I choose to keep her."

"Nobody's world is perfect," Cindy assured her.

Debby looked at her with a strange face. "Your world is."

The statement took Cindy by surprise. "Why would you say that?"

"You've got everything," Debby said as though it were common knowledge. "A great husband, a beautiful daughter ... a good life."

"You didn't think that a few months ago."

"A few months ago I wasn't thinking at all! I remember you telling me about your life and all the roads you had gone down and how empty they had left you. I thought you were crazy. You gave up so much to settle down into this ball-and-chain lifestyle. Now," she looked back and forth at Kyle and Cindy, "I realize that you do have it all. I wish I could have seen it before ... before I made choices I can never take back."

Cindy took her hand. "Believe me, I understand. But remember this: God is a God of redemption and restoration. He can even turn mistakes around into blessings if we will just be repentant and obedient." Then Cindy added, "I should know."

Debby took a deep breath and gently rubbed her tummy. "Thank you. I needed this today. You guys have been an encouragement."

"Then maybe you should come around more often," Kyle suggested.

"I don't want to interrupt your work."

Cindy shook her head. "Debby, nothing is more important than people. Not prayer lists or bulletins or even financial reports. When you need to talk, you come by. There will always be time for you."

Debby's eyes began to fill again. "Thanks. I just might do that." She straightened her shirt, wiped her eyes gently, smearing a bit of mascara in the process. "But right now, I have more errands to run. Daddy's trying to keep me busy."

After she left, Kyle and Cindy continued to stare at the door. It was almost baffling to see the humility that had grown in Debby Cramer since her return from Auburn.

"We need to invite her over," Cindy finally stated. "She needs to be with, well, Christian people, not that her parents aren't ..."

"I know what you mean. You're right." He then turned to Cindy, who was still standing, and pulled her into his arms. "God has changed your heart so much. I laugh when I think how unworthy you thought you were to be a minister's wife, but look at you—you're ministering every bit as much as I am."

"That's not ministry; that's just ... I don't know ... friendship."

"No," he corrected her, "that is very much ministry. You've never been friends with Debby Cramer. You're now becoming a friend to her because you want to see her life changed—you want to see her have the same kind of healing in her life that God brought into yours. That *is* most definitely ministry."

She looked up at him in thankfulness, but his face grew dim.

"What is it?"

"I was just remembering: Caryn never would reach out. I used to think she could help people so much, but she never outgrew her insecurities. We would pray together, and I would think that surely she would snap out of it, but she never did. I now realize it was because she was clueless about everything—everything."

He quickly turned his attention back to Cindy. He knew it bothered her anytime he talked about Caryn. "I have an idea."

"What?"

"Let's go out Friday."

"Just me and you?" She tightened her arms around his waist.

"Just us. And I know the perfect place."

"Do you think Mom will watch Kylla for us?"

Kyle laughed. That had to be a joke.

***

On Friday afternoon, Kyle wouldn't tell Cindy where they were going. They took her car for the first time in weeks. Since having the freedom to take Kylla out, they had done everything with her, thus always using his Jeep. He took several back streets in Tuscumbia to throw her off, but when he finally turned down the street next to the two-story Coldwater bookstore, she knew exactly where they were headed: *Oh! Bryans.*

"Very apt," she grinned as he opened her door and took her hand to pull her up from the car.

"Remember our first trip here?" he grinned at the question.

"Do I ever. I left the most flustered woman ever."

"Why? I rather enjoyed that evening."

"Oh, please! You were every bit as shaken up as I was. You were talking ninety-to-nothing trying to cover over your feelings after that kiss."

"That was *your* fault. I knew exactly how I felt; you were the one trying to tell me things wouldn't work out."

"That's baloney. You were just as out-of-sorts as me. You were doing your best to assure me that it would *not* happen again and that we should just forget about it."

"Perhaps, but it didn't work."

"Then you kissed me again before I went inside my house."

He chuckled as he placed his hand on the small of her back. "I was just curious … I guess."

She stopped and turned him to her. "Were you really curious? Is that the truth? That seemed really lame then … and it still does now."

He grinned and shook his head. "I thought that was it. In hindsight, you're probably right. It was all baloney, and I just wanted to kiss you again … desperately."

She kissed him gently and then started for the door. "Confession is good for the soul, isn't it?"

After eating, they walked up to the bookstore and glanced through a few photography books again as they sat on the same loveseat upstairs. This time, however, they sat close, with his arm around her shoulders, and his head leaned down next to hers.

"These national parks are gorgeous," Cindy sighed. "How many have you been to?"

"Most of them … even Denali in Alaska."

"I would love to see some of them. I've been to the Smoky Mountains and Mammoth Cave. That's it."

"Then let's go," he said softly in her ear.

She smiled as it tickled. "Just like that? Let's go?"

"For vacation next year."

"How? I mean, do we just drive there or what?"

He closed the book and stood up, reaching down to pull her to her feet also. He then led her to the very spot where they had shared their first kiss.

"How does *this* answer my question?" she asked curiously.

"The last time we were here, everything in our lives seemed impossible. You were depressed, I was in mourning, and as much as we felt for each other at that moment, we believed our situation was hopeless. But now, right at this time in our lives, we can do anything. If you want to travel and see the country, so do I. We can take Jonathan's camper and go anywhere you want."

"Really?" Cindy asked a little excited. "Have you ever gone camping?"

"Never. You?"

"A couple of times with the Wrights when I was a teenager. It was fun."

"I'll bet it'll be even more fun now," he grinned.

"Why is that?"

He didn't answer with words but simply pulled her close. He stared into her eyes and gently began to kiss her forehead, her cheeks, her nose. When he found her neck just behind her ear, she squirmed again at the sensation.

"You win," she giggled. "It'll definitely be more fun."

"Told you," he smiled as he finally found her lips.

The August heat was unbearable. It would be hard to stand the outside for the final service. Cindy rubbed her tummy as she, Kyle and Kylla followed behind the silver hearse from the church to the cemetery. The twins obviously felt her turmoil as they seemed to be fist fighting each other inside. She gasped for a moment as one gave a hard kick to her ribs.

"You okay?" Kyle asked quickly as he reached for her other hand.

She managed a smile. He was always attentive, and since the pregnancy, it had doubled. "I'm fine. Your children are wreaking havoc with my rib cage."

"Mama?" asked three-year-old Kylla from the middle seat of the new minivan. "Why did Granny Sue go?"

Cindy closed her eyes, hand still on her stomach, as she leaned her head back against the seat. They had discussed this many times the last two days. "It was time for her to be well again. Jesus took her to His home, heaven, so she could be with Grandpa James."

"She's not sick now?" Kylla asked for probably the fiftieth time.

"Not at all." Cindy could actually smile at the thought. "She's probably running around up there. The angels are trying to catch up with her so they can show her to her new house."

"But I want her to stay at our house."

Cindy was silent this time. She and her mother had become close the last two and a half years. When Sue's cancer came back in April, it was massive and inoperable this time. The church had been wonderful about giving Cindy time off to spend with her mother knowing these last few weeks would be their final moments together on this side of eternity.

Cindy thought of Saturday afternoon, just two days before Sue passed away. She had been sitting beside her on the bed, holding her hand tenderly, soaking up the last few moments of life her mother had. Sue had come to deal with the pain admirably because she didn't want to be so strung out on the medicine that she couldn't speak. She wanted to be lucid with her family before she left.

"I won't see my grandchildren," she said sadly. "That's what hurts the most about all of this."

Cindy had wanted to tell her not to talk like that, but she knew death was imminent.

"At least I've had Kylla these past two years. Sometimes, Cindy, I completely forget that she's adopted. She is so much a part of my life now that it just seems as though she was always here."

"She adores you, you know?"

"She'd better," Sue coughed slightly. "I spoiled her rotten."

"Tell me about it. You were the best grandmother ... and mother."

Sue had smiled weakly. "Not the best mother. I made my share of mistakes. You and Billy had to suffer through my ineptness by making your own mistakes and finding your own ways in this world. I could have done much better."

"Don't say that, Mother." Cindy squeezed her hand. "You did just fine. Billy and I were hardheaded and chose each path we went down. God is working in our lives, though, and has been for some time." She gasped as one of the twins gave a solid kick.

"There you go," Sue had said with a sweet smile. "Now, it's your turn."

"Tell me about it. These two are gonna give me a run for my money."

"You'll be so thankful for Kylla's tender temperament when you start juggling those babies around. You do realize that you have no idea what you're getting yourself into?"

Cindy laughed. "I've wanted these babies for two years now ... although I think God has a deeper sense of humor than I do. I really wanted only one at a time."

"Make me a promise," Sue said with a twinkle in her eyes.

"Anything."

"Don't get sentimental and name the poor things James and Sue if you get a boy and a girl."

"Mother!" Cindy exclaimed. "Why not? Don't give me that ultimatum. You know I wanted to ..."

Sue had put up her hand to stop her. "Promise me. James and Sue are old, fuddy-duddy names. Give your children names worthy of this age. I've gone back and forth over this since you told me your plans. I'm honored, but frankly, the thought nauseates me. Promise me, Cindy Sue, you won't name them after us."

She rolled her eyes and then flinched from another rib-bashing. "I think one of them agrees with you," she said as she reached up to her rib and tried to push the foot ... or hand ... or whatever it was away. The baby had simply responded with another pelt.

As the hearse drove through the cemetery to the awning over Sue's freshly dug grave, Cindy could feel her emotions begin to overwhelm her. She was surprised at how well she had done thus far. The way she was facing her mother's death was a stark contrast to how she had handled her father's. She had peace about Sue. She had seen the pain, the digression, and knew that death would be a welcomed friend in this situation. She also knew that her mother was ready to meet her Maker, ready to run into the arms of her Savior. Cindy had been so messed up and confused when her father had died, she could barely find a reason to go on. But with her mother, she had rebuilt a relationship, and had been a wonderful daughter for almost three years. Yes, there was peace.

"Ready?" Kyle asked her as he turned off the engine.

She only nodded. It was hard to speak right now. She opened the door to the van—the van her mother had insisted on buying a few months ago. Sue had traded in her big Buick for a new van, complete with a DVD player and the works. She claimed she was ready for a change, but Cindy knew it was because the twins were coming and a Jeep would not be a suitable family vehicle. Cindy made herself breathe. There would always be reminders of her mother; she had to come to grips with that. At least this time around, unlike the death of her father, the reminders would all be good and pleasant.

Kyle carried Kylla in one arm and reached for Cindy's hand with the other. "Let's go ahead and have a seat," he said tenderly, guiding her toward the awning.

She merely nodded. This couldn't be real. As cars passed the cemetery, it seemed so wrong. Her mother had died. The world should stop for a moment. How could life continue to go on when such a ripple had been forged in her world this week? She glanced up to see car after car pour into the cemetery. She was honored, and once again the peace found her.

A blue VW bug came down the highway and turned into the cemetery also. She knew that Jonathan and Barbara had one just like it. It had been Annie's from several years back. She looked over to the Wright's van; they were already parked and walking toward the grave site. She watched as the little car maneuvered its way past every other vehicle and came directly to the front.

Bold person, whoever it is, Cindy thought to herself. Kyle tried to direct her back toward the tent, but Cindy's curiosity got the best of her. "I want to see who's driving the VW."

"I think that's Jonathan's."

She shook her head. "I know, but it's not them. They're already here."

The Bug came to an abrupt stop, and Cindy watched as a tall, long-haired beauty stepped from the car. Her dark glasses hid her face, but as soon as Cindy saw the lips and the tan, she knew exactly who it was. Her hands came up to her mouth and a sob escaped.

"Cindy! What's wrong?" Kyle asked immediately. "Are you okay?"

Cindy pointed toward the lady and whispered, "It's Angie ... Angie's here."

Cindy slowly moved toward her, and then as Angie recognized Cindy, she practically ran to her. They were both very pregnant, and as they embraced they began to shake with sobs.

"I can't believe this," Cindy whispered to her through her tears. "How did you manage this? How did you get here?"

Angie wouldn't release her as she explained, "I didn't think our flight would make it in time. I left Michael at Moms' house with Cassie and I came zipping over here as quickly as I could."

Cindy pulled back to look at her dearest friend. "But how did you manage this?"

"How could I not?" she said warmly as she reached up to touch Cindy's face. She then glanced down at Cindy's belly. "Good lands ... what are you growing down there?"

"You're one to talk. Look at you." Cindy patted Angie's tummy.

"I'm not *that* big," Angie grinned.

"I've got two, and they're going at it right now as we speak."

Angie laughed heartily, the laugh that Cindy knew so well. She took her friend's hand and led her to the tent where Kyle and Kylla were waiting.

"Introductions aren't necessary," Angie said as Kyle stood. "I've seen more pictures than you can imagine. You are Kyle." Angie shook his hand, and Kyle wiped another tear. "And you," she reached over to Kylla, "are sweet, little Kylla. I've got a little girl at Pastor Jon's house named Cassie that I bet would love to play with you."

"I know Cassie!" Kylla piped out. "Mama has pictures. Can I see her now?"

"In just a little bit," Kyle told her. "We're almost finished here."

The four of them sat on the front row beneath the awning, with Kyle and Angie on either side of Cindy. As the service began, Jonathan did an amazing job of making this feel more like a homecoming than a funeral. Cindy could feel the peace again. To have Kyle beside her, with Kylla on his lap, her twins going full force inside, and Angie on the other side, she looked up toward heaven and whispered a *thank you* to the God who had come to mean so much to her. *Only You could have done this. Thank You. Thank You.*

As the graveside ceremony began to close, Jonathan looked toward Kyle and nodded. Kyle stood, took Kylla up to Jonathan and handed her to him. He then folded his hands and closed his eyes for just a moment.

"This is difficult for me," he said swallowing hard. He glanced down at Cindy, the love of his life, with Angie sitting next to her. He looked toward Jonathan who gave him a nod again as he tenderly held Kylla. He saw his parents off to the side and was thankful for their love and support and for the relationship they had forged with Sue too. Martin was also there, a permanent residence in Dockrey for a year now. Then he noticed Billy sitting at the back of the awning, tears burning his eyes. He had made some big changes for his mother's sake—going back to school in his thirties. She had been so proud of his new start.

He began. "When I first met Cindy and Sue, we all three were having a tough time. To see where we came from is almost unbelievable. Sue came to mean more in my life than I could ever tell any of you, and to know that she's gone right now hurts deeper than anything I've ever known. But even as I say that, there's still so much here in my life to live for. My wife, my children, my church, my community … all of which are here … right now.

"But during those dark times for us, Cindy said something that I think all three of us could relate to at that moment. She said life was like a winter midnight; it was the coldest and darkest point possible. I've never been able to let that go … those words have haunted me all these years. Right now, I have to confess, it seems like its winter midnight again. The best days of my life have had Sue Marcum stuck right in the middle of them. I know that Cindy and I will move on, but to lose her is hard … very hard."

He swallowed again and tried to regain his composure. "When Sue found out her cancer had returned, and that it couldn't be cured this time, I wept so hard I felt my insides would surely burst. I had to express my frustration somehow, so I did something I had never done before: I wrote a song."

He smiled at the look of complete surprise on Cindy's face. She had no idea.

"I wrote it pretty quick. The emotions were strong, and the words just came. Stephen Williams had promised me earlier that if I wrote it, he would record it. I sent it to him last month knowing that Sue wouldn't hold on a whole lot longer. I wish I could sing it for her today … right now, but there's no way. But if you wouldn't mind, I'd like to play you Stephen and Annie's version … of my *Winter Midnight*."

He pulled out a large CD player from behind the coffin and actually placed it on top. "Before I sent it to the Williams, I played it for Sue on my guitar. She said the words were absolutely beautiful and expressed it all perfectly. However, she said the music was downright mournful. She said to tell Stephen and Annie to put some *pep* into it." He grinned. "They did."

"When I played this recording for her last week, she said, *Kyle, you put that boom box on top of my casket out there at that cemetery, and you crank it up and let it go. If everybody starts dancing, let them know I'll be looking down and dancing with them.*"

Several laughed gently at the thought. He pressed a button, and a strong, steady beat began to pulse. When the singing started, smiles began to grow. Sue surely had to be dancing …

> *I don't know the future, I just know the past*
> *I long for tomorrow, this pain cannot last*
> *The night is so dark and the wind is so cold*

But there's more than today and trials turn me to gold

The sun always rises, the cold always fades
The winter will leave me, just as it came
Fate holds nothing over me, I'm not up for grabs
I may have no answers, but I know Who has
My faith, it knows, during winter it grows
As much in darkness as in the light
And it won't always be Winter Midnight

I don't have an answer, not a single one
My heart feels such sorrow, I can't see the sun
But I know it's there 'cause I've seen it before
And I know that some day in its light I will soar

The sun always rises, the cold always fades
The winter will leave me, just as it came
Fate holds nothing over me, I'm not up for grabs
I may have no answers, but I know Who has
My faith, it knows, during winter it grows
As much in darkness as in the light
And it won't always be Winter Midnight

Though His trials are like fire that burn through my soul
I've learned that each trial is making me whole
And even though trials may seem dark and cold
They bring forth new life in measures untold

The sun always rises, the cold always fades
The winter will leave me, just as it came
Fate holds nothing over me, I'm not up for grabs
I may have no answers, but I know Who has
My faith, it knows, during winter it grows
As much in darkness as in the light
And it won't always be Winter Midnight

As the music faded, no one moved. This was a dark moment in life, but the sun would shine again. Kyle turned off the player and placed it back on the ground. Before he could finish, Cindy came to her feet and walked over to him. When he stood back up, she placed her arms around his neck and pulled him to her. She knew that the song was as much about her as her mother. How blessed to know someone knew her as deeply as Kyle, yet could love her just as deeply. She pulled back to let him see her smile.

Reaching up to erase a tear on his face she gently kissed him in front of the crowd. Small sobs began to burst forth from several.

"It's not Winter Midnight anymore," she whispered so that only he could ear. "Not as long as you're with me. Not even today."

Summer Sunrise

(Book #4 in the Autumn Sunset Series)

Deception, whether accidental or deliberate, always carries a price. Annie Williams has held a secret from her husband for years, but can the well-meaning intentions of her heart erase the hurt such a secret could bring? Billy Marcum has almost pulled his life together, but the lies of his past seem to dog his heels at every turn. Can he possibly turn the page at last and build a life that is no longer self-centered and no longer destructive towards those he loves the most? The church in Dockrey has grown too large for Jonathan and Kyle to handle. As a new staff member comes on board, will he be a team player in the ministry or a tool of deception and divisiveness? When the truth is interwoven with lies, each life will be affected in some way.

www.ingramcontent.com/pod-product-compliance
Lightning Source LLC
Chambersburg PA
CBHW021125260626
47169CB00005B/1456